Ariel was standing motionless,

heedless of the cold kitchen floor under her feet, or the chill creeping up her bare legs beneath the tail of his shirt. The horror and pain in her eyes froze him in the doorway. The box of matches she'd gone to get was open on the floor, the blue-tipped sticks scattered like bits of the happiness they'd shared just moments before. His .45 dangled, ready to fall, from the fingers of her left hand. Her right hand clutched the damning file, the blood-red letters of her name on the cover screaming an accusation of him.

"Who are you? Where did you get this?" Her hand jerked, and the file fell, spilling its Judas contents over the cheerful blue and yellow tiles. "You knew all about me before you ever came. Dennis, the murder, everything." The guilt on his face brought her hideous suspicion to reality. "You *were* sent to spy on me!"

Dear Reader,

When two people fall in love, the world is suddenly new and exciting, and it's that same excitement we bring to you in Silhouette Intimate Moments. These are stories with scope, with grandeur. These characters lead the lives we all dream of, and everything they do reflects the wonder of being in love.

Longer and more sensuous than most romances, Silhouette Intimate Moments novels take you away from everyday life and let you share the magic of love. Adventure, glamour, drama, even suspense—these are the passwords that let you into a world where love has a power beyond the ordinary, where the best authors in the field today create stories of love and commitment that will stay with you always.

In coming months look for novels by your favorite authors: Maura Seger, Parris Afton Bonds, Elizabeth Lowell and Erin St. Claire, to name just a few. And whenever you buy books, look for all the Silhouette Intimate Moments, love stories *for* today's women *by* today's women.

Leslie J. Wainger
Senior Editor
Silhouette Books

IMRL-7/85

Patricia
Gardner Evans
Flashpoint

Silhouette Intimate Moments

Published by Silhouette Books New York

America's Publisher of Contemporary Romance

SILHOUETTE BOOKS
300 East 42nd St., New York, N.Y. 10017

ISBN: 0-373-07151-5

First Silhouette Books printing July 1986

PATRICIA GARDNER EVANS

has lived in New Mexico all her life, and has traveled extensively throughout the west exploring old ghost towns, Indian ruins and abandoned homesteads. She avoids housework by spending much of her free time outdoors fishing, and raising her own fruits and vegetables. She gets inspiration for her plots and characters from the land and people around her.

To Fred—for what was.

Prologue

Y ou're going down the tubes, Ryan Jones."

The russet-haired, green-eyed Irish pixie sitting across the kitchen table from him was, he reflected, the only person he'd have accepted that from. He picked at the remains of his lunch. The hell of it was, she was right.

Annoyance thickened her brogue noticeably. "No wife, no family, nothin' but self-indulgence and pushin' your luck as far as you can. Well, congratulations!" Her little hand slapped the tabletop in frustration. "You almost pushed it too far this time. Why don't you find yourself a good woman and stop wastin' your life?"

One corner of his beautiful, almost cruel mouth curled up in a cynical offer. "Well, Mother Eileen, why don't you find one for me? How about a beautiful virgin over the age of consent, if any still exist, and I'll make the ultimate sacrifice."

"A virgin?" One russet eyebrow crooked in sardonic amusement. "Tell me, Ryan, is the lucky bride goin' to get a virgin, too on her weddin' night?" Her soft laughter chided him.

Eileen Jones studied the dark man slouched in the chair opposite her and wondered for the hundredth time how two brothers could be so unlike. Oh, physically they were quite similar, same features, same height, same lean build. Her husband's bright blue eyes and rusty-red hair turned his older brother's aloof, dark elegance into an open, friendly warmth, but one would still easily recognize them as brothers. But inside, in their hearts and souls, where it counted, the resemblance ended. She gave thanks that her husband was free of the devils that plagued his brother.

Ryan joined in the laughter, mocking his own chauvinism. Then he realized that he'd been more than half-serious. An oddly bleak look passed over his face. Unrealistic as it might be, he did want a woman who was untouched, his alone. Maybe her innocence could cleanse his soul.

Eileen Jones lay close to her husband in the wide bed. She was frowning absently at him. "I'm really worried about him this time, Rick. Watching himself slowly bleed to death out on that ocean made him take a long look at himself. I don't think he liked what he saw."

"I know, Eileen, but he sure as hell won't take any advice from me." His low voice was harshly bitter. "Not after what I cost him."

"Know what he told me when I said he should find a wife and settle down?"

"Geez, you have more nerve than I do, honey." He kissed his wife lovingly and settled her under his arm. "What'd he say?"

She told him. "I think he was half-serious. A virgin, indeed!" She sighed, disheartened. "He'll be well enough soon to go back to L.A. Then he'll have another chance to kill himself with one of his loony stunts."

"Oh, I don't know," Rick said slowly, idly playing with the short russet curls tickling his chest. "There just might be somebody for him. Exactly what he wants."

His wife pushed against his hard belly and sat up, catching the scheming glint in her husband's innocent blue eyes. Only she knew just how far from innocent they really were. "Oh, no. No, no, no, Rick," she moaned despairingly, giggling in spite of herself. "Surely you're not thinking what I think you're thinking. This isn't the Middle Ages, Richard," she reminded her husband tartly, stifling her laughter. "She isn't chattel to be given over to another man's protection. And besides, Ryan is hardly a white knight in shining armor."

"No," he admitted reluctantly, laughing, "he's definitely more like a black knight." He watched his wife's face grow thoughtful. The gleam in his eyes got brighter and craftier.

"You know, though," she said slowly, "they would make a very good pair. But how will you ever get them together? She can't leave, and you'll never," she declared flatly, "talk him into burying himself in some dinky town in Montana, even for a week."

With a slyly wicked chuckle, he pulled his wife back down firmly into his arms. "Oh, yes, I will," he growled into her ear with great anticipation. "In fact, I already know how I'm going to do it."

His wife caught an odd undertone in his voice, and she was suddenly stiff in his embrace. "You still think there's a possibility she's guilty, don't you, Rick? And your boss is convinced of it, isn't he?" Her small fist connecting with his solid shoulder was not gentle. "How can you think that after all she did for us while she stayed here? Caring for Erin, colic and all, and me, so sick with that infection I couldn't lift a finger to help myself? And she kept you together, too, Richard, in case you've conveniently forgotten."

Rick Jones sighed. He knew that deceptively soft tone in his wife's voice only too well. For the second time in one day she was about to lose her fine Irish temper with one of the Jones brothers. "The evidence, Eileen—"

"Evidence!" The rich disgust in her tone conveyed Eileen Jones's opinion of the evidence. "How you lawyers love evidence! You've said yourself that all the evidence against her is circumstantial. It could just as easily prove her innocence as her guilt."

Rick Jones placated his wife with his soothing voice and hands. "I know, Eileen, I know." He felt her relax, her temper cooling as quickly as it had flared. Then he glimpsed a flash of fear in her green eyes.

"You think she's in danger! That's why you're sending him."

"It's a possibility," he admitted reluctantly. "There have been some new developments in the case, and someone may decide to ensure her silence permanently."

His wife nodded slowly. "No one could protect her better than Ryan."

Rick Jones closed his eyes tiredly. Ryan would protect her, and she could settle a debt that had been outstanding far too long.

The woman closed her mailbox and began walking up the dirt track toward an old, red brick country schoolhouse. Her steps slowed and finally stopped as she read the open letter in her hands. The September sun caught her golden hair, glinting around her bent head. The large brown dog by her side sat automatically, resting against a long, slim leg. Patiently she waited for her mistress to resume their walk.

The small smile on the woman's striking face spread into a large grin as she laughed softly at the color snapshot in her right hand. The blond, bearded giant in the picture looked like a Viking marauder. He actually managed to make nearly six-foot-tall Suzi, who stood beside him with his arm draped possessively over her shoulders, look petite. From their goofy, beautiful smiles and the way the camera had caught their eyes sneaking back to each other, they were clearly very pleased with themselves and each other. The love shining out of those joyous faces was so obvious that it almost hurt to see it.

She refolded the letter and slipped it back into the envelope with the photo. She glanced up at the blue mountain peaks guarding the small Montana valley. They looked so cold, so lonely in the Indian-summer sunshine. Her grin faded. Curling into the soft fur, her fingers unconsciously sought the heavy head leaning on her thigh. She was truly overjoyed for her best friend, and the love she had found, but the letter brought back the awful, restless impatience once again. A tear glittered as it fell unnoticed down her cheek. When would she be freed from this life . . . and maybe have a chance to find love, too?

She spoke to the dog in a low voice, and they continued their walk, heads down, plodding through the dark dust toward the empty house.

The parcel bin in the self-serve post office sighed shut, and the package fell inside with a solid thump. The man in the nondescript trench coat strode briskly back through the air terminal.

She would probably notice the San Francisco postmark, but the note inside should allay any suspicions. He had heard the young assistant D.A. she'd once lived with laughingly refer to himself as her "secret admirer." Even when the police discovered that the district attorney hadn't sent the package, there was no way it could be traced to him. The odds were against the package even being traced back to this particular mailbox. Even if it was and someone had seen him mail it, no one would remember the man with the lank blond hair and scraggly, drooping mustache who'd taken the red-eye flight up, then gone right back. Even the stewardesses had been half-asleep.

One had to take risks in business every day. The trick was to calculate the odds and make sure they were solidly in your favor. He was taking an infinitesimal risk in order to buy a lot of insurance.

He felt a small twinge of annoyance. It really was unfortunate that his "insurance agent" had only done the job halfway. It had been easy to get the "agent's" name one night when the old man was in his cups, reminiscing about the good old days. It was the same way he'd gotten other names, other information. He'd tracked the "agent" down. A lot of money and a little blackmail proved to be an irresistible offer for the small exterminating business the man had for sale. The blond man smiled unknowingly at that choice of career; the man's second profession wasn't far removed from his first. The absent smile was returned by a porter trundling a heavy trunk through the airport.

Even if the man hadn't died before the police could question him, he would have been able to tell them nothing about the man who'd hired him. His widow, if she'd known anything, had wisely kept her mouth shut, mentioning only her husband's nonexistent despondency over his retirement. Then she'd moved to Bakersfield to be near her grandchildren and quietly spend her sudden wealth. No, he was fully covered. He'd waited nine months, but, before the week was out, the last premium on the insurance policy should be taken care of.

The old man had been a fool to let the business go, he thought, but it hadn't been all that hard to start it up again. He'd had the money and a marketable name. He'd kept a few items from the old man's line and introduced a few new ones. Everything was going quite nicely. It just illustrated the classic law of supply and demand, and for what he supplied, there was a very profitable demand.

If only Dennis hadn't become so unreasonable about that woman, although he supposed, in a way, he should be grateful to her. It was her innocent suggestion that had solved their courier problem two years ago. Of course, she was also the reason he'd had to find the "insurance agent" and a new courier, since it was because of her that Dennis had wanted out.

And now he was having supply problems again, although in all fairness he couldn't blame her this time. Garza had been betrayed. By whom and for how much didn't matter; Garza's people would take care of it, and Garza wouldn't talk. He was much too fond of his lovely teenage daughters. A new supply line had already been established, but the news of the arrest of the cocaine king of Guadalajara, as the papers had dubbed him, was still going to cause panic among all those with red, drippy noses, but no colds. It should be very good for business; he ought to be able to raise prices fifteen or twenty percent.

Garza's picture had been plastered all over the West Coast papers. Her copy of the *San Francisco Chronicle* would take a few days to reach Montana, but she'd see a picture sooner or later and remember a man who'd been someplace he shouldn't have been, talking to someone he shouldn't have known.

And for that she had to die.

Chapter 1

There she was—every California girl the Beach Boys had ever fallen in love with and immortalized in song, the star of his adolescent fantasies, hundreds of miles from the nearest beach. She looked a little older, wiser, definitely sadder, but all the golden radiance was intact.

Her body was slender to the point of thinness, bent now to catch the giggled words of the little blond girl running up to her. The laughing smile on her face was an echo of the innocent smile beaming up at her. Ryan hadn't decided yet if it was a beautiful face, but it was certainly arresting. Her features were sharp angles softened by almost oversize blue eyes with long lids and a surprisingly full, soft-looking bottom lip. They gave her narrow, aristocratic face a startling touch of sultriness.

He watched the little girl skip away and the woman smile after her fondly. After all that had happened, how could she retain an illusion of innocence? Seeing her now, the sun gilding a halo around her summer-blond head, it seemed impossible that she could be guilty of murder.

As if she felt his intent gaze, she turned, her golden smile flickering over the crowd to him. The smile faded into a wary curiosity. Guarded eyes, as blue as the Indian summer sky over his head, stared directly into his. He stepped forward, crossing the few yards between them, and smiled.

"Ariel Spence? I'm Ryan Jones."

The low velvet voice brushed over her, and she felt lower than dirt. She had been furious when Chief Dye told her that he had sort of promised the empty half of her schoolhouse to Ryan Jones, the son of an old friend. He knew she wouldn't mind, really. The poor guy had had this terrible accident and needed a quiet place to recuperate, only for a month or so.

She did mind. Really. "The son of an old friend" was being sent to spy on her, he wouldn't have so much as a hangnail wrong with him. It wasn't enough that the whole town was watching her; now they wanted someone actually living in the house with her, to tell them when the big payoff came, or to snag the hit man when he finally showed up. It was all so absurd that she would have laughed it off if she hadn't been so furious. The chief had waited to tell her until it was too late to stop the "son" from coming, but she'd fixed him anyway, plotting her revenge with a fiendish glee.

But now he was here, and he very obviously *was* recovering from some awful trauma. He was at least a head taller than she, a little over six feet, and that long, rangy body was carrying too little weight for those broad shoulders and narrow hips. He was terribly thin, downright skinny, actually. Ariel was suddenly seized with the strange urge to cook hearty, fattening meals to put some meat on that malnourished, but nicely proportioned body. She laughed silently at the thought. Her cooking would undoubtedly make the poor man even skinnier.

She glanced back up to his face. The mouth was hard, yet it was curving now in a sweet, disarming smile. His skin was stretched too tightly over his cheekbones and it had an unhealthy, prisonlike pallor. His eyes were the color of bittersweet chocolate, bright, no sign of illness there. They were hooded, slightly mocking, as if he knew a secret she didn't. The straight, blue-black hair was healthy looking, too, parted on the left side and brushed back.

What was he going to say when he saw the condition of the place that was to be his home for the next month? Probably demand directions to the nearest motel, just as she had planned. A sickly ghost of her usual smile haunted her face, "Mr. Jones, I'm happy to meet you." She reached out a welcoming hand and a strong hard one clasped hers in return.

Ariel's eyes widened, a slight gasp slipping out between her abruptly parted lips. A sharp tingle had traveled from those long fingers up her arm. This man might not be what she'd been expecting, but he could be a problem just the same.

One winged black eyebrow arched. The wonder in his eyes was replaced by speculation before they became carefully blank. "I'm happy to meet you, Miss Spence," he returned gravely. There was just a hint of laughter in the smooth, dark voice.

She was definitely not happy. She looked very nervous about something, worrying her bottom lip, smoothing down her blue slacks and tugging on the hem of her navy pullover. It was a very nice little sweater, short sleeved, with tiny white flowers, but it fit too loosely, as if she'd lost weight. She probably hadn't been eating enough the past few months. He decided suddenly to do something about that.

Ariel realized that he still had her hand, and that his thumb was caressing slow circles over the too-rapid pulse in her wrist. She pulled free immediately. "How did you know who I was, and where to find me?"

"I stopped to see why all the cars were here, what was going on," he explained, then finished with a smooth lie. "Someone pointed you out to me when I asked for directions to your place."

"Oh. Probably you would like to go out to the house now." She wished she could sound more enthusiastic. "Why don't we—"

"Are you leaving, Ariel?" She was given a brief reprieve by the arrival of an older man with grizzled faded red hair. A large paunch spilled over his polished Sam Browne belt. He hitched it up, adjusting the holster more comfortably, and eyed the dark stranger with less than friendly pale blue eyes.

"Yes, Chief, I'm taking Mr. Jones out to the house." His hostile look finally registered. "Don't you know . . . ?"

"Chief Dye and I have never met," Ryan answered quickly. "I just heard about your place from my—"

"Right!" The chief picked up his cue immediately. "Ryan. Ted Dye." The two men shook hands. "How is . . . ?" He purposely didn't finish, and Ariel never noticed, because Ryan filled in with perfect timing.

"He's fine. He sends his regards." Ryan's right hand lightly gripped Ariel's elbow, and he began to guide her toward the jumble of vehicles parked in a dusty field. "Miss Spence was just going to show me where my new home is. I'll check in with you tomorrow and fill you in on the news from San Francisco.''

The chief waved them away and walked back into the crowd gathering before a makeshift bandstand to hear the finalists in the fiddlers' contest.

Halfway to an older, orange Dodge power wagon parked off by itself, Ryan pulled Ariel to a stop. ''I'm sorry; I never thought. Maybe you wanted to stay awhile longer?''

''Not really. Three hours of old-time banjo and flat-top guitar music is about my limit.'' Honey-colored eyebrows shades darker than her hair rose questioningly. ''I thought you were from Los Angeles, but you mentioned San Francisco just now.''

The sunlight playing through her loose, shoulder-length blond hair held his attention for a long moment. ''My family lives in San Francisco. My law practice is in L.A. and, of course, I live there.'' He chose his words carefully. For reasons he didn't care to examine, he didn't want to tell her any outright lies. Tugging gently on her elbow, he started off again, but her feet were stubborn, rooted in the grassy field.

Cocking her head, her generous mouth pursed in consideration, she asked, ''How did you know I didn't come with someone today, Mr. Jones?''

What would that soft mouth taste like? He would find out. It was just a question of when. ''Because,'' he stated with utter conviction, ''he would never have left you alone.'' His fingers slipped down the bare skin of her forearm to clasp her hand, and he led her away.

He followed her in his truck. Eventually Ariel signaled for a turn off the two-lane highway, glancing in the rearview mirror to be sure he was still with her. The wooden roadside sign by the cluster of mailboxes and newspaper tubes had been weathered gray by a half century of snow and rain and sun. Burnt Fork School, Ravalli County, Montana. Est. 1912, it read in fresh, brick-red letters. She drove automatically down the dirt road, her thoughts on her new tenant.

He'd favored his right leg, grimacing a bit every time he took a step on it. His half of the schoolhouse might be a mess right now, but he couldn't spend even a night at the Rustic Hut Motel. Only the upper level was open, and those steep slippery stairs would have him in agony before he was halfway up.

She'd noticed a lot more than his limp. She'd never before been so aware of a man's looks, so aware of a man, period. There was a peculiar air about him that made even his casual clothes seem elegant. When he moved, even with the limp, there was another kind of elegance, fluid, without wasted motion.

That too-handsome face belonged to a Regency rake, or his modern counterpart—the male model. Yet there was nothing dandified about Ryan Jones. Instead of a snowy, starched cravat tied in the complicated Mathematical knot, there was the open necked rust chamois shirt. Loose corduroy jeans were belted around his thin waist, not skintight pantaloons. He definitely wasn't modeling plastic masculinity and designer clothing on the pages of some slick magazine, either. His masculinity was all too real. She had sensed a very male, very primal sexuality, kept in control by smooth sophistication, yet undoubtedly still hazardous. Unleashed, she suspected it could quite possibly be lethal.

His clothes probably did have designer labels, though. They were well-made, obviously expensive, but they'd seen a lot of use, just like his truck. Clearly he didn't discard something simply because the newness had worn off and he could afford to replace it. Except women, she thought, one corner of her mouth tilting with wry amusement. A woman, she strongly suspected, would have a very short tenure with him.

She inventoried his truck as he drove up and parked next to her silver Blazer. The four-wheel drive pickup had at least two gas tanks, heavy-duty tires, a winch on the front bumper, an empty motorcycle carrier and a faded orange camper shell. It was hardly the kind of transportation she had imagined for a single thirty-four-year-old attorney of the caliber Chief Dye had intimated. Odd that he seemed to know so much about his friend's son, yet had never met him until today.

Gingerly Ryan eased himself out of the truck. His leg was killing him. He swung up the back of the camper shell and pulled down the heavy tailgate. Alongside three well-used leather suitcases on the truck bed were a hand-tooled leather gun case and a cardboard carton of law books and file folders.

Ariel joined him, and they each grabbed a suitcase. Ryan picked up the gun case in his free hand and started for the front door.

Ariel frowned at the oddly shaped case. "Do you hunt, Mr. Jones?"

A strange smile crossed his face. "I used to."

She started to ask him just what he used to hunt when a movement at the edge of her vision made her glance sideways. To her horror, she saw a large, brown, furry blur barreling around the corner of the house straight for her new tenant. "Murphy! No! *No!*"

Ryan swung the suitcase between the wicked-looking fangs and his leg. Just as he was bracing himself, praying that his leg wouldn't buckle, the vicious dog dropped, stopped dead and began a wriggling dance of demented delight. She yipped ecstatically, tail wagging, trying to worm her head under the hand with the gun case. He glanced dryly at Ariel, who was standing stock-still ahead of him.

"Great watchdog."

Ariel snapped her mouth shut. Now the darned dog was making calf's eyes at the man as he scratched behind her left ear. "I don't understand it," she muttered, shaking her head. "She's always very hostile toward men, even the ones she knows."

He slanted her a look from under sooty eyebrows. "Like her mistress?"

Ariel smiled sweetly. "I'm just careful, Mr. Jones."

"And one can't be too careful, can one, Miss Spence?"

He'd said it innocuously enough, but his eyes were laughing insolently at her. Ryan snapped his fingers and her dog trailed obediently at the heels of his old leather sneakers. What magic did this man possess? He'd been here less than two minutes, and already he'd seduced her man-hating dog. The only male Murphy had even shown that deranged affection for was Dennis.

"Why did you name her Murphy?"

"I didn't, actually. I inherited her from . . . a friend." Setting down his suitcase, she fished her keys from a suede shoulder bag. She wiggled the worn brass key in the lock until she heard a click, then pushed the door open with her shoulder.

Ryan noticed a new dead-bolt lock on the door, but she obviously didn't bother to use it. That would have to change immediately, he decided. She wasn't going to leave herself vulnerable to an attack, or come home to find that some burglar had . . . The thought brought him up short just inside the front door. He had no right to tell her how to lock her doors, no rights to her at all.

Just the same, long dormant feelings of possession and protection began to stir.

Ryan pushed them aside, along with the door that he shoved open wider. Bright sunlight followed them inside, and he concentrated on his home for the next month. A long narrow hallway ran the length of the first floor of the schoolhouse, separating what had once been two large classrooms and were now two apartments. Opening off the common hallway were two more doors, with pebbled-glass windows, one on each side for each apartment. The doors looked like the originals, unrefinished, and Ryan began to wonder just how rustic his accommodations were going to be.

Ariel threw open the left-hand door with a small flourish and an inward groan. Now she'd find out just how good a sport a high-priced, L.A. superlawyer could be. "Here you are," she said brightly. "I've, ah, been doing a bit of remodeling. I'm not quite done, but by next Thursday, at the latest . . ."

Her voice trailed off like a music box winding down as she watched him furtively from the corners of her eyes. His had widened slightly as he'd glanced into the half bath near the door. A neat black cap was over the floor drain instead of a commode. The sink was also missing. His eyes narrowed when he walked into the kitchen and saw the gaping hole in the yellow Formica countertop where that sink should have been, the vacant space for the nonexistent stove and the floor only half tiled with yellow and blue squares. His eyes narrowed even more, and Ariel sighed resignedly, thinking of the surprises yet to be appreciated upstairs.

Ryan spared a brief glance for the dining area and living room, then began to climb a wrought-iron spiral staircase. Still lugging his suitcase, Ariel trailed after him, wincing and feeling smaller and meaner every time his right foot took another careful step on the stairs.

At least the two bedrooms were all right, if a little Spartan and small. Ariel had taken her half of the second floor and more in order to keep the bell tower for herself. Each of his bedrooms held only a double bed, rag rug, antique oak dresser and a straight-backed kitchen chair. The first also had a squat black wood stove tucked in one corner. He probably wasn't going to be too thrilled when he realized that all their heat came from wood stoves.

Ariel held her breath as he opened the bathroom door. She would bet he needed to take long, hot baths for his leg. That was going to be a bit difficult, with the tub missing. She heard him open the bathroom's other door, presumably to look around the second bedroom. No comment about the vanished tub, sink and toilet. The suspense was beginning to get to her.

Ryan walked slowly back into the bedroom, advancing silently with an unreadable expression on that wickedly handsome face. His dark eyes impaled her. Ariel backed up until the backs of her knees pressed against her bed. There was a vague feeling of menace in the sunny bedroom. Why didn't he *say* something. Complain? Yell, even? But yelling, she thought, wouldn't be his style. He wouldn't need loud words to be intimidating. Those blank eyes, the subtle cruelty hiding in that beautifully carved mouth, the way he moved, were adequately sinister.

She assumed a posture a Marine drill instructor would have praised and smiled sunnily. Stop being ridiculous, she scolded herself silently, and stop cringing! This is just a man, tired, in pain, who is being made to suffer unfairly the inconvenience of your childish spite.

"I know things look a little...rough, right now, Mr. Jones," she temporized, "but it's only for a few days, and in the meantime I'm sure we—"

"Weren't you expecting me?"

That low silky purr was definitely more intimidating than shouting. Ariel was suddenly, humiliatingly certain that he knew she had torn up his quarters out of maliciousness and that, somehow, he even knew why.

"Yes," she conceded in a helpless mutter. "Things just got a little...confused." She sidestepped neatly to escape being trapped between the bed and his body. "Let's go over to my side and . . . oh!"

With her usual devotion to duty, Murphy had positioned herself a few feet from her mistress. Ariel tripped over the dog and started to tumble. Her hand flailed through the air in her desperation to find something to stop her fall. As she fell, she clutched Ryan's leg with all her strength. His body, much heavier than it looked, landed squarely atop hers, squashing her into the bed.

An agonized groan echoed in the quiet room, followed by the jangling of Murphy's dog tags and her anxious whine. The dog's cold nose on Ariel's neck helped her jerk her face from its suffocating burial in the fine black hair at the open neck of his shirt.

Ariel gulped in a shaky breath that brought in much-needed oxygen and a citrusy, musky scent.

Ryan groaned again, and Ariel was suddenly aware of her left knee—and her hand. Trapped as it was between them, she could only relax her fingers, but not move her palm from the growing warmth beneath it. She closed her eyes tighter in mortification. Her thigh was firmly snuggled between the tops of his. She wasn't sure if the groans were caused by her knee hurting his injured leg or her thigh and hand unintentionally pleasuring a little higher up, and she really couldn't give it any more thought. She was desperately fighting the urge to moan a bit herself. His hand had found a softness, too, and his touch was much gentler than hers, molding, stroking.... Her body, which had been so obedient for twenty-seven years, was abruptly defiant. It refused to move, preferring to enjoy the sensations short-circuiting through her.

Ariel finally opened her eyes. Ryan's face was turned toward hers on the bed. Immediately she straightened her knee and tried to slip out from under him as gently and rapidly as possible. His mouth showed fine white lines of strain and his eyes were shut tightly, as if in pain. Long black lashes curled against his cheeks. He hardly looked like a man copping a cheap feel, she berated herself.

As she started to push up off the bed, an amazingly strong hand shot out and clamped her wrist to the gold bedspread. "Wait!" he grated. "Don't move yet."

Ariel was appalled to see moisture at the corners of his still sealed eyes and a clammy sweat on his pasty forehead. She lay tensely, in an agony of embarrassment. Her free hand made a fist and hit the bed helplessly. "I am so sorry I hurt you, Mr. Jones," she whispered. "We just seem to have gotten off on the wrong foot entirely; I—"

"Literally," he gasped. He lifted his head and looked at her, a wicked gleam chasing the pain out of his eyes. His lashes curled even when his eyes were open, she noted absently. "Although I rather enjoyed your direct approach. If you wanted me on the bed, Miss Spence, all you had to do was ask. I never refuse a lady."

She'd just bet he didn't, she thought as he allowed her to stand. And few would refuse him. She sighed regretfully. "I *always* refuse, Mr. Jones." Her only annoyance, if she was honest, was at her body's traitorous reaction to his caressing hand, and not to his teasing. She joined in his groaning laughter from the safety at the top of the stairs.

"I really am sorry this degenerated into a slapstick routine." She saw his smile stiffen with pain as he tried shifting his leg to roll over. "If you want to rest for a while," she suggested gently, "I can explain later what I think we can do about the bathroom and cooking situation." She started down the spiral steps. Just before her head disappeared from view, she flashed him a quick grin. "I'll be around all afternoon; just come over whenever you're ready."

Ryan eased onto his back and inched up toward the pillows, stuffing one gingerly under the throbbing in his right thigh. The contemptuous smile on his face was solely for himself. He linked his hands behind his head and settled more comfortably onto the narrow bed. He stared up at a boring white plaster ceiling, seeing big blue eyes full of dismay at causing him pain. She would have been shocked if she'd known of the sweet aching in the middle of his body and the tingling he still felt in the center of his palm. And she would be outraged if she knew the ideas that ache and that tingle were giving him.

The file folder on the table spilled out photocopies of newspaper articles, police forms, grand-jury transcripts and IRS returns. Long fingers, dusted with fine dark hair, gathered the contents together. Meticulously they straightened the edges of the papers and laid the file gently on the trestle table. Ryan rocked onto the back legs of his chair and braced his good leg on the edge of another, stretching his right leg across the seat. A couple hours' rest had greatly eased the ache of two days of travel and Ariel's hard knee.

He knew virtually every word on the 173 pages in the file, and still he didn't know exactly what he was supposed to be doing here . . . or why he had agreed to come. He was here in no official capacity, just doing a favor for his brother and making a few decisions about his life.

Both his brother Rick and Rick's boss, the district attorney for the county of San Francisco, wanted the case closed. There had been an ongoing investigation into the murder for months, costing time, money and manpower, and turning up nothing. According to Rick, the investigation had stalled and would remain that way unless there was some kind of a break. After so many months, that didn't seem likely.

Ariel Spence was a murderess, guilty of the cold-blooded killing of her fiancé, Dennis DiSanto. The D.A. was convinced of it. She hadn't pulled the trigger, but she had been on the scene, orchestrating the event. Rick, the chief assistant district attorney, seemed less sure, but he wasn't ready to declare her totally innocent, either.

As the D.A. handling the investigation, Rick had been free to make copies of everything he had on the case. He had done so, then given them to his brother, ostensibly just to seek Ryan's opinion on the difficult case. Ryan had gotten hooked on the mystery, the too-many "coincidences," in the case, just as Rick had known he would. Then Rick had casually suggested a month's recuperation in Montana, where he just happened to know about half of a comfortable, converted schoolhouse for rent. Ryan could relax, fish the little mountain streams, let his leg finish healing—and ferret out a few of Miss Ariel Spence's guilty secrets. What else did he have to do for the next month?

Nothing. Ryan had admitted to himself that he wasn't ready to resume his law practice; he wasn't even sure he wanted to. So he had pretended not to see through his brother's transparent ploy and agreed to come to this town on the road to nowhere. The only problem was that Ariel Spence didn't look like she had any secrets, guilty or otherwise.

He picked up the file, tapping it absently on the table top. So just how was he going to occupy himself for a month? Maybe he would just catch his mental breath. The five days he had drifted on the Pacific under a scorching sun, watching his life ooze red drop by red drop into the salty green water, had brought on a crisis he'd thought to avoid forever.

Whenever he thought about his life, which was as seldom as possible, he always thought it would probably end in a glorious blaze of recklessness. He supposed he should be grateful to the anonymous powerboat that had run him down, leaving him to die off the coast of Kauai. There had been no glorious blaze, only a misty red agony and a grinding determination to survive just one more minute. As he had dangled beneath the rescue helicopter, his only lucid thought had been that he had made it; the fight to stay alive was over.

When he left the hospital, he discovered that the fight wasn't over, it was just moving to a more difficult battlefield. His law partner had informed him that he would handle Ryan's three pending cases, but no more. He was tired of defending guilty scum, no matter how much dirty money they could offer. Either they changed the type of client they took on or the partnership was dissolved. Ryan couldn't blame him. He was tired, too, tired of defending human trash he knew to be guilty as hell, but rich enough to pay his price. There had to be more to his life than that.

So, here he was, catching his breath, helping out his brother. He glanced at the file. He was going to satisfy his own curiosity about the woman, too.

Dennis DiSanto's murder had made headlines even down the coast in Los Angeles. The wealthy, handsome dentist had been one of the most sought-after bachelors in San Francisco. Yet he had successfully eluded every woman determined to snare him. Then, about two years ago, it appeared that the thirty-five-year-old DiSanto overcame his severe allergy to matrimony. He was seen constantly in the company of a young blond librarian turned historical researcher, whom no one had ever heard of before. He made no secret of the fact he was now the one determined to get married, while the lady seemed decidedly cool to the idea. Cynics had predicted that his interest would soon flag, but it never did. On a blustery December day in Golden Gate Park, nine months ago, it was in the arms of the blonde that he had died. And suddenly everyone knew her name.

DiSanto's killer had suffered a heart attack immediately after firing the silenced rifle. He died without ever revealing the motivation for his murderous act. When his widow tearfully lamented his depression over his recent retirement from the exterminating business and publicly begged the forgiveness of the DiSanto family and Dennis's fiancée, the respectable newspapers let them all rest in peace.

Not so the more scandal-minded tabloids. Ariel Spence's name and face were smeared over their pages regularly. The story had all the elements of a long-running epic designed to titillate readers. Rich, handsome hero; beautiful, somewhat mysterious heroine; hero's uncle reputed to be an old-time organized-crime boss. There were whispers that the killing had been a gangland execution. There were louder whispers that the hero, while supposedly besotted with the heroine, had occasionally been seen picking up a one-nighter in a singles' bar. Through it all, Ariel Spence repeated her contention that the killing was just a random shooting by a pathetic, crazy old man.

The uncle had indeed had organized crime connections—twenty-five years before and on the opposite coast. When Dennis Di-Santo and his younger brother Robert were orphaned, the old man had divested himself of his old friends and "businesses" and moved cross-country to Bel Air. The real estate development company he had recently turned over to his younger nephew was totally legitimate.

Ariel Spence said she was a researcher for several best-selling authors of historical romances. She politely declined to publicly name them, saying it might hurt their reputations and credibility, and her income. Rick hadn't seemed to think that income remarkable; indeed, he'd been reluctant even to discuss it, but Ryan had been astounded. He'd dryly observed to his brother that if she could make that much from doing mere historical research, they'd both wasted their years in law school. He would see, over the next month, just how much research she did.

Dennis DiSanto had been more than a simple dentist, it seemed. After his death the police had discovered his very profitable, very illegal sideline of writing prescriptions for morphine and other controlled substances for addict "patients." He'd dabbled in some small-time drug smuggling, but he hadn't hit the big time until two years ago.

Two years ago Ariel Spence had met Dennis DiSanto when she was well into several months of on-site historical research in a remote area of Mexico, populated by Yaqui Indians, impoverished farmers and, coincidentally, drug smugglers. Dennis DiSanto had accompanied Ariel Spence on several of her trips, dispensing free dental care in as many villages as possible, making contacts all over the area, another coincidence. Suddenly DiSanto had become a very successful smuggler of whatever illegal drug was turning the most profit at the time. Coincidence?

DiSanto continued his charity missions, alone, one weekend a month, right up to his death, dispensing dentures, filling cavities—and taking delivery from an unknown middleman. A familiar sight to the U.S. border patrolmen, they'd waved him through each time, without even the most cursory search. Not one of them could believe that the good dentist who gave so generously of his time and skill could be guilty of smuggling in a fortune in high-grade cocaine and heroin in his pickup and camper.

Ariel Spence had certainly been shocked to learn about Di-Santo's little prescription business. The D.A. had dismissed her surprise as an act, a much better one than her restrained, dry-eyed grief. They hadn't let her know they knew about the drug running, hoping she'd get careless and give herself away. So far, she hadn't.

It was obvious to the D.A. that DiSanto had been set up by someone close to him, someone who knew where he would be that Wednesday afternoon in December, someone who could even have suggested the outing herself, then been on hand to see that there were no mistakes. And no one seemed to have been closer to Dennis DiSanto than Ariel Spence—the most incriminating coincidence of all. She was guilty. She had to be.

Proving it was another matter. All the district attorney's office had were the sworn statements of informants who would sell their mothers for a dime bag of heroin, oblique references, and too many "coincidences" that strained belief in her contention that DiSanto's murder was just a random killing. Rick had been told to come up with solid proof, not circumstantial evidence, responsible witnesses to produce in court, and a motive.

In the D.A.'s mind Ariel Spence was an opportunist who had formed a partnership with Dennis DiSanto that would earn both of them far more than research or dentistry ever could. The most likely motive was that opportunity to make even more profit had presented itself, and Ariel had taken it. Most likely someone wanting to get rid of the competition had approached her with the deal to set DiSanto up.

Both DiSanto and Ariel Spence's profits remained well hidden. DiSanto's rather modest estate had gone not to his fiancée or to his uncle and brother, who hardly needed it, but to endow a dental-school scholarship in his name. Ariel Spence had inherited only his dog, his guns and all his photographic equipment.

Her tax returns had been scrutinized under a ten-power microscope: every penny in her checking and money-market accounts, the cash that had bought her house in San Francisco and the Burnt Fork School, even the $76.95 she'd splurged on an angora sweater last month, had been accounted for. Ryan knew it was easy to hide income, though, especially income you didn't want to have to explain. Several of his clients had shown him the tricks to establishing secret accounts that were virtually untraceable and purchasing holdings that could be lost in a labyrinth of dummy corporations.

The San Francisco District Attorney hadn't given up. When every lead had been followed diligently to a dead end, he'd declared Ariel Spence a material witness and put her in Rick's custody for her own "protection." For the first two months she had lived with Rick and Eileen, helping with their newborn daughter while Eileen recovered her strength. Then Rick had come up with the plan to isolate her in her Montana schoolhouse, where her contact with the outside world could be carefully monitored, and sold his boss on it. Ryan didn't imagine Rick had had to do much selling to Ariel. Even isolation in this tiny Montana town, under the watchful eye of Chief Dye and with a tap on her phone, had to be better than house arrest in San Francisco.

The D.A. was sure that a final payoff was coming, or that the insurance of her permanent silence would eventually be attempted. In nearly eight months neither had happened. She lived quietly, occasionally renting out half of her schoolhouse to vacationers. The rest of the time she was alone, except for the dog.

Page fifty-eight of the file had been a shocker, although it had nothing to do with the case. Ariel had exhibited symptoms of a miscarriage a few weeks after the murder. A copy of the doctor's treatment record revealed that a pregnancy would have made medical—and possibly religious history. In an age of free-and-easy sex, Ariel Spence was a virgin, an anachronism belonging to the age she specialized in researching.

Ryan knew his brother had been expecting some snide chauvinistic comment on that bit of information. He had only felt wonder as to how she had held off, yet still captivated the reputedly sexually voracious DiSanto. The only truth he was certain of in all the half lies, innuendos and impossible coincidences was that Dennis DiSanto had truly loved Ariel Spence.

He had also been oddly outraged that even this privacy, the most intimate of all, had been invaded, revealed for all the boys in the D.A.'s office to snigger at and lewdly speculate on. Rick had assured him that the report had never been in the open file, had never been seen by anyone but the two of them and the D.A. himself.

The quiet tapping on his door roused him. He grinned wryly as he went to answer it. Perhaps she'd come to tell him how to cope with the results of her mischief. He sincerely hoped she would take pity on him and not condemn him to the tumbled-down privy and rusty pump he'd seen outside.

She was smiling shyly and, he liked to think, a little hopefully as he opened the door. "Hi. I've fixed some supper and thought maybe you'd like to share it."

"Thank you." He was genuinely pleased by her offer, even though he knew it had been made only to atone for the unwelcome surprises she'd had for him.

Relaxing in one of the captain's chairs around a round oak dining table, he watched her ladle bean soup from a big pot on the stove top. Her half of the schoolhouse was a gem, but then his own place had surprised him. He had been expecting second hand store castoffs, not good solid antiques and comfortable, very masculine, leather couches and chairs. Ariel owned the schoolhouse, but DiSanto had obviously furnished the half Ryan had rented, making him wonder just how much time the man had spent here with her. Whatever else he might have been, DiSanto had liked comfort and had good taste. Ryan focused on Ariel's straight back and softly flaring hips as she worked at the stove. He'd already known DiSanto had good taste.

His eyes wandered around what was essentially one large L-shaped living room. Her place was softer, more feminine, with more of the touches necessary to make it a real home. Most of her furniture was antique, too, but lighter in color and smaller in size. The carpets were softly faded Orientals that showed as much character as age. Overstuffed, deep green plush chairs and a couch were drawn close to an elegant cast iron and brass wood stove with etched glass doors. His glance lingered on the sofa. It was long enough to accommodate his height and wide enough for two bodies, if one of them was rather slight.

Behind the sitting area was a wall of books. A narrow door exactly in the middle led, he guessed, to the garage. The shelves were crammed, but orderly. Reference books for her research, perhaps, but most likely, he decided, a lot of recreational reading. His private little smile was scornful. She and the dentist would have needed something to do on those long evenings.

A massive rolltop desk holding a word processor stood at right angles to the outside wall. Papers spilled out of the countless pigeonholes. Across the oak floor from the desk was the original staircase to the second floor, a half bath and closet tucked under it.

He looked back across the green tiled countertop separating the kitchen from the dining area. Ariel was swinging down the black glass door of the oven and pulling out a baking sheet. Two shiny, narrow loaves of French bread slid free onto a wire rack. The aroma of the fresh-baked bread brought a low, ravenous growling from his stomach, and Ryan realized how starved he was.

She brought their dinner to the table and sat down. "I'm sorry there's not more," she began, "but I'm not—"

His hand, already holding a slice of bread, waved her apology aside. He took a bite, swallowed and grinned appreciatively. "Don't apologize. This is really excellent."

She smiled back, then frowned at Murphy. The dog had seated herself next to Ryan's chair and was looking wistfully at the bread in his hand. "I can cook a few things very well, and everything else very badly. Murphy, go—"

"She's okay." He fed the dog the bit of bread. "What few things?"

"What . . ." She would tell him later that she never allowed the dog to beg at the table.

"What few things do you cook well?" he repeated patiently. The devilry in his eyes told her that he knew she didn't like him feeding the dog, and he was going to do it anyway.

"Soup and bread."

One black eyebrow went up. "Why only those?" He took a cautious sip of the cloudy liquid in a glass by his soup bowl. It was the best apple juice he had ever tasted. He enjoyed a long swallow, marvelling at the contentment he felt sharing a very simple, ordinary supper with her.

"Because you can make a lot of soup and bread at one time," she stated succinctly. "So I do, and freeze the leftovers. Then I just pop them in the microwave later." She sliced more bread, popped a sliver in her mouth and grinned at him.

"That's all you eat. Soup and bread?" No wonder she was so thin. He got up for a refill, silently gesturing toward her blue stoneware bowl with the ladle.

"Salads, fruit." She shrugged. She accepted her full soup bowl back from him, frowning at it doubtfully. "I didn't want this much."

"Eat it," he said blandly. "You need it." He considered the glass in her hand and not the look of consternation tightening her soft mouth. "That apple juice is good. You make it, too?" He reached across the table. With the tip of his finger he blotted a fleck of brown foam from the corner of her mouth. Holding her eyes, he slowly licked his finger clean.

Her glass frozen in midair, Ariel stared at him. She was thoroughly unnerved. His casually intimate gesture unsettled her, she supposed, because it was so completely unexpected. "Umm...this place...came with an old apple orchard." With an effort she broke her trance, noticing the glass still in her hand. With a quick, jerky movement she set it down, feeling completely foolish. This was undoubtedly his standard operating procedure with any reasonably attractive female. She certainly wouldn't be seduced as easily as her addled dog. "There was a very good crop this year, so I made juice and froze it. It's easier to make than soup," she finished briskly.

Realizing that he was probably close to eating up those leftovers she was counting on, he regretfully passed up another bowl of soup. A few minutes later, spooning up some of the golden cherries in the dessert bowl she set in front of him, he savored a taste that could never have come from a supermarket. "Did you freeze these, too?"

"No, I canned them." She twisted in her chair, indicating a quart canning jar on the counter, half filled with cherries. "One of my neighbors traded me for some apples."

He looked at her in surprise. "Home canning? I didn't think anybody did that anymore."

She looked back in equal surprise. "It would have been wrong to waste them."

Ryan bit back a laugh that threatened to choke him. The dangerous murderess spent her time canning cherries. "So what else do you do, besides make apple juice and tear out the plumbing?"

Ariel shot him a wary look. She didn't see anything more threatening than polite interest on his face. "Oh, I refinish antiques I pick up around here and," she glanced at him guiltily, "I'm about done with remodeling the house." Her hand gestured vaguely. "I do some research for a couple of historical romance writers. Right now I'm interviewing some of the residents at the rest home in town, trying to get a better perspective on life around here at the turn of the century.'' It had been so hard at first to find enough to occupy her long days and empty nights. Finally she had managed to establish a routine that kept her from going crazy at the waiting.

He nodded interestedly, then pushed himself back slightly from the table. Propping an elbow on the edge, he rested his cheek on his palm. His free hand reached across, idly brushing her hair behind her shoulders. ''Now, Miss Spence,'' he said with deceptive mildness, ''suppose you tell me what I'm going to do for a bathroom until Thursday.''

What he was going to do was simple. He was going to use hers. She would leave her door unlocked, which he exasperatedly suspected she did anyway, so he could use the bath and shower whenever he wanted. She also offered him unlimited use of her kitchen. She was making it ridiculously easy for him. He would be free to poke around as much as he pleased until he found the evidence of her guilt.

Chapter 2

Ariel stared into the unblinking yellow eyes that had silently wakened her. Burying her head under the pillow, she groaned, "Darn it, Murphy, why didn't you think of this when I let you out before we went to bed?" Muttering under her breath, she climbed out of bed. Not bothering to put a robe over her short lavender nightshirt, she stumbled sleepily downstairs. She opened her door, traipsed down the short hall in her bare feet, and threw open the outside door to a chill, night breeze.

"Out!" she commanded fiercely. The dog scratched infuriatingly at the lawyer's door instead of going obediently outside.

"Murphy! What's gotten into you?" she scolded in an aggrieved whisper. Bracing her feet on the rough floor while the breeze whistled up her nightshirt, she tried dragging the stubborn dog by her leather collar. Murphy had passive resistance down to a fine art. She collapsed on the floor, curling her upper lip in a sly grin.

"Oh...phooey!" Ariel snapped. Mentally, she could swear with the best of them, but her oral vocabulary of four-letter words included only such hair-curlers as rats, nerd, snot and drat. It was all her mother's fault, with that toothbrush and that damned cake of soap.

"You are *not* going to bother that poor man," she informed the intractable dog sternly. "Now, come away from there and go...out...side!"

A low whining issued from Murphy's throat, and her eyes seemed suspiciously moist. Ariel knew what was coming next. The whine would become a loud whimper, then a full-fledged howl. Murphy was usually well-behaved, but she could be totally pigheaded on the rare occasions when she decided to challenge Ariel's authority. And Ariel always lost. She simply didn't have the heart to apply the discipline needed to win.

"All right!" she whispered furiously. "I'll let you in there, but, so help me, if you wake him up, I'll—"

Murphy never learned what her dire punishment would be. As soon as Ariel opened the door the sounds coming from the bedroom upstairs made her swallow the rest of her words. Murphy's nails clicked over the floorboards and up the spiral steps, finally galvanizing Ariel into scurrying after the dog.

She hesitated on the top step, uncertain of what to do. Should she intrude, or withdraw before she caused him any embarrassment? Dim moonlight seeped through the drawn curtains, and she could see Murphy's brown head resting on the man's pajama-clad knee. The dog gazed up sadly at his dark, bowed head.

Ryan sat on the edge of the bed, harsh sobbing breaths racking his body. His knuckles scrubbed dazedly at the tears still slipping from his tightly shut eyes. Suddenly his eyes opened wide, glazed by some inner horror. He locked his fists locked between his knees and shuddered violently.

The look in his unseeing eyes decided her. On bare feet she crossed the floor silently; then knelt beside him on the bed and gathered him into her arms.

"Ryan, it's all right." She spoke quietly, as if to reassure a frightened child. "You're safe here, Ryan."

Frighteningly strong arms wrapped around her, trapping her against him. Surprisingly she felt no fear, just deep compassion, a need to offer comfort, and another, unnameable emotion curling deep inside her. Her hands soothed over his bare back, warming the gooseflesh skin. Her fingers traveled over the too-sharp bones in the small of his back, the too-prominent ribs up his sides. Cords of hard muscle registered, too, and a long thin scar she wouldn't remember until later.

"Ryan. Wake up, Ry," she encouraged him gently. The darkness and his distress drew her into unconscious intimacy, and she unknowingly used the nickname again. "Wake up and talk to me, Ry."

He clung to the soft voice commanding him out of the shadow land he visited all too often. The voice called him back with a name out of his childhood. He eased his grip slightly, and his hands spread over her back and up into her soft, loose hair. Fingers like cool snowflakes were lifting the tangled hair from his clammy brow and combing it back. His harsh, uneven breath warmed her neck as he buried his face in silky, flower-scented hair.

God, he wished it were truly over. The dream was always the same. He was back on the surf ski, half crazy with pain and thirst. And the sharks were circling. A snow-white bird perched on the end of the board, looking at him with the dead eyes of the young girl he had found in the Cambodian hut. She had been one horror too many.

He had carefully moved the girl aside, then emptied the clip of his automatic rifle. The men he had surprised inside the hut had never had a chance to reach for their weapons.

He had left the silent girl with the dead brown eyes with the good French sisters in Bangkok. The nuns had sadly assured him that such cases were not uncommon, but with time and God's love the girl would forget and be healed. He had thought he had finally forgotten, but the ordeal on the ocean had brought the dreams back. He knew now that he had never forgotten, never been healed. God's love apparently didn't extend to him, but that wasn't surprising. He wasn't sure he believed in a God that allowed such atrocities to happen to innocents, then chose him as the instrument of His revenge. He wasn't even sure he believed in Ryan Jones sometimes.

Ryan hadn't heard his own hoarse whisper as he recounted aloud the nightmare he had been reliving in his memory. He didn't feel the warm tears soaking into his hair or hear the smothered sobs trembling through the body holding his. His rigid body relaxed, and he was suddenly freezing cold and too exhausted to sit up any longer. Collapsing back on the pillows, he pulled Ariel down with him. He was reluctant to lose the human contact, the comfort and warmth she offered. He felt her try to pull away, and he hugged her more tightly to him, patting her back with what he prayed was re-assurance.

"Please don't go," he whispered raggedly against her cheek. The warm wetness on it didn't register. "Stay just a minute longer." Hold me, he begged silently; don't leave me.

He felt her relax at last, felt her arms hug him back. Her heat began to seep into his chilled body, and he fell asleep, his heart and mind curiously at peace.

Ryan started to put his razor and toothbrush back into his kit bag, then decided he liked the way his things looked, jumbled in with hers on the bathroom counter. After splashing on after-shave, he set the bottle next to her cologne. He picked up the black fili-greed atomizer and sniffed. It was the same warm-sunshine and spring-flowers scent that had lingered on the nightshirt he'd found in his bed this morning, after the best night's sleep he'd had in years. The name etched on the gold cap was Femme. He took an-other whiff. The name and the scent suited her perfectly.

He gathered up his clothes and bag, then stood in the bathroom doorway, looking around her bedroom. She'd left a note on her door, saying she would be back from church at about ten-thirty and that he should help himself to whatever he could find in the kitchen for breakfast. He would, in a minute, but first he wanted a quick look around, and her bedroom was as good a place as any to start.

An elegant royal-blue-and-orange-enameled French parlor stove stood in one corner. The highboy dresser was a meticulously re-finished antique. There was an antique pier mirror and an old church pew under the window.

Her bed was fascinating. He was absolutely certain there couldn't be another like it anywhere. The roof under the cupola housing the old school bell had been removed. A platform bed had been constructed there, with three steps leading up to it. A built-in bookcase, with reading lights and mirrored shelves, formed the headboard, a brass blanket rail made the footboard. The upper walls of the little bell tower were now glassed in. Someone lying in that bed at night could look out at the stars in the black sky and almost feel a part of it. The word processor downstairs might be-long to a practical researcher of dry history, but this bed belonged to a romantic who indulged in a bit of fantasy.

Downstairs Ryan prowled through the drawers and cubbyholes in her desk. Everything was trustingly unlocked. There were innumerable sheets and scraps of paper covered with something that looked like the shorthand his secretary used. The word processor on the desk was the same model as his own. He switched on the machine and took a disk marked SA-I from the file box.

"Retrieve file SA-I," he commanded. The screen remained blank. He tried a couple of variations. Nothing. Apparently there was a code word. Maybe she did have secrets after all. He couldn't retrieve so much as a comma from any of the ten sets of disks in the file, all identified only by two initials and the Roman numerals I or II.

He supposed he should feel a bit guilty, but Rick had told him to nose around. He knew now that Rick and the D.A.'s suspicions were totally absurd. Murderesses did not hold virtual strangers in their succoring arms in the middle of the night. They didn't bake bread and worry about wasting fruit. There might be a problem about the inexplicable income, but he would stake his life that she'd had nothing to do with DiSanto's murder.

He moved over to the bookcase and gave the titles a cursory inspection. In fact, he was very suspicious of Rick's suspicions. Had Rick talked him into coming here hoping that he would find exactly nothing so the D.A. would finally be willing to close the case? There was another possibility, but he didn't think his brother was capable of such deviousness.

Hearing the sound of her returning Blazer, the tires crunching on the gravel outside, Ryan ambled into her kitchen and started the coffee. Murphy came in a couple of minutes later, ahead of her mistress. After nudging Ryan's hand she went to lie by the chair she had already decided was his. Ariel responded to the greeting he tossed over his shoulder and studied him while he finished making the coffee. This morning he was dressed in black chinos and a scarlet-and-black rugby shirt. Red was a good color for him; so was black. She fidgeted just a little. How would he deal with last night, especially when she'd had to leave her nightshirt in his bed? While she'd been searching for a spare blanket to wrap up in early this morning, she'd been in a panic that he would wake up and see her scampering naked around his bedroom.

Ryan knew she was waiting for him to turn around and talk, but he wasn't ready to, not yet. He wasn't too sure how she was going to react to the previous night. Oddly, he felt no embarrassment, but she might. He sliced some of last night's French bread and toasted it.

Ryan put the plate of toast on the table along with the coffeepot, while Ariel found apple jelly and butter in the refrigerator. Then, pulling out her chair, he seated her almost formally before pouring coffee into heavy mugs he'd found in a cupboard. She looked so fresh and pretty this morning. She'd wound her hair into a knot on top of her head, but it was refusing to stay there. He could have it down just by removing a couple of pins. Her dress was a soft peach, loose, but still clinging nicely here, floating there, and swirling around her knees when she walked.

"I didn't think to ask you if you wanted to go to church." There was a question in her soft words.

"I haven't been to church in years," he said almost wistfully. "Do you go every Sunday?"

"Usually."

His eyes followed the tip of her tongue as it darted out to lick a crumb of toast from the corner of her mouth. Forcibly he dragged them back to hers; she was watching him with a hint of unease. "I'm sorry if I frightened you last night," he said quietly.

The unease vanished. "You did, at first," she admitted, then smiled in understanding. "I've had a few nightmares myself and wished there had been someone—" the smile faded, and her eyes dropped "—to sit with me." Her eyes flickered up to his, then immediately back down. Someone to hold me, she added silently. To promise me that this limbo life would end soon, to tell me the bad dreams would go away and never return.

"I wish I had been here, Ariel." His fingers were as soft as his voice as he brushed a stray wisp of hair behind her ear. "I would have been happy to sit with you." To hold you, to keep the night demons away. "What happened?" he asked gently. His fingers drifted down the side of her neck and stroked lightly.

Ariel regarded him soberly for a few seconds. She felt the same curious feeling she had had last night in the darkness of his bedroom. She could only describe it as the fragile bonding of two souls. The brief moment passed, and she sighed, then shrugged tiredly. Chief Dye would no doubt give him all the dirt, anyway.

"I was involved in a murder," she said bluntly. "In San Francisco, where I live." She corrected herself with a sad little smile.

"Used to live." The smile turned bitter. "My picture was in all the papers. Maybe you saw it; I understand it made headlines even down in L.A. Your landlady is quite a notorious woman, Mr. Jones."

She turned her head and stared hard out the window over the sink. His hand rested on her shoulder, kneading the tight muscle. "I was a material witness. Actually, I'm still in the custody of Richard Jones, an assistant district attorney in San Francisco.

"He arranged for me to live here so I could move without two policemen constantly at my heels, but there's still not much freedom. I can't leave town, and there's so little to do here." She grimaced with barely contained frustration. "Give me bag ladies and winos, dirty fog and cheap tinsel any day."

She drew a deep, settling breath and faced him. Ryan's hand fell away. "That's why I was so tacky and tore up your place. I thought you had been sent to snoop, and I was furious."

With maximum effort he kept the guilt off his face.

"I'd been meaning to do it all summer, and now seemed like a better time than any what with the opportunity to make life miserable for the 'spy.' " She met his unreadable gaze levelly. "I am truly sorry about the mess. I've just let myself get paranoid the past few months."

"I'm sorry, too." His eyes, dark and full of secrets, locked with hers. "This can't be much of a life for you."

She was grateful that he didn't seem interested enough to ask for any of the details. Gradually his eyes resumed their usual blankness. Silently he reached over to the chair next to him and picked up her ruffled nightshirt. He bunched the soft lavender material in his hand and slid it across the tabletop to her.

"I guess I should explain that." She laughed sheepishly.

"I was hoping you would," he said conversationally. "I'd hate to think something special had happened last night, since I could remember absolutely nothing this morning." Something special *had* happened last night, he knew and the memory was precious.

Her eyes widened on the word "special"; then her soft mouth tightened primly. "Nothing happened, Mr. Jones," she stressed. "You were simply sleeping on part of my nightshirt. I couldn't move you, and I didn't want to wake you, so I just . . . unbuttoned . . ." She faltered, swallowing to wet her stubbornly dry throat. One long, dark finger had been rubbing the soft fabric of her nightshirt. Now his hand was fiddling with the buttons. She could feel skittering tingles under her skin, as if she was wearing the nightshirt while he was touching it, feeling the brush of those graceful fingers as they unbuttoned... "Unbuttoned it, slipped it off and left," she finished in a rush. A curious warmth flooded her body. She tore her eyes away from his hand and snuck a peak at his face.

He wasn't grinning, or looking smug, just staring at her with a vacant, dreamy little smile. His eyes suddenly focused. "It's Ryan, not Mr. Jones, Ariel. I think we got past the formalities last night." He paused, looking at her speculatively. "Why *did* you come in last night?"

"Murphy," she explained hastily. The dog raised her head languidly at the sound of her name. "She wanted to check on you, sleep in your room. I used to share the schoolhouse with... someone else sometimes. We left our doors open at night so she could go back and forth. Now, for some reason, she wants to resume the practice.

"I'll leave my door open, then," he promised with an odd little smile. He pushed himself back from the table, sweeping his clothes and bag off the chair, and stood up. "Maybe later you'll tell me where to buy groceries. I can't keep eating yours." After the fantasy he'd just had with her nightshirt, it might be best if she was out of his sight for a while. He would still think about her, of course. He had decided what he wanted from her, but already he was wondering if it would be enough.

Murphy got up to follow him across the hall, and Ariel called her back sharply. Reluctantly the dog returned to sit at her mistress's feet, gazing lovingly at the door.

Ariel aimed a disgusted look at the animal's head. "Traitor!" she muttered. "Really, Murphy, you're supposed to be protecting me." Yellow eyes granted her a brief, puzzled look. "The first handsome stranger who shows up, you nuzzle up to him like the worst kind of floozie!" Ariel wadded up the nightshirt in her fist and went upstairs to throw it in the hamper.

The sweat was running down into his eyes, blinding him. Ryan tore of the saturated sweatband and wiped the perspiration out of his eyes. He lay back down on the living room rug, his knees bent, and gasped air into his burning lungs. He really should have done the exercises before his shower, but his leg had just been too tight without the hot, pounding water to loosen it up. The sit-ups and push-ups were nothing, but the right leg lifts with a five-pound weight strapped to his ankle left him as drenched in sweat as if he'd run a ten-mile road race.

His door suddenly swung open, and Ariel stepped inside. "Ryan," she called, not seeing him on the floor at first. Then her sweeping glance found him. Quickly she crossed the room to him, her face paling noticeably. Falling to her knees beside him, she reached a hesitant hand toward the dimpled mass of white scar tissue and purpled flesh that was his right thigh.

"Oh, Ry," she breathed softly, her eyes clouded with distress. "Whatever did you do to yourself?"

She used the nickname she'd used last night naturally now, he noticed, as her cool fingers caressed his leg, sending fiery shivers up his groin to his belly. "It was more like what the propeller of a boat did to me."

His voice was hoarse, and she snatched her hand back, afraid she'd hurt him. "What happened?"

"I'm a little fuzzy on the details," he admitted with a harsh laugh. He sat up slowly, wishing she would touch his leg again. Her fingers seemed to drain away the pain. "All I remember is hearing an engine, seeing a light. When I came to, I was hanging on to what was left of my surf ski."

Her shocked eyes were still on his wound. "Did it take them long to get you to a hospital?"

"Five days."

Her head snapped up in disbelief. That explained part of his nightmare last night, the part about drifting on the ocean. "Five days?" Outrage sparked in her sky-blue eyes. "The person who ran you down didn't even stop? My God, you might have died!" Her anguished gasp was healing music to his soul.

"I almost did." He shrugged it off lightly. She'd taken down her hair when she'd changed into the tan slacks and green crew-neck shirt she had on now. As she bent closer to trace the scar with her eyes, her hair feathered over his belly, bared by his hiked-up sweatshirt. Involuntarily he sucked in his breath and held it. Finally she sat back on her heels, and he could breathe again.

"They even had to graft some muscle," she said slowly. She remembered something from the night before, and her hand went unconsciously to his back, unerringly following the long, thin scar it had found last night. "From your back." Her eyes returned to his, compassionate, but not pitying. "Are you all finished with surgery now?"

He nodded. "I just have to strengthen it now."

She glanced at the weight on his ankle. "It may not look too wonderful," she admitted with a rueful smile, "but the important thing is you still have it, and it still works." She patted the leg gently with approval.

Oh, love, he thought, where were you two months ago when I needed you? His hand threaded through her spun gold hair to bring her closer. I'm glad you're here now, he added silently, because I think I need you even more.

She was being drawn irresistibly toward him.

"Ariel? Where are you?" The deep, masculine shout came just before the door was thrown open.

Ariel was scrambling up off the floor as a curly-brown haired giant stalked in. Ryan stood up slowly behind her, measuring the man who was frowning at him through wire-rimmed glasses. Murphy sat beside Ryan growling quietly.

The giant was some four inches taller than he was and a good sixty pounds heavier. Ariel looked like a little girl standing next to him. Ryan shifted his legs slightly apart and tucked his thumbs in the waistband of his raggedy gym shorts. So, he had competition. He stared back at the man, who was also younger and darkly tanned, as if he spent most of his time outdoors. To fit the outdoor image, he wore worn Levis, scuffed boots and a khaki field shirt.

Ariel stood between the two unsmiling men. She knew they were sizing each other up like circling tomcats, and she sighed in vexation. Really, this was ridiculous.

"Sam Bass," she said a little sharply, "Ryan Jones, my new tenant. He's a lawyer from Los Angeles." Her hand gestured toward Sam, and he caught it before she could pull it back. "Sam is a fish biologist. He's working on a project on the Bitterroot River."

"Bass." Straight-faced, Ryan extended his hand. So Bass's life's work was studying his fishy cousins. The fish biologist had to drop Ariel's hand and step forward to take Ryan's. There was the briefest of handshakes.

"Jones." Sam Bass's deep voice rumbled. He turned to Ariel, effectively blocking her view of Ryan. "Ariel, I'm going up to the bridge to check my fish traps. Want to come along for the ride?"

"Okay. I just need to tell Ryan where to get groceries and—"

"I'm sure he can find the store by himself." Sam's soft brown eyes shot Ryan a hard look. "There's only the one, and it's right on the highway. He can't miss it."

"Go ahead, Ariel," Ryan allowed generously. "I'll see you when you come home." He let the giant digest the fact that he was living there, and the giant wasn't. "Will you be back for lunch?"

"No. She won't," Sam answered pleasantly, and wrapped a bear paw around her shoulder to take her away.

Ariel opened her mouth to protest, then decided it would be wiser to keep it shut. Later she would make it clear to them both that she wasn't an old chicken neck for them to fight over.

The fish biologist's voice rumbled in through the open window minutes later. "I thought all the plumbing fixtures were out of there, Ariel. What's he doing for a bathroom?"

Ryan heard her blithe answer. "He's using mine." He bent down to unstrap the weight and smiled to himself.

He wasn't smiling hours later as he slouched in one of her armchairs, his right leg stretched over the hassock, nursing a nearly empty glass of dark rum. He was watching Humphrey Bogart bid goodbye to a tearful Ingrid Bergman at a snowy airport. It wasn't snowing in Casablanca; it was snowing inside Ariel's television. Her reception was lousy. He supposed he was going to have to do something about *that*, too, along with his competition, the unused door locks and her skinniness. She hadn't been back for dinner, either. He'd finally given the extra spaghetti to a most appreciative Murphy.

Tilting his head against the chair back, he watched the credits roll and drained the glass. He didn't particularly care for movies with "noble" endings, where the hero gave up the girl to the "better" man. He'd always been more than a little skeptical of this one in particular. He had a sneaky hunch that ol' Rick would look Ilsa up after the war. That's what *he* would have done—if he had let her go in the first place.

A car drove up outside. He stayed where he was. One door slammed. If two slammed, he was staying right where he was all night, if necessary. The engine revved and the car left. Fish biologists were apparently a little short on manners. Sam hadn't even walked her to the door and seen her safely inside, Ryan thought perversely. Dr. Bass wasn't going to make any points that way. Ryan silently saluted his departing competitor with his empty glass.

Ariel closed her door quietly, started toward the stairs, then abruptly halted. "What? You're still up? It must be after midnight!"

"Twelve thirty-seven," he supplied obligingly, and turned his head to see her face. "What happened? Did he run out of gas? Have a flat?"

"No, he didn't run out of gas or have a flat," she denied with syrupy annoyance. "I didn't know he meant the bridge down by Darby. It was after five before he finished his count, so we just decided to have dinner in Darby and go to the movie there."

"Mmm." He turned back to the snowy test pattern. "I hope you had a nice time." Sam the Bass was a wilier fish than he'd given him credit for.

Ariel scowled at the back of his head. Why had she felt obligated to explain her lateness. As if she was back in high school and he was her father? "I've got a headache," she announced. "I'm going to bed. Please—"

"Wait." He was out of the chair and between her and the stairs before she had taken two steps. "We leave our doors open tonight, right?" The corners of his mouth quirked up in a strange anticipatory smile. He took a step forward, trailing his thumb down her smooth cheek to her jaw.

"For Murphy." The words were a little breathless. She felt timeless longings stirring at long last to life, coiling their first, shyly eager tendrils deep inside her. She stepped back.

He closed the distance between them again, in the oldest of dances. His thumb followed the line of her jaw, stopping in the soft hollow beneath her chin. It took only the slightest pressure to tilt her mouth to his. "I just wanted to make sure," he whispered. His breath, rum scented, cooled her suddenly flushed face.

The kiss wasn't what she'd been subconsciously expecting for the past twenty-four hours. His mouth was surprisingly soft, incredibly gentle and unscrupulously experienced. His lips nibbled and sucked at hers, subtly coaxing her to respond. She would have resisted a rough demand, but she was utterly defenseless against this insidiously smooth persuasion. Only the top of his right thumb and his lips were touching her, and she felt melded to him, unable and unwilling to move.

Her warmed lips parted on a sigh, and his right hand dropped to her throat, long fingers circling it lightly. His left hand came up to comb through the hair at the back of her head. As he held her with a magician's light touch, his tongue delicately stroked over her moist lips, beguiling her mouth with magic. Her tongue met his with a shy sorcery of its own. As her arms rose to bring his body closer to satisfy a sudden craving, he pulled back and the illusion ended. She didn't hear her quiet moan of protest as her hands fell, frustratingly empty, to her sides.

His dark gaze searched her flushed face and smoky eyes. There was a hint of satisfaction in his velvet voice when he spoke. "You're very responsive," he murmured. His fingers traced her lips. "I wasn't expecting that." He brushed a whisper soft kiss over her forehead. "Goodnight, Ariel Spence. Sweet dreams."

He silently disappeared across the hall, leaving her thoroughly confused and not a little panicked by the unfamiliar hungers slowly winding through her. She'd wondered what sort of magic he possessed that had worked so well on Murphy. It seemed it worked just as well on her.

Chapter 3

Ariel, I don't think your heart is in this today, dear."

Ariel started guiltily. She looked back at the elderly woman sitting across from her in the sunny bedroom at the Valley View Rest Home. The woman's face was seamed, a line for every hardship and tragedy in her long life. Yet they gave her a timeless beauty, reflecting her triumphs and the defeats she'd had to accept with quiet dignity and unflagging spirit. Despite the near uselessness of her body, she sat erect in her wheelchair. Bessie Ruff dealt with infirmity with the same fortitude that had seen her through being widowed, left penniless with five small children sixty years before.

Flipping off the tiny recorder, Ariel replayed the past few minutes through her memory. It was no use; she had no idea what Bessie might have been telling her. Ever since that first galvanic handshake with Ryan Jones, she had been slightly out of kilter. It was not an uncomfortable feeling, though, more like the anticipation of some unknown delight that would soon be hers.

She sighed contritely. "I'm sorry, Bessie; I'm just wasting your time. I have . . . other things on my mind today."

"Don't apologize. I always tried to think of something else myself," the old lady confided dryly, "when I had to help my mother make soap. Are you still going to try it?"

"As soon as the butcher gets me the fat. I already have the lye."

"Well, you're certainly going to extremes for a little authenticity. You must remember what I said, and don't inhale any lye dust or splash the stuff on you. Lye burns are more reality than you need."

"I will." Ariel gently patted the arthritis-gnarled hand curled on the table between them. The age-spotted skin looked so fragile.

"I hear you've got a new tenant." Her ninety-six years and a stroke might have slowed Bessie's body, but her bright brown eyes still saw very clearly through her trifocals. Something, or someone, had finally put a sparkle in those sad blue eyes.

It had ceased to amaze Ariel that Bessie, without leaving the rest home, could know everything about everybody in the valley. "He's a lawyer from Los Angeles, recuperating from an accident. He has this terrible scar on his right thigh." Bessie's sparse white eyebrows rose just a bit. "He's awfully thin, but—" Ariel cleared her throat "—he's rather good-looking."

The little nurse's aide had seen him at the fiddlers' contest and said he was a "hunk." Maybe there was hope for the girl yet. The big-city lawyer might be the one to dig her out of her piles of research books and convince her that there were better ways to waste time than making lye soap. "How long's he staying?" Bessie asked interestedly.

Murphy's cheerful yipping and Ariel's oddly out-of-breath voice trying to hush her had nudged him awake that morning. After climbing a little stiffly out of bed, Ryan had stood at the side of his open bedroom window. He'd watched her pound across the last few yards from the orchard through a withered garden in an all-out race with the galloping brown dog. The golden wash of early-morning sunlight rinsed through the blond hair flowing behind her as her long legs gracefully lifted her over a pile of frost-blackened tomato vines. She'd looked like a carefree twelve-year-old out playing with her dog.

Her green nylon running shorts pulled over the tight curve of her bottom as she bent over, hands on her knees, gulping air. Even under the sexless, white UCLA sweatshirt, he had seen her breasts heaving with effort. Murphy had shoved her cold nose into the small of Ariel's back, and she had straightened with a shriek, then glanced up guiltily to his window. He knew she couldn't see him.

Severely admonishing the dog again, though with a wonderfully silly giggle, she had led the way through the back door of the house. During his exercises the diesel rumble of her Blazer had announced her departure, and Murphy had come to see what was keeping him.

Taking a second mug of coffee with him, Ryan wandered to the wall of books. He looked much more closely today, pulling out the contents at random. There were albums of faded photos, yellowed newspapers, tattered diaries and bundles of letters with exquisite Spencerian script, as well as crudely bound little volumes from long-defunct local presses. He decided that she must have grubbed through endless dusty boxes at estate sales and in junk shops to acquire a literary collection of early Western Americana most museums would covet.

There was also an eclectic range of recreational reading, just as he had figured: science fiction, novels, poetry, mysteries and Westerns, of course. His eyes were drawn to a nearly empty shelf. All the others were full, the books crowding each other, yet this one held only ten thick paperbacks by the same author. Why were these ten segregated to themselves, and what was she saving the much-needed space for?

Choosing the first, he scanned the cover. A beautiful blond girl, her old-fashioned dress artfully revealing, clung to the massive, mostly bared chest of a copper-haired cowboy. He was cradling her lovingly, if a bit lasciviously, in one arm, while the other cracked a bull whip.

Ryan grinned knowingly to himself. So Ariel was fond of the romances she did the research for, except . . . His brow creased in puzzlement. The book looked like it had never been opened, much less read. He idly flipped through it, then stopped to skim a page. He read with greater attention, going back a few pages to get the background.

The hero and heroine were out in the open wilderness. Blinding snow devils from an imminent blizzard were swirling around them. They stumbled on, practically into a river, where the hero saw steam rising. A hot spring! They were saved! They could wait out the storm in warmth and relative comfort.

The hero, obviously a quick thinker and ever resourceful, convinced the doubtful heroine to take off her clothes and stash them with his in a tiny cave so they would have dry clothes when the storm ended. They sank to their necks in the steaming water. One thing led to another and they ended up making love in the lifesaving water in the middle of a snowstorm. The heroine melted in the hero's arms as satisfyingly and completely as the snowflakes in the hot water.

Ryan felt a little steamy himself as he finished the scene. He would love to try it sometime; a hot tub would pale by comparison. The author, Felicia Fury—the name had to be a pseudonym—had either really done it or had a fantastic imagination. Either way he would like to meet her. Then he grimaced at his foolishness. "She" was probably a he, or a frustrated, fat, fiftyish old maid.

His eyes drifted back to the open book in his hands. The passage was undeniably erotic, but beautifully written. He could feel the heated water lapping his own body with every thrust, while the steam and storm mingled around their naked bodies. The same shivers of delight raced through him as the heroine's hot, slick tongue licked icy crystals of snow from the hero's chest, curling around his hardened nipples.

Ryan shut the book with a snap and reshelved it. The fantasy was becoming a little too real; Ariel's face had replaced that of the girl's on the cover. Maybe later he would find out what other fantasies Felicia Fury had. As he strolled out to the backyard, the coincidence of the characters' names struck him; Spence Tucker and Ariel March.

Ariel was following the measured thunk of an ax. She stopped short at the back corner of her schoolhouse. Sunlight flashed off the newly sharpened and cleaned ax as it rose and fell solidly into the chunk of dry apple wood. Ryan's back was to her, the fabric of his chambray shirt straining across it as the ax swung again. It paused for a pulse beat at the top of its arc as those strong, elegant hands slid along the smooth handle to a new grip. His slim hips shifted in old khakis, his thighs tensing as the ax arced down and neatly split the log.

Unconscious of his audience, he set another log on the block. He rested the hickory ax handle along his long leg, unbuttoned his shirt and shrugged out of it, then he tossed it carelessly aside into the scattered, fragrant wood chips. Ariel's fingers remembered the feel of his back. The muscles in his arms and shoulders bunched and slid smoothly as the ax flashed again. They pulled tight under the sweat-shined skin, and her palms began to itch oddly. The metal drove into the wood, and she felt the impact herself, the sense of something cleaving through her.

Murphy's welcoming woof broke his rhythm on the next piece. He turned to find her watching him. A soft warmth lit his dark eyes. "Hi. Been home long?"

He reached down for his shirt and slowly slid into it, flexing his shoulders to find a comfortable fit. He left it hanging free, unbuttoned, and took a couple of steps toward her.

"Ah...no." Her answer had a curiously wistful sigh in it. Pulling herself out of a languorous fog, she added, avoiding the glint in his chocolate-brown eyes, "Thank you for chopping the wood, but you don't—"

"Did you cut this all yourself?" he interrupted. The sweep of his arm indicated the cord of neatly stacked logs and the stumps of dead apple trees in the orchard.

Her thin shoulders lifted carelessly. "It takes a lot of wood to heat the house, and it's good exercise."

He suppressed a smile, raking her slender body. He couldn't think of any other woman he knew who would consider using the heavy chainsaw he'd found next to the ax "good exercise." "What's that in your hand?"

"The mail. You've already got a couple of letters." She handed over the envelopes and frowned puzzledly at a package in her hands.

After scanning his mail quickly, Ryan stuffed the letters in his back pocket. "What's that?" He pointed to the box under the brown wrapping paper she'd already torn through.

Ariel shook her head. "I don't know. There's no return address, and the postmark is smeared." Suddenly her face lighted with a golden smile as she read the enclosed note, and she laughed delightedly. "Oh, I think I know who this is from!" Ryan bent down and idly picked up the paper she'd discarded. "There are these two high school boys, Billy Greef and Davey Severson, who always want to help whenever I substitute for the school librarian. I think," she confided with a shy smile, "they have a crush on me."

He squinted at the postmark, trying to make it out. The city and the date were hopelessly smeared, but he could decipher, barely, the two-letter abbreviation for the state at the bottom of the circle:

CA—not MT for Montana. He seriously doubted that Billy and Davey had made a quick trip to California to mail a surprise to their teacher. That sixth sense he'd learned to trust in jungle shadows years ago raised the hair on the back of his neck.

Ariel lifted the yellow lid of the three-pound box of candy and offered it to him. "Here, would you like a piece?"

Being deliberately clumsy was not easy, he discovered. He acquired new respect for clowns and their seemingly effortless pratfalls. His foot apparently tripped on the uneven ground as he reached for a piece of candy, and his hand hit the box and sent it sailing. Chocolate rained down on the white woodchips.

"Uh—oh. I'm afraid I owe you a new box of candy." His tone was deeply apologetic.

Ariel looked from him to the empty yellow box to the sawdust-covered candy on the ground, then finally back to his chagrined face. An odd expression crossed hers. "That's all right," she answered shortly. "Actually, I don't really care for chocolate. I probably would have taken it to the rest home anyway." Her eyes narrowed, closely studying his face. "Are you okay?" she asked softly.

One shoulder lifted negligently. "Sure. My leg just buckled."

She gave him another close look, then stooped to gather up the candy. His left leg?

As he bent to help her, Ryan gave Murphy's nose a surreptitious swat when it came sneaking under his arm to snitch a piece of chocolate. He took the box from Ariel's hand when he was sure every piece was back in it, then picked up the wrapping and the note by their edges. He tucked the box under his arm, careful not to smear his sleeve over it.

Brushing a loose curl off her cheek, he pulled Ariel up with him. "I'll treat you to lunch in town to make up for the candy you didn't really want." His fingers guided the errant curl behind her ear again. "Anyway, it's the thought that counts." He almost laughed at his macabre joke.

She finally smiled at him. "Thank you, but I should warn you—it's going to cost you a cheeseburger with everything on it, fries and a strawberry shake."

"Even onions?" he groaned, laughing.

She grinned evilly. "Piles of onions."

Detouring to his kitchen, Ryan placed the papers and candy box in an empty grocery sack. Nearly every drugstore in the United States sold this brand of candy. The cheap white paper and wrapping paper were even more readily available. The note was a single line of handwritten block letters—"FROM YOUR SECRET ADMIRER." The attempt was rather crude and definitely amateurish, and Ryan was absolutely certain the candy had been meant as a deadly, not sweet, surprise.

But why? He refused to believe that the district attorney was right, that she'd had anything to do with DiSanto's death beyond being unfortunate enough to witness it. Yet the D.A. would seize upon this incident as further proof of her guilt. He would say that her partner was getting worried that she could become a liability and had decided to ensure her silence. The D.A. would still see her as a suspect, not a victim.

And just how did Ryan Jones see her? As a puzzle, a fascinating puzzle with a few key pieces missing that, inexplicably, he felt compelled to find. She had a sweetness, almost an innocence, about her that was startling combined with her sly wit. The prospect of sharing greasy French fries with her at a seedy drive-in was more exciting than taking the most beautiful, experienced woman in Los Angeles to an elegant restaurant and then home for a long dessert, and he couldn't explain that, either. The thought that someone was trying to harm her filled him with cold-blooded rage.

Ariel sat on the worn seat of Ryan's power wagon, watching him lock first the old schoolhouse lock, then the new dead bolt. Chief Dye had installed it personally, but she never took the time to bother with it. That's what comes from living in Los Angeles and having only criminals for clients, she decided self-righteously. You don't trust anyone.

Then she sighed. And you, Ariel, you chump, you trust everyone. Will you never learn? This is how it started with Dennis, and look how *that* turned out. Just a snack, he'd said, as if they were simply going to the drive-in after school. The next thing she knew, she was planning to marry him. And she would have, never knowing how he'd lied to her. He had let her believe him to be nothing more than a handsome, charming, successful dentist. Never had she suspected the even more successful career he'd had writing very proper, very aboveboard—and very illegal—prescriptions for dope.

The police had told her the truth, and she suspected there was more
truth that they hadn't told her.

Yet she must have suspected, unconsciously, that Dennis wasn't
quite what he appeared to be. That must have been what had kept
her from making the ultimate commitment to him.

She followed Ryan's progress toward his truck. His easy stroll all
but hid the limp. *And this one is even more handsome and charming than Dennis,* she realized, *and even less what he appears to be.*

After lunch Ariel vanished into her half of the house. When
Ryan stuck his head in her door an hour later, he found her kneeling on the floor. Gold-rimmed half-specs had slid halfway down
her straight nose as she busily sorted through the indecipherable
scraps he'd found in her desk. Whispering to herself, she seemed
to be arranging them in some order only she could ever hope to
understand. Despite the absentminded wave of her hand, he knew
that she hadn't heard his promise to fix dinner.

He had to use the pay phone at a gas station. There were no
phone jacks in his apartment, and he could hardly use Ariel's
phone for this call. After half an hour and a pocketful of quarters, he found a private lab in Missoula that assured him that they
could test for the more common poisons in a couple of hours. He
glanced at his watch as he hung up. It was too late to make the two-
hour trip today, but he'd be there when they opened their door in
the morning.

Stopping next at the Forest Service barracks, he got a map of the
hiking trails in the area. The doctor in San Francisco had pre-
scribed walks or easy hiking as part of his therapy. A few more
stops and he realized his brother's wisdom in sending Ariel here.
There was no one he had met, from the gas-station attendant to the
grocery clerk to the retired schoolteacher chattily pointing out the
treasures in the little town museum, who didn't know who he was
and what he was doing in town.

He got back to the schoolhouse in time to fix most of their dinner. Ariel defrosted and warmed a loaf of cracked-wheat bread and
a jar of broccoli-cheese soup. Ryan made cottage fries and grilled
two thick pork chops. They made a salad together while he told her
about his house on the beach in Malibu, and she wistfully described her restored row house, almost on the bay in San Francisco.

Ryan probed delicately into her life in San Francisco and her acquisition of the Burnt Fork School. He wanted her to mention DiSanto, to see what, if any, feeling she still had for him. She'd been engaged to marry the man. One could reasonably assume she'd been in love with him, yet she hadn't even mentioned his name yesterday when she said she'd been involved in a murder. She certainly didn't seem to be grieving for a lost love. Nor was she exhibiting anger over a love betrayed when she found out that Dennis DiSanto wasn't quite the hero she'd thought. She'd obviously been genuinely saddened by his death, but just as obviously she had had no great passion for the man. Of course love and passion didn't necessarily go hand in hand, he reminded himself cynically, yet he still felt curiously pleased.

Adroitly Ariel avoided the subject completely, saying little about San Francisco and nothing about Dennis DiSanto. She did mention that she had fallen in love with the vacant schoolhouse two summers before when she was in the area doing research and had bought it for a vacation home.

Ryan's hand dropped casually below the edge of the table, and there was a gulping noise. "Ryan," Ariel began hesitantly. He had supplied and cooked most of the dinner, but rules were rules. "We don't feed Murphy at the table. That's the first rule I made for her when she came to live with me."

"I noticed *we* don't," he agreed easily. "Only *I* do." He leaned toward the dog and advised in a stage whisper, "Chew with your mouth closed, Murph." Yellow eyes gazed up at him adoringly. "It's okay, girl. Stick by me; I'll see you don't starve."

There was an unladylike snort of disgust from across the table. Ariel glowered at the both of them. "Starve? Look at her! She's overweight!" Picking up her fork, Ariel stabbed determinedly at a piece of pork chop, her eyes fixed on her plate and not his impertinent grin. "Don't feed her at the table," she ordered firmly. "She'll just become a drooling mooch." A drooling mooch pooch. A giggle almost escaped, and she clamped her teeth together. Her lamentably irrepressible silliness insisted on surfacing at the worst time. This man was definitely a bad influence on her and Murphy both. Increasing the severity of her scowl, she glanced up at him. He was looking at her oddly. "What's wrong? Is there something wrong with the food?" She hadn't tasted the bread yet and hastily took a bite.

He continued to regard her thoughtfully for a moment longer, then resumed chewing. After swallowing, he finally spoke. "She's not overweight, Ariel. She's with puppy."

It took her a second to fully absorb the deadpan joke. "She can't be pregnant," she denied flatly. "I was *very* careful."

"I imagine you always are," he said blandly, "but Murphy definitely wasn't."

Giving him an exasperated glare, she went on doggedly. "But I never saw . . ." He laughed, and she groaned. "How soon?"

"When was she in heat?"

"Toward the end of July."

"And this is the end of September. I'd say about anytime."

Ariel turned on the dog and wailed woefully. "Oh, Murphy, how could you? Your father and I raised you to be a good girl."

"Father?"

"Well, you have to say that," she explained. "It's traditional."

"I see. You've had this discussion with her before, then?" His lips were twitching.

"No." Ariel shook her head mournfully. "She was a virgin." Addressing the dog once more, she scolded sadly. "Oh, Murphy, I warned you about smooth-talking strangers." Her desperate straight face finally dissolved into laughter, as she patted the bewildered dog.

Ryan laughed with her, a trifle uneasy. He might well be described as a smooth-talking stranger, and she was definitely a virgin.

Shortly before midnight, he lounged in her open doorway, his hands in the pockets of his black pants, a yellow sweatshirt pulled hastily over his tousled hair. He'd looked over a case and polished off the last of his rum. Then he'd gone to bed, tossed for an hour and gotten up. The soft light diffusing through the pebbled glass in her door had drawn him like a moth.

The funny little glasses were sliding a little farther down her nose every time she wrinkled it at the letters on the screen of the word processor. She shoved them up impatiently, hardly breaking the rhythm of her fingers flitting over the keys. He sighed to himself. He was having fantasies about historical researchers lately.

Ariel dragged a hand through her hair. Suddenly she looked up, catching the almost hungry look on his face. It vanished as soon as he met her eyes, a slow smile taking its place.

"I see you couldn't sleep, either." He eased away from the jamb and came to lean over the top of her desk. "I thought—" he glanced toward the bookshelves "—I'd come over and get a boring book to put me to sleep."

Ariel switched the machine off. Casually she crossed her arms over her chest, wishing she had broken this bad habit she had of going to bed and then getting back up to empty her overactive mind without putting her clothes back on. No telling how long he'd been watching her with that absolute stillness he had, like a predator choosing the moment for the kill. The long sleeves and high neck of her sturdy nightshirt more than adequately covered her, but his lazy, appreciative look up and down her body had made her feel stripped.

She eyed him over the lenses of her glasses. It wasn't a book he was after. She suspected that hotshot L.A. lawyers had a very low boredom threshold, and she'd known right where he would come looking for entertainment first. Maybe she was bored, too, though, because she didn't feel as irritated as she knew she should. She stared at his feet, not seeing them. No, it couldn't be boredom, because there was gentle, oh-so-willing Sam, and she had never felt the slightest urge to take him up on his unspoken offer. Urges...this man aroused urges, sweet, confusing, dangerous urges.

"Do you have a foot fetish?" The polite, velvety voice disturbed her musings.

"What?" Finally she saw what she had been staring at, and then saw that he was staring at her feet just as hard. "No, do you?" she responded just as politely.

"I haven't decided yet," he murmured. "Are those your typing clothes?"

She didn't need his barely contained laughter to tell her that she looked ridiculous. Most people did not wear red-striped nightshirts, mismatched fuzzy knee socks and seedy slippers to type in. Most people wouldn't be caught dead in an outfit like that. Well, it ought to at least induce him to take his boredom elsewhere. "The dryer, or Murphy, ate a couple of my socks," she mumbled inanely. "Besides," she looked at him pointedly, "I wasn't expecting company."

He did laugh then, and went over to the bookshelves. Behind him he heard noises from the direction of the stereo system on the opposite wall.

Ariel was riffling through plastic cassette cases looking for something noisy. She fed a tape into the machine and set the volume up a bit too high. A raucous voice rasped out a song about "Hot Legs." Maybe he'd take the hint that she'd gotten out of a warm bed to work, not to talk.

Apparently he did, departing through the door with a book and without a word. Resolutely she ignored a niggle of disappointment and squinted at the little green blurs on the screen. Entertaining Malibu beach boys in your nightgown at midnight was not particularly wise anyway.

An hour later Ryan shut his book and let it drop to the floor. Kicking off his shoes, he stretched his legs over the hassock and slid down in the chair. He watched her through slit eyes, listening to a sexy saxophone and the lazy rhythm of a snare drum coming through the stereo speakers. He'd never realized that historical research was so riveting. She'd never even noticed him come back or lower the volume on the stereo. Occasionally her hand would dart out and seize one of the bits of paper tacked across the front of the desk with Scotch tape. She would study it intently for a few seconds, crumple it, then toss it in the general direction of an old pickle crock she used for a wastebasket. Then she'd type furiously again for long minutes.

The words of the song on the tape insinuated themselves into his subconscious. Sung in a rusty-hinge voice by a jaded rock star was the blueprint for a sweetly tender seduction. The tape continued to wind unnoticed through both the cassette player and his subconscious.

She was frowning again, worrying that soft lower lip. Her slender hands were clenched together, as if she was praying fiercely for divine inspiration. Somehow he didn't think she needed it.

Gradually he became aware of the silence after the tape ended. He roused himself and silently padded across the carpet. Ignoring her tapes, he pulled one from his back pocket.

Ariel shut off the computer and pushed the swivel chair back from the desk with a satisfied sigh. She cocked her head at the unfamiliar tape. Quizzically she stared at the chair across the room.

He'd come back, and with his own music. The Beach Boys—how appropriate.

His long body was sprawled over the chair and hassock, his thin fingers laced peacefully across his chest. His eyes were almost shut against the orange firelight flaring through the glass doors of the wood stove. The glow played over a hazy smile softening his hard face. She waited quietly until the tape clicked off. He deserved to listen to reminders of a simpler, happier time undisturbed.

"'Be True to Your School'?" Her soft laughter filled the sudden silence.

"'Hot Legs'?" He rose from the chair with a slow, fluid motion, rather like a sleepy cat that didn't particularly want to move. A luxurious stretch pulled his sweatshirt up, exposing his taut, concave belly. Her eyes lingered on a silky black swirl and pale skin, and then dropped, reluctantly, when his arms did.

Ryan walked leisurely across the room to her, took off the glasses carefully, then pulled her unresisting body out of the chair and into his arms. The action seemed peculiarly natural, comfortably familiar. Bemused, Ariel let herself rest against his hard chest. The soft sweatshirt under her cheek was still toasty from the fire, and she snuggled unconsciously into its warmth, shutting her eyes with a contented sigh. The fire's heat seemed to have intensified his scent of soap, citrus and warm male.

"If you didn't sleep alone," he breathed into her hair, "You wouldn't need socks." His long, bare foot slid down the back of her smooth leg, catching the top of her knee sock and dragging it down her calf to her ankle.

Ariel's eyes flew open as the erotic tickling moved back up her leg to the top of her thigh, and she jerked back. Ryan let her move only a few inches, his hands tightening just enough to remind her that she wasn't free.

"Let me go." Neither the words nor the fists pushing on his chest were as determined as they were supposed to be.

"No. I don't think I will." He rocked her gently in his arms, his soft eyes teasing her. "Look, but don't touch. Is that another of your rules, Miss Spence? You seem to have quite a few of them."

"It shouldn't bother you, Mr. Jones." Her husky voice was sweetly scathing. "Rules appeal to you lawyer types, don't they?"

He laughed and hooked a finger in a loop of the red bow tied at the neck of her nightshirt. A gentle tug and the ribbon pulled loose, opening the throat of her gown. "We lawyer types are always looking for ways around the rules. Didn't you know that? It's ninety percent of our business, especially us criminal-defense types." His soft lips whispered against her prim mouth, "And your defense of your many charms is truly criminal, Ariel Spence."

It was supposed to be a light kiss, a hint of things to come, but her response caught him off guard. With a moan Ariel's mouth softened and clung to his, relishing the subtle flavor of dark rum. The mellow taste seemed to burn through her as if she'd swallowed the liquor herself, making her drunk on the kiss. Her fingers laced through his blue-black hair to hold his head so she could enjoy the taste again. The hunger that had been awakened the night before made her suddenly ravenous for the feel of his mouth nourishing hers.

Before he could consider the wisdom of it, Ryan's right hand clamped over the back of her skull. His mouth crushed down on hers, driving her deeper into passion. His left hand moved up to the four white buttons of her nightshirt. Her mind was too tangled in the onslaught of sensations swirling through her to appreciate how deftly his fingers freed the tiny buttons. Her body appreciated it, knew that its hunger to be touched was about to be satisfied. It throbbed, even before his hand slipped under the chaste flannel and covered her heart, hard calloused flesh over soft.

She clutched at his shoulders desperately, as if she was on a sinking ship and he were the only lifeline. She was sinking into a dark pool of sensuality. She couldn't swim out of it; she could only hold on and let him save her—or pull her deeper into the whirlpool.

Ryan took her softness into his rough palm, ignoring the inner voice reminding him that he had decided to move slowly with this woman. He gave in to a pounding impulse too ancient and too fundamental to be ignored.

The ruthlessly skilled hand on her breast stroked, shaped, maddened. His other hand slid down her spine to the base of her naked back. He pressed her firm flesh, and her knees turned liquid.

"No." Ariel's voice was a breathless whisper in the midnight stillness of the room. She arched against him helplessly as drowning waves of unbelievable pleasure washed over her. "Oh, don't."

His mouth was greedy against hers, silencing her weak protest before he sought satisfaction at her bared throat. Ariel breathed his name in a thin, tremulous groan.

Ryan's head came up. He shook it, as if surfacing from deep underwater, and gazed into the vulnerable face below him. Eyes closed, lips trembling as her breath stuttered over them, Ariel waited. He could take her now; on that wide sofa. And she would hate him for it in the morning. It was much too soon. His smoky eyes cleared, and his hands moved to the safety of her shoulders. He could wait. It would be just that much sweeter when he satisfied his hunger . . . and hers.

Her blue eyes opened, clouded, questioning. "I . . ."

"Should go to bed," he said completing her sentence. He pulled her back for the light teasing kiss he'd originally intended, then released her.

Swaying slightly, she grabbed at her desk for balance. She glanced around the familiar room, as if seeing it for the first time. "Yes, it's late." She pushed a trembling hand through her disheveled hair. "I should go to bed," she echoed faintly.

Clutching her open nightshirt closed, she turned toward the stairs, still half-dazed. "Good-night, Ryan."

He switched off the lamp on her desk and moved to the door. "By the way, Miss Spence." His dark eyes glittered in the firelight as he grinned back at her over his shoulder. She stopped halfway up the steps, watching him uncertainly. "You have *very* hot legs."

Chapter 4

Damnit, Dye, she has to be told!"

"The odorless, almost tasteless poison on the report you keep shoving under my nose, Jones, is used by half the exterminators in the U.S. Isn't it just possible that the candy got sprayed along with the cockroaches in some warehouse?"

Ryan spun away from the chief's desk, jamming his hands in his pockets so he wouldn't break something. The chief played devil's advocate with maddening reasonableness. Ryan stood for a long time at the station window, looking at nothing.

"All right," he conceded grudgingly, his back still to the police chief. "It's possible, but pretty damned unlikely. I still say Ariel should know."

"Know what? That someone, we don't know who, *might* have sent her a box of poisoned candy? Anyway, your brother's boss doesn't want her upset."

Ryan's opinion of the San Francisco D.A. was short and obscene. "He doesn't want her upset," he repeated tonelessly, his mouth curled in a sneer. "He's using her to draw out the real murderer. If she just happens to get killed in the process, that wouldn't bother *him*."

"The guy's tipped his hand. If he tries again, we'll be ready for him," the chief said noncommittally.

When, not if. Ryan lit another of the cigarettes he thought he had given up three years ago. He inhaled deeply, trying to settle himself. This conversation was infuriatingly similar to one he'd had from a phone booth in Missoula two hours ago. His brother must have called Ted Dye as soon as Ryan had slammed the phone back on its hook.

He found himself in a position he should have been used to by now, defending someone everyone else seemed convinced was guilty. Only this time, the person he was defending was innocent.

He knew he was rationalizing his excuse for not telling her for purely selfish motives. The San Francisco D.A. be damned; he should tell her. But then he would have to tell her who he really was and why he was there.

Chief Dye swiped a hand down his well-worn face and heaved himself out of his chair. He was too old for this. That was why he had retired to this nice little town in the boondocks, where the biggest crimes he had to worry about were stolen chain saws and the Geilenfeldt brothers tearing up a bar on Saturday night. He laid a heavy hand on the younger man's shoulder.

"Rick told me a little about your military experience. If anybody can keep her alive, you can."

Ryan wished he shared the chief's confidence.

Arriving back at the schoolhouse at dusk, he parked his truck next to her Blazer. Telling himself that it wasn't cold fear he felt, just the autumn chill in the air, he shouted Ariel's name when he couldn't find her. At last he located her, crouched in a corner of his kitchen, calmly laying the last of the blue and yellow floor tiles. Her shocked look and stiff reply told him that she neither understood nor appreciated his growled curse or the snarled demand that she yell louder next time.

He came downstairs from using her shower an hour later to find her staring disconsolately at the smoking skillet in her hand. "What happened?"

"I tried to cook something that wasn't soup or bread," Ariel muttered. She dropped the skillet in the sink and switched on the exhaust fan.

Leaning over the sink, Ryan examined the brown mess in the pan. "What was it?" he inquired politely.

She sighed and resisted the bizarre urge to smooth back the lock of damp hair falling over his forehead. "Two rainbow trout. They'd been in the freezer about a year; I guess they dried out."

"Hmm. Did you catch them?"

She was silent for a moment. Dennis had caught them on his last fishing trip. "A friend did."

Opening the freezer section of the refrigerator, Ryan pulled out a white package he'd put in yesterday. He put it in the microwave and punched the defrost button, then lounged back against the tiled counter. "Do you like to fish?"

Her nose wrinkled as she leaned against the opposite counter, facing him. "Not very much. I never catch anything, so I get frustrated." Apparently her rather shameless behavior last night was not going to be a topic for discussion, for which she was most grateful. It made it much easier to convince herself it had been just a temporary lapse of sanity.

Ryan laughed, a deep, cheerful sound, very pleasant in her too often quiet kitchen. "Look," she began firmly, "I can't let you fix my dinner again. I—"

His hand dismissed her objections. "I don't like eating alone." His smile was a genuinely friendly invitation, with none of the coolly sardonic amusement he usually treated her to.

Ariel looked at him doubtfully. He didn't look like the kind of man who minded eating alone. In fact, he looked like one who often preferred it. Self-sufficient . . . a loner . . . a solitary man, but by choice. She was quite sure he could fit comfortably into, or more likely control, almost any situation. A cool tingle shivered up her back. Who was he really? Not just some fancy lawyer. Several times his carefully civilized veneer had peeled back a little, allowing her a glimpse of a ruthless, cunning, rather dangerous man. She'd seen it during the retelling of his nightmare, as well as on the day he'd knocked the candy out of her hand in the accident that wasn't, and again this afternoon, when he was so peculiarly angry at her for not yelling loudly enough.

Three minutes later she was laughing at her absurd imaginings. The sinister Ryan Jones was standing in his bare feet, a blue-and-white checked dish towel tucked in the waist of his green rugby pants, expertly slicing steak into thin strips and pounding it with the edge of a heavy plate. Browsing in her refrigerator, he'd found two green peppers, and had plopped them in front of her. "Slice," he had commanded, and she sliced. They were going to have pepper steak, he had calmly announced.

Half an hour later Ariel savored her first forkful. His rice was moist and fluffy, not stuck together in gluey clumps as hers always was. The steak practically melted in her mouth. And he hadn't even used a recipe book. "Where did you learn to cook like this?"

"I learned while I was in law school." He refilled his plate and added more to hers. "I got tired of TV dinners and cheap restaurants."

"That's fortunate for the women you date and fix dinner for." She said it sincerely, ignoring a silly twinge of jealousy.

The sardonic smile was back in place. "The women I 'date' aren't into home cooking."

"Then maybe you date the wrong women," she said lightly.

The smile turned speculative. "Do you like home cooking, Ariel?"

"Of course." She smiled breezily. "Especially if it's my home and someone else is doing the cooking." She changed the subject abruptly. "Do you like to fish?"

Ryan had to think for a minute to remember the conversation before dinner. "When I get the chance." He looked at her curiously. "Why?"

"There's a lot of fishing stuff in the garage. I'll get it out for you," she offered ingenuously. "I noticed you got some maps, and there are lots of places around here to fish. Maybe you can catch me another trout." She grinned. "And maybe I can manage to cook it without incinerating it."

"I'll do my best," he promised gravely.

The television was on, but Ariel had turned the sound down. Curled up in her fattest armchair, she was making unkind faces at the sheaf of computer paper in her hand. Her glasses were sliding down her nose, but not far enough for her to bother to do anything about them. As she slashed through several lines of type with the red pen in her hand, she clucked her tongue in disgust. The paper was beginning to look like it was bleeding. Felicia wasn't doing well at all with this one. At this stage she should be fine-tuning, doing a little cosmetic work, not major surgery.

The heroes were usually the easiest, always rounders and rakes who were reformed, barely, on the last page by the love of a good woman. She had lost control of this one, though; he was suddenly behaving quite dreadfully. He was as much of a rogue as the rest, but he was arrogant to boot, full of insufferable male smugness.

As if that weren't enough, there was an inexplicable cloud of menace settling over the characters. Ariel heaved a huge sigh and shook her head resignedly. The glasses slipped to the end of her nose. As usual, she was the only one who could save the patient.

A shadow fell over her. She looked up and barely stifled a small shriek. Pressing her papers to her chest, she finally squeaked out, "Ryan! You scared the stuffing out of me!" He had crossed the old floorboards without one betraying creak. Since he'd left as soon as they cleaned up after dinner, she hadn't expected to see him again tonight.

He slid the glasses back up her nose. "What are you working on?"

"A mess," she muttered, trying to get to her feet and put the papers safely away in case he was planning on spending the evening. Grasping her hand, Ryan hauled her to her feet, and Ariel sidestepped quickly to her desk.

"You know," he said observing the silent TV, "the picture on that set is atrocious."

"Yeah, I know," she admitted, cramming the papers in the first half-empty drawer she could find. "There's a movie I want to see, though, so I guess I'll have to put up with it." She shoved hard on the overstuffed drawer, trying to close it.

"Why haven't you gotten a satellite dish?" He'd already checked; they were available even in this tiny town.

"Oh, I was afraid, with so little to do here, that I might get hooked on soap operas or something," she answered absently. Finally she gave up fighting with the stubborn drawer and went back to her chair, tucking her feet under her as she sat. "This way I only watch it when there's something I really want to see."

Ryan suppressed a grin; he couldn't imagine her avidly following the bed-hoppings on a soap opera.

"Are you going out?" Seeing the canvas jacket hooked over his shoulder, she hoped, and didn't hope, that he was.

As he sat on the arm of her chair, Ryan tried stifling the urge to see if her hair was as soft and silky as he remembered. "Yes." He wound one loose curl around his finger, then released it slowly. It was. Bending, he dropped a quick kiss on her startled mouth, then rose lithely from the chair arm. "I'll be back in a couple of hours."

From the doorway he added, in that damnable irritating velvet purr, "Keep the doors locked, including the dead bolts."

"I don't use the dead bolts." She gave him a cool look.

"Starting tonight you do." The outside door closed solidly, emphasizing his order.

Ariel blinked in astonishment and stared after him. Muttering to herself, she retrieved her crumpled papers and red pen and went back to operating.

Several hours later Ryan let himself back into the darkened schoolhouse. She had locked the dead bolt, he noted with satisfaction, then sighed heavily. It wasn't going to be that easy; no doubt he would have to remind her a few more times.

Murphy met him just inside the door. "Hi, girl," he whispered, scratching behind her ears. "Your mistress in bed already?" He started down the short hallway to his door.

Maybe his phone calls would produce a few leads. He would have liked to have taken Chief Dye up on his offer of the police-station phone again but the deputy had been a little too interested in the long numbers he was dialing. He'd had to use the pay phone at the gas station again, his conversations punctuated with dings from the service bell every time a car rolled over the hose.

There was a faint thump from the garage. Murphy cocked her ears and growled, then sniffed the air and relaxed. Ryan debated going for the .45 in his kitchen drawer and decided against it. Moving soundlessly through Ariel's living room, he reached the door in the wall of books. It opened on silent hinges.

The garage was lit by one dangling bulb. There was a jumble of cardboard cartons, a tall metal cabinet with a heavy padlock, and little else. Sitting on her heels in the midst of the boxes was Ariel, her golden head bent over the framed photograph in her hands. A dented, rusty tackle box and a fishing rod lay on the concrete floor next to her. Murphy padded over to sniff at the khaki fishing vest lying across Ariel's knees. Whining softly, the dog lay down, her head resting on the grimy vest.

Mindful of the start he'd given her earlier, Ryan spoke her name quietly to warn her of his presence.

One hand flew up to her eyes and brushed over them quickly. Keeping her face averted as he crossed the floor, she said in a thin voice, "I . . . I was just getting the fishing tackle."

He knelt in front of her, staying her hand as it tried to put the photograph back into a carton. He recognized the curling dark hair and handsome, sensual features of Dennis DiSanto. His arm was slung across the shoulders of a younger, slighter man. Both of them were displaying large fish with the exuberant pride of small boys. It was time, for several reasons, that the subject of Dennis Di-Santo came out in the open. "Who are the men in the photograph, Ariel?"

The harsh light overhead caught the wet sheen in her eyes. "The man I'm supposed to have murdered and his brother," she whispered, then burst into tears.

"So many tears, love." Ryan's low murmur in Ariel's ear was as comforting as the strong arms that held her. They relaxed a little and let her shift slightly on his lap. She only nestled closer; his warmth and gentle strength were assuaging a pain that had been gnawing inside her for months.

Rubbing the backs of her hands across her tear-clotted eyes, she thought reluctantly about sitting up. A larger hand brushed hers aside and gently wiped with a clean handkerchief. The soft cloth wrapped around the end of her nose. "Blow."

With a self-conscious giggle she obeyed, working up the courage to look at him. His smile was warm and gentle. She smiled back damply, then looked down at her lap, trying to think of some way to explain her bizarre behavior. The soft orangy glow and heat from the wood stove made her realize that they were no longer in the garage, but sitting together in her favorite chair. "How did we get here?" she asked huskily.

He laughed quietly, lifting her to a new position on his right thigh. "I carried you," he said simply. "That cement floor was hardly the spot for a good cry."

She plucked a piece of invisible lint from her pants. "I'm sorry," she mumbled. "I'm not generally so . . . hysterical."

Strong fingers raised her chin, and his serious eyes held her embarrassed ones. "You were hardly hysterical, Ariel. I think you've been saving those tears for too long. I'm just glad I was here. Your answer about the men in the picture," he added with an encouraging grin, "could use a little explanation, though."

"I'll bet it could," she agreed softly.

He released her chin, and her head seemed to fall automatically onto his shoulder as his arm closed loosely around her. Her low voice floated with the firelight in the warm, peaceful room.

"You might remember some of the story. Like I said, it even made the papers in L.A. almost a year ago." Her small laugh was harsh. "The older man in the photograph was Dennis DiSanto. He was a dentist, came from a wealthy family, knew everybody who was anybody in San Francisco. I was just a nobody, and perfectly happy that way." He felt her small sigh, then a deeply in-drawn breath. "I met him down in Mexico where I was doing research. We saw a lot of each other down there, and then, the next I knew, all my spare time was spent with him."

His hand stroked slowly over her soft hair. "Were you in love with him?" His tone was casual. His hand paused as he waited for her answer.

"No. I loved him, but I wasn't in love with him."

Ryan's hand resumed its slow play. "Was he in love with you?"

"Yes. He would ask me to marry him about once a month. I would say no; we'd laugh, and he'd say he'd wear me down sooner or later." She laughed ruefully. "Finally I guess he did. I decided I was never going to find any knight in shining armor, and having someone love me the way Dennis did was very special. I knew I could make him a good wife. The next time he asked me, I surprised him and said yes."

Her voice fell to an almost inaudible whisper, and unconsciously she settled deeper into his arms. "Only we never had the chance to get married. Dennis liked to take pictures of little kids and old people; it was quite a hobby with him. He was even thinking of trying to put together a book of his pictures. One day we were in Golden Gate Park, taking photos, and he was shot—killed by a crazy old man."

The last memory of Dennis filled her. She saw again the small ring of shocked and ghoulishly curious faces staring down at them as he lay in her arms. She felt again his warm, red life seeping through her frantic fingers, swallowed up by the thirsty ground. Once more she heard, dimly, the shouts echoing off the serene slopes of the park. She heard clearly Dennis' final, rattling whisper—her name.

Ryan felt her shudder, and folded her closer. Her tortured whisper seemed a shout in the quiet room. "At first I wished I'd said yes sooner, so I could have made him happy, at least for a little while. Then I found out he wasn't quite the man I'd thought he was."

She pulled free to look intently into Ryan's face. He could see the bitter tears glistening again. "Between the guilt and the disillusionment I felt, I couldn't even cry for him, not even at his funeral."

The overwhelming sadness ravaging her beautiful face tore at his heart, and he felt an irrational hatred for the dead man who'd loved her. It made his words harsh. "You shouldn't feel guilty about having doubts and being honest about them, Ariel. Would you rather have married him and then learned he wasn't what you thought?"

She shook her head, answering softly. "No, I think I finally came to terms with it tonight, when I saw the picture."

She was silent, and he enjoyed the quiet pleasure of just holding her. He heard her smothered yawn and knew the storm of weeping and its emotional release had exhausted her. "I remember an article now," he lied. He knew every one by heart. "Wasn't his uncle supposed to have organized-crime connections? Didn't the police think maybe it had something to do with that?"

"That's what the district attorney still thinks." She was too tired to give the words much of her usual acid. "He also seems to think I was involved somehow. I think he thinks I set Dennis up to be shot." She pressed her hands flat on his chest and sat up to see his face. "I think that's really why I'm here, so he can have Ted Dye and probably half the town spy on me and let him know when they either send me the big payoff or come to shoot me."

Tears filled her eyes again, and she began shaking her head in anguished bewilderment. "I lived with Rick Jones, the assistant D.A., and his wife for two months before I came here. They told me it was protective custody, but it was really so they could keep me under constant surveillance. I took care of their baby as if it were my own when Eileen was sick, yet even Rick still seems to think I'm guilty. How can he?" she cried. Her fingers curled into the soft fabric of his shirt, and she shook him unconsciously to make him see the truth.

Ryan hardened his heart to her pain and resisted the almost overpowering desire to wrap her in his arms and simply tell her the truth. He needed to hear this, to hear her side. Unknowingly she might give him the clue he needed to prove her innocence.

Suddenly she seemed to realize how hard she was shaking him and dropped her hands to her lap. She struggled visibly for control and went on in a calmer voice that trembled only slightly. "The worst of it is, they've never been open about it, never charged me with anything, so I don't even know what evidence they think they have against me. It's like they're playing some horrible game, waiting for something to happen to me, and—" her voice broke in a sob "—I don't even know why."

Ryan's left hand moved strongly up her back. His fingers spread through the hair on the back of her head, and he gently forced her body to relax against his. For a moment she resisted; then he felt her snuggle sleepily against his chest.

"If it didn't make me so crazy, it would be funny. There was no cold-blooded murder plot; it was just a random incident, a terrible, senseless killing." Her voice trailed off as she drifted into sleep.

He wished that ass of a district attorney could have heard this and then tried to tell him that she had anything to do with DiSanto's murder. He sat there long after the fire had burned low, sifting her hair through his fingers, thinking of random killers and sinister plots and evidence that could be seen two ways, and the golden California girl asleep so trustingly in his arms. His hand slid down unconsciously and curled possessively around her soft breast as he wondered exactly when she had become so important to him.

Apparently his sweet gift had not done its work; he should have heard something by now. Maybe the poison hadn't been strong enough, or she hadn't eaten enough. Whatever. Some business problems demanded one's presence to be solved.

Fortunately he had anticipated just such a situation months ago, when he'd bought the isolated cabin above Tahoe. He prided himself on his ability to foresee problems and solve them before they could cause trouble. That was one of the reasons he was so successful and others weren't. They simply didn't give enough atten-

tion to all the variables that could adversely affect business then take care of them ahead of time.

Everyone was used to his occasional absences now, assuming he used the cabin as an escape from his tremendous pressures and his grief. No one knew how easy it was to hike through the wilderness for a few hours and be on the highway, waiting for the bus to take him to the nearest airport.

With his filthy knapsack, grubby patched clothes and too-long dirty-blond hair, he would be just another of the aging hippies come down out of the hills. The local cops paid them no attention, letting them cultivate their little patches of marijuana and live their useless lives undisturbed.

He would have to do something about that damned dog. He'd never get close enough to take care of the problem otherwise. That dog hated him. He had never understood Dennis's absurd fondness for her. She should be easy enough to dispose of, though.

Chapter 5

The extra mile she'd added to her run this morning hadn't helped. Standing here in her bright kitchen, grinding coffee beans in the antique delft mill as she had done every morning for months, listening to Murphy's snore in a patch of sunshine, did absolutely nothing to solve her problem, either. Had she finally met a man whose mere touch could produce that fabled tingle, that little sexual shock of instant attraction? She knew it existed—between the pages of romances. She had ten and a half books in the other room to prove it. But that it existed in reality she had not believed—until she'd felt those eyes on her back last Saturday.

That he knew she was attracted to him annoyed her no end. "No doubt," she muttered fiercely to her disinterested coffee maker, "like every other female he subjects to that ruthless charm." Yet his tender caring last night, his refusal to take advantage of her vulnerability, had her defenses in a shambles this morning. Under that devastating sex appeal was a decent, even tender, man, something she suspected he didn't even know and would ignore if he did. Leaning her head against a cupboard, she moaned and silenced the tiny imp at the back of her brain that was telling her to quit fighting and find out if the other things described in those romances might be true, also.

"What's the matter with Murphy?"

She jumped. That was another thing! He was always sneaking up on his cat feet, scaring her to death. Ariel turned around and sighed, disgusted with herself. Murphy had heaved her heavy body off the kitchen floor and was trying to wrap it around his legs in their worn black jeans. Even in the jeans, scuffed hiking boots and a ragged flannel shirt open over a faded black T-shirt he was, as Bessie would say, "drop-dead handsome." She glanced up to his black-and-silver baseball cap announcing the Los Angeles Raiders' victory in Super Bowl XVIII. "She sees your hat and thinks you're going to take her for a r-i-d-e. Dennis always seemed to wear one when he took her out."

He gave her a dry look. "Ariel, you don't have to spell in front of a dog." He squatted down and patted the furry head pushing into his hand. "Want to go for a ride, girl?"

Murphy went berserk, racing circles between him and the door, sliding on the slick floor, barking small ecstatic woofs. Leaping on Ryan's chest, she knocked him flat on his back. In the eye of the canine cyclone, Ariel stood calmly, her arms folded across her chest.

"I warned you," she murmured in a smug singsong.

Glaring exasperatedly at her as he sprawled gracelessly on the floor, Ryan fended off Murphy's frantic tugs on his arm. "What else do we have to spell?"

"C-o-o-k-i-e, or y if you're in a hurry." Reaching down, she gave him her hand to help him up. Ryan's wrist twisted, and suddenly she was sprawled on his lap.

As she struggled to sit up he tugged a strand of her unruly hair to bring her closer. His eyes fell to her mouth, lips parted, breath suspended between them.

"Kiss me good-morning, Miss Spence."

That damned, rakish charm in his smile got her every time. Ariel sighed, closed her eyes and obeyed. His mouth was sweet and tender, undemanding. As his arms closed gently around her she felt calmer, warm and . . . curiously safe.

He drew back, his sober eyes searching her face. "Are you all right this morning?"

"I'm fine," she said softly. "Thank you for putting up with me last night." She cleared her dry throat. "I was a tad surprised to wake up minus my clothes, though." Mortified was more like it, thinking of his hands on her, undressing her. Maybe just the tiniest bit disappointed, too, that she'd been asleep and unable to enjoy it.

Murphy finally settled down, barricading the door with her body, worry wrinkling her forehead at the man's unwarranted delay.

The slow smile reappeared. "I've found that women are generally more comfortable in bed without their clothes." He laughed delightedly at her scarlet face, and his voice dropped to a husky whisper. "Don't worry, I wasn't ogling your luscious, naked body. I didn't turn the light on; I took your clothes off by touch alone." He hadn't dared turn on the light; he never would have left if he had.

"Undoubtedly because you've had so much practice undressing women in the dark," she sniffed. She scrambled out of his arms and stood up rapidly. She had a mug of coffee ready to thrust into Ryan's hands by the time he was standing.

He added enough milk from the carton on the counter to cool it and drained the mug in one long swallow. "Mind if I take Murphy hiking today? I don't think it will be too hard on her, in her condition."

She agreed readily. "No. I'm sure she would love it." Having him out of the house was an excellent idea.

Settling the baseball cap more firmly on his head, Ryan gave her an innocuous smile while his knowing eyes gently mocked her. Murphy, with a long-suffering air followed him out.

Ariel spent the day doing everything but what she was supposed to be doing. Mr. Severson, the town plumber, electrician and whatever else was needed, showed up right after Ryan left, with the new plumbing fixtures and stove. Pressed into service as his apprentice, Ariel learned more than she'd ever cared to know about the intimate details of sewer drains, flexible gas pipe and plumber's putty. After waving him off, she had stood in Ryan's kitchen looking a little forlornly at the new stove. She was going to miss their meals together, miss his toothbrush hanging in the rack next to hers, and ... she reminded herself sternly that the meals he cooked were too fattening, and he always made her eat too much and, anyway, he kept leaving the cap off the toothpaste. She marched across the hall and gathered up all his toiletries from her bathroom and his food from her refrigerator, then put them where they belonged.

When Ryan returned late in the afternoon he saw Ariel standing in the doorway of the schoolhouse wearing a soft green dress. She looked as if she was trying desperately hard not to laugh. He knew the reason only too well. Murphy, he had discovered, did not ride in the back of a pickup like a normal dog; she rode in the cab, on the seat next to him. She'd jumped in when he'd opened the door, and no amount of halfhearted cursing and tugging would budge her. On the way home the dog had sidled over and casually draped a paw over his shoulder. He'd received several startled looks on the highway, the other drivers no doubt convulsed by his girlfriend.

Ariel smothered another laugh at his look of saintly suffering while he patiently held the truck door open for Murphy's careful descent. "You know, I used to tease Dennis that Murphy was the reincarnation of one of his old girlfriends. But now—" one golden honey eyebrow arched as elegantly as his "—I think she's just a reincarnated nymphomaniac."

"You said she doesn't generally like men," he retorted.

"Well, perhaps, a discriminating nymphomaniac."

He laughed. "I suspect the terms are mutually exclusive, but since it's the first compliment you've paid me, I'll accept it—left handed though it may be." His gently reproachful tone made her realize just how easily he managed to put her on the defensive.

He added disinterestedly, as he unloaded the tackle box, fishing rod and stringer of trout, "Going out for dinner again with the fish biologist?" The significance of the dress had finally struck him. He was sure it wasn't for his benefit.

"Yes." She eyed the fat fish and wished she weren't.

"Hmm. You seem to see a fair amount of him." He tried, but he couldn't quite keep the hint of censure out of his voice.

Ariel cast a sidelong glance at Murphy, who was leaning lovingly against Ryan's leg. With his free hand, he was absently fondling the dog's ear. Her murmur was sweetly snide. "At least I stick to my own species."

She held the door open for him. As he started to turn into her apartment, she threw open his door and announced, "Your kitchen arrived while you were fishing. It's all set up. The bathrooms, too."

Ryan gave her a wordless look and passed through his door. Ariel felt a perverse tickle of satisfaction at the brief flicker of disappointment she'd seen before his eyes had blanked over.

He tossed the stringer in the spotless white sink and set the tackle down on the new lemon-yellow countertop. "Got any newspaper so I can clean my fish?" His tone was cool. If he'd had any choice in the matter, the plumbing would never have been installed.

Ariel disappeared across the hall and returned in a couple of minutes with the past Sunday's issue of the *San Francisco Chronicle*. She slapped the fat newspaper on the counter.

"This is all I've got. It came today, but I've already glanced through it. Sunday's paper is mostly ads, anyway."

Ryan spread several sheets over the counter. He pulled open a drawer holding a jumble of old silverware and utensils and fished out a razor-sharp filleting knife. The flexible blade began whisking silvery scales from the iridescent skin.

Ariel leaned against the counter and watched as the fish were efficiently shorn of their scales. When Ryan moved to a clean area of the newspaper and began to gut them, she swallowed and looked away. Her gaze fell on the section of the newspaper he'd already used.

Out of the corner of his eye Ryan saw her lean closer to the paper, staring at something intently. "Careful," he murmured. "You'll get this mess all over that pretty dress."

She didn't hear him. With the tip of her finger she brushed several sequins of fish scales from the cheek of the man in the newspaper photo. Delicately she dabbed at the fish slime covering the lower half of his face and the caption. The small, precise mustache over his thin mouth showed briefly on the damp paper, and then it began to dissolve. The caption and the article underneath it were gone, too.

"I know this man," she muttered to herself. "I wonder why his picture is in the paper? He's not from San Francisco."

She felt Ryan leaning over her shoulder for a look. "Who is he?" His warm breath tickled the nape of her neck and wisps of hair that had escaped from the pins.

Her forehead wrinkled as she looked up at him. "I don't think they ever introduced me," she said wonderingly. "One afternoon I dropped by Dennis's office. He wasn't expecting me, and this man—" her finger touched the photo "—was with him, and somebody else.'' She frowned harder, trying to see the third man's face. ''Dennis's brother, Robert? Their uncle?'' She shook her head impatiently. ''I can't remember. I do remember this man in the paper had a heavy accent. Spanish. Dennis mentioned that I'd been the one who told him about the Mexican villages that were so desperate for dental care, and that I was going down with him to help with the clinics.''

She glanced at him hastily, sure that now he would have some question or comment about her relationship with Dennis. But Ryan seemed to be staring at the photo as hard as she had been. Ariel breathed a tiny sigh of relief. Ryan Jones was a very private person who clearly meant to respect her privacy... or maybe he just wasn't interested. She saw him glance up to the top of the page—for the date? page number?—and then farther up, to her. He was silent, as if waiting for her to finish the story.

''He was very angry with Dennis about it, said it was too dangerous. That man—'' she gestured again toward the soggy paper ''—was from Mexico, I'm sure.'' Her eyes shifted away to stare vacantly at the wall over Ryan's shoulder, and she smiled. ''I'd forgotten that. It was sweet of him to be worried about me. I left right after that, so we never got around to introductions. And Dennis never took me with him to Mexico again.''

The smile faded as she bent to study the photo again. She shook her head slowly. ''I wish I could remember who else was in the office that day, but—'' she straightened, dismissing the thought ''—it doesn't matter anyway.''

Ryan turned back to his trout, apparently losing interest in the whole matter. ''If you don't think about it,'' he advised, ''maybe it'll come back to you.''

Minutes later Ryan watched from his living room window as the woman he was trying so hard to protect drove off with another man. He broke the seal on a new bottle of rum and poured a tumbler full. What the hell was the matter with him? It wasn't that he consciously sought to avoid romantic entanglements, he just never found any. The women he did find knew the score as well as he did—good sex, good times, no involvement.

Now, suddenly, he wanted involvement with a woman who didn't even know the game, much less the score. A virgin, for God's sake! It was just the knight-in-shining-armor syndrome. Every man suffered from it at least once in his life. He imagined himself the protector of some pure and fair maiden, prepared to slay a dragon to save her.

Then he remembered the flippant comment he'd made to Eileen, his sister-in-law, the comment that had been more serious than he cared to admit. Maybe he'd found his untouched woman at last, one who could be his alone. Perhaps her innocence could give him back what he'd lost so long ago.

His armor wasn't shiny; it was dented and tarnished, like his soul. And the dragon only had two legs, but the maiden was certainly fair, and he was more than willing to do battle. His laugh was short and harsh. The black knight rescuing the golden maiden. Who was really saving whom?

He slammed the empty glass down on the table. At least he didn't have to go to that damned gas station again; he could use her phone. It was precious little consolation.

"Were you able to find anything out yet?"

Rick Jones heard the impatience in his brother's clipped voice. "You were right on three so far. I haven't gotten answers on the others yet. The exterminator—" Rick allowed himself a grim chuckle at the black humor in the chosen profession of DiSanto's killer "—sold his business three months before the murder for twice what it was worth. The purchaser was a dummy corporation. We're trying to ferret out the real buyer."

"What happened to the equipment, the poisons?"

"The equipment, building, trucks, everything was bought from the new owner by a young guy at a bargain-basement price. He never met the actual seller; everything was handled by an agent who sent all the paperwork to a P.O. box in San Francisco. Both of them are clean. The box was rented for just a month. Nobody remembers what the guy looked like who rented it, of course, or if it even was a guy. False name, false address, dead end there."

Ryan swore pungently. "What else?"

"As you expected, no fingerprints on the candy box; it was wiped clean. Also, you were right about the levels. The concentration of poison was higher on the inside of the box than the outside, indicating that it was open when it was sprayed. Nobody else thought of checking that, by the way."

"So we know it wasn't accidently contaminated sitting around in some storeroom." The satisfaction of being right brought no pleasure, just a greater gnawing of tension in his gut.

"Know who Felicia Fury is yet?" There was suppressed laughter in Rick Jones's voice.

For the first time in several hours Ryan felt like smiling. "I know. Why didn't you just tell me how she really makes her money?"

"Because I know your opinion of love and romance," his brother retorted dryly. "I wanted you to be surprised."

Surprised? Ryan's smile abruptly vanished. He had been surprised, all right. Just what game was Rick playing? Did he think Ariel was guilty or not? His boss sure as hell did. He changed the subject curtly. "Nothing on the DiSantos' various enterprises yet?"

"I told you, we checked them out before," Rick said patiently. "Since the old man moved out here with the boys, he's been so clean you could eat off him."

"I'm convinced there's something there, buried deep, and maybe not to do with the old man, either. Keep digging," Ryan insisted stubbornly, and heard his brother's weary sigh. "What about the exterminator?"

"We've gone back about twenty-five years, to before he opened his business. Nothing so far. His wife is no help. That's when she met him, and she says he was very close-mouthed about his earlier life."

"She could be lying," Ryan considered, rubbing the bridge of his nose tiredly, "but I doubt it. Reilly was probably too smart to tell her anything."

"We'll keep working on it, Ryan," Rick promised. He restrained himself from asking his brother how he and his landlady were getting along. "Anything else?"

"Yeah. Find out whose picture was on page A-4 of last Sunday's *Chronicle*."

The sound of a car's leaving woke Ryan. He had tried to stay awake until Ariel came home, but he'd had too much fresh air, too much exercise and too much rum, and he'd had to go to bed. He focused blearily on the luminous face of the travel alarm by his bed. He decided dispassionately that if it was the green government-issue pickup of Sam the Bass leaving, he would shoot him.

Ryan pulled aside the curtain on his bedroom window. Moonlight frosted the silver Blazer, its headlights aiming down the dirt road to the highway. Murphy nudged his thigh aside for a look. He stared again at the clock in disbelief. Where the hell was Ariel going at four forty-five in the morning? Alone, without even her dog. He and Murphy exchanged a worried frown.

The sun was already high when Ariel returned. She was met at the door by two reproachful faces. She walked inside and slumped wearily on her couch, letting it support as much of her body as possible without actually lying down.

Tossing another chunk of apple wood onto the fire he'd kept going in her stove, Ryan took the wing chair opposite the sofa. While he'd waited for her to return he'd discovered several new meanings for the word patience. "You were up early this morning," he commented mildly.

"Research," Ariel yawned, eyeing the sofa pillows.

"At four forty-five in the morning?"

His sharp, almost accusatory tone was puzzling, but Ariel was too tired and too cold to worry about it. "It was the only time I could do it. Have you had breakfast?" she asked hopefully, momentarily forgetting that they weren't sharing meals any longer and she'd have to fix something for herself.

"About three hours ago. Going to leave your boots and coat on all day?"

Her jaw almost popped with a second yawn. "Probably." She closed her eyes and savored the fire's heat on her wind-chapped cheeks, contemplating this morning's fiasco. It ranked right up there with the night she'd camped on a southern New Mexico desert during what the locals referred to as the "breezy" season—a period of gale force winds that lasted only three-hundred-sixty days a year, she'd learned later.

Whenever she did the research for a new book she tried a couple of the everyday activities of the period she was working on. Often she was guided or inspired by one of her local sources. It gave her a feel for the setting and characters that she couldn't seem to get otherwise. At the moment she was truly doubtful that she would ever feel anything again with her cold-numbed fingers.

Old Mr. Applebury at the rest home had been very inspiring when he had lyrically described the idyllic goose hunts of his youth.

He'd even solemnly given her his handmade goose-call to use. And she was giving it back. She'd honked herself silly and gotten only one scornful hoot from a scruffy owl in response, and that wasn't the worst of it.

She'd thought to incorporate an equally idyllic hunt into Felicia's latest book. The hero could enjoy a peaceful day's hunting as a respite from vigilantes and hired guns, ambushes and murders. She suspected now that he'd probably have welcomed an ambush or two to avoid such "respite." Mr. Applebury's memories had been rather selective. He'd forgotten to mention freezing to death on a muddy riverbank while a frigid wind whistled down his neck and up his pant legs.

Her left leg was suddenly pulled out straight. Reluctantly she sat up and opened her eyes. Ryan was crouched before her, sliding up the cuff of her stiff field pants and very efficiently unlacing her heavy boot. Balefully she regarded the drying mud she'd dropped on her clean floor. One boot came off, then the other.

Pulling her forward onto his chest, Ryan eased her out of her fleece-lined coat. Her arms fell naturally around his waist. Ariel closed her eyes again and relaxed against him. It would be so nice to go to sleep this way. She felt his warm fingers lingering on her chilled throat.

"What were you researching this morning?" he murmured.

"Goose-hunting," she whispered into his sweater.

"You didn't bring in a gun."

Ariel sat up quickly and looked at him, shocked. "Oh, I didn't want to shoot one! I was just . . . capturing the atmosphere." She shivered. "It was miserable."

His brow lifted. "Seems like a lot of work just for a little atmosphere."

"One of my greatest strengths as a . . . researcher is the thoroughness with which I do it," she lectured him loftily. "It adds immeasurably to the authenticity of the finished product."

The rest of Thursday and the next day passed quietly. Ariel deserted her computer long enough to drag the carton from Ryan's new stove back inside. After cutting down one side, she lined the box with old blankets to make a nursery. When Ryan returned with another stringer of trout he paused in the hall, admiring her efforts with a small smile. He was sure Ariel had impressed upon the dog the importance of using the box. He was just as sure that Murphy would ignore her.

An hour later he brought over dinner. The sound of the shower overhead detoured him from the dining table to the microwave to keep the fish warm.

The rolltop desk was festooned more fully than usual with little notes in that hen-scratch code. Out of habit he switched on her computer, absently playing with the command keys. The sudden whirring of the drive arrested his head, and he gazed at the screen, transfixed.

Ariel hadn't remembered to code access to what she'd been working on for the past few hours. The water was still running upstairs; he hoped she was fond of long showers. Settling in her swivel chair, he began to read.

Luke Tanner rocked back on the heels of his worn boots. His long legs, still in dusty bat-wing chaps, were spread arrogantly on the Persian carpet. He tilted his flat-brimmed hat with a careless thumb, letting it hang down his back from a knotted rawhide cord. Despite his rough clothes and the long black hair curling over his collar, he looked strangely at home in the elegant parlor.

Drucilla Sloan resolutely faced him. Her soft white shirt, streaked with dust was only half tucked into a black serge riding skirt. Her red-gold hair was a glorious tangle of flames around her beautiful, dirt-smudged face. She was exhausted—from the frantic ride, the choking dust, the frenzied shouting and shooting. The stampede had been diverted, only just, from the rim of a steep canyon. And now she had to fight another battle, worse than any range war, one she was far less sure of winning, not even sure she wanted to.

She squared her fragile shoulders. "I don't love you, Luke." She looked steadily into the farseeing gray eyes, lying through her teeth.

"Sure you don't, Drucilla," he drawled with a cynical curl to the black-bandit mustache.

Sapphire eyes flashing, she shrugged indifferently and turned to leave him. Amazed at her own acting ability, she prayed she wouldn't dissolve in heartbroken sobs until she was safely locked behind her bedroom door.

Steel fingers closed over her shoulders, digging in gently. His spurs jingled as he took another step forward. Her traitorous body betrayed her, yielding to the hard body behind hers. He widened his stance, easing her back full-length, trapping her between his leather-clad legs. The scent of cold wind and horse and musky male made her giddy, and her knees threatened to buckle.

Cupping her shoulders in his hard hands, Luke bent, trailing his hungry, open mouth up her neck. She felt a sharp nip on her earlobe that sent a gleeful shiver down her spine. Then his hot tongue bathed the tiny hurt before it dipped and swirled in her ear, freeing more delightful sensations. "Tell me again," his warm, moist whisper tickled deliciously through the sunset wisps escaping from her hairpins, "that you don't love me."

She shook her head frantically, unable to speak. Her arms rose and crossed over her full breasts in an instinctive gesture of protection. The silky mustache caressed her warming skin as he strung a line of softly stinging kisses down her neck. Helplessly she arched her head into his shoulder, tilting it to bare more of her throat to his pleasuring mouth.

"Uncross your arms, Cilla."

"I mustn't. It would be bad of me," she moaned like a small child. Trying to twist away from those insolent hands and glorious mouth, her body burrowed deeper against his hardening warmth.

"Be bad for me, Cilla." The seductive whisper came as his tongue grazed in the pulsing hollow of her throat. "Uncross your arms."

"Nooo." Her groan dissolved in an ecstatic sigh as her arms, with a will of their own, fell to her sides. His calloused hands slid over her shoulders and down the chaste, thin blouse to cradle the breasts that were aching for his touch. His long brown fingers teased exquisitely the taut peaks swelling under the fine white linen.

"Tell me you love me, Cilla." His mouth was busy again at her ear, while one of his hands began gliding slowly down, over her chest, her flat belly, lower, hovering, teasing. They brushed lightly over the damp heat of her femininity.

"Tell me, Cilla!" he demanded huskily, his mouth closing hotly over the heavy pulse throbbing below her jaw.

"Damn you, Luke Tanner! I love you!" she groaned, barely able to speak. "Now take me, dammit!"

"I will," he promised fiercely, sweeping her up triumphantly in his arms and striding into her bedroom. He kicked the door shut behind them. "You're mine, Drucilla Sloan! And when I get through loving you tonight, you'll never doubt it again."

Ryan's mouth crooked in reluctant admiration. The shower overhead had stopped and, filled with the images the words on the screen had evoked, he tried to shut his inner eye to another one, of her getting out of the shower, toweling off the glittering beads of water trickling down the curve of her thighs, the slope of her breasts, the rough terry-cloth caressing smooth . . .

His half-cocked ear and a squeaky hinge told him that she was dressing. He glanced at the empty diskette jacket lying next to the machine. LD-I was neatly printed on the cover. He considered it thoughtfully. Surely it couldn't be that simple, but then, the obvious was often the hardest to see.

"Retrieve file Luke Drucilla I," his long fingers rapidly tapped out. There was a note of victory in his quiet laugh when "Rangefire by Felicia Fury appeared in green letters. There was a brief synopsis, then the first chapter followed.

The time was 1892, and the setting was Johnson County, Wyoming. The heroine found herself caught in the middle of the Johnson County War. Her father having been killed in an ambush, she was trying to hang on to her thousands of acres of prime grazing land, beleaguered on one side by the ranchmen and their hired gunmen, and by the alleged rustlers and their friends on the other. The hero rode in on his horse Lucky one day. His only allegiance was to money, and for a price he agreed to help the heroine. In true romance style they fell in love, fighting it all the way, of course.

Ariel's light, almost skipping step sounded on the stairs. Ryan cleared the screen. He was setting her table as she hit the bottom step and swung around the corner into the living room.

"You forgot lunch," Ryan murmured twenty minutes later. Ariel had just polished off her third trout, easily half of the hash browns, and was now reaching for the last of the salad.

Her hand froze on the salad bowl. She gave her plate, empty save for three bare skeletons, a somewhat shocked look. Slanting him a sheepish grin, she forked the remaining salad onto her plate. "I tend to lose track of time when I'm working."

"I never realized historical research was so absorbing."

Ariel cocked her head, puzzled by the strange smile curving his mouth. "It can be," she answered with an odd, secret smile of her own. "I had a satellite dish installed out back today," she added casually. "If you'd, ah, care to watch something tonight..." Ariel wondered a little despairingly where this sudden urge to play with fire had come from.

His quick, surprised grin was a definite yes.

Frosted moonlight flowed through the windows under the cupola and over the sleeping woman burrowed under the quilts. He really hated to wake her up. A far better idea would be to slip into that cocoon of quilts with her. Her body warm and pliant and her mind hazy with dreams, it would be so easy to arouse her and realize a few of his own dreams. But she deserved better than that. Her first time should be special, unforgettable. It could be that the man who wakened all that latent sensuality, expressed only in print, would be unforgettable, too.

"Ariel, wake up, love." He shook her shoulder firmly. "Time to play midwife."

"I don't know anything about this," she said doubtfully, trailing down the steps after him. Why did babies always choose such uncivilized hours to come into the world? Pulling the belt of her old fleece robe tighter, she stepped into the cold hall and her toes curled. She should have taken the time to at least find her slippers. Ryan had gotten completely dressed. She envied him his warm-looking blue sweatshirt and navy cords.

Ariel stopped in the hall, frowning at the empty stove box. Ryan reached back and pulled her along after him, through his door and up the spiral staircase. "Ry?" There was sleepy bewilderment in her husky voice. "Where is...oh, no!"

His bedroom was lit by the small lamp on the dresser. By its dim glow she could see that one of the rag rugs and Ryan's velour robe had been scratched into a comfortable birthing bed; and it was too late to do anything about it. Murphy was placidly licking a squirming, wet body so tiny it seemed her rough tongue would surely crush the fragile bones.

"I'm sorry, Ryan; I really thought she would use the bed I made."

"Don't even worry about it." He sat at the dog's side and pulled Ariel down beside him, carefully arranging the robe over her crossed legs. Murphy rose unsteadily, whimpering, and Ariel grabbed Ryan's hand anxiously. "Maybe we should call the vet."

"Relax." He put his arms around her, drawing her closer. "Murph knows what to do. We're just here for moral support."

As the second puppy made its appearance, with its flattened ears, zippered eyes and mashed-in face, Ariel clasped his hand delightedly and whispered, "Oh, Ry, how beautiful. He's so precious."

In the cool, dim room her hair smelled like sweet, warm sunshine. His long fingers separated hers, sliding between them and bringing their palms together warmly. "You've never seen puppies born?"

"I've never seen anything born. My mom is allergic to animal fur, and we kids could never have any pets." She gave him a dazzling smile that brightened the dark room. "Did you and your brother have a dog when you were growing up?"

They'd exchanged the usual family information over dinner one night. Ryan had left out one or two significant details about his brother, along with the fact that his father had died when he was thirteen. Ariel had mentioned her twin sisters, still in high school, one brother who had recently graduated as an engineer and another in college. As she had talked Ryan had seen clearly the strong bonds of love and easy affection that held her large family together.

"Mmm, we had a dog." He laughed. "She was a mutt with the very original name of Lady, but she wasn't one. She had puppies with great regularity until my mother had the vet put an end to her wanton ways."

They laughed together softly. Murphy whined again, and Ryan stroked a soothing hand along her flank, murmuring gentle encouragement as more puppies entered the world. Ariel sat on the cold, drafty floorboards, watching silently. She shivered suddenly and snuggled unconsciously closer to him.

"Hey!" He looked at her in concern, his fingers rubbing her cold cheek. "You're freezing!" She couldn't argue; her bare feet had passed freezing five minutes ago. Drawing her up, he pulled back the bedspread and blankets, commanding, "Get under the covers. There's no sense in you catching pneumonia."

Amazed at her lack of maidenly reluctance to climb into his bed, Ariel sat in the middle, wrapping the blankets around her shoulders. She imagined that she could feel the heat from his body still trapped in the covers. She buried her cold nose in them, smelling his citrusy, musky scent. "Does it usually take very long?" Her voice was muffled by the covers.

"Not too much longer, I think. First litters are usually small, and she's already got five." He paused for a moment. "She was DiSanto's dog, wasn't she?"

"Yes. When Robert couldn't take her, I did."

"Why didn't he want her? If they were as close as you say, I would think . . ."

"She never liked him, almost seemed to hate him, in fact." Her face in the shadowy light became reflective. "Dennis and Robert were very close, but so different. The three of us spent quite a bit of time together. Dennis was basically an uncomplicated man, easy-going, with simple wants and needs."

And one of those wants was you, he added silently. How had DiSanto kept his hands off her for a year and a half, when his own fingers were itching right now, after only a week, to rip off that prim little nightshirt and show her the reality of those love scenes she wrote so imaginatively.

"Robert is very intense, very complex. He was two years younger than Dennis, but Dennis always deferred to him, just to avoid conflict, I think. Dennis didn't like arguments, any kind of a fuss. He'd always give in to keep the peace."

She smiled at a happy memory. "Robert's a terrific actor, does a lot of amateur productions around L.A. With just a little make-up, some clothes, maybe a wig, he can become completely unrecognizable. He came to Dennis's Halloween party dressed as a bag lady. He stood right next to me, talking for ten minutes, and I never recognized him."

"Is he married?"

"To his business, the one he took over from their uncle. He's the quintessential businessman, fascinated with figuring all the angles, profit margins, risks. No mere woman," she said, laughing "could ever hold his interest very long."

She scooted closer to the edge of the bed. The five damp fur balls were rooting around for breakfast already. The unruly lock of Ryan's hair had fallen over his forehead again, and she brushed it back without thinking. "You're not an easy simple man, either, are you, Ryan Jones?" she murmured.

He caught her hand and held it for a moment to his cheek. She had startled him. Just the light touch of her fingers had aroused him. He laid her hand back on the spread. "And just what do you think you know about me, Miss Spence?" he bantered lightly.

"I know you and your brother don't have a comfortable relationship. There's a strain in your voice whenever you mention him."

What was it about the dark that made confession so easy, he wondered. Maybe it wasn't the dark. Maybe it was the woman, instead, with her gentle, compassionate voice inviting the burden of his sins.

"We used to be close, like you say the DiSantos were. But we lost it a long time ago."

"What happened?"

"I was supposed to go straight on to law school after I graduated from Annapolis. Just before I graduated my brother wrote me that he was going to drop out of college and join the army so he could go to Vietnam. I guess he thought he was missing out on the fun or something." Ryan's cold smile was twisted with bitterness. "He looked just like our dad, and I knew it would kill my mother if anything happened to him. So I requested immediate active duty in the same area. I knew Rick would never be allowed to serve in a combat zone when his mother was widowed and his brother was already there."

Ryan held his breath, wondering if Ariel would catch the slip he'd made, revealing that his father, Chief Dye's "old friend," had been dead for years.

She didn't.

"And something happened to you instead."

It wasn't a question. How did she know? Was it so obvious? "Yeah, something happened to me. I really wasn't trained for anything, but I'm a natural marksman, so they put me in command of a company of snipers. We were very good." His low voice dripped gall. "We did ourselves out of a job after a few weeks."

"I know. The first night you were here, when you had the nightmare, you talked about some of what you were remembering." Her hand rested hesitantly on his shoulder. He looked down at the slim, strong hand, realizing suddenly that he hadn't had the nightmare again since that night. He slid her hand down and held it over his heart.

"I killed so many men I lost count. I stopped counting intentionally," he corrected himself. "Some were men whose faces I never saw. Others were men whose faces I sometimes think I'll never forget." He leaned his head back on the edge of the bed, his eyes tightly squeezed to shut out the memories. "After the fall of Saigon my men and I stayed in Southeast Asia. We were given new training; each man became an expert in infiltration, assassination, intelligence or weapons and demolition. Since I was the leader, I had to master all four."

Ariel's heart ached for the man who had showed such kindness and gentleness to her and her dog as he described the horror in a flat, unemotional voice. "You quit after the girl in the hut."

He nodded, swallowing back the bitter taste in his mouth, "I thought, I'd learned to handle the fact that you could buy anything you wanted there—drugs, of course, a man's murder, a woman, a child. Every unspeakable desire could be gratified and—" his harsh laugh sounded like it came from a raw throat "—the prices were amazingly low. The Navy gave us medals and sent us home. But they couldn't—" his soft voice was unbearably sad "—send back the naive innocent boys we'd been, or give us back even one of our illusions."

"What happened to your brother?" she asked quietly.

"Oh, he lost the supersoldier urge, finished school and feels guilty as hell, trying to figure out how to pay the debt he thinks he owes me. And I feel guilty because I can't figure out how to convince him that he doesn't owe me anything. I made my choice freely."

He shook his head tiredly. He opened his eyes and with his free arm, gestured with mock grandeur. "Now I brilliantly defend guilty clients who pay me exorbitant amounts of money when I get them off." He laughed mirthlessly.

"Why?"

He turned to smile sadly at her, her hand still clamped to his heart. "Because I just didn't care anymore, Ariel."

He sat for a moment longer, watching her quietly, then stood wearily and sat on the edge of the bed, his hip nudging hers under the covers. Obligingly she moved over and pulled the covers back automatically.

"I think Murphy's all right, but—" he muffled a yawn "—we ought to keep an eye on her just a little longer, okay?"

His yawn was contagious, and she collapsed back on the pillows, feeling totally exhausted. "Okay, I'll stay a little while longer. But don't," she admonished sleepily in the midst of another yawn, "let me fall asleep here."

Chapter 6

Ariel wriggled blissfully deeper into the lean, hard warmth at her back. Blinking at the sunlight burning through the crack between the curtains, she tried to turn away from it, then realized that the heavy weight across her chest wouldn't allow her to. The weight flexed and tightened. She recognized drowsily that the weight was a long, muscular arm with a hand attached that was—every cell in her body snapped wide awake—gently kneading her breast.

Every muscle as tight as a piano wire, she could scarcely draw even a shallow breath. What the hell had happened last night? After she had recklessly invited Ryan to watch TV, they had sprawled comfortably in her armchairs and viewed a grade-C Western. They had munched the popcorn Ryan made during a commercial and drunk the two bottles of beer Ariel had unearthed at the bottom of her refrigerator. When the movie ended they had solemnly agreed that the sidekick's mule should not only have gotten top billing, but also been the script writer, too. Then Ryan had taken his leave with one of those electrifyingly enthralling kisses that sent restless longings stirring crazily through her. Just when she'd finally fallen asleep, he'd gotten her back up to help Murphy.

Ariel let her breath out carefully. Nothing had happened. But she'd better get out of this bed immediately, because those feelings were clamoring for attention more insistently than ever, and if he woke up she would be terribly tempted to do something about them.

Furtively she tried to inch out from under his arm. His hand was reluctant to give up its hold. She shut her eyes in consternation. Now what? She felt the mattress shifting next to her. Opening one eye, cautiously, she stared up into dark chocolate eyes with a look of distilled wickedness.

"Oh dear," she whispered, trying to fight the giggle at the back of her throat.

Propped above her on one elbow, Ryan smiled down lazily. "Good morning, Miss Spence. It seems you fell asleep in my bed once again."

He'd moved his hand, but still having his arm stretched all the way across her wasn't any improvement. His arms and chest were bare, but her investigative toes told her that he was still wearing the soft cords. With a lightning move Ariel caught his arm with both hands and wrenched it away, scrambling out of bed without a shred of dignity. "And I've escaped again, Mr. Jones," she crowed.

Not quite. Her nightshirt was caught under his hip. Ryan reached out almost carelessly, seized it and hauled her back down on the bed. Rolling over swiftly, he trapped her under him. Her eyes grew impossibly wide and dark as his mouth descended. He watched the color draining from her face as he brushed his mouth teasingly over hers.

"Are you afraid, Ariel?" he murmured, tracing her lips lightly with the tip of his tongue.

Her breath drew in sharply; then he felt the warm, ragged explosion on his cheek. "Not of you," she whispered. "Me."

Ryan smiled briefly; then his eyes closed, and his mouth took hers stunningly, thoroughly.

Ariel could sense the barely restrained hunger in him. Her nightgown crept up with the aid of his nimble fingers as his warm palm slid over her thigh and hip, past the curve of her waist to rest on the underside of her breast. She felt his other hand pulling the quilt back over them. His tongue was probing, tasting, coaxing a response. Ariel sighed and gave in. Her legs tangled languidly with his, while their bodies began to nestle into each other's. Her fingers climbed up the taut cords in his neck, plunging into his thick blue-black hair. The strands of rough silk slid between her fingers as she pulled his mouth closer.

The soft warmth of the bed produced a drowsy coziness, and the feel of a hard male body against hers no longer seemed so unfamiliar. It seemed natural... and comfortable. His lips nibbled across her mouth with a slow thoroughness. When he reached the opposite corner he rose on one elbow to lean over her, his other hand still radiating heat on her breast. He seemed content for the moment just to look at her and to touch—slow, delicate, hypnotic caresses circling her breast, but never quite touching the ultrasensitive tip. His other hand reached up languidly to brush her hair away from her face and back onto the pillow. His palm and long fingers smoothed the hair back with long soothing strokes that matched the motions of his other hand.

Where only moments before every muscle in her body had been tight, ready to leap off his bed, now Ariel felt a languor seeping into her, relaxing those tight muscles one by one. She didn't know if it came from the warm quilts, or his body covering hers, or the heat his hands were spreading. Maybe it was the glow warming, softening, his hard dark eyes. She didn't particularly care; she didn't really want to think about it at all, just enjoy it and hope this delicious, weightless sensation didn't end too soon.

She brought her hand up as she studied his face. Her eyes followed her finger tracing over his winged, black eyebrows. Down it went over the sharp bones in his cheek and across his hard mouth, relaxed now in a soft smile. It ended in the hollow between his tooprominent collarbones. His pulse was fast and steady under the light touch of her fingertip.

"You're so thin," she murmured, her eyes too innocent to hide her concern and awakening passion.

Ryan's hand brushed lightly down her ribs and back up to the startlingly full undercurve of her breast. "So are you."

He rolled onto his back, pulling her on top of him.

She whispered a kiss over the sharp bones at the base of his throat. The tip of her tongue delicately traced around his strong pulse before she sealed a warm kiss over it. "The first time I saw you, I wanted to fatten you up, fix you all sorts of hearty, nourishing meals." She laughed, the tip of her tongue now tracing over the bones. "If I had tried, you'd be even thinner."

One dark brow lifted, and her finger returned to follow it. "I only inspire your maternal instincts?"

"A few others."

"Which ones?" His voice and smile were deep and lazy as he tipped her chin up to read the expression in her eyes. He was enjoying simply letting her play with him, getting used to the feel of a man in bed with her, as long as he was that man. The celibate habits of twenty-seven years wouldn't be overcome in a single morning, but he wanted to show her what it could be like to wake up every morning like this, to learn the fun of teasing banter in a warm cozy bed wrapped in each other's arms. "Which ones?" he repeated.

She laughed lightly, tossing her head. "Oh . . . passion, desire . . . to name two."

"Those are pretty good ones—for a start," he acknowledged with a lingering kiss. "Are you flirting with me, Miss Spence?"

"I'm trying to," she admitted honestly, laughing a little self-consciously. "But I'm not any good at it."

"Oh, no," he assured her, "you're *very* good. A little more practice and you'll be irresistible." He guided her mouth down to his.

Ariel linked her arms around his neck. My Lord, she realized absently, I didn't even know how to kiss before. Her virginal mouth was rapidly losing its innocence as his tongue thrust and explored and danced with hers. With a small moan she melted completely, her hips unconsciously settling into the cradle of his.

Ryan's other hand slipped down her back and under her nightshirt, skating across her hip to the small of her back. He held her tight against him as he rolled them to their sides. He tightened his thighs, tangling their legs tighter as his hand moved up her bare skin to her shoulder. His mouth smiled against hers as he felt the little shivers under her cool skin.

Ariel felt Ryan push gently against her shoulder. Her body as fluid as liquid gold, she leaned away until his hand closed over the sharp bones, caressing, stopping her. The hand that had been idling at her breast moved up to untie the satin ribbon at the neck of her shirt. It spread the soft flannel, and his mouth left hers. It cruised down, trailing a ribbon of smoldering heat. Ariel closed her eyes, her fingers tightening in the hair brushing the back of Ryan's neck, waiting. She felt the unruly lock of his hair that insisted on falling

over his forehead brush against her throat, and her head arched
back slowly. His head moved lower, brushing the rough silk of his
hair across her chest. His mouth was warm on the upper curve of
her breast. The hand on her breast drifted lower, pausing at her
waist, drifting again, seemingly aimlessly, across her belly to her
thigh. The long fingers stroked over the lean muscle on the outside down to her knee, then back up the softer silken flesh on the
inside.

As Ryan's hand slipped up languidly, Ariel's hand dropped to his
chest and pushed unconsciously. "Ariel." Her eyes opened slowly
when his soft whisper called her.

Suddenly she was standing unsteadily on shaky legs, his arms
around her for support. Uncomprehendingly she looked up at him.

To the unasked question in her dazed eyes, he answered with a
crooked smile, "Not an escape, Ariel, a rain check, until you're not
afraid of either one of us." When he had felt her push him away
and she had opened her eyes, he had seen lingering traces of fear.
He gave her a proprietary kiss and turned her firmly in the direction of the stairs, sending her down them with a friendly swat on
the fanny.

Ariel drifted slowly across the hall and up her own stairs. Be-
musedly she sat on the edge of her bed, hands folded in her lap.
She'd been right to think him dangerous. She shook her head,
trying to clear the confusion. Oh, yes, he was dangerous, even
more than she'd imagined, but she no longer cared in the least.

This was definitely the man, the one she'd risk her heart and the
beliefs of a lifetime for. Her hands clenched achingly on each other.
Now the question was, did she have the courage to do it? Especially when she had no guarantee that she wasn't just a little vacation fling?

As she stared across the room the clock finally came into focus.
It was past time to stop daydreaming and get dressed. Bessie was
expecting her very soon, and she still had Murphy and her puppies to move, and Ryan Jones to avoid.

After a hurried breakfast Ariel stepped into the hall. She found
Ryan had already moved Murphy into her nursery. Kneeling by the
box, she laughed softly at the puppies wriggling around blindly on
the old blankets like fat, furry grubs.

"You going to be a good mama, Murphy?" she crooned,
scratching the velvety head. Murphy opened her yellow eyes for a

moment, then closed them tiredly. "Poor girl, you didn't know the price you'd pay for a few minutes of fun," Ariel commiserated with a giggle and patted the dog's deflated abdomen. "That rat didn't stick around when you told him you were pregnant, did he? Was it that sneaky ol' Chester from down the road?" The dog opened one eye and moaned quietly. "I thought so. Don't worry, girl, we'll sue him for puppy support."

"I'll represent her for free." Ryan hunkered down at Ariel's side, reaching out a finger to gently stroke a mewling puppy back to sleep. He shot her a sidelong look. "What are you going to do today?"

She returned the look from under thick lashes. "Oh, just go to the Apple Fair in town. You wouldn't be interested."

"I like apples." He dragged her up with him as he stood.

She tried to sound as boring and discouraging as she could. "I'm taking Bessie Ruff from the nursing home."

"I'd like to meet her." He truly did want to meet the ancient woman with whom Ariel had forged such a strong bond.

Silent, Ariel picked up the shotgun leaning against the wall, cradling it in her elbow.

"Is there going to be an apple shoot?" He lounged in the doorway, blocking her exit.

"No, a turkey shoot." A crafty little smile lit her face. On second thought, she did want him to come with her. "Skeet shooting, actually," she added. "With a twenty-five-pound turkey for the prize."

"Alive or dead?" That explained the gray sweater she was wearing with her red slacks. The sweater, which made her blue eyes bluer, had a leather patch sewn on the front of the left shoulder, a shooting patch.

"Already plucked and dressed. Want to come? I'll even lend you a gun."

He followed her out into the garage to the tall, locked metal cabinet. He wanted to be sure he got the Browning Magnum he had seen when he had picked the lock one afternoon while she was out. She undid the padlock and threw the door open wide, silently indicating that he could have his choice. Without hesitation he took out the Browning twelve-gauge and a box of shells.

He stowed both guns behind the seat of his truck. "Yours is old, almost an antique."

"It was my grandfather's. He taught me to shoot."

She was sitting next to the door, too far away. He wanted to slide her across the seat hard against his side. "But you don't hunt. Why not?"

"I never liked the thought of killing anything." She grimaced. "I'm too soft-hearted, I guess." She said it as if it were a defect in her character.

"Don't apologize for it," he said harshly, then consciously softened his voice. "What will you do with the turkey if you win it? Make gallons of turkey soup?"

"*When* I win it," she corrected him gently.

"Care to make a side bet?" One raised black brow challenged her.

"Oh, I couldn't take your money," she said kindly. "I would be taking unfair advantage of you."

A small smile tugged at his lips as he stared straight ahead through the windshield. "I wasn't thinking of money. And you can take advantage of me anytime."

He was too sure of himself. He deserved to be taken down a peg or two; it would be good for his rascally soul, she decided selflessly. "When I win, you have to fix dinner for me. Whatever I want."

"I hope I don't win the same," he said in mock alarm, laughing at the horrible face she pulled at him. "Well, don't worry." He gave her a slow grin. "I'll think of something."

"I'm not worried," she advised him sweetly, shaking the hand he offered to seal their bet.

Bessie Ruff was waiting for them on the sidewalk outside the nursing home. She didn't seem to be surprised to see Ryan. Ariel made the introductions, and then Ryan carefully lifted the elderly woman while Ariel collapsed the wheelchair and hoisted it into the back of the truck.

Ryan was hardly aware of any weight in his arms. It was as if the fragile bones were no more than air, and the only substance Bessie Ruff had was the indomitable will that refused to let go of life just yet. He glanced at her sharply, an unconscious question in his dark eyes. Bessie met his gaze unflinchingly. Then her eyes shifted to Ariel at the back of the truck, and her head shook almost imperceptibly. Ryan smiled sadly at her, nodding once, and then his eyes rested on Ariel. There was tenderness on his usually unreadable face. Ariel was soon to lose someone else she loved. He was only grateful that he would be present this time to try to ease the pain. Bessie Ruff studied his unguarded expression, then looked back to the young woman she regarded as more of a granddaughter than those of her own blood. Her crinkled face softened in a contented smile.

The October day was as crisp as the red apples shining in the slatted bushel baskets filling the backs of the trucks parked along Main Street. Overhead the cobalt sky was unmarred by a single cloud and the sun glowed like a molten gold coin. It was as if Mother Nature had decided to grant one last perfect day before she allowed the long, cold winter to close down on the valley.

The still air was quintessentially autumn: a faint drift of burning leaves, a subtle taste of high-country snow, the warmth of pure sunlight on cool cheeks and the scent of apples everywhere. Ripe apples, cinnamony apple pies and apple butter, and freshly pressed apple cider tempted the noses of locals and tourists alike as the crowd browsed at the booths scattered over the lawn surrounding the county museum.

Ryan, Bessie and Ariel detoured to the baseball park across the street, where the turkey shoot would be held later. Already a number of men and a few women were practicing with the targets stapled to hay bales. Ariel handed over Ryan's gun and took the handles of the wheelchair. His hand curved around the walnut stock of the gun as naturally as a wino's around the neck of a bottle. Her stomach tightened as she remembered how that same hand had closed around her breast only a few hours before. She shook her head to banish the unsettling memory and offered some friendly advice. "That gun shoots high and a little to the left."

He nodded and took the box of shells out of his jacket pocket. His first shot was low and to the right of the bull's-eye. Resting the gun on his shoulder, Ryan turned to give Ariel a calculating stare. She responded with a gesture of exaggerated innocence. Grinning, he turned back, swung the gun down firmly against his shoulder, hardly taking aim and shot the center out of the target. Ariel rolled Bessie back across the street, wondering if maybe she should have practiced just a bit more.

The Mountain Fiddle Band was tuning up. Ariel parked Bessie so she could enjoy the sunshine and folded herself gracefully down onto the grass at the old woman's side so they could listen. She held a palsied, weightless hand in hers.

"He's a scoundrel, isn't he?" Bessie's strong voice was full of humor.

"Who?" Ariel looked up artlessly.

Bessie gave her a dry look.

Caught out, Ariel laughed. "Yes, I expect he is. Also arrogant, complicated and much too good-looking. But..." Her glance strayed across the street, where she could see his red shaker-knit sweater and wheat jeans standing out among the blue denim and cowboy shirts. "He definitely has style." Her expression turned wistful. "I've fallen in love with him." The words slipped out so easily that for a moment she didn't realize how naturally she accepted the knowledge. She examined the words, savored them and knew they were true.

Bessie's knobby hand tightened convulsively on Ariel's. She stared at the girl in rueful astonishment. She'd figured it would take Ariel longer to figure it out, and she'd never expected her to accept it so blithely.

Ariel didn't notice Bessie's reaction as she softly voiced her thoughts aloud. "I've only known him a week; it hardly seems possible. Isn't love supposed to come slowly, comfortably, after knowing someone a long time?" She sighed lightly. "Maybe it's just lust, and it will pass."

"Don't discount lust, girl; every marriage can benefit from a healthy dose of it." She smiled down fondly. "But you don't think it's lust, do you, Ariel?"

Ariel smiled back wryly. "No, Bessie, I don't." She gazed off into the distance again, her eyes automatically seeking out a flash of red. "And I think he may well break my heart," she added softly. She grinned up hopefully. "Any words of grandmotherly wisdom would be gratefully accepted."

"I knew John Ruff all of ten minutes before I decided I was going to marry him," Bessie said reflectively. "The only reason our first son wasn't born shamelessly soon after the wedding was because I talked John into getting married just two weeks after we met."

Ariel laughed in delight. "Why, Bessie! You impetuous, scandalous woman!" Her joyful face gradually sobered. "I don't think I could be that convincing."

"If you want him badly enough, you can be."

Did she want him badly enough? Was she willing to trade her solitary, placid, rather selfish life for excitement, passion, shared joy and sorrow...and the very real possibility of being terribly hurt? Ariel sighed in frustration. If only she could know how Ryan really felt. But that was part of the adventure, the excitement of falling in love, the not knowing, the risk of offering yourself with no guarantee of winning, gambling with the highest stakes of all— your heart. And she had never been much of a gambler.

"I've wondered why you never remarried, Bessie."

"Widows with five young children don't get that many offers," Bessie informed her dryly. "Especially with no farm or business to sweeten the pot."

"Still," Ariel searched the old face which still held traces of the beauty she had once had, "I know you must have been asked."

"If I had an offer soon after John died, I would have accepted. I was so frightened and alone." Remembered grief and fears sixty years old shadowed her eyes. "But after a while I got to enjoying my independence, hard as it was. I decided I wouldn't settle for less than what I'd had with John. And," she finished matter-of-factly, "I never found it."

"Well, I think I have." Ariel laughed dismally, burying her head in her hands. "But I'm not sure what I'm going to do with it."

Bessie's worn eyes spotted a blur of red moving toward them. "You'll figure it out soon, dear," she predicted reassuringly.

They did the grand tour of the booths. Ryan bought a jug of hard cider and five dollars' worth of chances, though on what he wasn't quite sure. Ariel bought a quilted pillow, and then she and Bessie spelled the women at one of the pie booths for a time.

After reclaiming his ladies Ryan bought lunch, and they settled on the rustling carpet of red and gold under a maple tree to eat it. Ariel watched Bessie closely, not liking her color or the increasing tremor in her hands.

"Bessie, would you like us to take you back before the shoot? There are so many people; maybe you'd like to get away from the crowd." Ariel always tried to phrase her suggestions that Bessie rest as innocuously as possible, but she was never able to fool her.

"I'm not ready to be put down for my nap yet," Bessie told her tartly. "And I certainly don't want to miss the shooting contest between you two." Her bright eyes fixed on Ryan guilelessly. "Did you know Ariel won the last two shoots, even beating the man who'd been the valley champion for four years?''

"So more than several people took great pains to tell me," Ryan confirmed dryly. He also knew it was one of her lesser accomplishments. Ariel Spence, with Dennis DiSanto as her partner, had won the mixed doubles and trapshooting championship for the entire state of California two years ago. He anticipated an interesting contest. He anticipated what he would get if he won their bet even more.

The shoot quickly developed into a three-person contest. Only Ariel, Ryan and a surly man with almost no neck and the build of a football tackling dummy progressed past the third shooting station.

The competitors had to hold their shotguns waist high, standing at each of eight stations. Without warning bright orange clay disks were released by the trap machine to whiz across in front of them at ninety miles an hour. Since there were two machines, one on each end of the firing line, the contestants never knew from which direction the flying saucers would come. Their guns had to be whipped up against their shoulders, aim taken and a shot fired in a little less than two seconds. Two consecutive misses and a contestant was out.

The former valley champion missed two in a row and had to stand with the rest of the crowd. He took up a position with his two brothers, near a tallish, slight stranger with lank blond hair. The stranger was watching the duel with great interest.

The acrid smell of burned gunpowder and blue smoke drifted over the field as Ariel and Ryan moved to the sixth station. They'd both had misses, but within a second had managed to fire again and shatter the target before it was too low to be safely hit.

At the seventh station the trap released the disk and Ariel threw up her gun in a smooth, almost careless motion. The target exploded. She moved aside, gesturing graciously to Ryan. He shifted his hips a few times, settling into an easy stance. The orange blur flew across in front of him and he missed. He fired a second shot immediately, and the blur blew up.

The eighth and final station was by far the most difficult, with the targets passing almost directly overhead. The avid crowd pushed forward, offering encouragement, and a few more bets were made.

Ryan decided it was time to shift the odds in his favor. As Ariel sank into a half crouch with her gun, he pulled her back up and planted a long, leisurely kiss on her startled mouth. Her free hand came up immediately to push him away, but it ended up lying limply on his shoulder. He tilted her face to a new angle, drinking a deeper kiss from her softening mouth, then set her firmly away from him, smiling down into her wide eyes. "For luck, Miss Spence."

"Yours, I think," she whispered back. Trying vainly to gather her scattered wits, she kept her back to the laughing crowd. Nodding to the trap operators that she was ready any time—though she wouldn't be for at least an hour—she tensed. She missed both shots.

There was a roar of male approval and feminine groans. She faced the crowd with a shrug and a sheepish smile. Ryan took her place, and she moved just inside his peripheral vision. Twice he looked at her suspiciously, obviously expecting some outrageous distraction. She smiled at him cheerfully each time. He was glancing at her once more when he heard the trap. He barely had time for two shots and both went wide.

Ryan and Ariel saluted each other gravely with a perfect Regency bow and curtsy, and then burst out laughing along with the people who had enjoyed their performance. After accepting joint custody of the turkey they began to make their way back through the crowd to Bessie.

The voice on the loudspeaker caught Ryan's attention, and he stopped Ariel with a touch on her arm. He pulled a handful of raffle tickets out of his pocket and listened more closely. "Hey," he said wonderingly, "I think I won the raffle!"

"What did you win?" Ariel asked, laughing at the boyish excitement on his face.

"Damned if I know." He grinned at her. Slinging his arm across her shoulders, he headed them back toward the bandstand. "Let's go find out."

Ariel and Bessie struggled to keep their giggles at bay. "Oh, no, Ry! What are you going to do with *that*?" The look of total consternation on Ryan's face was too much for them, and they gave up. The cool, unflappable Ryan Jones was at a loss for words.

"Uh, Mr. Jones." The foreman of the lumber mill that had donated the prize stepped forward. "We kinda have to deliver it today; we need the truck. We can let you keep the trailer for a week or so, though," he allowed generously.

Ryan looked at him in greater disbelief, if possible, and then back at his prize: a low trailer with a pyramid of logs, each about twenty to thirty feet long.

"Gee, there must be twelve to fifteen cords of wood there," a bystander said interestedly. "Hope you have a good chain saw, Jones." The man slapped his congratulations on Ryan's back and walked away. Ryan's mouth tightened fractionally.

A prudent woman would have kept her mouth shut, but Ariel was apparently not a prudent woman. "Let's see, you could ship them back to Los Angeles and build a log cabin," she contributed thoughtfully. "No, that might look out of place on Malibu beach. Oh! I know," she said brightly, giving him her best cheerleader smile. "You can give each one of your friends a log as a Christmas present; I understand firewood is *very* expensive in L.A. Be sure you buy plenty of ribbon," she instructed. "Red, I think."

His black look sent her off into another convulsion of laughter. Both of them nearly missed the foreman's comment that the lumber company had used the low flatbed instead of a standard logging trailer to make unloading easier. By releasing one particular chain in the metal web holding the logs in place, he explained, they would be able to tumble the whole load off the truck.

"Come on, Ryan," Ariel said plopping the fresh turkey into his arms, "let's take our prizes home." Pushing Bessie's chair, she led the way to his truck, muffled giggles escaping her every few steps.

"What do they usually do for fun on Saturday nights in this town?"

Ariel stuck the last dish in her dishwasher and kept her head down, not offering any suggestions. After delivering Bessie to her room at Valley View, she and Ryan had come home and eaten the leftovers out of both their refrigerators for supper.

Ryan stretched his long legs across the floor as he leaned back against the counter beside her. "What about that place just down the highway?"

Ariel straightened slowly and faced him, hoping he wasn't going to suggest what she was afraid he would, because she would go. "It's kind of a rough place, especially on Saturday nights," she said dismissively.

"The sign says they have a live band and dancing. It can't be too rough."

"It's all stomp dancing, and the band is two guitars and a fiddle."

"Let's go." He had grabbed her hand and was leading her out the door in one of those smooth, lightning moves before she could think of one good reason why they shouldn't.

Two happy loggers reeled out as he opened the scarred plank door of the Stumble Inn for her. "This place should be called the Stumble Out," Ariel muttered to herself. One look around the smoky, barebones saloon, and she knew it had been a mistake to come here tonight. There were few women, and those few looked as hard and tough as the men. She'd forgotten that the lumber company had brought in roughhousers to do the particularly nasty and dirty job of harvesting the timber burned in a forest fire last month. The usual neighborhood crowd had wisely stayed away tonight.

Ryan stopped just inside the door. Rocking back on his heels, he braced his legs slightly apart, elbows cocked, hands in the pockets of an old leather bomber jacket. He surveyed the rough interior and its even rougher occupants and checked to see where the fire exit was. He felt that old recklessness stirring. The bar reminded him of his favorite hangout in Bangkok years ago. The dress was a little different and the men a little bigger, but the atmosphere of good-natured belligerence was the same. He glanced at Ariel and suppressed a smile at the worried pull of her eyebrows. He was confident he could get her out before the inevitable fight got too rowdy.

They started toward an empty table, and Ariel's stomach hit the floor. It hadn't been a mistake to come here; it had been insanity. The slightly slurred voice caught them in the act of sitting down and directed all eyes to them.

"Well, well, if it ain't Annie Oakley and the big-shot lawyer from California." The word "California" sounded like an obscenity.

Ariel occupied herself with removing her jacket, keeping her head down. She could feel the hostility from the back of the room. A chair scraped on the wooden plank floor, and she knew their adversary was coming closer, like a foul-smelling cloud. She looked up and caught Ryan's eye. He smiled benignly, seemingly unaware of the menace in the air.

"I think we should leave, Ryan," she whispered hurriedly. She reached for her jacket and started to put it back on. "That's Shirley Geilenfeldt, the one we beat today. And he's got his brothers with him. We don't want—"

"Shirley?" Ryan checked a laugh. "What are his brothers' names?" Calmly he removed her suede jacket and arranged it neatly over the back of her chair.

"Beverly and Gus." Ryan's head went back, and he laughed freely. Ariel looked at him, incredulous. "Listen!" she scolded in a low, fierce voice, shaking his arm to wake him up to the situation. "The three of them collectively have the personality of a wounded rhino, and Shirley's the meanest. And the fact that he was beaten today by a woman *and* a city slicker won't have improved it. Now, let's go!" she hissed, trying to stand up before the walking tackling dummy with the nasty smirk on his face made it to their table.

Ryan's hand closed over her arm and held her in her seat. "Sit down, Ariel. We haven't even had a drink yet," he reminded her reasonably. He lounged back in the wooden chair, legs crossed, one ankle resting on the opposite knee.

Ariel caught the suppressed excitement and anticipation lurking in Ryan's eyes and glared at him. "You're enjoying this, Ryan Jones!" she accused in a disbelieving whisper. "We're probably going to get killed by those three apes and you . . . oh, no . . ." She moaned and hid her face in her hands.

"Where'd you learn to shoot like that, boy?" Shirley Geilenfeldt sneered. Good manners dictated that he exchange a few pleasantries before he rearranged the pansy's pretty face.

"Potshotting at the ducks in MacArthur Park." Ryan leaned farther back in his chair, balancing it on the back legs, his hands in his front pockets. He stared blandly into Shirley's washed-out green eyes. "Shot a few skunks, too."

A lanky man with stringy blond hair and worn Levis stopped by the front door, as if reluctant to miss what would undeniably be the best show in town that evening. The door opened and Chief Dye ambled in. The blond man and a couple of others decided that discretion was the better part of valor, slipping out the door before it closed. The chief's sousaphone voice reached even into the back room, where the poker game was going strong. Shirley squinted at him glumly, grunted one last opinion of city boys and rejoined his disappointed brothers.

The band began to play, and three couples got up to dance. Ariel watched Ryan stroll over to the bar and order two beers. The limp was gone. The hours he was spending in the mountains had strengthened his leg rapidly. He'd even gained some weight. He leaned an elbow on the bar, relaxed and totally comfortable, laughing with two burly loggers. His red sweater and Calvin Klein jeans and topsiders certainly weren't de rigueur dress for a Montana bar, but he was accepted here as easily as he would be at the poshest lounge on Nob Hill in San Francisco.

Women found him incredibly attractive, of course; she hadn't needed to see their appraising looks at the fair today to tell her that. Yet men instinctively liked him, too, sensing, she guessed, the cool toughness under the suave charm. Only a Shirley Geilenfeldt, full of drunken bravado, would be stupid enough to challenge him.

Chief Dye made the rounds, carrying a mug of beer that never lowered appreciably from table to table. He offered his congratulations when he reached their table, asked Ryan to stop in and see him on Monday, then moved on. The band swung into "Cotton-Eyed Joe," and Ryan pulled Ariel up to dance. He danced, she discovered, as he seemed to do everything else, with a consummate, easy skill. The band downshifted into a slow Texas two-step. Ryan closed his arms over her back, holding her body against his so closely that she had no choice but to rest her head on his shoulder and wind her arms around his waist. She let her body indulge itself in the deeply pleasuring sensations generated by his hips and thighs and chest sliding lazily against hers. They swayed to the languid beat of the bass guitar, and Ariel nestled her head closer into his sweater, catching the tang of his cologne and a wisp of crisp apples and clean fall air through the smoky, stale beer smell of the bar.

The band decided to take a break. Dropping a light kiss on Ariel's forehead, Ryan went to investigate the possibilities of the jukebox.

Ariel looked around for the ladies' room. On her way back to their table she passed a table full of loggers. An arm as hard and thick as a middle-aged pine tree shot out and clamped around her waist, dragging her onto the lap of the biggest man. Her startled gasp was cut short by a low drawl from over her head.

"The lady is with me."

Ariel looked up warily. The mood in the bar was suddenly very primitive. Ryan stood less than two feet away, balancing easily on the balls of his feet, his hands relaxed and loose at his sides. He reached out and jerked her up to his side, his arm around her unmistakably possessive.

"If she's your woman, you should keep a better hold on her," the logger grumbled.

"I will," Ryan agreed with a slow smile.

"I am *not*—" Ariel started in a clear voice.

"Shut up, Ariel," Ryan said pleasantly as he began to guide her back to their table. "Unless you want to be fair game for every man in here, including Shirley."

She gave him a disgusted glare and turned to give one to the logger, too. Instead she reached down to the table they were passing and grabbed the first thing her fingers touched—a full heavy mug of foamy beer. The Geilenfeldts had seen Ted Dye leave and apparently decided they had waited long enough to avenge Shirley's honor. All three of them were closing in on Ryan from his blind side. She yelled a warning and swung the sloshing mug at Beverly Geilenfeldt's head at the same time.

Chapter 7

Oh, Ry, brawling—making a public spectacle of myself!" Ariel was desperately trying to look both ashamed and disapproving and to avoid Ryan's eyes. They caught hers, and she cracked up. He had managed to drag her out through the fire exit, almost unscathed, just as Chief Dye and two of his men had charged through the front door of the Stumble Inn.

Her stern mouth widened in a huge grin, her blue eyes filled with unholy glee, and she collapsed on her sofa in gales of helpless laughter. Ryan caught her contagious insanity and stumbled to the couch, too. Just as they began to regain control of themselves, they made the mistake of looking at each other, setting them off again.

Finally, hugging her aching sides and groaning, Ariel bent over, trying to catch her breath. She controlled hiccuping giggles long enough to gasp, "Did you see the big one's face," she wiped her teary eyes and caught another jagged breath, "when you hit him over the head with the spittoon?" She dissolved again.

"Dammit, Ariel, they were all big! Why the hell did you have to start a fight with every damn one of them?" He rested his head on the back of the sofa, his streaming eyes wide, trying to stifle his giggles.

"Me?" she squeaked indignantly. *"Me?"* She fell on his chest, too weak with laughter to sit up. Ryan's left arm automatically came around her, his hand threading through her disheveled hair to hold her. "You were the one," she felt constrained to point out, "who kicked the chair out from under the one with the red beard and then called him a—"

"I know, I know," he admitted, chuckling again. "But you didn't have to dump the other one's pitcher of beer over his head and then call him a fat twit." He heaved in a huge breath, trying for control again until the air exploded in another gusty burst of laughter. "A twit!" he groaned. "My Lord. I've got to teach you some better words if you're going to hang out with me. I've got a reputation to maintain."

"It's all my mother's fault. Every time I start to say what I'm thinking, I taste soap and I choke." She lay half sprawled over him, relaxed, an occasional giggle still vibrating through her body. At last she realized exactly where she was and struggled to sit up, pushing on his hard chest and thigh.

Ryan let her up, but tightened his fingers around the back of her neck. "Well! I, ah, guess I should see to your eye," she said in a small voice, refusing to look at him. She stared at her hands, folded prissily on her lap.

Ryan hardly felt the abrasion from somebody's fist. "Forget my eye," he commanded huskily. He flexed his wrist and gently forced her face to tilt up to his. "You swing a mean beer mug, Ariel Spence. I'm glad you were on my side."

Almost against her will her eyes, wide and uncertain lifted and were instantly trapped by his, half-lidded and sultry. "Y—you were?" She was unable to move. His free hand was opening the top button of her shirt and sliding under the fabric, his thumb feathering over the satiny skin at the base of her throat.

"Uh-hmm, I was," he reaffirmed softly. His warm breath fanned over her parted lips, making silky wisps of her hair tickle her cheeks and neck. "I like to raise hell every now and then. I think you have a secret desire to do it, too." His mouth touched hers briefly. "What other secret desires do you have, Ariel?"

His eyes slid shut, and his lips closed over hers, taking possession as his hand slipped up her throat to her chin, keeping her mouth where he wanted it.

She moaned regretfully, her eyes closing, too. "I can't tell you." Her arms stole around his waist as he bore her back slowly on the couch. One of her legs bent; the other stretched straight on the sofa, trapped between his. The kiss deepened, sweetened, his tongue curling leisurely in her mouth. Hers joined in, hesitantly at first, then gliding slickly along his to taste him, dark, tangy, male. His knee bent, sliding up her thigh to rest snugly at the apex of her legs nudging gently with a slow, seductive rhythm.

A husky sigh purred deep in her throat, and her eyes, hazy with rising passion, opened to look into his. "I really shouldn't be doing this. I don't know you well enough."

"Miss Spence, the librarian, might feel obligated to say that, but the woman who coldcocks bullies in barroom brawls knows it isn't true, doesn't she, Ariel?" he asked quietly, rubbing his moist mouth lightly over hers. "I think we knew each other before I ever got here," he added whimsically. "We just hadn't met yet."

For an answer her arms tightened around him, her fingers slipping unconsciously under his belt with a will of their own. They tugged up his sweater and trailed down the groove of his spine to the cool hollow at the base. They rubbed, pressed, urging his hips and knee tighter against her, sliding, straining to relieve that deep, sweet ache.

With a deep groan, Ryan moved his hand rapidly down, freeing the buttons of her silky cream shirt. Leaving the hungry softness of her mouth, he rose above her and spread the shirt wide. His head bent again, his mouth nibbling at the hollow in her throat. His hands swept slowly across her shoulders and down her chest. He was learning her, savoring the taste and texture of her skin with his lips and tongue and teeth and rough fingertips.

Her hand clenched on his sides as his fingers brushed the hollow between her breasts and freed the catch on her bra. His warm tongue touched the spot where his fingers had been, then slid wetly over her cool skin to a puckered tip. He drew it into his mouth and suckled gently. Ariel arched into him strongly with a sharp cry.

Ryan pulled back, his face full of tender concern. "Did I hurt you, love?" His hands moved up to frame her face, his thumbs brushing the soft hair off her flushed cheeks. His body was urging him to take her, but he forced himself to be patient as he waited for her answer.

"No," she whispered, her face flushing more deeply at her unsophisticated reaction. The women he was used to probably considered this casual petting. The trickles of liquid fire that his gentle mouth had sent through her were anything but casual, and she'd been totally unable to control her response. She desperately hoped he wouldn't guess just how little experience she really had. Yet she didn't know how she was going to hide it if his every touch sensitized nerves she hadn't known she had and made them stridently demand more.

She wouldn't meet his eyes, and he felt her embarrassment radiating in palpable waves. He slipped his arms behind her and rolled them to their sides. She buried her face in his shoulder.

"Ariel. Look at me." His hand prodded her chin up firmly. "Didn't Dennis ever make love to you?" He knew DiSanto hadn't introduced her to the ultimate act, but surely . . . ?

"Not much more than this," she whispered miserably. She felt like such a baby, but she might as well tell him the rest of it so he could have a really good laugh. "And I, ah, never had this . . . reaction."

He stared at her, trying to hide his astonishment. Despite those steamy books of hers, she was almost a complete innocent. She didn't even realize the power she had given him over her by what she had just admitted. "You two had a rather unusual relationship, didn't you?" he mused aloud. "You weren't lovers, yet you traveled together, shared this house."

Talking about a woman's lovemaking experience with another man, especially when he'd been in the middle of making love to her himself was out of character, to say the least. But suddenly, he wanted to know all about their relationship. He sensed that there were still a few ghosts for her to lay to rest. And perhaps, without that exorcism, his relationship with her could never be all that he wanted—and he found he was wanting more with each passing hour.

He could feel her still-aroused nipples teasing his chest even through his sweater, and it was too distracting at the moment. Deftly he redressed her and sat her up, his arm firmly around her waist to keep her close to him and the subject.

They had left off most of the lights when they had come in. The warm room, softly lit by firelight, was just right for telling secrets, and Ariel felt an odd compulsion to go on telling hers.

"It *was* a strange relationship." She leaned her head on his shoulder and smiled up sadly at him. "I've had months with little else to think about. I loved him, but that spark, the little tingle all the heroes and heroines in romance novels feel, was missing." She turned her head and stared into the fire. "I finally decided that was just another part of the fantasy. That's when I decided I would marry him."

"Did he feel the same way about you?" He knew DiSanto hadn't; everything he'd read pointed to a man crazily in love.

"You mean, no tingle, no spark?" Her head tilted on his shoulder, and she gave him a quick smile. She shook her head almost sadly and went back to studying the fire. "He had a very strong desire for me, but a lot of patience, too." Her low laugh was self-mocking. "Obviously. Then, too, he was nine years older than I am; perhaps he had some rather fatherly feelings, too."

Ryan grinned wryly at the top of the golden head resting on his shoulder. He was seven years older than she was, but his feelings for her were anything but fatherly.

"He used to build up a lot of frustration," she admitted softly, "and then he would find someone for the evening."

"He told you that?"

"No. But I always knew...somehow. I'm sure the police and Rick Jones did, too, but they were kind enough never to mention it." Ariel began to pleat the tail of her shirt into precise folds. "I used to worry that after we were married, he would be... disappointed with me, that he wouldn't want to give up those other women."

Ryan stilled her nervous hand and held it warmly against the strong heartbeat in his chest. He rested his cheek against her soft hair. "No, Ariel, he wouldn't have been disappointed, just very happy that you were finally his," he reassured her quietly. He was beginning to feel an odd kinship with the dead man who had unknowingly bequeathed him this woman. "But you would have been, eventually, knowing there should be more."

"No. I would have been perfectly content," she began without thinking, "as long as I never met..." She finished in a reluctant whisper, "You." She clucked her tongue and drew away. Throwing him a swift look, she whispered huskily, "Ah, yes. Well, now you know all my secrets."

Weaving his long fingers through her sun-rinsed hair, he brought their mouths together. "You have others, but I'd already guessed this one. We have far more than a mere spark between us." He took her mouth gently, rapidly fanned the spark to a full flame. He wouldn't let things go too far tonight. He had another plan for her seduction at the back of his mind, one that was a little foolish, romantic. But he did want something for himself now, and he wanted to make her a little hungrier.

His arms urged her closer; his impatient tongue opened her willing mouth and was welcomed. Vaguely they were both aware of an odd sound, like the collapse of a heavy body on the floor. There was a faint, sighing moan.

"Ry?"

"Hmm?" He was more interested in undoing the buttons of her shirt again than in conversation.

Suddenly she jerked away, her face white, her eyes on the floor. "I think something is wrong with Murphy!"

Ariel hated fluorescent lights. The fragile glass tubes seemed to be filled with the lifeless light from a cold, dead planet. They didn't glow like an incandescent bulb; they gave off no warmth, no comfort. Instead they seemed to suck the heat and color and life out of everything they shone on. They were, to Ariel, the lights of death.

Once upon a time she had never even noticed them, but now she never walked into a room without being immediately aware of them. Dennis's death and the mandatory visit to the morgue, the grand jury room and hours in an interrogation cubicle under that harsh sterile light had assured it.

She sat huddled motionlessly on the vinyl couch in the vet's cold waiting room. The only sound was the faint hum from a faulty ballast in the fluorescent panel above her head. Ryan had set her there with terse instructions to stay put. Coward that she was, she was obeying. She'd watched him disappear behind the closed door with Murphy. She had had to watch Dennis die; she couldn't watch his dog die, too.

She stirred, drawing in on herself more, shiveringly cold. The chilly plastic slipcovers, protection against the vet's nervous patients, cracked stiffly. Ariel wrapped Ryan's bomber jacket more closely around her body, like a small girl with her security blanket. She nuzzled her cheek against the worn fur collar, inhaling the comforting smell—aftershave, old musky sweat, Ryan. Her fingers twisted in the butter-soft leather, rubbing it between them.

Ariel had panicked when she had seen Murphy lying at their feet in convulsions. Ryan's calm, swift efficiency had infused itself into her. While he had wrapped the dog in a blanket and laid her in the back of his truck, Ariel had called the vet. He had even thought to load the puppies, too, box and all. During the endless ride to the vet's office she had cradled Murphy's wretching, convulsing body with her own.

The white door opened and both Ryan and Dr. Hughes, the lanky, sandy-haired vet, emerged. Ariel's eyes strained past them. Murphy was lying on the stainless-steel table, a silvery space blanket covering all but her brown head. A green plastic tube dangled from her slack mouth into a glass jar. A slow bellows on the jar pumped soundlessly. Another tube, darkly red, led out from under the silver blanket and up to an IV stand.

Not daring to hope yet, Ariel finally fixed her gaze on the two weary men, their grim faces seemingly drained of blood by the humming lights. Ryan's expression was a black study: eyebrows fiercely lowered in a slashing line, dark eyes narrowed dangerously, mouth turned down. Seeing Ariel's impossibly pale face grow even more wan every time her eyes snuck back to the motionless dog, he reached behind him and pulled the door shut.

Shoving his hands into his pockets, the young vet came over to her. "I think she's going to be all right. You go on home now; I'm going to stay with her just a little longer."

Ariel swallowed hard, forcing down the tears burning at the back of her throat. They settled in her chest, almost robbing her voice of any sound. "I know I should have called you to check her after the puppies were born. This is all my fault."

Dr. Hughes shook his head and started to speak. A sharp glance from Ryan silenced him. Ryan moved to the couch. Gently freeing her hand from its death grip on his jacket, he let her fingers wrap bruisingly around his. His other arm went around her thin, hunched shoulders. "It wasn't your fault. The vet couldn't have predicted this," he said with grim conviction.

Ariel looked to the vet for confirmation, and he nodded, clearing his throat. "What do you want to do about the puppies?" he asked gruffly.

Her eyes widened in horrified comprehension. Ryan felt the convulsive shiver jerk through her and pulled her more strongly to him. "Murphy can't feed them, of course," she whispered hollowly. "Could we..." Her voice trailed off as the vet's bassethound eyes grew even sadder.

Sniffling loudly, Ariel scrubbed her free hand fiercely over her eyes. Her voice was congested by unshed tears. "I guess it's silly to feel sorry over a bunch of mutt puppies you really didn't want in the first place." She took a deep, shuddering breath that ended in a sob, knowing what she had to say.

Ryan's low, calm voice saved her again. "What about your dog?" He addressed his question to the slumped vet who was raking his hand through his thin hair.

His hand stopped. "If she'll accept them, it would work out great." He looked to Ariel to explain. "My old Lab had pups last night; only two of them made it. She still has plenty of milk. If we can get her to take Murph's pups, they'll make it fine." His sudden grin was boyish and carefree. "Let's go see."

The golden Labrador retriever lay in a back room with her two glutted black puppies. She raised her head, gave her master and the two strangers with the big cardboard box a bored glance, and went back to sleep. Carefully the vet lifted out the pups one by one and laid them with their noses on his dog's swollen teats. Their tiny toothless mouths clamped on and began suckling greedily. They slurped and grunted like satisfied piglets. The old dog's head snapped up, and the three humans held their breath. She frowned at the tiny strangers pulling so familiarly at her, a hint of consternation in her cocked ears. After sniffing at their little bodies, she looked at Dr. Hughes with an obvious question in her eyes.

"It's okay, old girl," he murmured affectionately, patting her smooth head. He continued his reassuring motions until the dog laid her head back down with a resigned sigh, apparently accepting her role of wet nurse. The humans slipped out quietly, and Ryan took Ariel home.

She fell asleep on his shoulder during the short ride. When they arrived, he shook her awake gently. "Ariel, wake up. We're home." He eased her out of the truck and inside supporting most of her weight as she tried to go back to sleep under his arm.

"In you go. Watch the step, Ariel, dammit!" he scolded, laughing softly. Trying to maneuver her boneless body was like trying to manhandle a drunk. He wanted to carry her, but he didn't think his leg, after the fight tonight, would support both of them.

Ariel blinked open sleepy eyes to find herself half standing, half collapsed on Ryan, on the second step of her stairs. Grabbing the banister, she pulled herself a little farther upright.

"Can you make it upstairs by yourself, Ariel?" His concerned gaze flickered over her eyes which were smudged with exhaustion, and down the drooping line of her body. He sincerely hoped she could get herself to bed on her own. If he had to go up those stairs and help her, he wouldn't be crossing the hall to his own bed tonight.

"I can," she assured him in a drowsy whisper. She brushed a kiss over his unsmiling mouth. "Thank you, Ryan. Murphy and I would never had made it without you." He captured her soft mouth in a brief, intimate kiss, that ended before he awakened her too much. Firm hands on her waist turned her around and started her up the stairs with a little push. He stood below, watching until her shuffling feet disappeared around the bend in the staircase.

Rapidly he crossed the room, grabbed the flashlight on the shelf beside her door and went outside. There was one more thing he had to do before he, too, could go to bed.

He followed the white beam of light, searching slowly across the darkened ground. Murphy had been fine when they had let her out after coming home from the bar. Less than fifteen minutes later she had been dying. His sharp eyes and the flashlight found what he was looking for by Ariel's Blazer. He bent and picked up the half-gnawed chunk of raw, red meat.

Before storing it in his refrigerator he rechecked the dead bolts on both outside doors and climbed Ariel's stairs noiselessly. She had managed to get her shoes off, but nothing else, before she had crawled under the quilt. He pulled it back long enough to loosen her jeans and reach under her shirt to unhook her bra. She smiled in her sleep, mumbling something incomprehensible and nuzzled into the pillow. He grinned down on her ruefully, tucked the quilt around her and left for his own lonely bed.

Ariel rolled over, glanced at the clock radio on her dresser and groaned. They had already sung the last hymn, Reverend Todd would have given the benediction, and the congregation would be filing out of the beautiful little church in town. She shambled into the bathroom. Her brain still drugged from her exhausted sleep, she didn't immediately remember the reason for Murphy's absence from the foot of her bed. Over the past week she had gotten used to finding the dog gone in the morning. Although Murphy went to bed with her, at some point she always awoke and finished the night with Ryan.

Ariel yawned hugely and turned on the shower. Frowning down at her clothes, she stepped out of them. Why was she still wearing... Then she remembered Murphy's agony of the night before, and she was suddenly wide awake. She caught her hair with a rubber band, then stood under the shower only long enough to wash down her body, hardly rinsing off before she was reaching for a towel.

Tearing a comb through her hair, she raced down the stairs. She tossed the comb on the kitchen counter, then grabbed the phone.

"I've already called him. She made it through the night just fine."

Ariel sagged against the wall for a moment before straightening to face Ryan. With her total concentration and headlong rush down the steps she hadn't even noticed him standing by the wood stove, absorbing the warmth of the fire he had built.

He left the stove and stopped a few feet away from her across the counter. Tucking his lean fingers in the front pockets of his tan slacks, he shoved the sides of his black windbreaker back with his elbows. Her eyes followed the action that tightened the navy sweater over his chest and pulled his slacks taut across his hips and flat belly.

"Why don't you eat some breakfast and I'll take you in to see her?"

Ariel finally noticed the cup of steaming coffee, already creamed and sugared the way she liked it, and the plate of toasted muffins on the counter in front of her. Absently she spread jelly on a muffin and bit into it. "Thank you for this, Ry, and for last night," she said quietly. "I wouldn't have Murphy anymore if you hadn't been here."

One hand came out of his pocket to wave away her gratitude. "I'm just glad I was here to help you."

This time. The words, unspoken, echoed through the room as if they had been shouted. Last night had brought back the memories of Dennis's death too vividly; the lights, the panic, the hideous sense of helplessness had all been there. But last night Ryan had been there, lending his silent, calm strength. She had wanted only one thing more, but she had fallen asleep before she could ask him. She had wanted him to hold her while she slept, just for a little while. She had tried to tell him when he'd come back up to check on her, but he hadn't understood.

As she was putting jelly on another muffin her hand suddenly froze. "I forgot to ask the vet what made her so ill!"

"She was poisoned." Ryan heard her gasp. His hands knotted in his pockets, and he stared at the floor beneath his spread feet. If she saw his face, she might guess the truth. "Three other dogs along this road were poisoned, too. They weren't found until this morning."

"They..." She had to swallow to control the tremor in her voice. "They didn't make it?" She saw the shake of his downcast head. "How were they poisoned?" Even she hardly heard her croaky whisper, yet somehow Ryan did and answered in a neutral voice.

"Chunks of raw meat. Chief Dye says it was just a random incident; it happens every once in a while." He himself thought differently, but the lab in Missoula wouldn't open until eight-thirty tomorrow morning.

Ariel's stomach clenched, and she felt the clammy sweat of nausea. Mechanically she put away the jelly and carried her dishes and the remaining toast to the sink. She couldn't let herself dwell on this; it would be too easy to slip back into self-destructive memories. Her thin voice barely sounded over the sound of running water and the garbage disposal. "Whoever did it didn't know about Murphy's sweet tooth. S-she doesn't care much for meat. If they'd used a bag of chocolate-chip cookies they'd have had better luck."

Her macabre attempt at a joke failed wretchedly. Ryan heard her liquid sob and was pulling her into his arms before she could take another breath.

"Oh, Ry, who would do such a rotten thing?" Her despairing moan was muffled in his soft wool sweater. He shut his eyes tiredly and rested his chin on the top of her head.

"I don't know, Ariel; I just don't know." He heard the note of frustration in his voice. The only thing he did know was that the poisonings hadn't been just another "random incident."

They visited the vet's office and found that the puppies and their new family had adjusted well to each other. Murphy was still unconscious, but out of danger. Dr. Hughes wanted to keep her a few more days before he let her go. Ariel went home feeling oddly bereft.

As she and Ryan drove back to the schoolhouse, Sam Bass was just turning away from the door. Ariel climbed down out of Ryan's truck and hurried over. Ryan followed more slowly, but when he stopped next to Ariel, he draped an arm around her shoulders. She tried to ease away nonchalantly. The arm tightened.

Sam's kind brown eyes were filled with concern. "I just heard about Murphy. Is she okay?" he asked hesitantly. There was nothing hesitant in his eyes as they shifted from Ariel's upraised face to Ryan's arm.

"She's going to be all right," Ariel replied softly. "Thank you for coming by to ask about her." Whatever Ryan Jones's game was, she wasn't going to play. She would ignore both him and the hot spark skipping down her spine.

Sam's warm eyes grew perceptibly colder. "Perhaps you'd rather I didn't come for dinner tonight, what with the upset . . . and all." He stared pointedly at Ryan's hand as it closed over her shoulder.

Ariel hoped that her shock didn't show on her face. Unobtrusively she tried to shrug off Ryan's hand while scrambling for an answer that wouldn't let Sam know she had completely forgotten the invitation she had extended Wednesday night. She smiled warmly at him. "I want you to come tonight. Is six-thirty still okay?" Two long fingers began rubbing lazy circles through the red and blue flannel of her shirt. Ariel discovered that the back of her right shoulder possessed a previously unknown, tremendous erogenous potential.

Sam returned her smile. "Six-thirty it is." He glanced back to Ryan, his friendly face hardening again.

Ryan shifted his stance slightly. His feet moved a little wider apart, his thigh brushing Ariel's lightly, his body straighter, his head thrown back a fraction more. The stance, the faintly wolfish smile, the cold eyes staring directly into Sam Bass's, delivered a primitive male message far clearer than the arm around Ariel's shoulders.

She could see that Sam understood the agressive challenge only too well. Tonight she was going to gently tell him that there wasn't much point in seeing each other anymore. She'd planned to tell him a week ago, but had delayed, unconsciously using him as a buffer against the bewildering attraction she had felt for Ryan Jones from the very first.

Sam would believe her, but for all the wrong reasons now. He would never believe that it was because Ryan Jones or not, she could never offer anything more than the easy friendship they'd enjoyed all summer. Sam would think it was because of this dark stranger who had moved into her house only eight days ago and already staked his claim.

Her body tensed with the struggle to control her rising temper and her reaction to that secretly caressing hand. Ryan's eyes never wavered from the bigger man, but his fingers tightened warningly on her shoulder. He needn't have worried; she wouldn't give him the satisfaction of a scene.

"Good," she said firmly. "I'll see you at six-thirty."

Sam turned away with a nod and climbed into his battered pickup. Ariel wrenched her shoulders strongly, throwing off Ryan's arm. After unlocking her front door, she stalked into her kitchen. Ryan, she knew, was right behind her.

He propped himself against the kitchen wall, following her quick, stiff movements with hooded eyes. "What are you going to fix him for dinner? Soup and bread?" His voice was mildly bored. "He'd probably like some of that apple juice."

Ignoring him, she took a package of T-bones out of the freezer and jerked open the door of the microwave.

"I'm glad you're not planning to fix our turkey," he said conversationally. "It would never defrost and cook in time."

She slammed the door shut and jabbed viciously at the buttons. She had hated the hurt, defeated look in gentle Sam's eyes, something she had been trying so hard to avoid. Regardless of her feelings for Ryan, Sam Bass deserved better than that.

She turned on Ryan. "You're very good, aren't you? It's quite a trick, intimidating a man who's so much bigger than you." She advanced on him, her blue eyes like glittering ice chips, her voice as frigid as an arctic wind. "Was it an inborn talent, or did you work long and hard to cultivate it?"

Ryan moved away from the wall, seemingly relaxed. He had curled his hands into fists in his jacket pockets to keep them from curling around her stiff, fragile neck. The hunger to sample again her sweet, mysterious taste turned his thin smile cruel. "And just what else," he sneered suggestively, "will you be sharing with the good doctor tonight, Ariel, besides a meal?" He knew she was making him lose control, and he hated it, yet was helpless to stop himself.

"That's none of your damn affair!" she exploded. She turned her back to him, gripping the counteredge until her fingers were numb. The emotional elevator she'd been riding for the past two days had left her ragged, and she knew she was dangerously close to falling down the empty shaft. "I am sick to death," she gritted between clenched teeth, "of people poking their noses into my business."

Ryan paled, remembering the nastily insinuative news clippings in the file in his kitchen drawer. "You're absolutely correct," he agreed expressionlessly. "I have no right to ask." He turned away and took a few aimless steps into her living room. Frustration tightened his lips into a thin, bloodless line. "It's just hard to be right across the hall, knowing he's over here with you, wondering what he's doing with you." Ryan rammed his hands deeper into his pockets, feeling completely frustrated and murderously jealous. They were new emotions to him; and he found he despised them.

It was only then that she understood how truly furious he was. The taut empty face, the even, emotionless voice, were the usual careful sham. His naked eyes betrayed the truth: cold rage warred with hot passion in them, and something else—entreaty? A vein jumped in his temple, near the tumbled lock of hair that her fingers habitually itched to brush back. Despite the explosiveness of the situation an exultant thrill surged through her.

"There's nothing between us, Ryan."

"He wants it, Ariel." Bitter chocolate eyes pinned her remorselessly.

She met his gaze unflinchingly. "But *I* don't." She turned on her heel, then looked back over her shoulder at him. "And as far as rights are concerned, counselor," she advised shortly, "perhaps you ought to think about establishing a few."

There was a low hiss of indrawn breath behind her, and suddenly she was spun around. Fingers locked bruisingly on her shoulders. "I believe I will. Right now."

His hard, punishing mouth swooped down. Her avid lips melted under his, enticing him deeper. His mouth softened over hers after the first stinging nip of his sharp teeth. He saw her blue eyes beginning to heat before they slid slowly shut. Her hands pressed against his back to bring him closer. He resisted, not allowing full contact.

"Ryan, please." Was that breathless voice really hers? Ariel couldn't be sure. The room was suddenly much too warm, muddling her brain as his mouth wandered along her throat, blazing a trail of soft kisses.

"Ryan, please, what?" he mocked gently, his warm breath whispering across her moist skin. "Please kiss me?" His lips moved back over hers, which were parted and swollen from his rough kiss, her breath hurrying raggedly between them. The tip of his tongue lightly teased hers.

"Please, Ryan, touch me?" His hands roamed down her back and over her hips, loitering to span her waist before one glided up her ribs. His fingertips traced and counted the fragile bones under the soft flannel. His hand came to rest on her breast, cupping its weight, molding its softness to his palm. "Please love me, Ryan?"

"Is that what you want, Ariel?"

His husky voice whispering in her ear, his gently demanding touches on her body, his mouth, all were cajoling and leading her further into passion. They promised so much more gratification if she would only surrender to him.

"No, no," she lied, moaning against the mouth that was now biting softly at hers. "I don't want it." She forced her hands to drop from his back. Empty, desperate to touch him again, they balled into fists and hit weakly at his shoulders.

"Yes, Ariel, yes," he countered in a lulling whisper. "You do." His palm moved up, rotating hypnotically over her hardened aching nipple that begged for release from his delicious torture.

"No, I can't." The moan became a mournful sob. "Not now." Desperately she pushed herself away from him, staggering a little. He steadied her with a hand on her elbow, then let go. Gasping air into her starved lungs, she stared at him, striving to regain her tattered composure.

He caught the wild excitement in her eyes before it began to fade. As he lit a cigarette with hands that shook only slightly, his eyes narrowed and he watched her over the yellow flame and curling smoke.

"I've, ah, got to start dinner now." Ariel willed her jellied legs to walk into the kitchen, silently cursing the faint undertone of hysteria in her voice.

Ryan nodded once, the habitual sardonic smile back in place, and strolled toward her door. "Enjoy your meal," he said blandly. His goal was more than accomplished. She wouldn't be thinking about the fish biologist tonight.

The poison hadn't been necessary after all; the dog didn't seem to be around anymore. The expense for the meat had been negligible, however, against the anticipated reward. Besides, the local police chief and his force of three would be too busy investigating the rash of poisonings by the dog hater to worry overmuch about any accidents befalling the owner of the Burnt Fork School until it was too late.

Who was the guy living with her? Bodyguard? Lover? Obviously not just a temporary tenant, not from that kiss. He wouldn't have minded being her lover himself, but smart women and business didn't mix. Dennis had shown remarkably poor business sense, becoming infatuated with a smart woman. They asked questions, and sooner or later they got the wrong answer. In his business, he couldn't afford risks like that.

He'd gotten the man's name from someone in the crowd at the fair, and it nudged at the back of his mind. He frowned puzzledly for a moment, and a stewardess stared in his direction. He dismissed the subject. Whoever Ryan Jones was, he shouldn't be any problem.

He waved off the hovering stewardess and leaned his head tiredly on the high back of the airline seat. It was going to be nice to have his weekends free again. And he could sell that damned cabin. He'd always hated roughing it.

Chapter 8

She was up earlier than usual this morning. When the back door had creaked open, Ryan had wakened instantly. He was at his window in time to watch Ariel running toward the river. It hadn't seemed right to see her without a big brown dog at her heels.

Nearly an hour later he was at the same window again, dressed now, with his second cup of coffee, waiting for her to return. He saw the flash of gold and pink at the far end of the orchard. Her hair was loose, floating, catching the first rays of the sun rising over the valley. As a concession to the cooler weather a pair of hot-pink sweatpants hid her long, driving legs. She flitted through the long shadows and bare twisted trees in the old orchard like an exotic gazelle. Effortlessly she cleared the only portion of the split-rail fence still standing, guarding the ancient apple trees.

Ryan made it down his staircase and across the hall just as she came in the back door, wiping the light sweat off her forehead with the sleeve of her white sweatshirt. He followed her into the kitchen and leaned over the counter, sipping his coffee and watching her hop around on one leg like a wounded flamingo as she tried to get the sweatpants off over her running shoes.

"Here." He pulled out a chair and pushed her into it. "Sit down before you fall on your butt." She collapsed on the chair, still huffing from her run. Obligingly she lifted herself off the seat as he squatted down and grabbed the soft pants. He pulled them impersonally down her legs and over her shoes, letting his palm slide back up over the smooth, warmed muscle of her calf.

"You're up early. Are you doing something special today?" Ryan stood back up and tossed the pants carelessly over a chair.

"I have to play librarian at the school for the next three days." Her voice was still slightly breathless. From the run, he thought. From his hand, she knew. She scooted back on the chair seat, tugging down the legs of the old purple running shorts she'd worn under her sweats. She watched him set down his mug of coffee and dig a brownie out of the pan on top of the stove.

"You make these for the fish biologist?" he asked around a mouthful of rich chocolate and pecans. He chewed thoughtfully and swallowed, a look of frank surprise on his face.

Ariel wrinkled her nose in complaint. "He was too full to eat very many, and now I'm stuck with them. Brownies are my one weakness," she moaned. "I'll probably eat every one." She tossed him an upward glance as he snitched another from the pan. "You can have them, if you want," she said offhandedly.

His eyes danced with secret mischief. "Only one weakness, Miss Spence?"

Ariel laughed, her head down.

"Brownies are one of my weaknesses, too." He licked crumbs delicately from his fingers. "And these are the best I've ever eaten." He slanted her a look. "I thought you could only cook soup and bread?"

She gave him a pained look. "I spent an entire summer when I was in high school learning how to make brownies. Lord only knows how many pans I threw out before I finally succeeded."

He held a brownie in front of her mouth. "You're only going to be working through Wednesday?" he asked casually.

"Mmm-hmm." She opened her mouth and he stuffed in a huge bite.

"So you won't have to get up early on Thursday?" he persisted.

Ariel was sneaking a sip from his mug, grimacing at the sugarless coffee scalding her tongue, and missed the speculative look that went with his question. "Not if I don't want to."

"I'll fix dinner Wednesday night," he mentioned carelessly. And I'll guarantee you won't want to get up early Thursday, Ariel Spence, he thought grinning to himself.

"That would be very nice." Her surprised, pleased smile warmed him more than the sunniest California day. Ariel glanced at the clock and leaped up. "I better get moving. I want to stop and check on Murph before school starts."

Thirty minutes later she stuck her arm out the window of her Blazer and waved goodbye. He was in his truck close behind her. She turned left onto the highway, toward town. Watching in her rearview mirror, she saw Ryan turn right, toward Missoula.

"That's the most common, over-the-counter rat poison sold in the United States." Ted Dye's voice was infuriatingly calm, almost bored. "Hell, they have it next door for $1.98 a box. I bought some last week...."

Ryan tuned him out. He'd had this conversation before, six days ago, to be exact. He had been totally frustrated then; now he was incensed—and, even more, frightened. He stood at the chief's office window, shoulders hunched, knotted hands cramping in his jacket pockets, staring out. Same cars out on the street, too. Well, he'd done what the technician in the Missoula testing lab had hinted at so pointedly. He had talked to the police. But the police weren't listening. He tuned out the disembodied voice of his brother asking a question from the phone speaker on the desk, too.

Chief Dye watched gilded dust motes drifting lazily in the afternoon sun rays burning through the front window of his office. The role of apologist had been assigned to him. "Look, Jones, these random poisonings happen every once in a while. There is *nothing* indicating that Ariel's dog was the real target and the others were just a smoke screen."

The dark, oddly menacing silhouette at the sunny window finally spoke. "I'm going to tell her. She's got to be aware of the danger so she'll be more careful."

"No!" Even after traveling a thousand miles, Rick Jones's voice was sharply forceful. "What if she gets scared and runs, Ryan? We'll lose her."

"She won't run."

"Can you be sure of that? You've known her little more than a week. I've known her nearly a year, and I can't predict what she'll do."

"I'm sure," Ryan said evenly, turning away from the window to stare at the black speaker on the chief's desk. It was just one more frustration to have to talk to that box instead of his brother, face-to-face.

Rick offered a sop. "You know that newspaper photo you asked about? It was Antonio Garza, the so-called cocaine king of Guadalajara." There was a brief pause. "Why *did* you ask?"

"Ariel saw the picture, but the caption was missing. She remembered seeing him in DiSanto's office one day and wondered why his picture was in the paper. Why was it?"

"He was just arrested by the Mexican authorities for drug smuggling. She pretended not to know him?"

"She wasn't pretending. If she'd known him, if she was guilty as you and your boss Davidson are so sure she is, she'd never have mentioned it at all."

"Maybe she just wanted you to think she didn't know him?" Rick ventured.

"Now why in the hell would she do that, Rick?" Ryan asked with exaggerated patience, trying to hang on to his temper. "She doesn't know who I am, remember?"

Rick's sigh was audible over the phone speaker. "Davidson doesn't want anything to alert her that we know about DiSanto's smuggling. If you tell her about the poisonings you'll have to tell her everything. Give us another week. I have a gut feeling we're getting close to that hidden truth you have me digging for."

"Jesus Christ!" Ryan didn't know if he was blaspheming or praying, probably both. One fist came out of his pocket and slammed down impotently on the glass-topped desk, making everything on the surface, and the chief, jump. "One week, Rick, and that's only if nothing else happens."

Ryan felt a little sicker, knowing only too well how easy it was for a determined man to kill. And whoever this man was, he was not only determined, but clever. Murphy's poisoning had obviously been intended to get her out of the way so the killer could set up some sort of deadly "accident." He'd spent most of Sunday afternoon and evening unobtrusively checking out the Blazer, the

rowdy exhilaration singing through her that came just from seeing him and receiving a measly peck goodbye on the cheek. I will not make a fool of myself over you, Ryan Jones, she vowed, steadfastly ignoring the imp inside her laughing uproariously.

When she got home after school, Ryan was hard at work in her half of the house. Law books, papers and manila file folders were scattered over her round dining table. Ever since he'd arrived he had been working on a very involved case, when he wasn't hiking in the mountains or distracting her. There had been several long discussions with his partner Jack Smith on her phone, and twice he had used her computer to transmit information over the phone line to his L.A. office. She had enjoyed a private laugh when she'd learned his partner's name—Smith and Jones. It sounded as if they used aliases, just like their shifty clients.

"Hi," Ariel said brightly.

"Mmm," he answered absently, not even looking up from the file in his hand. His lips moved silently as he read over the pages, making rapid notes in the margin.

Ariel went over to her desk. There was a package that Ryan had signed for waiting for her. She gave him a peculiar look that he didn't see. The package had been opened, the contents disturbed, as if it had been . . . searched.

She shook her head, dismissing the crazy notion. The package just hadn't survived its rough handling by the postal service; there was no reason for him to be searching her mail. She pulled out photocopies of local newspapers from the time of the Johnson County War. She'd ordered them from the Buffalo, Wyoming, museum over three months ago and given up on ever seeing them. At the moment she couldn't seem to work up much enthusiasm for them.

Ryan snapped the file shut and closed his eyes. He let his head roll back, working the kinks out of his neck.

Ariel sat in her old swivel chair, idly rocking it a little, back and forth. "Is that the case you've been working on all along?"

He didn't open his eyes. "Mmm-hmm."

"From what you've told me this client is actually innocent. Can you get him off?"

He finally opened his eyes and favored her with a perturbed look. Then he grinned wryly at the mischief in her oh-so-innocent, big blue eyes. "After getting so many guilty ones off, it would be a hell of a note if an innocent client went to jail, wouldn't it?'' Ryan sighed, rubbing the back of his neck tiredly. ''His ex-partner really has him framed, though. The whole tax-evasion scheme looks like my client's work, while the partner plays the outraged innocent. Unfortunately for him, however,'' he shrugged modestly, ''I know the setup from the inside out.'' He gave her an ingenuous grin. ''I've had one or two of these cases before.''

''They were all framed, too, no doubt,'' Ariel murmured dryly.

Ryan merely laughed and started to gather up his papers.

''Want to stay for dinner?'' Ariel tried not to sound too hopeful. ''I have curried potato soup and fresh sourdough—''

''I've got other plans tonight.''

''Oh.'' She managed to keep most of the disappointed surprise out of her voice.

The comically startled look on her face almost made him laugh. He knew what she was thinking. What would she say if she knew his ''date'' was with his favorite pay phone at the gas station? Working on the tax-evasion scam had made him think of another angle on the DiSanto case Rick could check out. A whisper of suspicion in the right ear would be enough. More than one criminal had gotten away with murder, only to be tripped up by a dogged IRS agent.

''See you later,'' Ryan waved breezily and was gone.

Ariel wandered aimlessly around the house. Murphy wasn't even around to keep her company with her crazy romping gyrations. The vet had said today when she'd visited that he wanted to keep her a few more days. She really missed that dumb dog. That was undoubtedly why she suddenly felt so lonely and cold.

Building up the smoldering fire in the wood stove took only a little of the lonesome chill out of the air. She went upstairs and changed into a wool sweater, blue wool pants and her floppy fleece slippers, but she still felt chilly.

She spread the papers from the Buffalo museum over the living room carpet, then put on her spectacles and plopped cross-legged on the floor. She read through the papers, taking notes, until a supper break at eight o'clock. Sipping the curried potato soup, she wondered somewhat wistfully what Ryan had had for dinner...and where...and with whom. It wouldn't take an old beach boy like him long to find a warm and willing body or two.

It was after eleven when she heard his power wagon pull up outside. The outer door slammed; then he tapped on her door and stuck his head inside. His black hair was damp, fitting his well-shaped skull as sleekly as a seal's. With a small start, Ariel realized that it was raining; she hadn't even heard the soft pattering of raindrops on the windowpanes.

"Remember—dinner, tomorrow night," Ryan instructed. "Don't bring anything but yourself."

Before she could think of a subtle way to find out what he'd been doing half the night, the door was shutting on his cheerful, slightly off-key whistling of an old Beach Boys tune. Grumpily she gathered up the papers she'd been squinting at for hours and put her notes in order.

Well! she humphed to herself. He might have stayed to talk a bit. No "Hi, Ariel, guess where I was?" Not even a "What are you working on?" No . . . nothing!

She caught herself remembering those treacherous, calculating, consummate good-night kisses. She would do better to remember, she reminded herself severely, that regardless of her feelings for him, he no doubt thought he'd acquired her with the month's rent he'd paid—stove, refrigerator, bed warmer.

The next morning the weather was still damp and dreary. Yet the dripping clouds, layered like sodden, dirty fleece over the valley all day, couldn't drown her inexplicable happiness and the persistent, peculiar sense that some special surprise was about to delight her. Giggling at her foolishness, Ariel shooed the last of her faithful, male high school helpers out the library door and locked up.

She swung by Dr. Hughes's veterinary clinic. Murphy was much livelier, the dull, death-shadowed look out of her eyes. Assured that she would be able to take her dog home the next day, she left the vet's office. She had one more stop to make before going home.

She had expected to find Bessie in the large lounge of the rest home, her wheelchair pulled close to the fire in the stone fireplace. Instead she found her already tucked in bed, her body only a faint mound under the wedding-ring quilt she'd brought from her home.

"Bessie? Are you all right?" Alarmed, Ariel chafed a hand that seemed to be nothing more than one layer of thin, age-spotted skin stretched over glass bones.

"I'm fine, girl." The fragile fingers gripped Ariel's with surprising strength. "This blasted gloomy weather just gave me a chill, and I got into bed to warm up." Her faded brown eyes were shadowed, as Murphy's had been. "You get your soap made yet?"

Ariel shook her head. "Mr. Hankins, the butcher, say's he'll have the fat I'll need to melt down Friday."

The chitchat dispensed with, Bessie got down to what she really wanted to know. "How's that handsome devil, Ryan Jones? You two cooked your turkey yet?"

Ariel flashed her a bright smile. "As handsome and devilish as ever, Bessie. We haven't cooked the turkey yet; maybe we'll have to find a special occasion." No, the turkey wasn't cooked yet, but she had the sinking feeling her goose was. Suddenly restless, Ariel got up to wander around Bessie's tiny bedroom.

Her back was to Bessie, but the old woman saw the unguarded expression on Ariel's face in the mirror over the dressing table. It showed the mixed longing and fear she felt about making a one-sided commitment to a man she was so unsure of. Bessie ached for her, yet felt a sentimental envy. She remembered the sweet joy and desperate agonizing that came with gambling your heart on a risky love.

"You know, you remind me of myself in many ways, Ariel. Be careful that you don't let your independence become a habit you can't break," she warned softly. "Be willing to take a chance, my dear. You can get to like living alone too much. After a while, you become too selfish to share your life with anyone else."

Ariel toyed with the delicate petals of a yellow spider mum. When she turned back, Bessie's eyes were closed. She seemed to have drifted into a nap. Ariel patted the covers around her friend and tiptoed from the room.

Ryan grinned happily to himself, looking over his equipment. It had been years since he'd planned a seduction. It had become disgustingly easy over the past few years to get a woman into bed. But then, maybe he'd had the wrong kind of women . . . and the wrong word. Seduction implied that the woman was tricked or otherwise led astray. He didn't want Ariel that way. Although he expected to lead the way, he wanted her following willingly, joyfully, cooperating fully in what they would share.

The sound of the outside door closing snapped him out of his anticipation of the evening ahead. He met Ariel as she was hanging her wet trench coat on a hook in the hall.

"Hi. I'm sorry if I'm a little late." Her smile was a ray of pure sunlight brightening the rain-gloomed hallway. Shaking the raindrops from her hair, she started to go in her door. "I'll just go change and be right over."

"No," he said quickly, staying her with a hand on her arm. The plum dress under his fingertips seemed to have been spun from the fur of the softest kittens. His gaze swept the sweater dress with its row of tiny pearl buttons running from the collar diagonally down across her breast. "You look fine; I don't want you to change." His hand rested against the middle of her back, lightly urging her through his door.

He guided her to the leather sofa by the old potbelly stove. "Dinner will be ready in a few minutes."

"Can't I help?"

"Not tonight. I'll do it all."

Ariel sank back against the sofa's fat arm and pried off her gray pumps, wiggling her cramped, chilled toes appreciatively. Tucking her feet under her, she smoothed her dress over her knees and rested her head in the corner of the sofa. She soaked up the dry warmth of the potbelly stove that had heated two and a half generations of little bodies. Heated a little too much. Absently Ariel loosened the first four buttons of her dress.

She could hear Ryan's quiet movements in the kitchen and the occasional hiss of rain falling down the stovepipe to boil on the crackling apple wood. The sweet scent of the burning wood and the rain and the smell of hot cast iron masked the odor of whatever he was fixing for dinner. She watched fat raindrops leave wet trails along the smooth, dark glass of the living room window.

Ryan came silently across the oak floor and handed her a glass of wine. Ariel's mouth crooked wryly when she saw the glass holding the clear, pale gold liquid. He'd filched two dime-store wineglasses from her kitchen cupboard. It wasn't class, but it was definitely a step above the gas-station-giveaway plastic tumblers stocking his own cupboard. Without tasting the wine, she looked at him, bending down to adjust the damper on the stove. She realized with surprise that this was the first time she'd seen him in anything but the most casual clothes. Now that he'd gained some weight the charcoal wool slacks were perfectly tailored to his slim hips and strong thighs. His black shirt had a dull sheen, like silk, and was formfitting, pulling tight over his broad shoulders as he stood up. His days outdoors had darkened the sickly pallor of his face to a healthy bronze. He looked more rakish and impossibly handsome than ever.

Ryan sat in the leather armchair across from her and picked up his wine.

"Are you planning on seducing me tonight, Ryan Jones?" she inquired watching the tiny bubbles fizzing slowly to the top of the glass in her hand.

"The thought had crossed my mind."

"It's also crossed mine a time or two," she admitted softly with a small smile. Raising her wineglass and smoky, fathomless blue eyes, she toasted him soberly. "Here's to the success of your plan."

He touched his glass to hers with equal solemnity, his mouth twitching. Damn you, Ariel Spence, he demanded with silent laughter, are you going to let me do this right or not?

Ariel met his eyes over the rim of her glass. She drank the contents in one long swallow. Perhaps the wine would drown the butterflies in her stomach.

Ryan took the empty glass from her unresisting hand and pulled her to her feet. Wrapping an easy arm around her waist, he walked her to the table. "Dinner is served," he announced with a charmingly crooked smile. "Then we'll see if my plan's going to work."

The table wasn't set with fine crystal and china, or spotless linen and sterling. The ordinary white wine was poured into her cheap wineglasses; the plates were chipped blue spatterware; the utensils were mismatched and worn stainless; and the placemats were faded brown calico with frayed ruffles. No tall, elegant tapers lighted the polished old table, just the stubby candle she'd stocked in a kitchen drawer for the occasional power outage.

Ariel enjoyed every mouthful of crisp salad with tangy homemade dressing and trout stuffed with wild rice. He had really outdone himself on the meal, and maybe the setting wasn't the most glamorous and expensive, but it couldn't have been any more romantic or perfect. Her nervousness vanished along with the food on her plate. For this night, at least, she was giving herself over into his care, implicitly trusting him with her body and her heart.

Ryan drained the last few inches of wine into their glasses, then led Ariel back into his living room. He settled easily on the couch beside her, his arm around her. He played with her hair, winding silky wisps around his fingers and freeing them. He raked his hand slowly through her heavy hair, letting it slide between his fingers as if trying to free the golden sunlight trapped in its depths. "You have the softest, silkiest hair," he murmured, tilting his head to watch his hand play. "It's just like a baby's."

Her mouth curved in a teasing smile. "Maybe that's to make up for being totally bald as a baby."

"Shh, don't make jokes. You'll ruin my plan." His grin was slow and sexy, his eyes half closed as they focused on her mouth. His arm tightened, and he leaned over, kissing her wide eyes shut before brushing her lips with his. His mouth closed over hers, his flicking tongue demanding an entrance. Her lips parted, and he rapidly deepened the kiss. His hand slid around her throat, the thumb measuring her pulse. It had jumped when his mouth first touched hers, then settled into an accelerated, slightly ragged beat, like his own.

Ariel felt as if she was spinning, slower and slower, sinking down smoothly at last to rest. Somewhere in the endless spiral she had lost her wineglass. Her arms opened and closed around a hard, male body, her palms sliding up over silk warmed by the heat of the long, tight muscles shifting underneath. She lifted heavy eyelids and stared into the depthless, dark eyes above, softer and warmer than she'd ever seen them.

She was lying back on the wide leather sofa, Ryan's body a satisfying weight on hers. He raised himself on his elbows, watching his thumbs brushing her hair back from her cheeks and temples, watching the sharp, aristocratic angles of her face softening into the sultriness he'd glimpsed the first day.

"You are so lovely, Ariel Spence." His smile was a little blurred as he bent to string a long necklace of kisses around her throat, following his hand as it undid the rest of the pearl buttons on her dress.

"I'm not," she murmured in a little sigh. "But it pleases me that you think so."

His head snapped up, and his suddenly fierce eyes burned into hers. "You are. And before the night is over you'll believe it." He took her mouth a little roughly, as if impatient to prove to her the truth of his statement.

She breathed in sharply as his right hand moved down to her straining breast. She released her breath in a long sigh of pleasure as his thumb and finger began to shape her flesh gently. "I don't know all that much about this, Ryan," she whispered.

His mouth began nibbling its way down her arched throat, and she bit her lip. "In fact, I may have been the only twenty-seven-year-old virgin left in San—"

"I know," he muttered against the heavy pulse in the hollow of her throat. His tongue tickled back up her neck. "In just a few minutes it will be my very great pleasure," he whispered gravely in her ear, the tip of his tongue circling the delicate rim, "to correct that serious flaw in your education."

He pulled back to see her face, full of shyly hesitant excitement. Desire burned hotly in his bright eyes, yet sympathetic understanding and an oddly tender humor were in his smile.

He spread the edges of the soft, clinging dress wide. Moving down her body, his lips and teeth and tongue worried a hardening, dusky-rose nipple through misty lace.

Each tug of his mouth was a hot wire uncoiling deep in her belly. Her hands skimmed over his shoulders, down his chest and even lower, impatient with buttons and zippers that kept her from feeling skin gliding on skin, smooth muscle working under her questing hands, a hard fullness to fill that aching emptiness inside her.

She found herself at the foot of Ryan's bed with no clear memory of how she'd gotten there. The small lamp on the dresser filled the room with soft shadows and softer light. "The light," she mumbled. She felt the resurrection of the butterflies in her stomach.

"No hiding in the dark," he admonished softly, holding her anxious eyes, his strong hands gentle on her tense shoulders. "From the first, Ariel, I want no secrets, no shame between us. I want to see you and you to see me, to see us together and know how right it is."

Wordlessly he undressed her, her clothes falling away under his hands. He stood relaxed before her, his arms and legs spread slightly, silently indicating that she should return the favor. His shirt and belt joined her clothing, but he had to finish his own disrobing when her faltering fingers could go no further.

He tipped up her chin until she opened her miserably embarrassed eyes. He kissed her again, slow, drugging kisses, bringing their bodies together gradually, letting her get used to the feel of naked, male flesh on hers. She shivered once as he brought them into full contact, and she felt his body's heavy desire for hers.

When he ended the kiss he just held her tightly to him until he could feel her begin to relax, her softness filling his hard empty hollows. Turning, he drew back the spread and sheet on the double bed. He sat her on the edge of the bed, then sat beside her, carefully pressing her down until she lay on the virginal white sheet. Her hands were clasped primly over her chest as her trusting eyes locked on his.

Linking his hands with hers, he stretched her arms above her head. He let his frank gaze wander over her slim body, over its gentle curves and high, firm breasts. "You are beautiful, Ariel," he whispered. At the melting heat in his chocolate eyes, she began to believe it.

Raising her right hand, he kissed the palm; then, starting at her wrist, his tongue traced the blue veins under her creamy skin. Past her elbow, over the sensitive flesh of her inner arm, his mouth whispered across her shoulder and down her chest to the pale softness of her breast. He spiraled closer and closer to the swelling, dusky aureole and nipple. His tongue flickered and tasted delicately until she was whimpering with need. Finally his hot mouth fastened over the hard nub, his teeth scraping with a tiny pleasure-pain before he began to suckle and soothe. She cried out, desire pooling between her thighs. Her hands dragged at him desperately, urging him up, closer.

"Please," she begged. "Please now, Ry."

"No." He captured her grasping hands, imprisoning them on the sheet by her restless thighs. "Not yet." He watched her flushed, writhing body, held her pleading, passion-heavy eyes with his. "There's more."

"I don't think I can take any more." Her throat was already so tight with wanting that she could hardly speak.

"Yes, you can." His beautiful, chiseled mouth was almost stern. "I'm going to give you much more."

"No. No," she moaned, shaking her head slowly in sweet agony. "I'll go crazy."

"I know," he agreed with a slow, satisfied smile.

Still shackling her straining wrists, he moved to her ankles and began the sensual assault once more. He lavished attention behind her knee, to the top of her thigh. He went back to her other ankle. Lingeringly he finished the wet mapping of her body, testing the outer limits of his control.

Shivers raced through her. To be so totally in his thrall should have terrified her, she understood dimly, but it didn't. She felt only an incredible excitement and the expectancy that the impossible was going to get even better.

When Ryan reached the top of her thigh he paused, looking up at her. Her eyes were squeezed shut, as if in pain, and her small perfect breasts heaved, her fingers twisting into the bottom sheet. Tears of frustration were seeping from under her dark lashes. "Ry, *please!*"

Her hoarse cry exulted him. She was more responsive than he had dared dream and completely in his power, his power to please and satisfy her totally.

Her eyes slit open, glittering down at him. "Ryan Jones," she gasped raggedly, "you're driving me out of my mind."

His fingers slid into her, and she arched violently, moaning. She was so tight and warm and so ready for him.

Her hand wrenched free, and she dragged him up her body with a strength that astonished him. "Now!" she demanded fiercely.

"Now," he agreed hoarsely. Before I go out of my mind, he thought in abandon. He surged strongly into her, and then was still.

She hardly felt the small, stretching pain as her body adjusted and accepted the newness of his.

Stretching out flat over her, he imprinted the soft surface of her body with the hard, male feel of his. His hair-roughened skin slowly rubbed against her smoothness. After tonight her body would never forget his; never would she be able to let another man touch her without remembering Ryan and what he was doing to her. He knew his action was unforgivably chauvinistic, but he felt the overwhelming, primitive need to make her his in the most basic, undeniable way possible.

He moved inside her, steadily building the rhythm. "Tell me you want me," he rasped. Her physical surrender wasn't enough. He wanted all of her.

"I want you, Ryan." He could barely hear her choked whisper. "Oh, God, I want you." She flexed against him. She'd learned the rhythm, and suddenly he knew he had surrendered himself, as well. His body would never forget hers, either, never be satisfied with any other woman's.

She was losing track of time and space, lost in exquisite torment. Slowly, torturously, her body was being stretched with a tension that must break soon or she would surely fly apart.

"No," she groaned desperately, her nails raking urgently down Ryan's back, her teeth sinking into his shoulder. "No, I can't!"

"Don't fight it, Ariel. I'll take care of you." His mouth moved over her face, down her throat. "Just go with it. Let it take you. It'll be so good, Ariel," he crooned. "So good for you." His lips softened on hers, coaxing, his hands encouraging.

Her voice high and thin, she began shaking her head frantically, tears slipping faster and faster from her closed eyes. "Nooo, I-I—"

He was laughing! Laughing triumphantly as he controlled her wild body to his rhythm. His hard hands dug into her hips, holding her tightly to him to meet his demands...and hers. Behind her closed eyelids every color imaginable whirled faster and faster. Her body was tautening, tautening, too tight. She splintered in a sweet, glorious explosion, the snapping tension flinging pieces of her into a consuming fire.

The flames died down. Her body had somehow managed to put itself back together. She lay trembling with a delicious weakness. Gradually she became aware that he was still lying over her, his body a wonderful, warm weight on her.

Tenderly he caressed the damp wisps of hair off her forehead, his eyes searching hers deeply. "Are you all right?"

"I'm more than all right." She smiled. "I'm deliriously happy. Your plan was an unqualified success."

He laughed quietly, as if well pleased. The motion made her aware that he was still inside her, full and pulsing.

He nodded slowly at the wondering realization he saw in her face. "The first time was for you, love." He inhaled deeply as his hands began moving in a languid exploration of her body. His body picked up the rhythm of his hands and began stroking, too, leisurely, long. "This time—" he bent his open mouth to catch hers "—is for me."

Minutes later, recovering from a galvanic implosion that left her feeling gloriously fulfilled, she decided that it had been for both of them. He held her still beneath him, soothing wordless sounds in her ear, stroking her hair, gently kissing her stunned eyes shut, absorbing the tremors still pulsing through her body.

Finally he rolled to his side and stretched out next to her, dropping a kiss on her nose. "I wish I hadn't had to hurt you," he murmured, continuing on to her mouth. "It will never be like that again."

Her vastly disappointed voice froze him. "It won't ever be like that again?"

Slowly he raised his head and examined her sad face. Finally he asked carefully, "What exactly do you mean, Ariel?"

Her blue eyes glinted up at him as a slow, provocative grin spread over her face. "I want it to be like that again. Every time." One of her hands came up lazily, and her fingers brushed back the lock of hair that had fallen over his forehead, staying to weave through the heavy silk strands.

"You didn't hurt me, Ry," she assured him softly. "It was . . ." She shrugged helplessly. "Indescribable."

Her face was suffused with a glowing, inner light that took his breath away and filled him with an incredible surge of power and love. She started to reach up for his mouth, but he turned her on her side, clasping her possessively to him. Burying his face in her rain-scented hair, he whispered achingly, "Oh, my virgin girl, you are truly in my heart and soul." Smoothing back her tumbled hair, he kissed her forehead. "Sleep now."

She relaxed against him, her breathing slowing gradually. "I love you, Ariel Spence." He whispered the words he had never spoken to another woman into the quiet of the bedroom. He wasn't sure if she were awake to hear him or not.

He lay awake for a long time afterward, listening to the rain on the tin roof over his head and her soft breathing as she slept. He reveled quietly in the simple joy of holding her. He knew he could never let her go now. When he had recovered from that mindless, shattering ecstasy, he had felt pure and new again, his soul cleansed. Her totally unselfish gift of innocence had given him that.

He had thought that knowing he was the first was what was important. Perhaps it was, but now it was knowing, being absolutely certain, that he would be the last was what really mattered. His arms tightened around her pliant, sleeping body. Mine, he thought fiercely, my woman. He fell asleep before his happiness could be dimmed by the thought that she was his only if he could keep her alive . . . and only if she chose to be.

Ariel awoke by degrees, absorbing the marvelously right feel of Ryan in bed with her. She lay very quietly, not wanting to disturb the man sleeping beside her, or that feeling. The weight of his arm, thrown over her waist and fitting the curve so naturally, told her that if ever she woke up again without him, she would be incomplete.

The heavy curtains at the window blocked most of the early-morning light, but there was enough to see him clearly. He lay sprawled on his stomach, his head turned toward hers, sharing the same pillow. Easing carefully away, she studied his face. With his hair sleep-rumpled and his firm mouth not quite so hard, he looked younger, almost . . . vulnerable. The sharp bones seemed to have softened in sleep, the cynical curl of his mouth gentled. The long, curling eyelashes, so unfairly wasted on a man, shuttered the eyes that usually showed the world nothing, or only sardonic amusement at the goings-on around him. They had shown her many things last night. She just wished she knew if one of them had been love.

Rolling onto her back, she studied the patterns of light and shadow on the white ceiling. If anyone was vulnerable this morning, it was she, frighteningly so. Falling in love was a heady, magnificent feeling, but she was discovering that it was also rather terrifying. It took great courage to speak your love when you didn't know if the other person returned it, or ever would. Had Ryan really whispered those five words as she was falling asleep. And if he had had they been anything more than a meaningless cliché said to every woman he slept with? She'd heard that practically everyone said those words, words that once were so special and private, to the "love" of the evening. Did they say them because it was expected, or because they had to reassure themselves and their partner that casual sex with strangers really made them feel pleasured and socially sophisticated, and not empty and just a little sleezy?

She really shouldn't condemn anyone for saying "I love you" when he didn't. After all, she *did* love Ryan, but she hadn't said so. She just wasn't brave enough yet to risk the pitying rejection in his eyes if he refused the gift of her love, or the heartache she would feel if he accepted and gave nothing in exchange. She knew one should not give a gift, especially love, expecting, or even hoping, to receive anything in return. But she was too selfishly human to be able to do that.

Closing her eyes, she sighed dejectedly. She had another problem, too, though much more minor. Those books on the sixth shelf of her bookcase, full of heroines rapturously rhapsodizing about love and their lovers, were laughably poor and lacking. She was embarrassed to realize just how inadequate they were, but then, she'd had no way of knowing before. Two-dimensional black letters on white paper that could be appreciated by only one sense couldn't possibly convey an experience that involved at least three dimensions, all five senses and every conceivable color. She could certainly improve her heroines' future experiences, but she already knew with depressing certainty that never could they equal the love she felt for Ryan and the wonder of their physical response to each other. "Felicia" simply didn't have the words.

Turning back on her side, she tucked an elbow under her head and watched him sleep. Slowly she realized that her nose was turning numb. The room was frigid. Neither of them had stoked the little stove and banked it to burn lowly through the night. Her mouth curved into a satisfied smile as she reviewed the reason why. She buried her nose in the covers. There was a lingering trace of her cologne and his, and the musky earthiness of love.

The spread and top sheet had slid down to the middle of Ryan's back, and his bare skin was exposed to the chilly air. Ariel's gaze drifted over his relaxed muscles. Her palms itched slightly as she remembered the feel of those muscles, rippling in straining ridges and ropes under her hands last night.

Her hand snaked out of the warmth of the covers and pulled them up over his shoulders, her fingers lingering in the hair at the nape of his neck. The raw silk texture was so different from her own hair. She had never been aware of the differences in texture between a man's and a woman's body. They were as obvious as the visual differences, and they fascinated her. She'd been careful to let him sleep before; now, perversely, she wished he'd wake up.

Her hand stroked around his neck, and her leg inched closer to his. She was like a greedy child sneaking into a cookie jar. She wanted to experience everything she had last night, but with the time to savor those fascinating differences: the feel of a hair-roughened thigh sliding up between silky smooth ones, a sandpapery cheek brushing over a satiny one, a hard muscled chest easing over soft cushioning, nipples tickled by wiry hair and the best—hot, sleek strength gliding into a snug moist welcoming.

Ryan moved suddenly, and Ariel found herself trapped in the two strong arms that had lashed around her under the sheet. After a hard hug and harder good-morning kiss, he levered himself up on one elbow to peer over her shoulder at the clock on the dresser. She saw his sleepy eyes widen in horror at the time. He flopped down, groaning and twisting onto his back at the same time, pulling her over him.

Nuzzling fiercely into her neck, he growled, "Ariel Spence, you are a heartless woman. I thought this morning, of all mornings, you would sleep late."

"Why?" Her innocent tone was ruined by a giggle as her fingers scaled his ribs. "Did something unusual happen last night?"

Ryan nipped warningly at her throat while his hands roamed down her back. "Brat," he muttered, shoving her tousled hair back to get at her ear. "I'll show you unusual."

His shoulders, bared to the cold air by the slipping covers, flinched, and he looked up at her blankly. "It's freezing in here!"

"Mmm." Ariel rubbed her cold nose against his, her hair a golden curtain around their heads. "Maybe that something unusual you're going to show me will warm it up," she said hopefully.

Ryan let his head fall back weakly onto the pillow and moaned disconsolately. "Good Lord, I've created a monster." His eyes rolled wearily upward, and he addressed the ceiling. "The woman's insatiable already."

His eyes slid back to hers, filled with a satanic anticipation. "Lucky for you, so am I." He leered evilly while Ariel laughed in delight. Then, in a lightning move, he slid out from under her and stood up. He shivered convulsively. "Unfortunately, even that wouldn't be enough to warm this place up."

Wincing every time his bare feet had to touch the icy floor, he grabbed a paper and kindling and relit the stove.

Ariel buried herself in the warm bed, laughing heartlessly. As Ryan crouched before the open door of the wood stove, the flames spread a glow over his face and bare chest. They reflected in his eyes as he turned to give her a happy grin. Ariel was a little shocked at herself. She was feeling decidedly insatiable and rather uninhibited. She felt no shyness at all, looking at him as he came back to bed. Maybe, she mused, it hadn't been inhibition at all that had kept her from looking at naked men before but simple lack of interest.

The gleam in his eye should have warned her. Ryan ripped away the covers, and Ariel scrambled up with a shriek. "You are completely vicious, Ryan Jones! It's like an icebox in here!"

"We'll take a shower and warm up." As he dragged her up off the bed, he let his eyes wander appreciatively. Holding her in a loose embrace, he saw her eyes flick down and around. He grinned over the top of her head. Miss Spence was still just a little shocked by casual nudity. Rocking her bare body against his, he watched her blue eyes widen a little more and begin to turn smoky.

Ariel felt herself color. Well, perhaps there was an inhibition or two left, after all, but she doubted they would last much longer.

Ryan gave her an exuberant kiss and released her. He tossed her his black shirt from the night before as he shrugged into the brown corduroy jeans he had draped over the chair. "Put that on until the shower's ready. You're turning an interesting color." His eyes teased her unmercifully.

"From the cold," she sniffed primly, then gasped. The silk shirt was like putting on a layer of frost. "You have a lot to learn, Mr. Jones," Ariel told him severely, "about hospitality. It is *not* hospitable to let your guests freeze to death."

"Actually, I'm the guest," he informed her, disappearing into the bathroom. "*You* own the place."

"Then I'm going to get a fire going downstairs and warm my place up a little faster," she called, skipping down the circular staircase.

Ryan smiled to himself and leaned into the shower to turn on the spray. He felt so fantastically good this morning, better than he could ever remember waking up feeling before. There were one or two things he did need to tell her, but he would pick the time and the place. He was confident that he could explain his deception without getting her too upset.

She was yelling something at him from downstairs. Sticking his head out into the bedroom, he heard her call again.

"Where are your matches?"

"In the kitchen drawer by the stove," he yelled back. He went back into the bathroom to check the water. Abruptly, with an explosive curse, he turned off the shower so violently that he nearly tore the handle out of the wall. Desperately he ran for the stairs. He had just remembered what else was in that drawer.

Chapter 9

Ariel was standing in the middle of the kitchen, heedless of the cold tile under her feet, or the chill creeping up her bare legs beneath the tail of his shirt. The horror and profound pain in her huge eyes and bloodless face froze Ryan in the doorway. The box of matches was open on the floor. The little blue-tipped sticks were scattered like bits of the happiness they'd shared just moments before. His .45 dangled, ready to fall, from the fingers of her left hand. Ryan thought furiously, trying to remember if he'd left the safety on.

Her right hand clutched the damning file, the blood-red letters of her name on the cover screaming an accusation at him. "Who are you? Where did you get this?" Her voice was that of a little girl trying to understand some incomprehensible tragedy. Her hand jerked, and the file fell, spilling its Judas contents over the cheerful blue and yellow tiles. "You knew all about me before you ever came. Dennis, the murder, everything. You even knew I was a virgin."

The agonized guilt on his face brought a hideous suspicion to reality. "My God!" she breathed, the horrifying indictment glazing her eyes. "You *were* sent to spy on me!" Rationality fled.

She brought the gun up in slow motion, frowning at it puzzledly, as if trying to remember how it had gotten into her hand. Every cell in Ryan's body tensed. If she shot him, perhaps it would be no less than he deserved. Suddenly she flung the gun away with an inarticulate cry, as if it were indescribably evil and filthy. It skittered across the floor and came to rest with a small thump against the baseboard.

Ryan went limp, as the breath he didn't know he'd been holding burst out. Then the look of helpless panic on her stark face shocked him immobile again.

In a soundless whisper that seemed like a scream in the quiet kitchen she demanded, "Were you sent to kill me? Have you been toying with me, playing some perverted cat-and-mouse game?" Her head began to shake slowly from side to side as she tried to deny the truth. Her thin, disbelieving wail echoed loudly in Ryan's ears.

Her sense of betrayal was complete and totally devastating. She had opened herself physically and emotionally to the dark man standing across the room from her, so silent, denying nothing. The only man, ever. She had joyously shared her body and her love, freely offering it in the most exquisite, soul-satisfying experience in her life. He had profaned it, turning it into a brutal, vicious rape, violating her in the most fundamental, soul-destroying way possible. The recognition of her own all-too-willing, ecstatic complicity physically sickened her.

The realization that Ariel's knees were buckling thawed Ryan's frozen body. He sprinted across the kitchen and caught her just before she hit the floor. "No!" he roared in helpless rage. She recoiled from him in abject terror, and he forced himself under control. "No!" he repeated strongly as he compelled her cringing body into his arms. Heaving sobs racked at him.

"No, no, no, Ariel." His rough voice gentled into a deep soothing litany. "It's not what you think. It's not what it seems."

Over and over he crooned the words as he rocked her gently against him, like a mother cradling a hurt child. Her bitter tears warmed his bare chest. His hand tangled in her hair, pushing her head tightly into his shoulder as he tilted his own head back, swallowing the tears burning his throat and blurring his eyes. He felt a deep, angry despair at the possibility that Ariel would twist the most beautiful night of his life, the only shared fulfillment he'd

ever experienced, into something sordid, another selfish emptiness. He couldn't allow that.

Slowly her sobbing eased. A shudder passed through her as she
drew a deep breath and then, too weakened to resist, sagged completely against him. Ryan's wet cheek rested on the top of her head,
his arms tight around her.

"That's the only trouble with this place, not enough drawer
space," he muttered inanely. Easing her away so he could look into
her face, he gripped her shoulders. Shell-shocked blue eyes finally
focused on his grim face.

"Ariel, I'm going to explain that damned file to you, and a hell
of a lot more. Please, please believe," he shook her roughly for
emphasis, "that I am telling you the truth." The lost, hopeless look
on her face would haunt him to the end of his days. He sensed that
she had retreated from him completely, like a mortally hurt animal that crawled into the deepest corner of its den to lick its
wounds.

Her robot body obeyed his hand on her arm. She walked across
the room. She sat when he pushed her gently down into one of the
hard, wooden chairs at the table. She stayed, staring at nothing, as
he lit the fire she'd never had a chance to start.

He waited until the kindling was well caught, then placed two
logs on the fire and shut the small door. He was readying himself
for the most important defense of his life, with himself as the de-
fendant, knowing she had probably already convicted him on the
evidence in that damned drawer.

Taking the chair opposite her, with the narrow table between
them, he reached for her frigid fingers. He held them tightly,
warming them in his. Maybe she would feel the truth if her ears
refused to hear it. In a quiet voice he began answering her first two
questions.

"I am Rick Jones's brother. He gave me the file and sent me to
watch over you."

He was drained, emotionally and physically. He wanted nothing more than to take her back upstairs to bed and prove the truth
of his feelings in the most irrefutable way possible. His wish wasn't
going to be granted; he knew it all too well. Shock still haunted her
blue eyes, and there was a wariness about her, as if she were ready
to bolt at the first wrong word.

Ariel withdrew her hand from Ryan's. "You lied to me, Ryan." Her voice was deadly calm.

"I never told you a single word that was untrue," he denied quietly, each word slow and clear, looking for an acquittal on a technicality.

"There are silent lies as well as spoken ones," she reminded him neutrally. "They're the cruelest ones of all. You had numerous opportunities to tell me who you really were."

Her tone took on an exaggerated carelessness. "Oh, by the way, Ariel, Rick Jones is my brother. He sent me to keep an eye on you, snoop around, find out what dirt I can on you." Her voice lost the carelessness, lowered, throbbing with the intensity of her anger. "That was the plan, wasn't it, Ryan? What a sweet little setup! Cozy up to the suspect, entice her with the oldest lure in the book— sex. She'll spill everything. And it worked, didn't it?" Ryan saw that the tears were back, bitter tears at her own gullibility and his betrayal. "I fell right into your bed and loved every second of it."

His heart made a cautious leap at her unconscious confession. "But it was for nothing, because I don't know anything!" Ariel's fists bunched against the edge of the table as she strained across it, fairly screaming the words at him.

She slumped back in her chair, defeated. "I didn't even know about Dennis's prescription racket until the police told me."

Ryan looked at her for a long, silent moment, seeing his dreams fading like the illusions they were. "I'm sorry, Ariel," he whispered softly. And she didn't even know the worst of it yet.

"I'm sorry, too." She could barely get the whisper past the tears clogging her throat. Hugging her arms around herself, she dragged in a deep, trembling breath. Gradually she became aware that the room was still uncomfortably cool, and that he was wearing only a pair of pants, while she had on only his shirt. "You ought to get a shirt on," she remarked absently, her voice husky from crying. "You'll catch cold."

His mouth quirked with the ghost of his usual sardonic smile. "You're wearing my shirt."

Her eyes thawed slightly. "Then we may both catch cold." But she made no move to get up and find something warmer, and neither did he.

Her voice even huskier than before, she asked almost diffidently, "Why did you come?" Her eyes stayed on his fingers toying with the wooden salt and pepper shakers on the table.

He knew what she was really asking. Why had he gone along with Rick's harebrained suggestion? "I was bored, not ready to go back to work." He gestured toward the papers still littering the floor. "Rick gave me the file, and I read it. You intrigued me. He knew you would."

He watched her eyes follow his hand and saw her mouth tighten. That file really disturbed her, as well it should. It was an obscene invasion of her privacy, but the motive behind it had been pure. "No one but the D.A., Rick and I know what's in that file, Ariel," he reassured her quietly. "We're the only people who have ever seen it." It was obvious she hadn't had enough time to see the reports on DiSanto's smuggling. He made an instant decision.

Ariel finally looked up at him and nodded briefly. Her eyes remained on his, the oddly pleading defiance in them a sharp contrast to her flat emotionless voice. "Did you think I was guilty of Dennis's murder?"

His hand sought hers and tightened gently before he answered her just as flatly. "Yes." Her eyes closed as if in pain, and she tried to jerk her hand away. He wouldn't let it go. "I thought you might well be implicated; the evidence could be interpreted that way." He tugged on her fingers until she opened her eyes to glare at him. He grinned back, "By the morning after I met you, I was convinced you weren't guilty of anything."

"What changed your mind?" The curiosity in her voice overrode the cold stiffness.

"Cold-blooded murderesses don't make homemade soup, and they don't hold strange men in their arms in the middle of the night and tell then not to be afraid," he responded softly, his dark eyes even softer.

She searched his face, finally nodding slowly. This at least wasn't a lie. "What is the evidence against me?" Her voice was amazingly matter-of-fact. "Why do your brother and Davidson think I murdered Dennis?"

Ryan understood now how her tremendous self-control had worked against her. Her seeming lack of emotion after Dennis's death had been taken as yet another sign of her guilt.

He followed through on the decision he'd made moments before. "Dennis was involved in more than writing a few illegal prescriptions for painkillers, Ariel." Her pale face grew whiter as she instinctively prepared herself to even more pain. There was no easy way to tell her. "He was smuggling in cocaine and heroin every time he came back from one of his mercy missions to Mexico. One of those little villages was his supply point."

Ariel sat very still. The numbness settling over her had nothing to do with the coolness of the house. "My God," she whispered, "and I actually used to accompany him down there." Staring sightlessly past Ryan's shoulder, she understood immediately part of the evidence against her. "How could I have been that blind?"

"You saw only what he wanted you to see, Ariel."

Her eyes came back to his. "And I thought he wanted to help those people. He was just using them, like he did me."

"He did help them, Ariel," Ryan reminded her quietly. His thumb stroked soothingly over the pulse in her wrist. It was still much too fast.

"I don't think he ever intended to use you. On the contrary, I think he tried to keep you from being tainted by his 'business.' The one thing he never lied to you about was that he truly loved you." Why was he defending a man who didn't deserve it? Because, Ryan thought bitterly, he was defending himself, too, subtly justifying his lies because of his own selfless concern for her. He ought to be honest with himself, at least. His concern was purely selfish. He didn't want what they'd had together for so brief a time to be irretrievably lost.

"Does your brother really believe I'm guilty, Ry?"

Ryan shook his head wearily. "I honestly don't know, Ariel." The cautious hope in her eyes died, and they were filled with a bleak despair.

He rose from the table and picked up the scattered pages of her file. He offered it to her, and after a moment's hesitation she took it.

"Read it, Ariel. You can see the facts of the case and how Davidson sees them as evidence against you."

Ariel opened the file reluctantly. Seeing all the tabloid articles again made her feel physically ill, yet she couldn't bring herself to shut the folder. She skipped over them to the lengthy report on

Dennis's smuggling. She read every word with a morbid thoroughness.

She was unaware of the quilt Ryan tucked around her. She absently drained the mug of coffee he placed near her hand, never noticing as it was refilled. Ryan moved around the kitchen quietly, preparing breakfast. As Ariel closed the file she felt the warmth of the old quilt around her and smelled the mundane, somehow comforting scents of coffee and bacon and toasting bread.

She stared vacantly at the closed cover of the file; her name in red letters seemed like the name of a stranger. The evidence the police and the district attorney's investigators had unearthed after Dennis's murder was very convincing. All circumstantial, of course, nothing that could be presented in court without more solid substantiation, but still convincing. It all pointed very clearly to her. Anyone reading the file would at the very least wonder if Ariel Spence had not been Dennis DiSanto's accomplice.

A couple of motives for her part in setting him up for the killing were advanced, but the one the district attorney seemed to favor was the classic one; greed. Ariel had seen a chance to increase her share of the profits by murdering her partner and taking it. Davidson expected that she would eventually disappear, so she could spend her ill-gotten wealth. He had it all worked out. The only flaw in his reasoning was that he was wrong, but how could she prove it? She was guilty until proven innocent, and she began to understand that she might have to live with that supposed guilt haunting her for the rest of her life.

Ryan set a plate with crisp bacon, two fried eggs and toast in front of her. She glanced over to him; he was already back at the stove, his back to her, dishing up his own plate. She wasn't up on the new etiquette for lovers, but she suspected it dictated that he should provide the breakfast, since he had provided the bed.

Lovers. Ariel salted the eggs absently and began to eat automatically. The numbness that had frozen her emotions was beginning to wear off. Ryan sat down across from her silently.

Lovers. This meal should have been a very intimate special celebration of the night before, their eyes making promises of more such nights. But she had been cheated out of that, the promises broken before they were even made. Here they sat, only the narrow trestle table between them, but they might as well have been light years apart, so perfect was their isolation from each other.

With a violent motion Ariel shoved her half-eaten breakfast away. She rose abruptly from the table, her usual grace gone as she tripped over a leg of her chair. She could no longer bear to be in the same room with him.

She was suddenly mad, gloriously, furiously *mad*. Mad at closed-minded district attorneys with tunnel vision, mad at liars, cheats and sneaking spies, all of them with the name Ryan Jones. She reveled in her anger, wallowed in it, stoked it to a white-hot fury—to keep at bay the soul-wrenching hurt, the emptiness threatening to destroy her.

Ryan half rose from his seat, starting to call after her as she rushed from his apartment. He sagged back in the chair without speaking a word and stared after her bleakly. Nothing he could say would bring her back. The only words that might have done it stuck in his throat. They'd been so easy, so natural, in the warm aftermath of loving last night, but now, when he desperately needed them, they wouldn't come.

Ariel took her shower alone. No matter how hard she scrubbed, how scalding the water, she couldn't seem to wash away the feel of his body on hers, the lingering warmth of him, his scent.

She stepped out of the bathroom to find her clothes from the night before neatly folded in the middle of her bed. She ignored them; she would not wear that dress again. She pulled a neon-pink sweatshirt and baggy carpenter's pants from the closet, dressing automatically.

She dried her hair with even less attention. She turned her head in the hot stream of air, her fingers automatically lifting the wet, heavy hair. He would leave immediately, of course. Let him explain it to his brother. She switched off the dryer, combed through her almost dry hair and went downstairs.

She couldn't shake the feeling that something had been missing from the file, something she sensed between the lines, something talked around, but never clearly stated. Yet what more could there be?

Pausing by her front door, she shrugged into her blue ski jacket. Before she told him to get out, she wanted Murphy back. The house would be too quiet, too lonely, without . . . her.

She fastened her seatbelt and started the Blazer. As she turned the truck around she glimpsed the tall dark man standing on the front step. He was watching her over the rim of his mug. The steam from the hot coffee framed his sober face, those dark hooded eyes following her.

She started off down the muddy track to the highway. They hadn't spoken since he'd handed her the file. The road in front of her was suddenly blurred by fresh tears. The conflict inside her was so strong that she felt she was tearing apart.

He'd betrayed her trust, her love. This morning's revelations had destroyed the trust, but the love was still there, insidious, like a weed pulled out of the garden. The top was gone, but the deep taproot remained, the plant waiting to spring up again.

The memory of the night before stubbornly refused to die. He had orchestrated the evening to provide her with a memory that was not of a disappointing loss, but of a special gift full of joy. She might not have had much experience with passion, but she knew that he'd exerted tremendous control over himself to ensure her pleasure before he took his own. How could he have been so sensitive to her needs...and yet so full of deceit? Had last night been the ultimate deception?

Ryan meandered aimlessly across the muddy yard. A stiff breeze was chasing the tattered tail end of the storm over the western mountains. His shoulders automatically hunched at the chill wind whipping through his plaid flannel shirt, but it cleared the dull ache from his head. The sun was shining brilliantly from a rain-washed, azure sky. The air was invigoratingly brisk, freshly cleaned by the storm and scented by the damp prairie surrounding the schoolhouse.

He would take it one day, one hour, at a time. Little by little he would coax her back to him. She would retreat again, when he told her the one detail the file hadn't contained. He hadn't thought she could bear any more bad news this morning. His hand clenched on the stoneware mug in his hand. He *would* have her back.

He frowned at the ground where Ariel's Blazer had been parked, vaguely disturbed by something out of place. The coffee-colored dirt underneath the truck had dried out overnight. Suddenly Ryan bit off a violent curse, flinging the coffee cup aside as he raced for the house and his keys. The significance of the four identical wet spots on the ground where the wheels of the Blazer had rested had finally dawned on him.

Ryan leaped into his truck, grinding the reluctant engine into sputtering life. Ruthlessly he jammed the cold transmission into gear and floored the accelerator. The wet mud sucking at the deep treads on his tires made his progress hideously slow. He had a clear view of the silver Blazer following the straight fence line to the highway. The heel of his hand slammed on the horn, but even he could hardly hear it over the noise of his truck.

He watched her approach the intersection with the highway in agonized desperation. If there was no oncoming traffic he knew just what she would do; he'd watched her often enough the past thirteen days. His subconscious recognition of the superstitious number bypassed his rational mind and sent a chill down his spine. With no traffic to worry about, Ariel would ignore the stop sign, let the truck slow down on its own, gear down, lightly tap the brake pedal and pull out onto the highway. With the mud dragging at her tires, slowing her more than usual, she'd never notice that her brakes weren't working.

Then she would climb the steep hill, top it and start down the long twisting road leading into town. There was a solid granite wall on one side of the road and a drop-off of two hundred feet to the river below on the other. Either would provide an adequate, if fatal, brake for a runaway vehicle.

Through the stinging mist clouding his vision he saw the brake lights ahead of him flash briefly, then stay lit, the blood-red light seeming to mock his useless attempt to stop her. Angrily Ryan swiped a hand across his eyes to clear them, just in time to see a fully loaded logging truck barreling down the hill toward her. The Blazer slewed wildly as Ariel, obviously trying to avoid a collision, wrenched the wheel hard to the right.

Slippery mud had been tracked onto the highway by other cars before hers, and Ryan watched in oddly detached horror as the silver truck slid inexorably closer to the logging truck. The action seemed to be taking place in slow motion, each detail of the deadly scene before him brilliantly clear. In petrified fascination he saw her coolheadedly turn the wheels into the skid, still fighting for control.

The truck driver, too, was trying to take evasive action, but the pavement was slick and he ended up jackknifing his rig across the highway.

Without being aware of it, Ryan had stopped his power wagon a scant hundred feet from the intersection. His white knuckles locked around the steering wheel, and the bitter taste of panic mixed in his dry mouth with the salty, metallic flavor of blood from his bitten-through lip.

At the last possible second before impact Ariel gunned the engine, twisted the wheel again and prayed that just one tire might grab enough to send her past the wall of logs looming inches from the front bumper.

The right rear tire hit a dry patch of asphalt. The vehicle spun just enough to slide past the tail of the logging truck with the screeching sound of tearing metal. The additional acceleration destroyed the precarious balance of the Blazer, and Ariel began a crazy roller-coaster ride as the truck rolled. Hanging on to the steering wheel grimly, she watched through the bursting windshield as the trees in front of her swung insanely upside down and the sky changed places with the ground.

Ryan was shocked out of his terrified trance. He nearly tore the door off its hinges as he slammed out of his truck and began running toward the tree-lined shoulder of the highway. The Blazer rolled onto its roof and rocked there for a few heart-stopping seconds; then its momentum carried it over onto its side. It trembled to a shuddering halt with a metallic sigh like a dying mechanical elephant. The only sounds were Ryan's harsh breathing as he reached the overturned truck and the last, quiet tinkle of glass from a smashed window.

He paused by one rear wheel that was still spinning lazily. Diesel fumes were burning his eyes; the fuel was less volatile than gasoline, but an explosion was still very possible, and even the fastest way to get her out might be too slow. He bypassed doors that might be warped shut by the wreck and crashed through thigh-high cockleburs to reach the open windshield.

"Ariel!"

"What?" A strong voice that sounded more exasperated than scared answered him. A moment later a white face with a smear of bright blood on the left cheek appeared in the opening formerly occupied by the windshield. A body that seemed none the worse for wear, judging by the speed with which it was crawling through the window, immediately followed.

"I think we'd better get away before it blows," Ariel advised calmly, albeit somewhat breathlessly, as she scrambled across the crumpled hood. "I can smell—"

Steel fingers hooked into the sweatshirt under her gaping jacket and dragged her down off the hood to a hard, heaving chest. Before Ariel's sneakers could touch the ground she was being hauled and shoved through the brambles.

There was a soft whoosh behind them, then a deafening roar. The force and heat of the explosion hit them in the back, sending them sprawling over the wet prairie grass.

Ryan and Ariel staggered to their feet, their arms unconsciously seeking each other, holding on as if to reassure themselves that they were truly all right. Silently they watched the truck driver try to battle the inferno with a puny fire extinguisher. He gave up after a few minutes and came to stand with them, his hands brushing absently over his face. Wordlessly, all three of them saw the ravenous flames consume the Blazer, their faces grimly sober. Pungent smoke and fine ash drifted over them like a dirty snowstorm.

The scream of sirens announced both Chief Dye and the county sheriff's deputy. Although technically out of the village police chief's jurisdiction, the deputy deferred the investigation to him. Ted Dye stood by himself, considering the already dying fire and twisted metal. Then he trudged over and called the stunned truck driver aside.

Ryan felt a strong shiver run through Ariel's body. He looked down at her, his face darkening with concern. Underneath the grime and blood her face was pale and composed. The eyes looking up at him were smoke-reddened, but sharp. The trembling under his hands said she wasn't as calm as she appeared.

"The brakes failed, Ry." Her voice and face expressed her bafflement. "Completely. If they were only wet, they should have grabbed at least a little, shouldn't they? I don't under—"

"They weren't wet," Ryan said tersely. Out of the corner of his eye he had seen the chief pat the truck driver on the shoulder, dismissing him.

"And you were right behind me," Ariel said slowly. His comment deepened her puzzlement to disturbing suspicion. "Why were—you . . . ?"

"Ariel, can you tell me what happened?" the chief asked as he lumbered up. His grizzled eyebrow lifted as he noted Ryan's arms linked possessively around Ariel's shoulders, her body drawn protectively into his side.

Ariel answered the chief with a distracted air that he put down to shock over the accident. When she mentioned the failed brakes he glanced sharply at Ryan, who nodded almost imperceptibly. The chief's questioning ended abruptly. He seemed to lose interest in her and wandered back to the dying fire.

Ryan took Ariel's hand and led her toward his power wagon. As if it were an afterthought, Ted Dye called him back.

"Wait for me in the truck, Ariel, I'll be back in a minute, and then we'll go get Murph." Ryan's smile was easy as he shut the door firmly after she'd climbed up. It vanished immediately as he headed back to the police chief.

"You're sure?" the chief asked after a few minutes' discussion. He glanced sideways from where his boot toe was destroying the ash skeleton of a weed to the stern man staring at the smoldering, blackened framework that had been a shiny silver truck. Greasy black smoke still coiled around the wreckage and the two men.

"As sure as I can be without any proof." Ryan sighed tiredly and scuffed through a pile of ash with a frustrated kick of his hiking boot. "Luck still seems to be with our unknown 'friend.' The proof burned up with Ariel's Blazer." He swore bitterly as he turned to leave. As a bodyguard he was a joke. If Ariel hadn't been as lucky as her would-be killer, she would be part of that smoking pile of metal right now. Impotently he thrust his hands into his pants pockets. He hoped the gods were enjoying their obscene little chess game. Which mortal pawns would be sacrificed to gain a win?

Ariel accepted the vet's concern over her accident with a lack of concern that raised Ryan's eyebrows and detoured the vet back to his usual cheerfulness. She responded to his instructions for Murphy's convalescence with polite monosyllables. Before letting her leave, he sat her on his examining table to wash her filthy face and examine the cut on her cheek.

Leaning in the doorway, Ryan watched Dr. Hughes's stubby, clumsy-looking fingers clean away the soot and dirt and blood. The veterinarian kept up a constant stream of soothing nonsense. Ryan's impassive face showed neither the irrational jealousy burning in him as the vet's impersonal hands touched Ariel, nor the acute self-disgust that jealousy was causing him. He had wanted to be the one to care for her, but she was undeniably better off in Dr. Hughes's care—and that galled him.

"I hope the local doctors don't find out I've been treating two-legged patients as well as four-legged ones." Dr. Hughes grinned at her as he swabbed disinfectant on Ariel's cheek. He called Ryan over and showed him the hairline slice from a stray sliver of glass. A single drop of bright red blood oozed onto her pale cheek.

"She certainly doesn't need stitches, but I'm going to put two butterfly Band-Aids on it, to be sure the edges stay together. There won't be a scar," he murmured to Ryan. Both of them ignored the fidgetings of the patient. "Be sure she doesn't get any dirt in it."

"Perhaps *I* could see it?" Ariel suggested caustically.

Dr. Hughes blinked and looked at her in confusion for a moment; then a sheepish grin split his good-natured, homely face. "I'm sorry, Ariel. I'm used to patients who bite, not talk, and to anxious owners who are worried about their precious pets." He handed her a small mirror.

"Ariel wouldn't make a very good pet," Ryan murmured blandly, his dark eyes laughing slyly. "She's not very obedient." But she was infinitely precious.

Ariel sent him a sugary, withering glance, then solemnly accepted a giant dog biscuit from the vet for being a good patient.

Murphy jumped into the back of Ryan's pickup, content to cede the cab to Ariel, and Ryan slammed the tailgate. Despite her brief show of spirit in Dr. Hughes's office, Ariel was still far too quiet and self-controlled. Ryan knew that she'd already had more than enough shocks for one day, yet the worst one of all was going to have to be faced in a very little while. He'd hoped to spare her for a few more days, until her strength and defenses were not so weak, but that was no longer possible.

The ride home was silent. Murphy leaped out of the truck and tore around the yard, obviously fully recuperated. She took off after a pair of imprudent ground squirrels that had decided to take up residence under the front step during her absence. Ryan escorted Ariel into the house with an unobtrusive hand at her back.

He sat her in her favorite armchair, put a log in the stove and sat on the couch across from her. He waited. She looked at him for a long minute, her face closed, her eyes as cold and empty as ice. When she finally spoke her question was so quiet Ryan had to strain to hear it over the popping of the wood in the stove.

"My accident wasn't an accident, was it, Ryan?"

"No, Ariel."

She considered his toneless confirmation. Her voice was as expressionless as his. "How was it done?"

"Probably with Xylene, or any of several other solvents, replacing the brake fluid. Xylene is the easiest to obtain. You drain the master brake cylinder and refill it with the xylene. It eats away at the rubber seals for a few days until the fluid leaks out all at once. The brake failure is total." His smile was faint and humorless, his eyes far away for a moment. "It's an especially successful tactic in hilly terrain."

He answered the stark question that pierced the blankness in her eyes. "Vehicle sabotage was a specialty of mine once. Doing the brakes is particularly effective. There's a fatal crash, and no proof that it was anything but ordinary brake failure. No one suspects a thing."

Her hands were gripping her upper arms so tightly that he knew she would have bruises tomorrow. She breathed in suddenly, deeply, and consciously relaxed, unlocking her fingers and taking hold of the fat arms of her chair. She dug into the green plush viciously.

"And Murphy?" She took another quick breath and conquered the slight waver in her voice. "The other poisonings were simply camouflage. Someone needed to get Murphy out of the way to work on my Blazer."

"Yes."

"That candy you knocked out of my hand that day... was that...?" Her lips worked but were unable to form the awful word again.

"Poisoned?" he finished for her. "Yes, it was." His voice was quiet and steady, his heart aching as he read the emotions she could no longer mask flitting across her face; stunned disbelief, anger, then recognition of her terrifying vulnerability to an unknown killer.

"This is what you left out this morning," she whispered. Her eyes closed again to shut out the horrible truth. "I knew there was something you weren't telling me, but I thought it was that you had guessed...'' A hysterical giggle bubbled up in her throat, and Ryan started off the couch. She swallowed it down, her body rigid as she battled to control her fear. Ryan sat back, seeing her fingers whiten on the chair arms. He wanted so badly to hold her, but she'd shown no sign of wanting him. She didn't trust him enough any longer to seek his comfort.

"Who is it?" she demanded in a fierce whisper.

"I don't know, Ariel." All his frustration and unacknowledged fear were in his answer.

The tension went out of her body, and she slumped in the chair. Two tears seeped out from under the dark fringe of the lashes resting on her white cheeks. With a soft curse Ryan rose in one furious, fluid motion and scooped her out of the chair. The hell with what she wanted; he knew what she needed. Her eyes flew open, and she stared warily at his set jaw as he took her place in the chair. He settled her on his lap, surrounding her with his protection. There were no more tears. He wished there were; she needed the release.

"Why does someone want me dead, Ry?" Her poignant whisper expressed the total incomprehension that he himself had known the first time he'd been shot at and realized, to his astonishment, that someone was actually trying to kill him. At least he had had a glimpse of his enemy.

"We think it might have something to do with Dennis's death," Ryan said hedging a little.

Ariel sat up, almost clipping Ryan's chin with the top of her head. He loosened his arms only enough to let her lean away to see his face.

"That was only a random incident, Ryan," she argued forcefully. "Your brother tried to prove otherwise, but even he couldn't turn up anything concrete. He even searched through all of Dennis's photographs, looking for someone in a picture who shouldn't have been there, or something suspicious happening in the background." Something in the look on Ryan's face made her eyes narrow suddenly. "You've looked at them, too, haven't you," she realized quietly. "You picked the lock on the cabinet."

"It was an easy one," he said neutrally, shrugging off the heat from her gaze. "I didn't see anything, either."

"Is there anything of mine you haven't snooped into, Ryan Jones?" Her tone was a little too silky. "Is there *anything* you haven't lied about?"

Yes. There were the five words he'd whispered in the warm darkness last night, five words he couldn't repeat in the cold, bright daylight. He knew she thought they were the biggest lie of all.

Actually, he preferred her anger. It would counteract the effects of the accident and keep her out of the dangerous apathy that fear could produce. And it was putting some color back into her chalky face.

Ariel tried to stand, outrage stiffening her body. Ryan held her easily, hauling her up against his chest. One implacable hand caught the back of her skull, holding her face so close to his that she felt his breath cooling her hot cheeks. A struggle would be undignified, and she would lose, anyway. She had to content herself with staring coldly into those eyes that caressed her pursed lips as effectively as teasing kisses. At least, she recognized dimly, when she was angry with him, she couldn't be afraid.

Ryan spoke quietly. "I was looking for anything that would give me a clue to the killer's identity. Compared to saving your life, violating your privacy didn't seem like much of a crime."

· The sudden tears that flooded her eyes startled both of them. She tried to turn her head away, and he released it immediately. Raising her chin, she sat stiffly on his lap. She sniffed, vainly trying to blink back the tears. "I'm sorry," she said thickly. Her fingers were twisting the hem of her sooty pink sweatshirt hopelessly out of shape. Ryan stilled them and kept them captive gently in his own. She whispered so softly that he had to lean closer to catch the words. "You've lied to me, yet you saved my life, and Murphy's, too." She turned back to him, her eyes achingly vulnerable. "I-I can't . . ." She was unable to put her conflicting emotions into words.

"Oh, Ariel," he murmured helplessly as he kissed her cheek tenderly. He tasted the salty moisture on her skin then drew her head down to his shoulder. He laughed grimly. "All that's happened to you in less than twenty-four hours is that you've lost your virginity and thought the man who took it was sent to kill you, but he only turned out to be a liar instead. You've survived a near-fatal accident and then discovered someone really is trying to kill you. I suppose—'' he rubbed his cheek over her smoky, silky hair ''—you're entitled to a few tears.''

Ariel nestled against the smoke-soured flannel of his shirt and closed her eyes in sudden exhaustion. It was despicably weak of her to lean on him, she knew, but those strong arms around her felt so good, and she was so alone, so frightened. She sighed sadly, ''If you have any more little surprises for me, Ry, maybe you could save them for tomorrow.'' Within seconds she was asleep.

Ryan held her for a while longer, her softness melting slowly over his hard angles. Finally he stood and laid her on the sofa, then removed her sneakers and covered her with a rainbow afghan. Sighing heavily, he kissed her sleep-soft mouth. Her mouth curved in a dream smile, and he echoed it unconsciously. Reluctantly he straightened and went to her desk; then dialed the eleven digits of his brother's phone number.

Ariel moved slowly through murky dreams to fuzzy awareness. She blinked her eyes open and stared around her living room dazedly. The sunbeams slanting through the side window were nearly horizontal. It had been a little before noon when Ryan had brought her home; now it was nearly sundown. She must have slept for hours. She listened; everything was quiet. Where was Ryan?

The crash of wood against metal only a few feet from her head made her start violently with a small scream. A growled curse came through the cast-iron door of the the wood box built into the wall near the stove. She rose stiffly from the couch and padded over to the small square door.

Bending down, she swung it open and peered through the square tunnel in the brick wall. The corresponding door in the outside wall was open. Ryan was squatting in front of it.

''Hi.''

Ryan's head snapped up from the log he was carefully laying inside. He grinned ruefully at the woman shoving the tangled blond hair out of her sleep-flushed face. ''I was trying to be quiet so you could sleep.''

''You blew it with the first log.'' Against her will her eyes pleasured themselves on the man framed by the hole in the wall. The last rays of the dying sun picked out the blue highlights in the black hair ruffled by the cold breeze. Apparently he had been chopping more wood, because wood chips clung to his black jeans, and his flannel shirt hung open over a white T-shirt despite the chill. The exercise had given his face a healthy flush and his eyes a dark sparkle. He looked like a man who'd simply been spending a quiet afternoon around the house, enjoying ordinary, everyday chores. The traumatic events of the morning and his duplicity receded to the back of her mind for the moment.

Without thinking about it, she reached through to flick back the stubborn cowlick over his forehead. He caught her hand in his and brought it to his cold lips, warming them with a kiss on her palm.

He felt her shiver and released her hand. "Shut the door before you get a chill. I'll be in in a few minutes."

Ariel shut the door with a small clang. The cold draught of air that had come through the wood box had cleared the sleep from her brain, but one last, jaw-stretching yawn snuck up on her as she went into the kitchen. There she saw two thick steaks marinating on the counter and a loaf of her Italian bread defrosting beside them. Her stomach reminded her that she'd slept through lunch.

She pulled open the refrigerator to see what she might throw together for a salad and found one all ready in a wooden bowl on the glass shelf. He had been busy this afternoon.

She leaned over the door of the refrigerator, staring vacantly at the crisp green lettuce and red tomatoes. There was no possibility of his leaving now. She would have to accept his preparation of dinner tonight as the first gesture of the uneasy truce that was going to have to exist between them. She suspected that Rick Jones could, through some fancy legal finagling, force her into letting his brother remain in her house, but that wasn't why she would allow him to stay. She couldn't accept his deceit; she couldn't forgive him, but the sense of how truly alone she was against this unknown terror threatening her was overwhelming. She needed him.

The cold air pouring out of the refrigerator onto her stocking feet finally roused her from her daze. The door slammed shut with a little more force than was necessary.

Hunkering down before the cabinet under the sink, she looked inside. She could at least make the gesture of baking a couple of potatoes for their dinner. Her eyes skimmed over her pants, pulled tight over her left knee. A long, nasty scratch she hadn't even felt showed through a wide rent in the cloth. She must have acquired it during the wreck, or more likely in the mad scramble after it. At the same time she caught the nauseating smell of burnt upholstery and melted plastic trapped in her sweatshirt. Her nose pinched involuntarily to shut out the odor, but it was too late. Her brain registered both the sight and the smell, and her memory all to easily supplied the details.

Was it only this morning that her safe little world had been so ruthlessly destroyed along with her Blazer? But then, she had been living an illusion all along, for twenty-seven years. She'd been lucky to enjoy her illusions about life longer than most people did, certainly longer than Ryan Jones had. And his lessons had been much more painfully learned, and not at the hands of a tender lover.

It was past time she came out from between the covers of her books and acknowledged that life wasn't always neat and tidy with a "And they lived happily ever after" ending. It was messy, unpredictable and even ugly at times. Sometimes people disappointed you, especially the ones you loved the most.

She knew she was spending an inordinate amount of time sorting through the potatoes. Irrationally, she felt safe, crouched here on the floor, hiding where no one could see her. If only she could crawl into the little cupboard and pull the door shut after her. No one would find her. She could huddle in the dark like a little girl pulling the covers over her head until the bogeyman went away.

Strong, gentle hands closed around her arms, pulling her up against a warm, solid body. Ryan had come looking for her. She felt no surprise; her subconscious now recognized him automatically. Wordlessly he turned her, shutting her in the safety of his arms. She stood passively, letting him support her, her head pressed against the strong, even heartbeat under her ear. He nuzzled his chin into the silky hair at her temple, rocking her slowly in his arms. She shut her eyes, her brain registering and savoring the ordinary scents of fresh-cut wood, cold autumn air, Ryan.

At last he put her from him and stopped to pick two potatoes out of the sack. "If you're through playing with these," he commented lightly, "maybe we can bake a couple for dinner."

After dinner they each took books from her bookcase and kept up the pretense of reading for nearly two hours. Ryan felt her eyes on him, looking at him covertly, anxiously, many times. He had a pretty good idea what was worrying her. He raised his eyes from the twelfth page of the mystery he wasn't reading. She managed to shift her gaze back to her own book just before he caught her watching him.

"I think I'll go to bed," he announced, rising from the chair.

Ariel said nothing, merely nodding, keeping her head down, apparently too absorbed in her book to spare him even a glance. How on earth could she be wanting him to stay? The words to ask him were already in her throat. She swallowed them back.

She was still completely off balance, teetering between despair and disaster. Her anger with him was abiding and deep, smoldering inside her, but so was the desire she felt for him. She didn't have to try to recall last night; the memories came unbidden—those lean dark fingers on her virgin skin, stroking with unforgettable pleasure, his mouth hot and demanding, her mouth, her body, meeting his demands.

Her chin lifted, and she looked at him squarely. Maybe she couldn't help the desire, but she *could* control what she did about it, which would be nothing.

Ryan paused by her chair, looking briefly at the thin stern face meeting his gaze unflinchingly. He leaned down and brushed a light kiss over her set, beautiful mouth. He tasted a trace of desperation and felt the tiny quiver of her lips. He almost stayed.

If he could have honestly believed that they would share her bed in sleep only, he would have. Danger, as he well knew, was a powerful aphrodisiac, and the physical spark between them generated a desire that was incredibly strong. The near loss of her life today would only have distilled that desire, making it more potent and pure. Despite what she thought of him, her body was craving the release of his. He didn't want them to use each other for that kind of release and temporary gratification. She would wake up tomorrow despising herself and hating him even more.

"Good night, Miss Spence," he said softly.

She smiled back crookedly. "Good night, Mr. Jones."

Chapter 10

"What are you doing this morning?" Ryan leaned against the schoolhouse and watched Ariel feed kindling to a small fire fighting the wind for its life. It was trying to heat a cast-iron pot hanging from a rusty tripod. His nose wrinkled at the evil odor wafting in his direction. The rig looked and smelled exactly like a witch's cauldron.

"Making soap," she answered blandly. She glanced at him and sighed. The wind was teasing his hair into a black halo around his head. A fallen angel. She laughed grimly to herself. His eyes were squinted against the smoke, his hands stuffed into the pockets of the old bomber jacket. His tan pants were almost as scruffy as hers. As usual, he looked fantastic.

Shouldering himself away from the brick wall, he sauntered over to her. Holding his breath, he peered into the pot, though not too closely. He arched a black eyebrow and slanted her a look. "Of course. I should have guessed." A corner of his mouth kicked up in a sly offering. "I'll share mine if you're that desperate."

She gave him a long look before turning back to her pot. "I'm doing research."

The wind rolled an empty can with a large skull and crossbones and large red letters spelling out "LYE" under the log trailer. Ariel reached for the stout stick leaning against the trailer. Planting one fist on the hip of her paint-splattered jeans, she leaned as close as she dared to the kettle and stirred.

Ryan observed her stirring and scowling at the struggling fire, as if daring it to go out. Another gust of wind whipped her hair into her face and flapped the tails of the faded denim shirt she wore. He grinned to himself. She looked like a beautiful, down-and-out witch, with her hobo clothes and wild hair, trying to conjure up a powerful spell to change her luck. His smile dimmed. Maybe she could conjure one up for both of them.

After reading two of Felicia Fury's books, he could testify to the skill of her research and writing. Just as she had with the more interesting scene involving Ariel and Spence in the hot spring during the snowstorm, she infused even mundane happenings with extraordinarily vivid life. The love scene, naturally had come mainly from her imagination, but much of the rest was obviously the result of painstaking research and actual experience.

In one book the reader shared with the characters a pot of beans flavored with mesquite smoke and blowing gypsum grit. Ryan had tasted the smoky beans, felt his eyes grow red and scratchy, and chewed the sand in his teeth. The readers of *RangeFire* were apparently going to know the reality of having the linings of their noses cauterized by lye fumes.

Absently Ariel brushed the hair out of her eyes. Ryan tugged out the bandanna he'd shoved in his pants pockets earlier. He stood in front of her, taming her windblown hair with the red-and-black cloth. Reaching his arms over her shoulders, he knotted the scarf at the nape of her neck. His hands subtly cajoled her closer in a loose embrace.

"You look a bit tired this morning," he murmured, scanning her upturned face critically. Before she could respond his hands tightened across her back as his mouth covered hers.

Ariel froze; then the stirring stick dropped unnoticed as her arms locked around his slim hips. After the miserable night she'd spent, her coldly rational mind warring with her hotly unreasonable body, she needed this kiss. Perhaps it would be enough to satisfy the irrational cravings she was still trying to ignore.

When it ended she leaned on him, breathing deeply. "I didn't sleep very well last night," she muttered.

His chuckle was rich with rueful understanding. His decision to leave her last night hadn't been made out of any sense of chivalrous nobility. It had been purely selfish, as had been most of his decisions concerning her. He had wanted nothing, not even temporary pleasure, to ruin his chances for the permanent right to that soul-satisfying joy he'd found two nights ago . . . and the right to the woman he'd shared it with.

"Did you sleep well?" Ariel murmured. She used the excuse of needing a windbreaker to burrow under the open edges of his leather jacket and snuggle against his soft chamois shirt. The warmth of his body and his familiar scent dulled her resolve to stay out of his reach. It was so easy to believe she could do it when he wasn't around, and so hard to do when he was.

"Mmm." He bent his head, his warm mouth finding the wind-chilled skin under the collar of her old shirt and heating it.

He laughed soundlessly. He had slept lousily. At first light he had given sleep up as a lost cause and left his lonely bed to drink too much coffee and try to straighten out the convoluted case he was helping his partner with. Not long after he'd gotten up, he'd heard Ariel whistle softly for Murphy, who had been stretched out under the table with her nose on his foot. The dog had nudged the door open and trotted across the hall to accompany her mistress on her run. He became so absorbed in the case that he was only peripherally aware of their return an hour later. When he'd crossed the hall to use her phone, he'd been surprised to find her house empty. Looking through the back window, he'd seen her doing her "research."

With a deep sigh she began to untangle herself from his jacket and his arms. It was time to get back to work.

Ryan tucked an escaped strand of gold back under the bandanna and squeezed his arms around her in an exuberant bear hug before he released her.

Ariel started to stir yellowish lumps in the cauldron.

Ryan looked in warily at the foul-smelling mess. "What's that?"

"Fat. The butcher gave it to me. I melted it down and strained it last night." She leaned a little closer to check the consistency of the seething, dirty-white mess. Bessie had said it should be the consistency of butterscotch, whatever that meant. She'd never made butterscotch, either. "If I was really going to do this right, I should have made my own lye water by dripping rainwater through wood ashes," she commented absently. "This should be enough for authenticity, though."

"I should hope so," Ryan murmured dryly. He wondered if her readers appreciated what she went through to provide them with realism. The wind shifted. "It certainly smells authentic."

"I know," she agreed with a small laugh, her nose wrinkling. "Proctor and Gamble doesn't have to worry about competition from me."

Ariel kept stirring with her makeshift paddle, her face averted to avoid breathing the fumes. Suddenly the pot belched rudely and the boiling soap splattered over her hand. Ariel snatched it back, uttering a curse that would have guaranteed her a mouthful of soap as a child. She caught herself just before her scalded hand clapped itself over her astonished mouth.

Ryan threw back his head, roaring with appreciative laughter as he groped for the hose. He doused her hand with icy water. "You're learning, Ariel. Maybe I won't have to teach you too many words after all. That's a pretty good, all-purpose one." He chuckled approvingly.

Pulling her numbed hand out of the hose's spray, she tried to look both contrite and vexed, but only succeeded in laughing. "Oh, Lord," she groaned helplessly. "My mother would faint dead away if she ever heard me say that."

"Really?" Ryan asked interestedly, taking her hand to examine the reddened skin. "Why? Surely she'd heard it before."

"Not from any of her children," Ariel mumbled. "I have to finish making the soap. And you—" she gave him a stern look "—have to come up with an idea for all the firewood you won. They're coming for their trailer on Monday."

He gave her hand a final pet and released it. "You're okay, no burns." He turned and regarded his raffle prize balefully.

Ariel gingerly stirred her soap one last time and began setting out foil-lined cardboard flats. Very carefully she ladled out the liquid soap with a long-handled, blue enamel spoon. It had been Bessie's.

With the last of the soap cooling in the improvised molds, Ariel filled the kettle with clean water and drowned the fire. Glancing around to make sure she hadn't forgotten anything, she dusted off her hands in satisfaction, then looked over at Ryan. With his hands on his hips and his feet braced apart, he was still frowning at his logs.

What game was he playing this morning? He was acting as if everything was normal, maintaining the easy relationship that had been growing between them until she'd found him out yesterday morning. Did he honestly think she was going to go along with that?

He'd *lied* to her, for God's sake! Just like Dennis had, only Ryan's lies had been much crueller, because she hadn't been in love with Dennis. She hadn't felt this pain, hadn't realized with such humiliation what a fool she'd been. He must have been secretly laughing at her as she'd tearfully poured out the whole sordid little tale he already knew by heart.

She watched him rake his hand through his wind-tousled black hair, and her fingers unconsciously mirrored the motions, remembering the feel of those rough-silk strands. He shook his head at the wood and shifted his stance, his hands shoved now in the back pockets of his tan pants.

Her fury vanished as suddenly as it had come. No, he hadn't laughed at her; she knew that instinctively. And the lies had been gently not cruelly meant, intended not to harm her, but to keep her safe. If he had told her the truth when he'd come, she would have refunded his rent and cheerfully kicked him out. And she would have taken the candy to the rest home, then eaten a piece or two with Bessie and the other old people she loved. She would never have known the fearful, glorious wonder of falling in love with him.

But still he had lied.

Finally she stepped forward, slapped her palm on the butt of one of the lower logs and offered her suggestion. "Why don't you—"

There was an odd sound, like the distant rumbling of an avalanche. The next thing Ariel knew a body had slammed into her, tackling her and rolling them both under the log trailer.

With the sounds of wood splintering and smashing echoing and reechoing in her ears, she raised her head. The sight of Ryan's white, too-tight face above hers choked off her words. His mouth had thinned to a straight slash across his face, and his jaw was clenched. Ariel stopped struggling against the unintentionally cruel hands biting into her arms. She turned her head, following the direction of his cold, empty eyes.

The wind was already clearing the air of the dirt and wood dust that had been stirred up when the full load of logs had rolled off the trailer. Ariel felt the blood drain from her face and her body turn frigid. Anyone standing by the trailer would have been crushed, every bone in his—or her—body smashed.

Her voice startled her as she spoke at last. It was amazingly calm and matter-of-fact. "Another accident-that-wasn't?"

Ryan's head turned sluggishly, as if he was awakening from a drugged sleep. He looked down at her. She'd been wrong about his eyes; they weren't cold and empty at all. They were burning with an out-of-control rage.

The hands on her arms tightened until she thought the bones would splinter. She couldn't stop her small cry of pain. Anguish replaced the fury as his black eyes slowly traveled down her body, looking for the cause of her distress and stopping at his own white-knuckled hands.

A choked cry broke free from deep in Ryan's throat. It ended in a strangled laugh as he instantly relaxed his grip and rolled them onto their sides in the dirt. One hand slipped up to the back of her head, his long fingers sliding through her tangled hair to cradle her face against his shoulder.

"Oh, Ariel, I'm sorry." His harsh voice was unsteady. "I'm not much of a bodyguard if I save you from disaster, only to break both your arms." He buried his face in her throat, and Ariel could feel his warm, stuttering breath playing a ragged counterpoint to her skipping heart.

He shuddered once, and she wrapped her arms strongly around his body. She was strangely clearheaded and composed. It was as if, during the miserable night she'd spent, she had reached a silent understanding with her unknown killer. She accepted that he was going to continue his deadly game of attempted assassination, but he would have to accept that she was determined to survive until she succeeded in outwitting him and learned his identity. She was, admittedly, depending heavily on Ryan Jones's help.

"Ryan." There was a trace of unlikely laughter in her raspy voice. "I can't breathe."

Ryan's head lifted and he stared down at her, frowning. His eyes narrowed warily. He suspected she had slipped over the edge into hysteria. Not that he blamed her; he felt a little hysterical himself. Her wobbly smile was marginally reassuring as she pushed against him, silently asking for release. He let her go reluctantly. She began crawling on her belly toward the front of the trailer. He was right behind her when she stood up and brushed the dirt and wood chips from her clothes.

"How did he do it, do you think?" she asked, absently fending off Murphy, who had come over to sniff curiously at the fallen logs.

Ryan bent, groped under the trailer for a moment and pulled out a heavy chain. "Did you unhook this chain?" he asked almost idly. Mutely Ariel shook her head. "Neither did I."

Wordlessly they stared at the chain in his hand. It was the chain that the lumber man had shown them last Saturday. Simply open the spring hook, he had said, and the carefully balanced load would come tumbling down at a touch. Neither of them had unhooked it, and it couldn't have come unhooked accidently, yet the logs had come tumbling down at her touch.

"Very likely he was standing just a few feet away from us last Saturday, listening to everything the guy from the mill told us," Ryan said grimly. He tossed the chain down in frustration. It whipped into the rusty side of the trailer with an angry clank.

Ariel wrapped her arms around her chest to ward off the cold wind. "Well, at least this solved part of our problem about what to do with the wood."

He responded to her black humor with an obscenity hissed between his teeth. Then he turned at the light touch on his arm and looked down into her huge blue eyes.

"Ryan, thank you," she whispered.

He closed her carefully in his embrace. "That one was too close," he breathed into her ear, staring sightlessly across the orchard, seeing instead the slow shift of the logs and feeling again the terrifyingly leaden motion of his body as he tried to reach her before they did.

"Do you think he booby-trapped anything else?" Her words were whispered, but steady.

She really astounded him. The stricken look on her face when she'd first seen the avalanche of logs had told him that she understood the lethal reality of her situation quite well. Then her body had stiffened and her chin had lifted, and he had known that she had no intention of dissolving into a puddle of helpless hysteria.

There had been resolution, not resignation, on her grim face. She was every bit as strong and courageous as the heroines she created.

Turning her in his arms, her back against his chest, he rested his chin on her head. His arms were crossed tightly over her breasts as he surveyed the yard.

"I don't think so," he said slowly. "He didn't have that much time, and the brake job would have used most of it."

"Then I guess we wait until he pays another visit," Ariel answered tiredly after a minute.

"Maybe not. Rick had some interesting information yesterday afternoon when I called him." She let his arm curl loosely around her waist as they ambled toward the back door of the schoolhouse. "I called him while you were sleeping, but I didn't tell you, because I thought you'd had enough for one day."

"Yeah," she agreed softly as the door swung shut behind them.

A little while later Ariel pushed Ryan onto her sofa and sat on the edge of the chair opposite him. She looked at him with barely disguised impatience. "So what did Rick say yesterday?" They had cleaned up, eaten lunch, stuffed their turkey and put it in the oven to roast, but Ryan had yet to utter a word about his conversation with his brother.

"It bothered me from the beginning that a retired Los Angeles exterminator would go all the way to San Francisco just to shoot somebody at random. If that's all he'd had in mind, he'd have stayed home to do it."

Ariel prayed for patience. The Perry Mason in him was finally coming out. She'd suspected all along that beneath that controlled, cynical exterior there was a secret love of courtroom theatrics and playing to an audience. She'd had many glimpses already of his mischievous humor and carefully hidden almost boyish delight in pulling surprises. He was going to make her suffer through the opening statement and the presentation of exhibits *A*, *B*, etc as he built up to the surprise witness.

"Dennis's killer worked for his uncle back in New Jersey. Reilly was his enforcer, only his name wasn't Reilly then: it was O'Fallon. Rick did some checking on old man DiSanto's background in Newark and found the connection." He saw Ariel pale and tense, but she said nothing.

"Reilly, or O'Fallon, was an ex-cop who apparently decided that enforcing DiSanto's law was more lucrative than enforcing the city of Newark's. An old desk sergeant who's just about to retire remembered him, even had a picture. They were in the same police-training class. Rick says it may be thirty years old, but there's no doubt that Reilly and O'Fallon were the same man.

"DiSanto set him up in the exterminating business and then, as far as Rick can find out, there was little or no contact between the two men for the next twenty-five years."

Ariel understood the implication immediately, and she shook her head emphatically. "No, Ryan. Whatever else Mr. DiSanto may be guilty of, he did not have his old hitman kill his nephew. He loved Dennis very much."

"From what I've read of the reports, I'm inclined to agree with you, Ariel. I doubt that Reilly even knew who Dennis was. There was an almost obsessive loyalty between him and his old boss. He was the only one of his men that DiSanto brought out with him. I don't think Reilly would have knowingly harmed anyone DiSanto cared about."

Ryan shrugged. "Why Reilly took the job, I don't suppose we'll ever know. Maybe he was being blackmailed; maybe the offer was too good to refuse." He was silent, letting Ariel puzzle through this unexpected information.

Her dark gold eyebrows lifted as she stared at him distractedly. "Whoever hired Reilly obviously knew about his old life and connections. That almost guarantees he knew Mr. DiSanto, probably very well." Her hands chopped the air in helpless frustration. "But who is he? That report in my file showed that they've investigated everyone close to Dennis. Not just me, but Mr. DiSanto, Robert, his friends. There just weren't any leads, except—" her mouth twisted bitterly "—all that circumstantial evidence they're using against me."

"There's been a new lead," Ryan revealed quietly. "Do you ever remember hearing Dennis mention an Antonio Garza?"

Ariel thought hard, finally shaking her head. "Never. Who is he?"

"The man in the newspaper photo you wondered about, the man you saw in his office. Until his arrest two weeks ago he was the main distributor of cocaine in western Mexico. Apparently Dennis was his best customer, but Garza's not talking."

Ariel passed a hand over her eyes tiredly. "My God. No wonder he was so angry with Dennis for taking me with him on his trips to Mexico." She laughed mirthlessly. "And I thought he was worried about my safety."

"Have you ever ~~been~~ able to remember who the third man in the office that day was?"

She rubbed her forehead, shaking her head in frustration. "No. I've replayed that scene in my mind a hundred times." From the vacant look in her eyes he knew she was replaying the scene for the one hundred and first time. "I can see Dennis sitting behind his desk, Garza on his left, but the other man . . . ?" She sighed wearily. "Nothing." She stared at Ryan helplessly. "I can't even remember that he said anything."

"Maybe you won't let yourself remember," Ryan said thoughtfully. At the angry frown threatening to darken her face he explained himself quickly. "It might be too painful a shock if you remembered right now. Perhaps it was someone close to Dennis, someone you liked."

"I don't think there can be many more painful shocks for me after yesterday, do you, Ryan?" She laughed harshly.

Ryan returned her accusing gaze, his face revealing nothing of his thoughts. Ariel looked away first. *No, love, I don't,* he agreed silently. His elbows resting on his widespread knees, he bowed his head. He studied his clasped hands, which hung loosely between his knees. *If only we'd met under different circumstances,* he thought.

Ryan raised his head and stared at her, his eyes empty and bleak. *If only I could start fresh with you, love, no lies between us. If only—the two most useless words in the English language.*

Ariel was grimacing at the floor. She hadn't seen the look that had passed across Ryan's face. Consciously she relaxed and whispered to herself. "Whoever he is, maybe he's the one who's hired another killer for me."

Ryan's cool answer startled her. "I don't think he's hired anyone. A professional killing is generally very straightforward, something none of the attempts on you has been. They've been very amateurish, although fairly clever. I think he's after you himself."

Ariel's gaze sharpened on Ryan until he could almost feel it cutting through him. "You have a suspect, don't you?" she deduced, her voice devoid of emotion. "Who?"

Ryan matched her impassivity and raised it. "I don't want to tell you yet. It's someone you know rather well." He watched anger flush her cheeks, and her eyes acquired a hard glitter. His smooth words cut through her first, hot burst of anger. "If I do tell you, and I'm wrong, you'll have lowered your guard against the wrong person. I want you suspicious of everyone, it's your best chance of staying alive."

He hated telling the facts to her so cruelly, but he would hate losing her a thousand times more.

The cold brutality of his words shocked her into silence. The realization that the killer stalking her was someone she knew, most likely someone she trusted and liked, was devastating. A faceless, nameless murderer was hard enough to cope with, but the idea that it was probably someone she considered a friend made the situation all the more unbearable. She understood what Ryan was doing, but she almost wished he'd left her in ignorance. At least she could wrap ignorance around herself like a warm old sweater. Ryan had stripped it away, leaving her to face the cold, hard reality with no protection at all.

Her heart suddenly started racing, pumping icy blood through her body. Her courage faltered. Was he also warning her against himself, warning her not to trust him, either, not to expect too much? Maybe all he had to offer her was a few nights of passion.

Too agitated to sit still any longer, she leaped to her feet and began pacing the small area in front of the sofa. "This is such a tangle of mystery men, hidden motives..." She wheeled and faced him. "I feel as if when it's unraveled, all the loose ends will be neatly knotted into an obvious answer everyone's missed." She shivered suddenly in the toasty room. "I just hope I'm around to know the answer," she whispered softly, staring into the orange flames in the stove.

Ryan rose and gathered her carefully into his arms, ready for her resistance. There wasn't any. "You'll know the answer, Ariel, I guarantee it." He felt sick at heart. It was the first outright lie he had told her. He couldn't guarantee anything. He could only try with every skill learned in the old days and every ounce of intelligence he possessed to keep her alive.

She believed in him, though. At last she lifted her head from his shoulder and looked up into his hard face, her hand tightening on the back of his soft shirt. Her eyes were even more vulnerable than they'd been the morning when she'd found the file.

What then, Ryan? she wanted to ask. What about us? She felt a giggle bubbling up in her throat. Maybe she was getting hysterical. Why else would she be wanting to ask such an insane question? Hadn't she had enough misery over the past two days? Why would she intentionally lay herself wide open for more?

Certainly she was due the luxury of a little hysteria after all she'd been through. What a release it would be to scream, rant, cry, totally lose control. But she couldn't risk it. If she ever lost control she might never find it again.

Ariel gave herself a mental shake. She wasn't really close to hysteria. Last night she had been in her cold bed in the dark, alone, but not now. She was asking about her future with Ryan because the answer was as important to her as the identity of the killer.

The bitter pain growing inside her was becoming unbearable. What did they really have between them besides one night of passion and lies? Ariel cringed inside when she imagined just how many such nights Ryan had enjoyed. No doubt many, most of them much more enjoyable with much more practiced lovers. Only she had believed it had meant to him what it had to her. Certainly he hadn't had any foolish dreams based on one romp in the sack.

Maybe, when it was over and he left her, she would be lucky. Perhaps the memory of his lies would leave her enough self-righteous anger and pride to forget that night.

Ryan saw the questions in her eyes, but he wasn't ready to answer them. Instead he offered a curiously sexless kiss rife with boundless love and affection. He held her against him for a moment longer before he set her free.

"I'll carve the turkey if you'll get the rest of the dinner on the table," he said. The rest of the evening passed as had the night before, the wary truce continuing.

Something had obviously gone wrong—twice. There had been a wreck; she'd mentioned it when he'd called her on the phone for their monthly visit. But she'd walked away with only a scratch. Then she'd made a brief comment about a "peculiar" accident with a load of logs.

He'd finally remembered why the name and face of the man living with her had seemed familiar. Ryan Jones. He'd filed the

*name away in his memory a couple of years ago; in case he ever had
need of a good defense attorney. Jones was reputedly one of the
best. He laughed humorously to himself. Jones would hardly be
willing to defend the man who deprived him of his lover, although
he'd heard, if the price was right . . . and everyone had a price.*

*He toyed with the rolled playbill on his desk. It had seemed too
much of a coincidence that the assistant D.A. and her new "tenant" had the same last name, no matter how common. They had
been too careful with her, allowed too few people close to her. Still,
it had been a bit of a jolt to have it confirmed that they were indeed brothers.*

*Had Richard Jones sent his brother to watch over her? Was that
the reason his "accidents" hadn't worked? Could they be suspicious—of him?*

*He killed the thought as soon as it came. Not possible. He was
utterly confident that there was no way they could tie him to anything suspicious.*

*It was a pity the candy hadn't worked. The mail was so conve-
nient. Too bad he knew nothing about letter bombs. Unconsciously his nervous fingers unrolled the playbill and smoothed it
over the desk top. He wasn't free this weekend, but he was the next.
And, coincidentally, it was the start of the deer-hunting season in
western Montana. He knew about that the same way he'd known
about the apple festival and the old biddy in the nursing home who
she was fond of, from the occasional, chatty letters she sent him.*

*The annual fall rite would bring out plenty of hunters who would
be only too eager to shoot at anything that moved. They would be
along the river, waiting, where the deer liked to come for water in
the early morning, where she liked to run in the early mornings. He
would also be waiting. Who could know where a stray bullet had
come from.*

Chapter 11

"What are you going to do for transportation?" Ryan sat at Ariel's dining table, looking on as she attempted French toast. In a minute he was going to have to get up and save it from cremation.

"I guess I'll have to go dicker with the car dealers in Hamilton on Monday." She wrinkled her nose disgustedly, whether at the French toast or the unpleasant prospect of haggling with car salesmen, he wasn't sure. "The insurance adjuster says I should have a check within a week."

"Why not go today?" He rose from his chair and sauntered across the floor to stand by her. She had on a blue heather tweed suit with a navy silk shirt. It was obvious that she was going somewhere. He reached around her, his arm brushing the swell of her breast, to flip the toast. Unconsciously she leaned back into him. Even if he hadn't seen her wearing her running clothes earlier, he would have known she'd been out. Her cheeks had a healthy, outdoor rosiness, and he could smell the cold, crisp morning in the silky hair grazing his chin.

Abruptly she stiffened and stepped from between him and the stove. "I have to go to the monthly birthday luncheon at Bessie's rest home." She gave him a sidelong glance. "I was hoping I could borrow your truck." She left the sentence dangling.

"Will there be enough cake for one more at the party?" he inquired idly, concentrating on the French toast on the griddle.

"If not, you can have mine. The Valley View ladies would run me out of town if I didn't bring you," she informed him dryly. "My 'drop-dead handsome' boarder has been the main topic of conversation for two weeks." That too-rare, boyish grin lit his face, and her heart contracted.

Ariel was placing the last dirty plate in the dishwasher when Ryan walked back into her kitchen. She smiled approvingly at the gray herringbone sports coat, charcoal slacks and soft yellow open-necked shirt he'd changed into. The ladies would certainly be enthralled. She had seen him every day for two weeks, and she still was. But then, she sighed hopelessly, she would be even if she saw him every day until she was as old as Bessie.

She opened the refrigerator and pulled out a two-and-a-half gallon kerosene can. The fractional lift of his left eyebrow was his only comment.

"Research," she explained.

"Naturally."

"Also our contribution to the party," she added, laughing at the skeptical look he threw the blue metal can. He took the heavy container from her, noting the roughly cut circle that had been cut near the spout. The patch covering it had been sealed with a shiny ribbon of dribbled lead.

"Bessie and I made it a couple of months ago." Ariel whistled up Murphy and let her inside as they went out. Ryan shot her a despairing glare she didn't see and turned back to lock the dead bolt.

Ariel slid onto the truck's worn upholstery. She raised her voice over the growl of the engine. "When Bessie was a girl, her mother used to preserve fruit in empty kerosene cans. Every wash day they'd fill up the cans with the used wash water and rinse them until the kerosene smell was gone." She caught Ryan's faint look of distaste directed toward the can on the floor mat. "Don't worry," she reassured him in a grave aside, "this can never had dirty washwater in it.

"Anyway," she continued the history lesson, "in late summer they'd gather whatever wild fruit was around and pick any that was left on their trees and boil it together in a sugar syrup. Next, they'd pour it into the cans and seal them with lead. Then, if the cans didn't swell they'd have fruit all winter. Bessie said whenever they opened one, it was like opening a can full of summer.''

"Why did the cans swell?"

Ariel shrugged blithely. "Boiling didn't always kill all the bacteria, and sometimes the fruit spoiled."

"Did this can swell?"

Ariel laughed at the slightly ill look on his face. "No," she assured him sweetly, "it didn't. Bessie and I decided we'd open it this winter and do just like her family and their neighbors did—share it around with everyone." Her forehead wrinkled. "I wonder why she decided not to wait for winter?"

"What kind of fruit did you use?" he asked quickly. He didn't want her thinking about Bessie's reason. "Apples?"

"Hmm? Oh—peaches, wild plums, pears. No apples." She grinned at him, then made a face. "The pears were horrible. I had to peel them, and sticky juice ran down my arms. Ugh. And Bessie made me do all of them, too."

"You love Bessie very much, don't you?" He glanced away from the road to her, his eyes soft and a little sad.

"Yes, I do," she answered quietly. "Most people grow up knowing their grandmothers, maybe even one of their great-grandmothers. Mine were all gone before I was old enough to remember them." She smiled back at him a little mistily. "Bessie is like all my grandmothers and great-grandmothers in one."

His arm came around her hard, dragging her close for a quick hug before she could pull away.

As soon as they entered the gathering room at the rest home Ariel had to choke back a laugh. As if they were all connected to the same radar, Valley View's residents materialized as one. The ladies fluttered like elderly butterflies around the young, handsome *man*. The old men looked on, disgusted, until they could pull him aside to talk about really important things, like the memories of youth only another man could appreciate.

"He's a fine man." Bessie's voice behind her was like dry, dead leaves caught in a winter whirlwind.

"Yes, he is." Ariel knew Bessie was seeing more than the good-looking face and lean, graceful body. She wheeled her friend closer to the fire, lit at midday for this special occasion. Bessie had looked cold, huddled under the daffodil-yellow afghan the two of them had crocheted together this spring. Her usually neat hair was a wispy cloud around her head, and her eyes were dull and rheumy.

Ariel threw another of the home's carefully hoarded logs on the fire and suddenly knew what Ryan could do with his raffle prize. She looked across the room. Ryan was lounging on the sofa, apparently quite content to be Mr. Applebury's new audience for his long-winded rhapsodies about goose-hunting. Ryan had, of course, charmed all the old ladies and gentlemen in less than ten minutes.

The preserved fruit brought back so many childhood memories as it was spooned over angel-food cake that Ariel wished desperately for her tape recorder. She sat on the carpeted floor of the gathering room, surrounded by a dozen surrogate grandparents. All were intent upon sharing their reminiscenses with her, to be sure someone would carry them on to the next generation. Absently she noted Ryan taking Bessie back to her room.

It was another hour before she wandered down the east hallway to say goodbye. Bessie was already asleep, both her exquisite wedding-ring quilt and the yellow afghan covering her withered body. Ariel sat by her bed for a few minutes anyway, trying to organize the priceless memories her elderly friends had stored in her mind. Finally she rose, tucked the covers more firmly around Bessie and tiptoed out.

She went two doors down to visit with Mrs. Donner, who was recuperating from a broken hip. It had kept her from the party today, and Ariel knew she would be dying to hear whatever gossip Ariel might be able to spread.

Enid Donner was Bessie's first cousin and only a decade younger, but there was no family resemblance. Where Bessie was spare and tall, Enid was short and as plump as a comfortable, overstuffed chair. She dyed her hair a brilliant red that Bessie had confided tartly one day had *not* been her natural color when she was younger, even if she did tell everyone that. It was curled in an elaborate style popular thirty years before, but, curiously, it went with her remarkably smooth rose milk skin and sharp black eyes. Despite the impression she gave of being a vain and silly old lady, Ariel knew her to be as true an example of a real pioneer as Bessie. She also possessed an incredible motherlode of memories, one Ariel had mined for fascinating bits of treasure many times.

Ariel recounted the highlights of the party. Glancing down at Mrs. Donner's bedside table, she picked up an open paperback.

"Mrs. Donner, I'm surprised at you! Reading books like this." She laughed a bit uneasily. She'd never dreamed Mrs. Donner would read this book.

"Like what, dear?" Mrs. Donner seemed fascinated with something over Ariel's left shoulder.

Ariel held up the book, *StarFire*. The cover depicted a half-fainting, raven-haired woman in danger of losing her blouse. She was clasped in the muscled arm of a Western hero, his black Stetson pushed back on his curly, golden hair, his shirt unbuttoned halfway down his impossibly virile chest. His perfect white teeth flashed under a luxuriant mustache as he blazed away with a sixgun.

Mrs. Donner tore her gaze away from whatever she was finding so captivating and spared a glance for the book. "Oh, I just love Felicia Fury's books," she enthused. "They're so..."

"Trashy?" Ariel supplied.

Mrs. Donner flushed a delicate shade of rose. She reproved Ariel gently. "They may be a bit naughty, dear," Ariel barely kept a straight face at the eighty-six-year-old lady's choice of adjective, "but they are like a very exciting history book, too, full of so much detail, and very accurate." She sighed appreciatively. "The stories are really so good, full of action. The hero is always so handsome and always gets the beautiful girl."

"Yes," Ariel said knowing nearly deaf Mrs. Donner couldn't hear her dry murmur, "numerous times." Old ladies, she decided, had their dreams, too, or memories. There was an odd sound behind her, like a strangled snort, and she turned to look over her shoulder. Ryan was standing in the doorway, his hands in his pockets, enjoying her verbal footwork. He gave her a pleasantly innocuous smile, and she was instantly wary. She barely heard Mrs. Donner's next comment.

"But then, I don't have to tell you about her books, do I, dear? You must know her very well."

Ariel's head snapped around. "Why would you think I know Felicia Fury, Enid?" she asked, aghast. How was she going to get Ryan out of here within the next five seconds?

Mrs. Donner indicated the book Ariel still held in her hand. "Because in her newest book, the same thing happens to the heroine as happened to my sister on her wedding night." Ariel tossed *StarFire* back on the nightstand as if it had suddenly burst into flame. "She hears a pack mule braying and is sure it's a cougar. The hero has a hard time convincing her it isn't until he thinks of a way to make her forget about it entirely." The elderly lady's sly giggle was surprisingly girlish. "I know I'm the only one alive who remembers it, and I haven't told that story to anyone in years—except you." She gave Ariel a sharp look. "I hope she appreciates all the research you do for her, dear." She added hopefully, "Do you suppose you could get her autograph? She *is* my favorite author."

"I don't know her, Enid." She could feel the heat of dark eyes on her back. "I just do general research, and then the editor gives it to whoever needs it." Ariel scuttled to the door. She relented a little when she saw Enid Donner's profound disappointment. "If I ever meet her, though, I'll get it for you."

Mrs. Donner's happy smile returned. "Oh, would you, dear? I would be so pleased!"

Ariel smiled goodbye stiffly, then grabbed Ryan's arm and began dragging him down the hall. He hung back long enough to wave to Mrs. Donner, then let her lead him on. Casually he looped his arm around Ariel's shoulders, glancing down at her innocently. "I wonder if Felicia does appreciate all the hard work you do for her, dear."

"I wouldn't know, Ry," she said irritably. "Oh, look!" She skidded to a stop, grateful for anything to change the subject, even a terminal bore. "There's Mr. Caldwell! I need—"

"Another time, Ariel." His arm tightened implacably as he led her through a side exit to his truck.

They drove in silence for several minutes. His offhand question broke it. "Are you going to give her the autograph, Felicia?"

Ariel waited until she could breathe evenly again. "You think *I* write those . . . ?" She struggled for an adequate word.

"Louis L'Amours with sex?" he offered.

Pretty good, she silently congratulated him. She sounded properly affronted. "How could you think I—"

"I know, my dear Miss Fury." He parked the power wagon in the grocery-store lot. Draping his long arms over the steering wheel, he turned and grinned at her. "There was a mystery of your astoundingly large income for doing mere historical research." At her look of surprise, he confided, "My brother didn't see fit to tell me how you really made your money. I had to find out for myself."

She remained silent, waiting for the rest of his evidence.

"First there were those ten sexy books on the sixth shelf of your bookcase. Then—" he got out and walked around to open the door "—there's the matter of your name, your real name, which you just happened to use for the hero and heroine of your first book, *WildFire*." He headed her toward the store with a firm hand on her back. "You also left your computer on one day. I figured out the code on those sets of discs you have and . . ." He let his insufferably smug smile finish for him.

"Damn!" Ariel's fist bounced off the fender of the car they were passing. "I *knew* you'd be sneaking around someday when I left it on accidently." She sighed disgustedly, gave him a black look, then sighed again.

"How should I sign the autograph, do you think?" A grin flirted with her mouth. "Just 'All my love, Felicia'? Or 'To my dear friend, Enid, love from Felicia'?"

He pushed open the heavy glass door, and Ariel grabbed a cart, one with a wobbly, noisy wheel. He calmly took it away from her and exchanged it for a better one. "Oh, I think she deserves the full treatment, don't you?" He leaned over and whispered in her ear as they reached the frozen-food cases, "Don't worry. I won't betray your secret, Felicia." He turned her mouth to his and kissed it gently.

When they got back to the schoolhouse they unloaded their groceries, then parted company in the hall to put things away and change clothes. Ryan had agreed that Bessie and her friends should have some of his raffle prize, even suggesting that he and Ariel cut it up and deliver it.

The sky was a watery blue, partly overcast, and the pale sun gave little warmth. By the time Ariel got out to the backyard Ryan had already parked his pickup by the pile of logs and gotten her chain saw and ax out of the storage closet in the back hall. She slapped an old pair of gloves she'd scrounged up into his hand, pulled on her own and they got to work.

It was one of the happiest afternoons Ariel could remember, and she spent it doing nothing more exciting and exotic than cutting and stacking firewood. With a great deal of wonderful silliness as she tried to follow Ryan's contradictory directions, they managed to wrest the awkward, lightweight camper shell off his truck. Both of them had to put on heavy flannel shirts with their jeans and sneakers against the chill of the day, but as soon as they'd staggered over to the orchard fence to prop the shell against it, they stripped down to T-shirts.

Muscles that had been tight with tension for several days warmed and loosened. They traded off on the chain saw and ax several times, and the pile of split pine grew steadily. Despite the hard, physical work Ariel felt oddly relaxed. There were long silences between them, broken only by an impersonal word or two commenting on the work, but the silences were companionable, filled with quick, flashing grins and shared smiles when their eyes happened to meet. They made, she realized, a good team.

Turning the twenty-foot logs into fireplace-size chunks demanded strong muscles, but not much thought. The monotonous drone of the saw, the metronomelike thud of the ax and the smooth steady rhythm of her body as Ryan swung up chunk after chunk of wood, which she caught before turning to stack it neatly in the bed of his truck, seemed to clear the clutter in her mind.

Life is hard, Bessie was fond of saying, and then you die. Ariel had found she was giving a good deal more thought lately to dying than was usual. There was so much of life that she hadn't even experienced until Ryan Jones had come to rent her schoolhouse and spy on her, and then the experience had been much too brief to be satisfying. Even though she didn't plan on obliging her unknown killer by dying anytime soon, she didn't want to waste time, either.

She sat down on the roof of the cab, waiting for Ryan to split the last few logs to top off the load of firewood. He'd really seemed to enjoy the afternoon, maybe because it was such a novel way for him to pass a Saturday. She doubted that he spent many weekends in Malibu chopping wood, yet he'd been relaxed, his attitude carefree and happy. Ariel unknowingly echoed the grin he flashed up to her. It faded slowly as her expression grew thoughtful and a little sad.

The novelty of a small backwater town would soon wear off, though, or the mystery would be solved, and then he'd leave. Before he did Ariel wanted some more of that life she'd experienced all too briefly. The love that had been quietly growing for him, impossible as it seemed, refused to die, even though she knew she couldn't trust him any longer. Indeed, it still seemed to be growing.

There was a chemistry between them that was very rare; even she, with her paltry experience, knew that. Whether it was good or bad chemistry she couldn't predict, but she couldn't resist experimenting to find out. The reaction might produce a brilliant blinding flash, like Fourth of July fireworks that burst gloriously across the night sky, then died all too quickly, leaving her with a broken heart. Or it might produce what the ancient alchemists had dreamed of, solid gold, a love that would last.

Whatever the final result, Ariel was willing to risk it. She had no way of knowing how long they had together; she wanted all the experience, all the memories, she could have.

Ryan's imperious whistle brought her down to her feet just in time to catch the log he'd tossed her. The last few were piled on, and then he reached a hand to swing her down to the ground.

"I'm going to take this on over to the rest home. I'm sure I can find someone to help unload it and be back pretty quick. Why don't you—" he flicked a speck of sawdust off her nose "—take your shower and heat up some of that turkey chowder you made yesterday for dinner?"

Ariel nodded, and he bent to pluck the flannel shirt out of the wood chips, where she'd carelessly thrown it. He shook off most of the chips and held it out to her, but he didn't let go when she reached for it. Ariel looked at him questioningly.

"Build a fire in your bedroom, too," he suggested quietly. He'd seen the answer to his unasked question in her eyes. Tonight he was staying.

They lay close together in her bed in the bell tower, the first, impatient demands of passion satisfied. They were reluctant to sleep, wanting instead to savor for as long as possible the joy they'd found in the sanctuary of the tower. Here, for a few precious hours, the specters of death and suspicion and distrust were forbidden.

Ryan's hand tangled in her hair, weaving moonbeams through the gold, letting it fall over his chest like a silken blanket. "How did a virgin manage to write such good love scenes?"

She twisted over onto her stomach to give him an innocent look. "My mother always said I had an excellent imagination." Her finger traced lazy circles through the silky black hair around his navel.

He detained her wandering hand. "Why did you remain a virgin so long?" he asked curiously. "I'm not complaining, you understand—" he gave her a quick kiss "—but you certainly bucked the trend and, as beautiful as you are—" she was starting to shake her head when his mouth stopped her again, longer this time "—you must have had countless opportunities." He rolled them onto their sides, and an easy arm around her waist kept her close.

She shrugged off the question with a studied casualness. "My parents impressed on all us kids that sex wasn't a form of aerobic exercise, but a part of a very strong commitment to another person—a commitment to build a life together, maybe raise a family—and I just never wanted that with anyone."

"Marriage," Ryan murmured, watching her closely.

She gave him a quick glance, then looked away. "Yes." She was silent for a long moment; then he felt her release a long, quiet sigh. She continued in a matter-of-fact voice, "Then, too, I'm the oldest, so I had the responsibility of setting an example for my brothers and sisters.

"But maybe—" her hand unconsciously sought his as she smiled softly "—the greatest reason was seeing my parents' marriage, how devoted they still are to each other. Yet they've allowed each other to develop as individuals, too. I want that."

"So you planned to save yourself for your husband?"

"Certainly a ridiculously outdated notion." She dismissed it with a flip of her hand.

"No." He looked deep into her shadowed blue eyes. "A lovely notion."

Ariel swallowed, her throat suddenly dry, then managed to send him a look of pure devilment. "Of course," she added thoughtfully, "being the daughter of a minister in a very small town also might have helped."

He laughed in delighted surprise. "A preacher's kid. No wonder you didn't know how to cuss." He looked at her suspiciously. "But I thought the preacher's kids were always the wildest ones in town."

"I didn't know how to do a lot of things, Ryan Jones, until I met you," she retorted wryly. "And I was the most disgustingly sedate preacher's kid you ever saw until a little-old-lady writing professor convinced me that my future lay in racy novels." Ariel's grin was irresistible. "Even if she didn't think my first book was sexy enough."

Ryan's hand smoothed the bright fall of her hair. "Maybe they're too romantic for most men," he said resting her head on his shoulder as she laughed in rueful agreement, "but they are everything Mrs. Donner said. I can see why you've been so successful."

His lips brushed over the top of her head. "Your family doesn't know who you are, do they? That's why you give out that story about being a historical researcher."

She grimaced, picking at the white piping on her navy sheets. "I've always been afraid it would embarrass my parents if people knew their number-one daughter wrote sexy—" Ryan nipped her shoulder warningly "Okay, *historical* romances," she conceded. "Part of my college education was paid for by a scholarship from my father's church. The members raised the money with bake sales, church suppers, raffles. I never wanted them to know what I did with the education they helped pay for."

"You have nothing to be ashamed of, Ariel." A long forefinger trailed up her bare arm and across her milky shoulder to the hollow in her throat. "And I doubt your parents would be as embarrassed as you seem to think. Their values come through in your books quite clearly." He knew they were her values for all her blithe talk. Marriage, a man's and a woman's affirmation of faith in each other and a future together, was what all her heroines believed in. She did, too. He just wished he had her faith.

He nibbled up her throat to her ear. "Did Dennis know?"

She shied a little from the exquisite tickle of his warm breath. "Mmm-hmm. I had to tell him." She giggled. "He had this crazy idea I was somebody's mistress."

Ryan didn't laugh. He would have had the same crazy idea and hated it at least as much as DiSanto undoubtedly had. Sliding down in her bed, he pressed his arms around her to bring their bare bodies together. In the dead quiet of the house, they drifted off to sleep at last.

A hand had slipped between her knees and was sliding inexorably upward. "What are you doing?" she murmured sleepily. Sable lashes fluttered open, then closed again as she rubbed her cheek over the silky-crisp hair and warm flesh of his chest.

The dark velvet voice drawling in her ear sent shivers up her back. "I would think it's obvious."

Her body was soft and warm with sleep. With languorous deep kisses and slow hands he brought her to full wakefulness.

Ariel sat up and leaned over him, the sheet caught over her left shoulder. Ryan lay quietly, his hands still, to see what she would do. The midnight moon shone through the glass walls of the bell tower, silvering her blond hair and turning her skin to translucent white porcelain. The figure bending over him might have been a beautiful, cold and lifeless statue, but the fingers brushing through the hair down to the smooth skin of his chest were warmly alive. They hesitated, then caressed lightly over his nipples, making his breath catch in his chest. He looked into her face, illuminated by the pearly cataract of light.

Her expression was intent as he allowed her to satisfy her curiosity about his body. His right hand reached up and idly brushed aside the sheet. It floated to her waist, revealing her breasts, moon frosted white skin and dark, mysterious centers. A slow, seductive smile curved her mouth. She trailed one set of fingertips over the sensitive skin of his abdomen.

"What are *you* doing?" He grinned lazily. His hand slid around the back of her neck to bring that giving, wonderfully sensual mouth closer.

She resisted, one raised eyebrow expressing her sly surprise. "Exploring. I would have thought it was obvious." Her instinctively clever fingers teased his navel, then moved lower over his twitching skin.

He inhaled sharply and felt the sharp claws of desire deep in his belly. "Two," he breathed, "can cover more territory." His free hand glided up her back, bending her to him as he arched up. The top of his tongue touched her breast.

Ariel felt her stomach clench with anticipation as her body began to change, heating, softening, opening. Her breathing deepened and slowed, as did the movements of her hand.

Ryan's lips closed around her nipple. He suckled gently, letting her unique taste seep slowly through him. Her wordless murmur of pleasure was echoed by his, as his lips and tongue and her hand fell into the same rhythm, languid and soul deep. Her head lolled back as Ariel arched nearer to his delight-giving mouth. His hips shifted, telegraphing his need for more of her touch.

But their caresses became too exquisite, crossing the line between excrutiating pleasure and pain. The bed shifted as Ryan pulled himself up. The iron grasp of his hand on her wrist stopped her poignant torture of him. She felt the stroking of his strong fingers through her hair as he cradled her head a breath away from his. "Ah, witch, I want this to last," he whispered hoarsely as he took her mouth.

She wanted it to last, too, but with the first delicate probing of his tongue, she knew it was too late for leisurely pleasuring. Her hand captured his jaw, and she returned his kiss with a furious urgency, telling him how great was her hunger, her need, her love.

Ryan groaned deep in his chest, rising above her. Ariel's head fell back deepening their kiss. Her hand was freed as his other arm slid around her waist. His hard body and avid mouth forced her slow, backward fall onto the tangled sheets. His hand explored her hip and thigh, back up the soft inner flesh, teasing at the top, then moving to clamp her arching hips to the bed, holding her still as his mouth worked down deliciously from her breast. He could feel the headlong race of her heart falter, then pound even faster. His tongue flicked over the quivering skin of her stomach like a liquid flame, burning intricate patterns, lower and lower.

The anticipation of its ultimate destination became a maddening torment. When his searching mouth at last touched the heated core of her, madness overcame her.

Ariel's hands clawed at his back, digging into his tight muscles urging him over her. Ryan heard her incoherent cry, then his name on the breath that shuddered from her body as he drove her to the first peak. He thrilled to that cry, determined to drive her higher yet. He was greedy for the dark, sweet taste of her, high on the power he felt as he relentlessly controlled her mindless body with his.

Ariel was beyond pleading with him to take her. Speech was no longer possible. The most primitive need to fill the sweetly aching void inside her ruled her. With a sudden surge of impossible energy, her slender hands locked over his shoulders and wrenched his heavier, stronger body up hers. Her trembling thighs tightened around his hips, demanding that he satisfy the need he had created.

Ryan's ruthless command over his own need was destroyed. "Next time," he groaned against her arched throat. "We'll make it last next time." He thrust into the moist heat that was so ready for him. Gritting his teeth, he held himself still above her, denying his body's insistent demands that he enjoy the deep, pulsing pleasures immediately. "Ariel, look at me," he rasped.

Midnight-blue eyes, hazed with passion, opened to see his own eyes glowing fiercely above her.

"We belong together now," he said almost violently. "Do you understand, Ariel? Nothing," his voice was harsh with passion as his body began to move, emphasizing the truth of each word, "nothing is going to take you away from me."

"Or you from me." Her eyes closed as she began to move with him.

The fierce exhilaration that surged through him at her words swept away his control. He joined her straining reach for the apex of perfect pleasure. They found it together with a brilliant burst of heart-shattering joy that banished, for a time, the dark shadow lengthening over them.

Ryan lay on his back, utterly relaxed, totally sated. He could, he thought, happily spend the rest of his life here, like this. He tried to fight off the sleep that had claimed Ariel almost immediately. What greater contentment could there possibly be, he wondered, than to lie in this fantastically comfortable bed, holding your woman, soft and warmed from loving, asleep in your arms as you gazed up at the beautiful diamond stars glittering in the black velvet sky? His eyes closed on a sigh of pure pleasure as one of the beautiful stars fell to its death across the inky night.

Chapter 12

Ariel was dreaming that the telephone was ringing. She hoped someone would answer it soon, because she certainly wasn't about to, not when it meant leaving a warm bed and the even warmer body curled around hers. She dreamed on, not hearing softly growled curses when bare feet hit a cold floor and colder air hit a bare body. She woke up only when she realized that, while the bed was still warm, the body was gone.

She threw off the quilt and danced naked over the icy floorboards until she found her fleece slippers behind the mirror. Her teeth were chattering by the time she shivered into the pink nightshirt she grabbed off the back of the closet door and tried to button up the countless tiny buttons with stiff fingers.

She reached the bottom step in time to hear Ryan's quietly despairing curse. He was leaning against her desk, running a hand through his rumpled black hair distractedly as he listened to whoever was on the other end of the phone. His eyes had closed in an angry scowl before he could see her, and he rubbed the bridge of his nose absently. He'd slipped on only his jeans, zipping but not buttoning them. His ankles were crossed, his long bare toes curled against the cold floor. The skin on his belly and shoulders was roughed into gooseflesh, yet he seemed oblivious to the cold, concentrating only on the obviously bad news coming from the other end of the phone line. Ariel felt a chill that had nothing to do with the lack of heat in the house.

To give him privacy she slipped out into the hall and opened the front door a crack. Sometimes the neighbor at the end of the lane brought by the Sunday paper from Missoula and left it on her doorstep. Ariel stooped down and picked up the paper and a package that had apparently been left in his mailbox by mistake.

Ryan was still on the phone when she came back in. With his back to her, he didn't see her as she set the paper and package on her desk and moved toward the kitchen. When she turned on the water to fill her coffee maker he heard her and turned, his eyes tracking her automatically as she moved quietly around the room.

"No!" he shouted forcefully. "Don't worry about that, I said. There's no way in hell he can do that. I'll file a writ of endangerment so fast it'll make his head spin." He paused. "No, I'll come up with something and leave as soon as I can." He spoke for another minute or two, then hung up.

He shivered violently. "God, it's cold in here!" Ariel was in the living room kneeling before the stove, laying in kindling. As he crossed to her, he gathered up the rainbow afghan she had thrown over the back of the couch. He crouched behind her, draping the afghan over his shoulders and then wrapping it around her as his arms crossed over her breasts.

"What did we do, forget to stoke the stoves again when we went to bed?" He chuckled, burrowing his cold nose into the warm curve of her shoulder.

There was no humor in the tension she felt radiating into her back from his taut body, and there had been none in that phone call. "Yes," she murmured, striking a match and swinging the door shut. She turned in his arms, and her fingers whisked the tousled black hair off his forehead. "Who was on the phone, Ry?"

"You can keep this nightshirt," he murmured, his gaze wandering down the front of the soft pink material to the shirttail brushing the carpet behind her. His darkening eyes ticked off the Victorian ruching high around her neck, the fuzzy smocking over her breasts and the tiny shell buttons marching primly from her neck to her knees. "I can have such fantasies while I'm undoing all these buttons," he growled against her throat.

He arched her tightly to him under the afghan, his hands rubbing leisurely up her back. Ariel was caught between his thighs as his hands ran back to her hips, securing her warmly in the saddle of his. His strong fingers flexed, and an involuntary moan escaped her as he pressed her closer to his hard warmth. One hand slipped around and up to the first button of her shirt.

Ariel caught the hand at her throat. She kissed his fingers quickly, then cradled them to her breast. As she sat back on her heels the afghan slid off their shoulders. With the fire's heat, neither noticed. "What's wrong, Ry? Please tell me." Her worried blue eyes, huge in her pale face, searched his. They were shuttered once again, revealing nothing.

A muscle in Ryan's cheek twitched; then he sagged back on his heels. He brought up his other hand and laced their fingers together tightly. Was there no end to the lies he had to keep telling her? When would things finally be open and honest between them?

"There's trouble with that case I've been helping my partner with. He wants me to come back right away and help him out."

Ariel controlled her voice carefully to keep the ridiculous panic she was beginning to feel out of it. "You have to leave? Today?"

He nodded. "The trial resumes tomorrow." His tone became very casual. "Too bad you can't come with me, but you'll be safer here, of course."

Ariel's shock was showing clearly in her face, and he felt it in her suddenly icy hands. Unconsciously he began to chafe some warmth into her freezing fingers.

"I would be safe with you. Whoever's after me wouldn't know where I was," she suggested hesitantly in a whisper he could barely hear.

"If you change the routine you've had for so long, he's liable to be scared off. It may be months before he thinks it's safe to try again." His voice was so damned reasonable that she wanted to scream. "And you'll have to wait those months." *And so will I,* he added silently. "Don't you want it over with, so you can get on with your life?" *A life we might share.*

She said nothing, just stared at him as if not really seeing him.

"Don't worry; you'll be fine here. I'll let the chief know I'm leaving. There won't be any problems while I'm gone, I'm sure." Who was he trying to convince, he wondered, Ariel or himself? "Just keep the home fires burning till I get back."

As soon as the flip words left his mouth, he knew it had been the wrong time for a lousy joke. She was stiff and cold in his arms.

"This isn't your home, Ryan," she pointed out expressionlessly, "and I'm not your wife."

He answered her very softly. "I know where my home is, Ariel, and what you aren't." He dropped her hands and stood up slowly, like a tired old man. "I have to call the airline."

Ryan walked back to the phone, and Ariel went back into the kitchen as if she were sleepwalking through a bad dream. Automatically she poured two mugs of coffee, adding exactly the amount of milk Ryan liked to one. So, the novelty had worn off sooner than she'd thought it would. Her harsh laugh turned into a sob, and she almost choked on the gulp of coffee she took.

The case was just a flimsy excuse to leave. She could see through his lie as clearly as if it were glass. He just didn't care about her as much as she did about him. How could he? If he did, he couldn't leave now, when she needed him so badly. Didn't he understand that even with a whole army division surrounding the schoolhouse to keep her safe, she wouldn't *feel* safe unless he was inside it with her?

She glanced at him as he hung up the phone without speaking and walked toward her, his face unreadable. Maybe he did understand; he just didn't care.

"The line was busy," he said as he picked up his coffee.

"That's too bad. I'm sure you'll get through in a minute," she said tonelessly, calmly sipping her coffee.

She didn't notice how badly her hand was shaking, he realized. The scalding coffee sloshed onto her wrist, and she didn't even seem to feel it. God, what an impossible position his brother had put him in. Did he leave her in ignorance, sure he was lying to her again and hating him for it, or did he tell her the truth? Davidson wanted her back in San Francisco to make the bait more accessible...and to ask her why a Bahamian bank had sent a letter to her house telling her that she was now the owner of an account with over half a million dollars in it.

Rick felt they were close to the real murderer now; there was no need to expose Ariel to any more danger. If someone could just hold off Davidson for a week or so... And who better than Ariel's new attorney, Ryan Jones—who just happened to have an appointment at nine-thirty tomorrow morning to discuss his client's not very-protective custody? Rick's machinations were peculiar indeed for a man who had professed to believe Ariel was as guilty as his boss did.

The hard bitter lines Ariel hadn't seen for days were back in Ryan's face. "It shouldn't take more than a few days to wrap everything up, and then I'll be back."

Her face lit with a curiously wistful smile for a moment before the mask of utter impassivity slid back into place. "Of course you will."

Ryan's mug slammed down onto the table. Ariel jumped at the sudden violence in his action. Milky coffee began seeping from the crack in the bottom of the mug. His temper was at the flashpoint. The quiet desperation in her eyes and the frigidly dignified words were threatening to crack his control like angry screaming never could have.

He turned his back to her and stared sightlessly through the window over the sink. If he had to look at her, his control would break completely.

The heavy silence in the kitchen was darkening the sunlit room. Ariel sighed shudderingly, and fierce arms closed roughly around her. She turned, giving herself up to the temporary luxury of his protective embrace.

His words whispered over the bare skin of her neck, melting a little of the fear icing her heart. "Please try to understand, Ariel. It just isn't safe for you to go."

His arms cradled her tenderly, when what he wanted was to crush her to him and hold her forever where he knew she would be safe. His fear at leaving her alone, unprotected, was ripping him apart. They stood in each other's arms for a long, silent moment.

The phone lines into the Missoula airport seemed to be permanently busy, and Ryan finally went across the hall to dress and pack. He reappeared in a navy pin-stripe suit, the jacket hooked over his shoulder, carrying one suitcase. Ariel was just putting their breakfast on the table. She had managed bacon and toast and a perfect omelet that Murphy ended up eating. They made careful small talk that completely avoided what was uppermost in each of their minds.

Unable to sit still any longer, Ariel shoved back her chair and left the table. Remembering the package she'd found on her doorstep, she sat again, this time in the swivel chair at her desk. She pulled the package onto her lap and glanced at the postmark, then began to tear off the brown wrapping paper.

The package was jerked rudely out of her hands. "Where the hell did this come from?" Ryan demanded furiously. He turned the parcel over gingerly, examining all sides carefully.

"It was on the front step this morning. It must have been delivered to Mr. Hanson by mistake, and he brought it by with the paper." She calmly grabbed it away from Ryan and proceeded with her unwrapping.

Ryan jerked it away again and held it up over his head, out of her reach. "Who's it from?"

"My mother," she said evenly. "Ryan, I am not going to wrestle you for it. Now hand it over."

He lowered the box, but didn't give it to her. He walked into the kitchen very carefully, set the box on the counter gently and began filling the kitchen sink with water. Out of the corner of his eye he saw Ariel reaching for the package.

"Do not touch that package, Ariel." His voice was low and dangerous.

"Ryan, I don't know what you think you're doing, but this is from my mother and—"

"Uh-huh, and you thought the poisoned candy was from two lovesick high school boys, too," he reminded her.

He started to lower the parcel toward the water-filled sink with one hand.

Ariel hissed in frustration, her eyes widening with disbelief. With both hands she seized his wrist, staying the package inches above the water. She forced herself to speak calmly. "Ryan, the postmark on the package is Weaverville, where my parents live. That's why you were suspicious of the candy, wasn't it—the postmark wasn't from anywhere in Montana?"

Ryan nodded, but didn't release the package.

Ariel nodded in return. "That's what I finally figured out. John, the postmaster, knows everyone in Weaverville, and he knows me. No stranger could mail a package to me without him remembering it. I don't think the killer would be that stupid."

Ryan stared hard at the box in his hand, as if trying to see through the brown paper, and finally handed it over.

Ariel sat down at her desk and returned to her unwrapping. "Why were you going to put it in the water?" she asked curiously.

"I thought it might be a bomb," he answered matter-of-factly. "Water would ruin the detonating mechanism, but not any fingerprints. I'd have called the state police to disarm it."

Ariel blanched. The funny incident was suddenly not so funny. The last bit of wrapping paper tore free and out tumbled eight copies of *RimFire*, Felicia Fury's latest romance, available in bookstores and supermarkets everywhere.

With numb fingers and a feeling of dread, Ariel reached reluctantly for the note on her mother's blue stationery that had fallen out with the paperbacks.

"What does she say?" Ryan asked interestedly, trying to read the note over her shoulder. It was a short one.

Ariel looked at him dazedly over her shoulder. "She says..." Her voice came out in a squeak, and she tried again. "She says she would like me to autograph these, one for her and the rest for her friends." Ariel had to stop to clear her throat. "She mentions that she was suspicious about Felicia Fury's identity with the last two books, but knew for sure with this one. She recognized the heroine's two little boys as my brothers. She wants to borrow my copies of the other books to read; she can't find any in the used bookstore." Ariel looked at him, shaking her head slowly. "I didn't even know my mother read books like mine," she whispered, shocked.

Ryan threw back his head, laughing at her astonishment. Sheepishly, Ariel joined in, and for a few moments the room was filled with laughter. Then their eyes met, and their laughter abruptly died. Ryan's suspicions about the very real possibility of a bomb and his imminent departure killed it very effectively. A pall of depression settled over her.

Wearily she bent to gather up the books. She supposed she was really very lucky. For some reason she was sure that the idea of a bomb had occurred to the killer. Fortunately for her, he apparently lacked the knowledge to make one.

The phone rang once more, and Ryan answered it. Ariel could tell by Ryan's end of the conversation that it was Chief Dye. Too upset to wonder how he'd known Ryan was leaving, she climbed the stairs to dress while he and Ryan discussed the least useless ways of keeping her safe.

She came out of her bathroom, still in her nightshirt, to find him standing by the bed, unbuttoning the cuff of his ivory, satin striped shirt. It was already hanging open, pulled free of his slacks.

"My plane doesn't leave until two o'clock," he said huskily. His fingers reached for the first small button at the neck of her nightshirt.

The fresh fire she'd built in the blue enamel stove was already heating the room. The curtains filtering the midmorning sunshine gave it a dusky gold light. The air was warm and thick with an almost tangible sensuality.

Ariel had been disconcerted by her body's sudden addiction to Ryan's, even a little embarrassed. Suddenly it became even more pervasive, as if her body realized that the fix it needed to get through the long days and longer nights was about to be provided.

They took the time to savor each nuance of taste and texture and response. Hands and mouths that could have been rough and demanding were gentle and coaxing. Pleasure that could have been rushed and desperate was unhurried and relaxed, drawn out to the fullest before a new pleasure was discovered and totally explored.

Ryan undid the tiny pink buttons, lingering over each new bit of soft flesh that was exposed to his fingers and eager mouth. As he sank to his knees her finger twined through the heavy blue-black silk of his hair. Her head fell back, and her stance unconsciously widened. When the pleasure of his agile, searching tongue became too delicious, she urged him up. His trip back up her body was leisurely. As he straightened fully, her nightshirt floated to the floor like a pink cloud.

Ariel took her turn to undress him. His shoes and socks were gone already. She took off his shirt and draped it carefully over a chair. The silky-crisp hair of his chest and belly slid between her cool, slender fingers as they followed the dark path narrowing down to his belt. Her body drifted down along his until her knees touched the worn rag rug. Her nimble hands unbuckled his belt, drawing it slowly from around his waist. She savored the little quiver of pleasure rippling through his muscles as she unhooked his slacks and slid them down his lean flanks. A touch on the back of his ankles and he stepped out of them gracefully. She folded them precisely and laid them across the seat of the chair.

She reached back up, and her hands slipped inside his briefs, dragging them free. She let her palms glide first down the warm satin skin of his hips, then enjoying the change as they caressed the hair roughened skin of his thighs and calves. He kicked his briefs free, and her fingertips brushed back up his legs.

Ryan breathed her name into the still, warm air. "Ariel. Oh, sweet, love." His hands seized her shoulders tenderly and she slithered up his body. He twisted unexpectedly and guided her gentle fall to the bed.

The room was peaceful, filled with the quiet sounds of their accelerating breathing, small sighs, bodies subtly shifting on crisp sheets, the faint hiss and crackle of the fire. The light fragrance of his citrus after-shave and her spring flowers-summer sunshine cologne mingled with earthier, natural scents.

His stroking hands wove an invisible web of desire over her body. His mouth grazed, licked and tugged, breathed hot whispers over her skin. The slow, delicious slide of his calloused palm over her hip and down her smooth leg sent cool shivers through her that melted into a shimmering pool between her thighs.

She wanted to give pleasure as well as take it. Rising up on one elbow, she splayed her hand across his chest and slowly pressed him back on the bed. The balance of power shifted to her as she leaned down to kiss him. Her lips traveled across his mouth, her teeth nibbling delicately at his bottom lip, inviting that beautiful, hard mouth to play. His lips softened and bonded to hers in a kiss that scintillated through her blood like burning gunpowder. Lazily they took turns taking the kiss deeper. Her lips wandered to the sensitive hollow of his shoulder, and a hot spark skidded down his spine. Then her mouth journeyed lower, following her adept hands. Her tongue tarried at the hardened brown nub of his nipple, then dipped into his navel. He tangled his hands into the sheet to allow her freedom to pleasure him . . . and herself.

The top of her silky head brushed the twitching flesh of his belly as she shifted between his thighs. Her warm tongue rasped languorously, sampling forbidden flavors, salty-sweet, tangy. His body slowly arched off the bed like a bow drawn back by a powerful archer, his head twisting sinuously on the pillow.

Her low laugh whispered over him. His fingers buried themselves in the golden floss of her hair and dragged her head up to his.

Her smile was primitively satisfied as she watched him lose control.

Suddenly she was on her back, pinned by the muscled thigh pushing imperiously between hers. The raw hunger in his face and the ruthlessness in his movements might have frightened her. Instead they exhilarated her, filling her with an exultant power that she could make this cool, self-contained man burn for her as he made her burn for him. She absorbed the shock of the primal joining of his body with hers, touched with a trace of savagery. Then the long, silken friction began, and she could think no more.

Their bodies flushed and totally spent, they drifted together in a golden haze. At last they were forced to rise reluctantly and dress, interrupting each other a time or two to wordlessly caress and kiss.

The two-hour drive to Missoula was quiet, each of them busy with private thoughts. In the parking lot of the airport Ryan showed Ariel how to lock the front wheel hubs and shift the balky transmission into four-wheel drive. It had been decided that Ariel would use his power wagon while he was gone.

At the boarding gate he prayed that she could control the tears that had filled her eyes and were threatening to spill over. If she cried, no force on earth would get him to leave her behind. Deliberately he riled her out of her tears.

"Four things," he said imperiously. His long fingers ticked them off in front of her nose. "One—keep the dead bolt locked at all times, even when you're home. Two—keep the pickup locked in the garage when you're not using it. Three—keep your lead foot off the gas pedal of my truck."

Ariel made a rude face and the tears receded. When he paused, she asked dutifully. "What's number four?"

His voice was low and fierce. "I'm coming back!" He wished he could be sure she believed him.

They exchanged a brief kiss as he held at bay his heartsickening fear and worry at leaving her. There was so much he wanted, needed, to say, but this wasn't the place, and the time wasn't right. Would it ever be? Gently disengaging the hands clinging around his neck, he held them bruisingly for a moment. When her hands were free Ariel clasped them tightly behind her back to keep her arms from winding around him again.

"I'll call you every day," he whispered. "Here are a couple of numbers where you can reach me if you need me." He stuffed a scrap of paper into her jacket pocket.

His thumb lingered over her cheek, as if trying to memorize it softness one last time. Then he was striding away from the frost-pitted concrete toward a red-and-white jet.

The trip up to the airport hadn't seemed as long as the one home. She dashed the foolish tears from her eyes as the feeling of abandonment finally swamped her. Of course he was coming back. Her grim laugh echoed in the truck cab. He had to get his precious truck, didn't he?

Watching him cross the runway had made her realize what an illusion their life together during the past two weeks had really been. He was going back to his real life, where beautiful navy blue silk and wool pin-striped suits, perfect tone-on-tone ivory shirts and burgundy satin ties were the standard dress, not old jeans and flannel shirts. Reality wasn't scuffed leather sneakers, a ninety-year-old schoolhouse in the boondocks of Montana, sitting around at night watching old movies on TV, fishing, splitting firewood or messing around in the kitchen fixing dinner.

Reality was scuffless black Italian shoes with elegantly smooth wing-tips, a house on the beach in Malibu, fancy restaurants, beautiful women, and the excitement of the courtroom. *That,* she reminded herself viciously, was his real world, a world in which he might decide she had no place.

She pulled down the garage door and let herself into her cold house. Murphy looked past her expectantly, then whined questioningly when she saw that Ariel was alone. "He'll be back soon, girl," Ariel assured the dog with a cheerfulness she didn't feel.

She awoke much too early the next morning with a familiar ache in the small of her back and the sudden awareness that she had been appallingly irresponsible. Unaccountably, the ache also made her a little sad. She forced aside the unbidden mental vision of a small scamp with a rascally grin and blue-black hair.

Ryan was accustomed, of course, to women who handled the modern little social niceties like pregnancy prevention themselves. Yet he had certainly known she was neither sophisticated enough nor experienced enough not to have committed the ultimate faux pas by becoming accidently pregnant. She'd never even given it a thought. And she knew quite well that he had done nothing to prevent it, either. It seemed a very odd oversight; Ryan Jones was hardly the sort of man to have "accidents" like that.

The trip to the doctor's office and the little town pharmacy wasn't as mortifying as she had feared. Despite her flawless impersonation of a red-faced, mumbling teenager, the prescription was written out routinely and filled without comment. There were no knowing smirks or raised eyebrows, no pointing fingers or outraged whispers.

Congratulations, Ariel she told herself dryly. At last you're a part of the sexual revolution. A three-months' supply of white dots assuring worry-free, socially acceptable and responsible *fun* is tucked in your purse.

Suddenly her free, helpless laughter filled the cab of the truck. Listen to you! she chided herself. You sound like a self-righteous old maid eating sour grapes.

She was irrevocably in love with this man. He was the one she had waited twenty-seven years to share herself with. And she had enjoyed every glorious minute of it. Whatever happened, she knew she would never regret her decision.

Maybe it wasn't particularly rational to fall in love with a stranger, but she really hadn't been given any choice in the matter. She *had* a choice of whether she would act on that love, and she had made her choice freely, joyfully. She wasn't naively confident that they would live happily ever after together. Her choice could have a very high price, but she was willing to pay it. She suspected that even if she lived as long as Bessie, loving Ryan Jones would be the greatest adventure of her life.

The second greatest was going to be staying alive. She wasn't naive about that, either. She was all too aware of her vulnerability. She was inclined to agree with what Ryan had told her and Ted Dye believed: that whoever wanted her dead had made only one lightning personal appearance so far. He'd set up his delayed strikes then left as suddenly as he had come. Strangers in the valley were always noticed. Only during some event that drew an out-of-town crowd, like the apple festival, would he be able to enjoy anonymity. The next logical time for him to strike was the coming weekend, when deer-hunting season opened and the town would again be full of strangers, drawn by the valley's large deer population. Still, she would take no unnecessary chances.

By Monday evening, only one day after Ryan's departure, she was already a little stir-crazy, Following one of Ryan's forceful "suggestions," she had locked herself inside the schoolhouse after coming home from town. She had baked pumpernickle and made turkey noodle soup that she wasn't hungry enough to eat, then worked on *RangeFire*. As the day had worn on the ache in her back had disappeared, but its vague echo seemed to be lingering near her heart. And Murphy kept looking at her accusingly, as if asking her what nastiness she had done to make Ryan leave.

She found herself reaching again into the tissue box on top of her desk. It was dumb to cry over a book, especially one of your own. And she was about to commit the unpardonable sin of writing a romance with an unhappy ending. No matter how she tried, she couldn't seem to get Luke and Drucilla to resolve their differences. Luke was about to ride off into the sunset—alone. James, her editor, would have heart failure, and she wouldn't make a dime.

She switched off the word processor, not bothering to save what she'd just spent two and a half hours writing. She stood, hugging her arms around herself. Damn, why was she still cold? Maybe she was coming down with something. She'd put on the green wool pants and cream fisherman's knit sweater she wore on the most frigid winter days and built up the fire an hour ago. Now she was sweating, for heaven's sake—and still freezing. Perhaps a hot shower would help.

Ariel kept twisting the hot-water faucet just a little farther as she stood under the steaming water until her scalded skin protested vehemently. After drying off she redressed in her mismatched fuzzy knee socks and a green-sprigged flannel granny gown that would really have made Ryan laugh. After locating her slippers which had migrated under the bed, she strayed over to Ryan's half of the house.

She told herself that she had to keep the stove going to keep the pipes from freezing, but she knew she wouldn't have to worry about that for at least another month. She just wanted to be someplace where she could still sense him. A trace of his after-shave lingered in the cool air, and he had left some books and papers scattered over the maple table. Murphy had bounded up the spiral stairs, sure he had to be around somewhere. Ariel trudged up after her when the dog refused to come when she was called.

Prowling around his bedroom, Ariel poked listlessly through the jumble on the oak dresser, some loose change, the bandanna he'd tied around her hair the morning she'd made the soap, the watch she'd seen on his arm every day for two weeks. A discreet gold watch had nestled in the dark hair of his wrist under his suit cuff when he'd left. She picked up the old skin-diver's watch and wound it carefully. The brass-and-chrome case was worn on the corners, and the crystal was scratched, but the steady ticking in her ear was oddly comforting.

He'd left clothes scattered around, too. She picked up an inside-out gray sweatshirt and rubbed the soft fleece over her cheek. It smelled of him, the clean scent of his ordinary soap and the musky sweat he worked up exercising his leg. She slipped the shirt over her head and felt suddenly warm and very tired. She went back to her own room to sleep, the brown dog trailing dejectedly behind her.

Lamplight gleamed dully on the long barrel of his hunting rifle. There was a brighter flash as the light caught briefly on the lens of the powerful scope mounted on the barrel as he slid the gun carefully into a custom-made, tooled leather case.

The rifle hadn't been dirty, he reflected, fitting the cleaning supplies precisely into their place in the kit box. Still, it was best to leave as little to chance as possible. He couldn't afford a misfire because of a speck of dirt.

He wiped the cleaning oil from his fingers on a clean rag. He would certainly have liked to have a silencer, but acquiring one would draw attention to himself. He would just have to do without.

He set the rifle case in an olive-drab, army-issue duffle bag, the type favored by the seedy hitchhikers he often saw along the highway. The bag gave the appearance of being full of all his worldly possessions. In fact, it held only the rifle and a quantity of crumpled newspapers. He would have to check it in as luggage at the airport; he'd never get it past the scanners as carryon baggage.

He stored it in his bedroom closet. Pity he wasn't the shot Dennis had been, but his skill was . . . adequate.

Chapter 13

Most people would never receive a letter from the Grand Bahama Bank of Nassau telling them that there was an account in their name with a balance of $622,300.48. Ariel had never received her letter, but the money was waiting for her just the same. Ryan tossed the letter back onto the kitchen table, the same kitchen table, he reflected, where he'd sat less than a month ago and told his sister-in-law to find him a beautiful virgin over the age of consent, if any still existed. His hard mouth softened in a smile; one *had* existed.

Rick had wisely never sent the letter on to its rightful owner, guessing that Ariel would be so shocked she would do something dangerous and foolhardy, like rushing back to San Francisco to find out what the hell was going on. His brother had guessed correctly, Ryan thought; that was exactly what she would have done, and Davidson would have been ecstatic. She would have been right where he wanted her.

Instead he was here, pretending to be her attorney, coming to negotiate her release from custody so she could spend her money. He stared at his brother, who was seated across the table, bouncing his tiny daughter on his knee and laughing at her squeals of delight. Would Ariel's daughters have their mother's blond hair, he thought absently.

He wasn't pretending, however. He was going to be fighting for Ariel's best interests tomorrow morning, harder than he had fought for any paying client he'd ever had.

He sighed and picked the letter back up. It wasn't going to be easy. This straightforward, innocuous letter was the most damning piece of evidence against her yet. It concerned the account of one Dennis Michael DiSanto. There had been no activity in the account for the past ten months so, pursuant to Mr. DiSanto's instructions, it was being transferred to Miss Ariel Spence. The bank extended a cordial welcome to its new customer and wanted her to know that it would be very happy to serve her in any way possible. Ryan had laughed cynically to himself when he'd come to that line. Any bank would welcome a customer with over six hundred thousand dollars.

Had DiSanto had some disturbing premonition, or had he simply been doing the equivalent of making out a will? The latter, Ryan suspected.

Davidson was convinced that the bank had already performed an invaluable service for Miss Ariel Maria Spence. Long a haven for tax-dodging Americans and a laundry for dirty money, Bahamian banks took in sacks full of soiled dollars and returned them squeaky clean. Ariel's new wealth would be untraceable, the chances of the Internal Revenue Service laying claim to any of it slim at best.

No wonder, Davidson had gloated, she'd put up so little resistance to moving to Montana. She'd known she had only to be patient for a time and the money would be hers. DiSanto had undoubtedly told her about it. She was being compensated twice for setting him up for the hit. The one thing she couldn't have known was that she would be double-crossed and set up for a hit herself.

The hell of it was that Davidson's theories had merit. They were plausible; they fit the evidence and a Grand Jury might well find them convincing.

Another piece of evidence against her, one Ryan knew the district attorney would never present to a Grand Jury but would consider almost as damning, was the fact that she'd retained Ryan Jones to represent her. Even in San Francisco everyone knew you only hired Ryan Jones when you were guilty and only a slick lawyer who knew all the dirty tricks could get you off. And for Ariel he would use every one of them and learn a few new ones besides.

His niece was reclaimed by her mother for the nightly bath, and Rick Jones turned to his brother across the kitchen table.

Ryan gave his brother a long, speculative look. "You're walking a very thin line, you know."

Rick rubbed both hands down his face. "Don't I know it!" he groaned feelingly. "But I didn't know what else to do. I've been sure she wasn't guilty since she lived with us, but Davidson is so sure he's right. I'd thought to let it just ride, that sooner or later he'd give up and she could come home. Then we got word that Garza was about to be arrested. We already knew his connection with DiSanto, and I got a bad feeling." He sent his brother a sidelong look. "That's when I thought of you. A hunch couldn't get her any official protection, but I was sure she was going to need it. You're better than a police bodyguard anyway."

Ryan gave his brother's flattery a dry look.

Rick leaned his head tiredly on his hands. "It turned out to be just as I'd suspected. She knew something somebody else was afraid of, something that seemed so insignificant at the time that she forgot about it." He glanced up hopefully at his brother. "Has she remembered who the third man in the office was yet?"

Ryan shook his head. "No," he replied shortly, "but I'll lay you a thousand to one it was our man."

"Ryan . . ." Rick reached hesitantly across the table and laid his hand on his brother's arm. "You realize that unless we can find some way to prove he acted alone, Ariel's still going to be under suspicion?"

Ryan shut his eyes wearily. "I know, Rick."

Ariel's nemesis was right on time for his nine-thirty appointment the next morning. Edward James Davidson, district attorney for the county of San Francisco, was a small man, slight, with a thin pointed nose that twitched occasionally, a wispy soft-brown mustache that matched his hair and bright button eyes the color of black coffee. If he'd been an animal, he would have been an innocuous field mouse. However, Ryan knew that this field mouse had the soul of a wolverine. Ferociously tenacious, Davidson would sink his teeth into his victim, worrying it and shaking it until he made his kill. And his next victim was going to be Ariel Spence, unless he could be tempted to attack a juicier one.

"How long have you been Miss Spence's attorney, Mr. Jones?" The district attorney smiled, showing sharp white teeth.

"Since she's gotten tired of people trying to kill her," Ryan replied blandly.

Davidson merely smiled again. He would be an interesting man to play poker with, Ryan thought.

He smiled genially at the D.A. and the other man in the office, Rick. "Suppose we talk about how you're going to keep my client alive, gentlemen?"

Edward Davidson explained his plan slowly and carefully. If Ariel came back to her town house in San Francisco she would be much safer with round-the-clock police protection and his personal guarantee of her safety. But Ryan read the silences between the careful words.

It would be leaked that she was home, to the tabloids, most likely. The waters surrounding the murders would be stirred up again with more salacious headlines and speculation. The killer would have to be blind not to know she was back when the headlines would be flaunting her presence from every supermarket checkout stand. The killer would make his move; the police would make theirs—and Ariel would be caught in the cross fire.

They argued it back and forth politely and then, at the properly orchestrated moment, Rick produced a confidential report from an IRS agent grateful for the tip Ryan, through his brother, had supplied. Suddenly the little D.A. saw a fatter victim to sink his teeth into.

Ryan stared out at the foggy drizzle while he waited for his brother to finish plotting new strategy with his boss. Davidson wouldn't forget about Ariel; he was just going to leave her be until he could prove that his new suspect and his old one were in league. Ryan knew the district attorney didn't expect it to take long; Ariel Spence and the man knew each other very well. But at least he'd bought her a little time.

Ariel had gotten up with the cool, mid-October sun. After dressing in a chrome-yellow sweater and bright blue pants to try to cheer herself up, she rambled downstairs. She turned away from the waiting word processor with marked distaste. Gazing longingly out the window over the kitchen sink, sipping coffee, she watched the weak yellow light grow stronger. It gilded the tops of the trees along the river, seeping slowly down through the shadows to sparkle off the silvery water. Long, lonely runs along the river bank weren't very sensible anymore, but she was dying to go outside. Why hadn't she ever noticed before how big and quiet this house really was?

After sharing her breakfast with Murphy, she gassed up the heavy chain saw and marched determinedly to the remains of Ryan's raffle prize. Gingerly she heaved and rolled a log off the haphazard pile. Four strong tugs on the saw's starter rope produced an ear-numbing drone, and the mechanical beaver began gnawing into the wood.

Several hours later she sat on the back step and lolled back on her elbow under the noontime sun. A slight breeze from the river dried the wisps of hair that had escaped from her ponytail and stuck to her damp neck. The strong clean scent of fresh pine was the smell of satisfaction. The pile of logs didn't look appreciably smaller, but there was a respectable stack of firewood beside it.

Ariel flexed her sore shoulders and rose from the steps. Hefting the saw and ax, she went inside to store them away until her next attack of cabin fever. She took the empty gas can and walked through the house into the garage to put it in the back of Ryan's truck. She left the garage door open so she would be sure to hear the phone if Ryan called.

He had been faithful to his promise so far, calling at least once each day. And, he'd only been gone two and a half days, she reminded herself. She'd spent those two and a half days trying to solve the puzzle of Ryan Jones. With his disturbing, distracting influence gone from the house, she found she could think about him a little more objectively.

She was in love with a man who, she suspected, didn't believe in love or in trust. For several years his very survival had depended on his superior talent for deception. Lies and mistrust had been a way of life, and those habits would die hard. She doubted that Ryan Jones had trusted anyone—man or woman—in years.

Did she trust him? She had examined her innermost feelings, the secret ones she seldom chose to confront except under duress. She'd found that she didn't know if she trusted him or not. She wanted to, desperately, because love without trust had little chance of succeeding.

Ariel believed staunchly in love. She didn't just write about it and deposit those healthy checks in the bank, laughing all the while. She knew she was as big a sucker for romance and love and happy endings as her avid readers—probably more so, because she created the illusion, yet still believed every word of it, every heated glance, every heartthrob, every tender vow. It was like a magician being taken in by his own tricks. He'd lied to her, and she knew it, and she loved him anyway.

As she lifted the gas can over the side of the truck she stubbed her toe on one of the cardboard boxes she'd shoved against the brick wall. They contained Dennis's darkroom equipment, cameras and photo files.

Kneeling on the concrete floor, she dragged over one of the three cardboard files and pulled open the drawer. Inside were hundreds of eight-by-ten black-and-white glossies. She and Dennis's brother, Robert, had packed up all the equipment and photos one afternoon and delivered the file boxes to the police. She remembered Robert patiently thumbing through the pictures one by one, seemingly fascinated by them. The boxes hadn't been opened since the police had returned them.

What she really ought to do was sort through this stuff. The chemicals probably weren't fresh anymore and should be disposed of. The expensive equipment wasn't doing anyone any good, either. She pulled a photo out at random, marking its place with her finger.

The picture was of her old neighbor, George Lu and his five-year old great-granddaughter, Amy. They were feeding peanuts to the park squirrels. The pair could be found somewhere in Golden Gate Park almost every Wednesday afternoon. She and Dennis had spent a lot of his Wednesday afternoons off there, too. Dennis had taken countless shots of the spare man who smiled only for his effervescent China doll, Amy.

Ariel smiled softly, remembering the prints in the file. She had persuaded Dennis to make some of them into a little album. Mr. Lu had thanked them gravely in his impeccable Hong Kong English that had always made Ariel's tongue feel clumsy. Then he had sat on a peeling green park bench with Amy, counting the visual treasury of their very special relationship, tears in his old almond eyes. Amy would be in school all day now. Grandpa George would be spending Wednesday afternoon alone.

She replaced the glossy and pulled out one of the last shots. It was of her. The files were full of pictures of her, too. She had been wading in the surf off Point Lobos, her jeans rolled to her knees, but soaked anyway, her hair in pigtails.... Dennis had delighted in taking pictures of her in all her ''best'' moments—hair flying away on a windy day, face fog-washed and utterly devoid of makeup or hanging upside down on the park jungle gym with Amy.

She kept waiting for the pain these black-and-white memories should evoke. It never came. She had Ryan to thank for that, she realized. He had helped her lay the past to rest at last. There was no pain anymore, only a bittersweet remembrance of all the good times she and Dennis had shared.

She slipped the photo back, but it wouldn't quite go down. She felt around on the bottom of the box and fished out a glassine envelope of negatives. They must have gotten mixed up with the prints when she and Robert had packed things up that day. There on the bottom of the box, they had probably been overlooked by the police, too.

She held a strip of celluloid up to a bright sunbeam burning through the dusty garage window. The picture was of her again, leaning over the arched bridge in the Japanese Tea Garden. It had been drizzling that day, the last time they had been to the park before the afternoon Dennis was shot. Her hair was plastered to her somber face. What had she been thinking?

She glanced rapidly over the remaining strips, light and dark reversed in the negatives. Dennis must never have printed them, because she had never seen the glossies. She scanned the last strip, then stopped at one in the middle, her forehead puckering.

It was a long shot of a grassy slope. Dennis had taken several shots of an elderly woman carefully matching her patient steps to those of a teetering toddler. In this one, something... someone... else was in the upper left corner, partially screened by a bush.

After tearing up the taped lids of three boxes, she finally found the cases with Dennis's cameras and lenses. She held an 80 mm lens over the upper corner of the picture like a magnifying glass, revealing two men. Their heads and chests, along with the pointing arm of the taller man, were magnified into sharp focus. Dennis probably hadn't even noticed them, but the camera's sharper eye had caught the figures hidden behind the shrub. The clothing and hair colors weren't accurate of course, but there was no mistaking the shorter, older man: Patrick Reilly; the man with him, she didn't recognize.

Squinting at the tiny negative, she mentally extended the line of the unknown man's upraised arm. What had he been pointing out to Reilly? Dennis? No, the angle was wrong, he should have been pointing directly at the camera, and he wasn't—he was pointing a little to the left. The left. She had always stood to Dennis's left, and a little behind, so she could pass his film or a lens . . . With a sickening certainty Ariel suddenly knew that she too, had been supposed to die that raw December day in the park. Only an opportune heart attack had saved her.

She blinked away the sudden tears blurring her vision and focused fiercely on the face of her killer. There *was* something familiar about him, about the eyes and the bone structure of his face, half-concealed under a drooping dark mustache and lank, dark hair. Blond, she mentally corrected; it only appeared dark because this was a negative. She ignored that. She did know this man, but she knew him with dark hair, not blond, and without the mustache.

When the name came to her, the blood in her veins crystallized into ice. "No!" she whispered in agonized denial while the name ricocheted in a scream inside her head. As the scream died she remembered at last the face of the third man who had been in Dennis's office with Garza that day. This was the same man.

She scrambled up off the floor and ran inside for Ryan's keys. Less than a minute later she was forcing the power wagon to bolt down the rain-rutted dirt road, ignoring the bone-jarring bucks of the vehicle and the stop sign at the highway.

Minutes later she screeched to a halt in the high school parking lot. "Billy! Billy Greef!" she shouted as she flung open the truck door.

A lanky, dark-headed boy paused in the act of climbing into his red pickup. He looked across the lot for his summoner. A look of shy delight and wonder brightened his homely face when he saw who was running toward him.

"Miss Spence!" His voice was amazingly deep for such a thin body. He shoved the heavy glasses back up on his hawk nose with a nervous gesture.

Ariel clutched his thin arm with steel fingers. "You don't have football practice or anything today, do you?" she demanded shaking his arm fiercely.

His Adam's apple slid up and down several times before he managed a bullfrog croak. "N-no, ma'am. Coach cut me from the team; said I was too sk—"

She cut him off impatiently. "Good! I've got a negative that needs printing. Can you do it right now?"

Billy felt the red flush creeping up to his ears growing hotter. His hazel eyes flicked around the rain-puddled parking lot, seeing a group of his buddies eyeing the interchange between him and the wonderful, so out-of-reach Miss Spence with great interest. He straightened his skinny shoulders and quit slouching. "Sure," he said easily. "I just got a new enlarger last week; I can—"

"Great!" She shoved the strip into his hand. "The third one from the top. Just as soon as you can."

He spared a glance down at the strip of celluloid in his bony hands. "I'll do 'em all," he promised eagerly. "It'll only take a few more minutes, and I've got plenty of—"

"No! Just that one. That's the only one I'm interested in."

"But I can do it easy," Billy persisted persuasively. "There might be something you want to see in one of the others, too."

Ariel felt a hysterical giggle of desperation rising. "No, no. Next time. You can do a whole roll if you want next time," she promised recklessly. "Today I just want the third one, and print it on the largest paper you have."

"Well, okay," he agreed reluctantly. "But I—"

"Thank you, Billy. You just don't know how grateful to you I am." Ariel kissed his cheek quickly and headed back across the parking lot. She called back over her shoulder, "I've got to see Bessie Ruff, and then I'll drop by your house about—" she glanced at the old skin diver's watch pushed halfway up her forearm "—four-thirty. All right?"

"All right," he answered dazedly. Then, catching the eye of his best friend, who was starting determinedly toward him, he shrugged his thin shoulders carelessly under his letter jacket and sauntered nonchalantly back to his pickup. He drove off with a cool flick of his hand to his openmouthed buddies, the spot Miss Spence had kissed burning like fire.

Two hours later Ariel was staring at the glossy prints spread over her round oak dining table. Billy had printed the negative in every size from three by five to eleven by fourteen. Any one would have been all the proof she needed. She would have to let him take whatever of Dennis's darkroom equipment he wanted, she thought absently. Even in the biggest, grainiest print there was no doubt about the identity of the second man.

She opened the closet under the staircase and pulled out the jacket she'd worn the day she'd taken Ryan to the airport. She found the crumpled scrap of paper with the phone numbers that Ryan had stuffed in one of the pockets.

Glancing at the clock in the kitchen as she crossed to the phone, she debated which number to call first. Given the one-hour time difference between Montana and the West Coast, she might be able to catch him at his office, if he wasn't in court. His secretary should certainly be able to get a message to him if he was.

As she smoothed the piece of paper, the better to read the numbers, it occurred to her that she had decided to call Ryan without consciously thinking about it. He, not Rick Jones, and certainly not Edward Davidson, had been the automatic choice to share her news and help her decide what to do about it.

The first number was probably his office. As she read the neatly printed numerals the hair on the back of her neck rose. She didn't know the area code for Los Angeles offhand, but 415 wasn't it. Four one five was the area code for her phone number... in San Francisco. Ryan was supposed to be in Los Angeles. Both of these phone numbers were in San Francisco. With numb fingers she dialed the eleven digits of the first number.

After one and a half rings a man answered. It was odd that she hadn't noticed the similarity between Ryan's and Rick Jones's voices before, even though she had known they were brothers. Ryan's was perhaps a touch deeper and smoother, but Rick's had that same tight note of impatience that she'd heard in Ryan's voice a few times. She hung up the phone gently without saying anything.

Sitting down carefully on the edge of the sofa, she took a deep, calming breath. Well, now she knew the answer to one question she'd been puzzling over. She did not trust Ryan Jones. Bleak, heart-destroying desolation turned into a fierce all-consuming anger.

She slammed one fist down on the coffee table by her knees, making Murphy leap up with a startled yelp. Dammit! He had lied to her again! And this time it was worse, much, much worse. All his protestations that she would be safer here than with him in Los Angeles had been lies. She saw immediately what he and his brother, no doubt with Davidson's blessing, had done. They had withdrawn her protection, leaving her alone and vulnerable. If they had sent the killer an engraved invitation they couldn't have made their intention any clearer. They were inviting him to take a clear shot at her. Of course, they were no doubt planning to nab him as soon as he did, but that would be small consolation to her.

Ariel leaped to her feet and snatched up the jacket, shrugging into it as she hunted up her purse and Ryan's keys. Well, she wasn't going to sit around here, moaning and wringing her hands like some helpless, terrified ninny. She was too furious to be terrified and the only thing she planned on wringing was Ryan Jones's neck! How could he *do* this to her? Twice! And how could she have been so stupidly trusting as to have let him? She knew the answer to that one already. She'd known he was lying the morning he'd left; she just hadn't wanted to admit it to herself. Because you didn't want to miss one last chance at him in bed, she reminded herself viciously, ignoring a wave of shame and fresh despair.

Ariel took a medium-sized print off the table and slid it carefully into her purse. She was going to stuff this damned photograph down their throats after they'd had a good look at it. Then, whether the Jones brothers and Davidson deigned to accompany her or not, she was going to confront the subject of the photo and ask him why he was trying so hard to kill her. Then... But she couldn't think beyond then. It was too painful.

Ariel backed the power wagon out of the garage and forced herself to drive slowly down the dirt road to the highway. She came to a full stop at the sign. She wanted to do nothing to draw attention to herself. Once she was clear of town, beyond Ted Dye's sharp eyes, she would have no trouble getting to Missoula and catching a flight out. She should be in San Francisco by early morning.

As she crested the long hill that led into town she glanced to the left at the steep canyon and the ribbon of river below. It was a pity she needed his truck. It would be so satisfying emotionally to simply let it roll over the edge and watch it crash onto the rocks below. She drove through town with a small prayer of thanks that the chief's patrol car was nowhere in sight.

Dusk was just deepening into true darkness when she drove onto the bridge that crossed over the Bitterroot River on the far side of town. The lights of the truck flickered down the length of the narrow span, shining off a white car parked across the other end, blocking it. Ariel moaned despairingly. Now she knew why she hadn't seen the chief's car.

She abandoned the idea of simply ramming his car and continuing on. She had no desire to have the state police scouring the highway for her between here and Missoula. She parked the orange truck a few feet from the white patrol car, lights on, motor running. She climbed down from the cab and strolled across the where the chief was lounging against the front fender of his car.

"Evening, Ariel."

"Chief."

"Out for a little drive?"

"Yes. It's a-a nice night for one." Ariel stifled a nervous giggle. Surely the chief wasn't buying this? She couldn't be so lucky.

Chief Dye pulled the toothpick he'd been sucking on from the corner of his mouth and examined it. "Thinking of going up to Missoula?" he asked idly.

No, she couldn't be that lucky. The chief might have perfected his hick-sheriff routine, but the "hick" had been a detective lieutenant with the S.F.P.D. and hadn't been fooled for a second. "I found some evidence I think the San Francisco district attorney should see. I'm going to fly out there with it tonight," she stated boldly.

"Let's see it." His hand was in front of her, the toothpick flipped away faster than she would have thought a man twenty years younger could move.

Ariel pulled out her photograph and gave it to the chief. He frowned at it a long time in the headlights of the truck.

"What's it supposed to prove?"

Ariel explained.

Ted Dye nodded, still considering the photo. He didn't point out to her that the picture could also prove that the taller man was pointing out to the shorter, older one the person he was *not* to shoot.

"I'll take it into Missoula and send it off on the state police wire-photo machine."

"No!" Ariel made to grab the picture back. "I have to take it myself, to explain it. Otherwise the D.A. won't believe it's the same man."

Dye's burly body easily blocked Ariel's arm. He reached through the open window of his patrol car and laid the photo on the dash. Privately he was certain Davidson wouldn't believe it whether she went or not.

"I'll send your explanation with it, Ariel," he promised. "Now go on home."

She stood toe-to-toe with him. "And if I don't? What are you going to do. Shoot me?" she demanded sarcastically.

"No. I'll arrest you for being disorderly and refusing to obey an officer, and throw you in jail," he answered calmly. "Jones told you to stay put. You can either stay at home or stay in jail. I imagine he'd bail you out when he gets back," he added as an after-thought.

If she had to wait for Ryan to come back she would rot in jail. Ariel blinked back tears of frustrated fury, she would *not* cry. She glared at the chief defiantly.

He stared back implacably. "Ariel, I can't go to Missoula until you climb back in that truck and go home," he explained patiently. "I promise you, as soon as you do I will drive up to Missoula and send the picture off. You can call Davidson first thing in the morning to confirm it."

Ariel gave him one last belligerent glare, then climbed back into the truck. If she wanted the photo to reach San Francisco, she would have to do it his way.

She slammed the door shut and started to put the truck in gear. The chief held up his hand and walked toward her. She rolled down the window, and he stuck his head in. A notebook and pencil materialized in his hands.

"Okay now. Tell me again, exactly, what this picture proves."

Ariel was curled into the comforting arms of an overstuffed chair, staring at her phone. Murphy's head on her knee spread a little warmth through her cold body. The dog gazed at her mistress, whining softly. Absently Ariel patted the brown head.

Should she swallow her pride and call the second number Ryan had given her? She'd checked her address book and her suspicions had been confirmed. The first number was Rick Jones's home phone. Ryan had probably never dreamed she'd use the numbers and had felt perfectly safe in giving them to her, to reinforce his image as the concerned lover, no doubt.

She roused herself from the chair, scrubbing away a half-dried tear with the back of her hand. No, she wouldn't call; she wasn't that desperate—yet.

Come on, Ariel, she chided herself as she paced the living room, Murphy pacing with her. You've plotted at least a dozen hairbreadth escapes from vengeful posses and irate Indians. Surely you can come up with something to get away from a middle-aged police chief.

She would not meekly wait around here for somebody's target practice. She would confirm the photo's arrival tomorrow morning, all right—in person. And she would be there with the police to see the look on the killer's face when he opened his door.

She paused in the middle of the floor, tapping her finger absently on her cheek as a plan took form. Ryan's orange pickup wasn't exactly inconspicuous, but Mr. Hanson's pickup was. Battered, rust-eaten, it looked like half the pickup trucks in the valley. Ever since he'd bought his new car, Mr. Hanson rarely drove the truck. If she told the right story of automotive woes he would be more than willing to lend it to her.

She could cut across his hay field to the levee road along the river. The road went close to the county line, well past Ted Dye's jurisdiction. If she called Mr. Hanson now she could still catch a late flight out of Missoula and be in San Francisco by morning.

Her hand was on the phone when it rang. She lifted the receiver expecting to hear Chief Dye's gruff voice making sure she was at home. It wasn't Chief Dye.

The bell on the wire-photo machine rang shortly after midnight, waking the police aide from his daydream of apprehending four dangerous bank robbers single-handedly and receiving sergeant's stripes on the spot. He waited by the machine, yawning until the photo and the message accompanying it were complete. Carefully he tore the paper free, scanning it briefly. Vaguely disappointed to see no mention of a bank robbery, he placed the photograph and message in a folder, dropped it in the basket for the district attorney's office and went back to daydreaming.

The folder was picked up by a courier promptly at eight o'clock the next morning. By eight forty-five it was in the hands of a secretary in the D.A.'s office. She was just about to carry it into her boss's office to lay it on his desk when the phone rang. She laid the file temporarily on the stack of files to be returned to the record room in the basement to be refiled.

A runner from records stopped by her desk, nodded at the stack of files questioningly, and the secretary, busy taking a message, nodded back absently. The runner scooped up the files and continued on his rounds. At ten, just in time for his break, he dumped the load of records in the refiling bin. The empty chair nearby was usually occupied by the pretty young clerk in charge of refiling. He'd hoped to buy her a doughnut and a cup of coffee and try again for a date, but she was still out with the flu. He sighed disappointedly; she would probably be out all week.

Chapter 14

The headlights of the rented Firebird cut a misty swath through the fog swirling over the highway. It was very late. Actually, Ryan corrected mentally, it was very early Saturday morning. He'd been extremely lucky; his had been the last plane to land before the fog had closed down the Missoula airport. But then, he'd been very lucky all day.

He guided the responsive car around a curve and was suddenly out of the fog. This was so much more fun to drive than his cumbersome truck. Maybe he could talk Ariel into replacing her Blazer with a sports car they could both enjoy. They weren't going to need two four-wheel-drive vehicles when they went back to California. And they'd be going back very soon.

Her would-be murderer would have been taken into custody about two hours ago, while Ryan was thirty thousand feet in the air over Oregon. He would have liked to have been there, but the shock was going to be hard for Ariel when she learned who it was. She was going to need him with her.

The man was in custody, but not for murder. The carryon suitcase of a tourist boarding a plane in L.A. bound for a little fun and sun in the Bahamas had suffered an unfortunate accident when it mysteriously fell from the overhead luggage compartment. The

other passengers were rather startled to see, not swim trunks and
Island shirts and tubes of sunscreen, but neat green-and-white
bundles spilling from the broken bag. The money wasn't the courier's and he hadn't been about to go to jail for it. The IRS agents
had offered a deal and he had taken it, giving them the name of the
man Ryan had already pegged for Dennis's death.

Ariel wasn't above suspicion yet, but Ryan was confident he
could find the evidence to convince even Davidson of her innocence eventually. And when he did, he knew the discovery would
bring a soul-satisfying sense of rightness that had always been
lacking when a guilty client was found innocent on a technicality.

He turned onto the narrow two-lane road that dead-ended in the
valley. It was finally over. He would clear the air between them,
then tell her what he wanted from her. She was probably going to
be a little shocked. He'd been rather startled himself when he finally realized that he had the decidedly old-fashioned intention of
carrying her off to keep forever, to bear him a brood of lively little
California girls and dark-eyed little boys. Well, one of each, anyway, for starters. No sense in getting carried away. He didn't see his
silly grin in the rearview mirror.

The low Firebird bounced cautiously over the ruts in her road.
What had happened during the past three days? The first time he
had called when she wasn't home, he had called Dye immediately.
The chief had said that his truck had been parked all day in the
Valley View Rest Home parking lot.

Ariel had given him her promise that she wouldn't leave the
house unless it was absolutely necessary. If Bessie Ruff had needed
her, he knew Ariel would consider it absolutely necessary to go to
her.

She was still gone at midnight the next night, but this time Dye
told him that his truck was at the small valley hospital. Yesterday,
with every call, he had known with the first ring that the phone was
ringing in an empty house.

Dye kept assuring him that she was fine, just staying with Bessie at the little hospital in Hamilton. If Bessie were that ill, why
hadn't she called him? He knew she would need him, need somebody.

She didn't even know he was coming back tonight. Not only had
he been unable to reach her today, but the chief, too, had been un-

available. At least he didn't have to worry about her safety anymore.

The L.A. police had had their man under surveillance for several days. When he was packing his car for what appeared to be a short weekend trip the L.A. police had checked to see if he should be picked up. After a brief council that Ryan had been privy to, it was decided to tail him instead, and to use a search warrant to legally ransack his house while he was away. He'd arrived at his cabin near Tahoe in midafternoon and, Rick had assured Ryan before he left, would be picked up by the county sheriff.

The schoolhouse was dark. He'd seen his truck through the garage window when the car lights flashed over it. At least she was finally home. The front door was unlocked and he felt the touch of an icy finger on his spine. He cursed quietly, fear making him choose words that were uncharacteristically vile. If he shouted for her and someone else was in the house . . .

He opened his door and moved soundlessly to the kitchen to get the .45. He stepped back across the hall just as silently, then paused outside her door and listened. It was half open. There was no sound. He pushed the door wide and stepped into the room; flattening himself against the wall. The fire in the stove was dead. The house was as cold as a tomb.

Weak moonlight barely illuminated the living room. There was a huddled figure at the end of the sofa, and a darker shape on the floor.

"Ariel?" he called softly. Fear formed a choking lump in his throat, and there was an obscene taste in his mouth.

For long breathless moments there was no answer. Then the figure on the couch stirred. The white light of the dying moon glimmered briefly on blond hair. The dark head resting on the daffodil-yellow afghan that was wrapped around the figure lifted with a welcoming whimper.

"Bessie died while you were gone, Ry," Ariel said dully. "Her funeral was this afternoon."

The gun fell soundlessly on the carpet as he dropped next to her. He crushed his arms around her, his voice gentle. "Oh, baby, I'm sorry, so sorry." He cursed again, silently. "And I wasn't even here for you." He rocked her gently as she lay passively against him. "Why didn't you call me, darling?"

A long shiver trembled through her. She closed her dry eyes, trying to keep the tears locked inside. It was no use. They began to seep silently down her cold cheeks, glittering in the even colder moonlight. He shifted her to his lap, wrapping the folds of the warm afghan more tightly around her chilled body.

Ariel's voice was a poignant whisper. "I've known she was dying for months, but I wouldn't let myself think about it. I tried to call you yesterday. There was no answer at your brother's house, and his secretary said she'd take a m-message for you when I called his office. I left the message, but I-I needed you r-right then." The thin, pitiful cry of a lost child filled the cold, quiet room. "I w-wanted you to come back so b-badly!"

Ryan closed his eyes, resting his cheek on top of her head. So she knew where he'd really been. When she heard his reason for lying to her, surely she would forgive him.

Ariel sniffled and tried for control. It was beyond her. "When you didn't call back, I knew you w-weren't ever coming back." With a broken sound she turned her face into the soft sweater under her cheek and gave into her grief.

Ryan gathered her closer, his body a shield against any more pain and hurt. "Oh, love, no. No, no. I'd have come back right away if I'd known. I love you." Silently he swore every obscenity he could remember. He'd never gotten the message.

Dennis's death, the long months here alone, Murphy's poisoning, the murder attempts that she'd barely survived—none of them had broken her spirit. But Bessie's death and then the thought that he'd betrayed her once again had shattered her.

Ryan's voice was a lulling wordless purr. His cheek soothed over the soft wisps of hair at her temple. With a strong gentle rhythm he slowly stroked her back. After a long while her last tear was spent, brushed from her cheek by his tender thumb. Her convulsive shivers eased as she absorbed his warmth, and her breathing evened. She lay still across his lap within the shelter of his arms. He brushed a kiss over her forehead, heard her quiet sigh and he was sure she had slipped into healing sleep. She was broken, and he would put her back together, restore her, tonight—and whenever else she might need him.

The grandfather clock on the opposite wall played its Westminster chimes and struck twice. "Ryan." He thought she was calling to him in a dream and drew her still closer.

"Ryan."

He felt the butterfly wing flutter of her lashes on his throat.

"Please make love with me."

Please comfort me, she was asking; please heal me. He answered with gentle fingertips raising her mouth to his. His lips, warm and unbelievably soft, held hers in a passionless, loving kiss. Then, silently, he rose with her in his arms and climbed the stairs, praying he would have the gentleness she would need tonight.

He laid her on the bed in a patch of gauzy moonlight. His hands, delicate as moonbeams, undressed her. She closed her tear-ravaged eyes against the pale light. The bed shifted, and he was naked beside her. As he drew the quilt over them, he reached out to bring her close to him.

For a long time he only kissed her, those incredibly gentle patient hands whispering over her, asking for nothing and giving solace, peace, tender care. Then his mouth followed the path of his hands, never arousing, never urgent, never demanding. He offered only sweetness to neutralize the bitter pain. His lips came back up to hers, the sweetness distilled to an absolute purity that seeped through her, dissolving the bitter ache.

He let the kiss deepen with the softest coercion, and her pain poured into him. As her body relaxed, she knew dimly that she was selfishly taking, returning nothing. Her boneless arms lifted toward him.

"No, love." He caught her hands, holding them loosely as he kissed the slow, steady pulse inside each of her wrists. Then, rolling her over onto her stomach, he eased her arms above her head and stretched them over the pillow. She felt the slight pressure of his knees at her hips as his strong hands began a tranquil massage up her back, across her shoulders, down her sides. Lean, sure fingers kneaded her waist, eased the last knot of tension in the small of her back.

Ryan's voice stroked over her, too, like velvet, telling her how much he loved her, how much he had missed her, how precious she was to him. She drifted, serene and wonderfully slothful, in his loving care. His breath warmed the nape of her neck a fraction of a moment before his light kiss. Ariel felt the first mild sting of passion as he continued the trail of soft kisses down to the base of her spine.

Time seemed to cease its flow and began to swirl and eddy around them. His sensitive fingertips noted the quickening of her body. He turned her back to face him again, his mouth and his hands treasuring her body. They were still unselfish, giving subtle pleasure, cosseting her. Ariel luxuriated in the feel of his hands. She felt as if she was something exquisite to be appreciated at his leisure, lingered over.

The clock downstairs chimed again. Three deep tones reverberated through the quiet house. The moon floated from behind a thin cloud, its light washing her body in white translucence. Ryan saw clearly how slight, how perfect, she was, like a fragile, priceless statue of the rarest porcelain. Eyes closed, the statue barely moved, save for the shallow rise and fall of her breasts.

He lowered his mouth to one nipple and felt, rather than heard, her low moan. As he inhaled her familiar, bewitching flower scent, his lips dawdled. She moaned again, her body beginning to shift, inviting him to take more. Ryan's tempo never varied, still easy, still unrushed.

He wanted her; the flames licking deep in his belly were ravenous, but love damped them down. Tonight was solely for her, her pleasure, her needs. He would find his pleasure in hers.

Ariel basked in the warmth of his hands and mouth. When his tongue laving her breast changed mere warmth into heat, her body began to thrum, stronger with each soft touch. All the pain was gone; even the sweet pain of desire was absent. He permitted only succoring pleasure. She concentrated on the gift of exquisite bliss he was giving her body.

His mouth pressed to hers, and she met him mindlessly, lost in his flavor and scent and feel. He reminded himself of her fragility and took her with infinite tenderness and care and love. She wept again—with joy.

The coppery October sun rose and hung high overhead. Only a few mares' tails, the leading edge of a storm front, swished over the northern horizon, marring the empty perfection of a pure azure day. They slept on in each other's arms like exhausted children. Finally Murphy's apologetic whimper woke Ryan. He shook his sleep-fuzzed head and laughed into Murphy's yellow eyes. His hand left its warm hold on Ariel's breast and reached out to scratch the dog's ears.

"Glad to see me, girl?" he whispered.

Murphy's eyes rolled ecstatically.

Easing his angular body away from Ariel's soft heat, he swung his legs over the side of the bed and stood. He stretched sinuously and then, not bothering with his clothes, bounded down the stairs.

He swore feelingly under his breath. Energy conservation was all very well, but they were going to have to get some reliable heat in this place. He was tired of freezing to death every morning. But even the shivering gooseflesh covering his bare body couldn't lower his spirits. He hadn't had a chance to tell her last night that the killer had been apprehended. She was finally free, and they were going home. First he had to get dressed, though, and get some coffee in her to be sure she would understand what he was going to say to her.

He let Murphy out, then picked up his suitcase which was still standing by the door. As soon as he got a fire started in the wood stove he went back upstairs. He built one more fire in the little French parlor stove, watching the top of the tousled blond head showing above an old wedding-ring quilt for any sign of life. He went into the bathroom, shutting the door quietly. When he came back out twenty minutes later she was peering owlishly at him from her nest of quilts.

Ariel blinked the sleep out of her eyes. It hadn't been a dream; he really was here. His hair was damp; it must have been the sound of the shower that had woken her up. He was wearing a smile and an old pair of jeans, one of the first ever made, from the looks of them. They were faded gray-blue at the knees and blue-white at the fly, the cuffs and pockets frayed. The waistband was a little loose. Whatever he'd been doing the past week, he'd lost weight.

Ariel stared at him silently as he crossed the bare floorboards.

"Going to stay in bed forever, lazybones?" He reached out to ruffle her hair affectionately. He glanced significantly at the little clock on the dresser. "You've already been there most of the day."

"I may." Ariel closed her eyes again. She wasn't ready to deal with this. She'd convinced herself that he wouldn't be coming back, and now here he was, calmly walking out of her bathroom as if he'd never been away, never lied to her again. Had he left her in the hopes of drawing out the murderer or not? And what smooth lie did he have all prepared for her this time?

His hand caressed over her temple, smoothing back the tangled hair. "Are you feeling better this morning, love?" His chocolate-colored eyes were loving and kind.

"I'm better," she answered softly, with a bittersweet smile. She pulled his hand down and for a moment held it to her cheek. "I should never sit on your lap. I always end up crying."

He bent down to give her a gentle kiss. "I wish I could have been here sooner." His dark eyes were shadowed with regret.

Ariel laid his hand carefully on the bed and sat up, drawing Bessie's quilt protectively around her. She wished she had on one of her nightshirts instead of being naked. Her nakedness under the soft quilt was too sharp a reminder of his tender, selfless loving of the night before.

Ryan sensed her withdrawal even before she had released his hand. He waited, tension slowly tightening his stomach.

She looked at him for a long time, saying nothing. When she finally spoke, her question was quiet and very clear. "Why did you lie to me again, Ryan?"

"Davidson was going to bring you back to San Francisco to make you an easier target for the killer." His tone was neutral. "He was sure you would draw him out, and Davidson would be able to catch him. I went back to talk him out of it."

"Why didn't you tell me the truth?"

Ryan answered honestly. "Because I was afraid you would go."

Ariel felt suddenly cold. She would have gone. "Why now, all of a sudden, did he want to do that?"

"Because of the money Dennis left you, Ariel," he told her gently.

She started to shake her head uncomprehendingly. "Dennis didn't leave—"

Ryan explained. As he spoke he watched her eyes widen in disbelief at the amount. She shook her head violently. "I don't want it!"

"We'll figure out what to do with it," he assured her quietly. "Ariel, it's over. We can go home now. The man who was after you was arrested last night."

She looked at him, dazed. "It's over?" she whispered. Why didn't she feel something? Joy? Jubilation? Even just relief? She felt . . . nothing, nothing but incredible weariness.

Ryan nodded. "Ariel, love, I'm sorry; this is going to hurt. It was—"

They said the name together. Ryan looked at her, stunned. "You knew? For how long?"

"I realized it a couple of days after you left." His puzzlement didn't dawn on her for a few moments. "I was poking through Dennis's picture file when I found a bunch of negatives that he'd never printed, and I saw Robert in one with Reilly. One of the high school boys printed the negative for me and—" His deepening frown finally registered. "Wait a minute! Didn't you see the photograph Chief Dye sent Davidson?"

"No."

Ariel laughed bitterly. "He never sent it! I was going to take it to Davidson myself, but I never got out of town."

"Thank God," Ryan murmured.

"The chief took the photo and said he'd take it to Missoula and send it on the state-police wire-photo machine. Obviously he didn't. I was going to call Davidson to confirm it, but then Bessie..." Her eyes dimmed; then something else occurred to her. "Then what was he arrested for?"

"Tax evasion, for starters," he said tightly. "Ariel, why the hell didn't you call me when you found it?"

She looked at him bleakly. "I was going to. That was when I realized you were in San Francisco, when I saw the numbers. I thought you'd left me unprotected to lure the killer," she finished softly. "I didn't think you'd be back."

"I'm so sorry, Ariel." He pulled her into his arms. "Of course you'd think that." He laughed mirthlessly. "What else could you think?"

He rocked her gently in his arms until he felt her begin to relax. Nuzzling his mouth through her silky hair to her ear, he whispered with gentle humor, "You should have known I would come back. I had to get my truck and the rest of my clothes." He felt her flinch. "And you," he breathed. He looked down into eyes filling with a hesitant hope and kissed her softly. He took another kiss, longer, infinitely sweeter.

When he at last relinquished possession of her mouth, her face was luminous with the overpowering happiness suffusing her body, but her husky voice was cautious. "What exactly are you saying, Ryan?"

His smile was tender and oddly uncertain. "I'm saying I love you, Ariel." His hot, insistent mouth reiterated his vow.

For a few precious moments Ariel allowed herself to wallow in the glorious feeling of being loved and desired, ignoring the niggle of doubt that still persisted at the edge of her mind. She pulled back, and he held her loosely in his arms, a question in his eyes.

"It was hard to be sure," she admitted softly. Her eyes didn't meet his.

Ryan felt a jab of heartache. What she was saying was that she found it hard to believe him. He couldn't blame her; he'd hardly given her much reason to.

"The first night we made love, you told me you loved me, but I thought you were just saying it because everybody says it in those circumstances."

He bit back his laugh at her attempt to be casual and sophisticated. "You didn't," he pointed out solemnly.

She shrugged slightly, her voice nonchalant. "Umm, well, I'm a novice. When I have more experience I'll undoubtedly say it, too." Her eyes flickered up to his, then quickly back down. She was leading him shamelessly, but she desperately needed more reassurance.

His arms shifted, his hold a little rougher. His voice was nearly as careless as hers, but with an underlying warning. "Then you'll be saying it to me, because you're going to be getting all your experience with me."

Ariel felt her heart stop, then restart with a rapid jerk. She still couldn't let herself quite believe what he was implying about their relationship. "I'd been thinking...maybe you were attracted to me out of boredom—you know, something to do while you were stuck in a small town." Her anxious eyes belied her complaining banter.

Ryan finally exploded in helpless, disbelieving laughter. "Boredom? Ariel Spence, if you can't tell the difference between recreational sex to pass the time—now *that*'s boredom—and a man making love to you because he's crazy about you and can't keep his hands off you, you do need experience." He started to nuzzle her neck ferociously. "A *lot* more," he warned ominously, taking tender love bites up to her ear lobe.

Though she was laughing delightedly, she reluctantly pushed him away. "I should get that photograph to show you." Oddly, it didn't seem so urgent anymore.

His eyes searched her face, a faint frown replacing his smile. She was thin, almost gaunt. She probably hadn't eaten a decent meal in days. The violent shadows under her eyes bespoke too much grief and too little sleep. "It can wait, Ariel," he said gently. "He's not going anywhere."

He stood and pulled her up after him. The quilt caught and she was suddenly shivering, naked, in the middle of the cold room. A low fire burned in his belly. He tamped it down. They had a few things to settle first.

He spotted his old sweatshirt under the quilt. Wordlessly he held it up, one black brow arching.

"I was . . . cold," she explained.

"Of course." He nodded with an arrogant grin. He pulled the shirt over her head, kissing the top of her cold nose as her head popped through. "Get dressed," he ordered. "I'll scrounge us up some lunch, and then we'll decide when we're going home."

She nodded solemnly and turned away. She took a few steps toward the bathroom, then suddenly whirled. She ran back, flung her arms around his neck and gave him a jubilant kiss. "It's over, Ry!"

"Yes, love," he affirmed softly, smiling into her eyes. "It's finally over."

Half an hour later he watched her devour the second plateful of scrambled eggs he had fixed. She fed the last bite of her bacon to Murphy, laughing for the sheer joy of it. The sadness that had shadowed her face ever since he'd met her was gone, her golden radiance shining brightly.

She got up for more coffee and refilled his cup, flashing him a brilliant smile.

Why wouldn't she say it? he wondered. He knew she loved him. After twenty-seven years of chastity she hadn't surrendered for casual sex or out of curiosity. She had given him her heart as well as her body, so why wouldn't she say it, dammit? He wanted, *needed*, to hear the words; actions weren't enough.

The left corner of his mouth curled in self-derision. Hell, he knew why. A bittersweet pain settled near his heart. He had betrayed her trust twice. She was just protecting herself, making sure she had a little pride and self-respect left in case he did it again. He sighed in resignation. He could wait until he had her complete trust again; he had nothing but time.

They cleaned up the few lunch dishes; then Ariel took Ryan by the hand and led him to her desk. "I want to show you the photograph, Ryan. I'm sure it would be enough proof to convince Davidson that Robert was the one who hired Reilly." She pulled a large manilla envelope from the bottom drawer of her desk and undid the clasp. "He was wearing a disguise, and I don't think even I would have recognized him from the photo, but I saw the negative first." She lifted the flap and began to ease out the largest print. "With light and dark reversed, the blond hair was dark like his really is, and he used to wear a mustache a couple of years ago."

The photograph lay on the desk. Ariel stared at it sadly. "As soon as I saw it I remembered who the third man was in Dennis's office that day; he and Dennis must have been doing the smuggling together." There was agonized bewilderment in her voice as she raised her haunted eyes back to Ryan. "But why would he kill his—"

The rest of the question froze in her throat. Ryan had lost his color, and a look of sick certainty had tautened his features. He bit off a savage, impotent curse halfway through, staring at her starkly. "That man—" his lean finger stabbed the blond man in the photo "—sat across the aisle from me on the flight to Missoula last night."

So the last act in this deadly drama hasn't been played out after all, Ariel decided wearily. She sat on a rickety folding chair in a corner, ignored by the rest of the crowd in Chief Dye's small office. The chief had called his three men back to duty, and the county sheriff had arrived with one of his deputies.

Ryan stood at center stage, listening to the others deliver their lines about roadblocks and bloodhounds, awaiting his cue. Or maybe now he was the director. Occasionally he would ask a question or make an even quieter suggestion.

The chief had been vindicated. As Ryan and Ariel had been leaving the schoolhouse to confront him, the phone had rung. Rick Jones had been on the other end. The photo had apparently been languishing at the bottom of a file basket for most of the week. It had finally made its way to the district attorney's office after Robert had been fingered by the courier—and after they realized that he had given his tail the slip and was probably already on his way to Montana. Ryan had told him that Robert had already arrived.

Ted Dye hung up the phone and slumped back in a tired swivel chair. The chief's faded blue eyes looked worriedly to Ryan, who was now sitting, seemingly totally at ease, on a corner of his desk. "He rented a car about ten minutes after you did, false name on the credit card, of course." Dye tore a sheet off a notepad and tossed it across the desk. "Here's the make on the rental car and the license number." Ryan flicked a glance over the sheet. The other men pulled out pocket notebooks and pens and dutifully wrote down the information. They each had a photograph of the suspect already.

Ryan ambled over to the large map of the county mounted on the back wall. He stood before it, rocking a little on his heels. His right hand was shoved loosely in his jeans pocket, jingling his keys and change. The men who had served under him years before and numerous prosecuting attorneys who had faced him since could have testified that now Ryan Jones was at his most dangerous.

His dark eyes narrowed and traveled over the relief map. His left hand reached out and curled around Ariel's neck, his thumb fondling her cool satin skin almost absently. He found he had the wholly understandable compulsion to keep her in sight, preferably within reach. He took his right hand out of his pocket, his forefinger pinpointing exactly the location of her schoolhouse on the map. Then it traced idly over the nearby river. The banks, he remembered, were thick with concealing brush and trees. A man could easily keep watch on the schoolhouse and its owner with binoculars—or a rifle scope—and never be seen himself.

Ryan's left hand slipped across to her shoulder and prompted her to rise. "I think we'll go now." He said it as if they were leaving a rather boring cocktail party after putting in a polite appearance. "If anything develops, you know where to find us."

Ariel murmured her thanks and goodbyes, Ryan's arm solidly around her.

Since he had discovered earlier that her refrigerator was almost empty, Ryan made a quick stop at the grocery. He was sure she had lost the few pounds he had managed to put on her and a couple more besides.

Later Ariel choked down enough of her dinner to loosen the tight lines around Ryan's mouth. He slid a large slice of cheesecake in front of her and gave her a hard look. Murphy enjoyed most of it while Ryan was occupied with clearing the table. They finished putting her kitchen to rights in a silence that communicated more than hours of conversation could have.

The oddly telepathic silence continued as they sat on her sofa, paying little attention to the television. Ariel curled up against his side, under the arm that had seemed to be around her all day. Eventually they went up to bed. There they made love with hands and mouths that were greedy and a little rough, their movements driven by an almost desperate urgency neither wanted to acknowledge.

Ariel jolted awake violently. She lay in the dark, her heart racing. The sheet beneath her was clammy with perspiration. Left with only the vague dread of some horror she found the nightmare that had awakened her all the more terrifying than if she could remember the details. Carefully she eased from under the heavy arm that tried to hold her. She wanted no more of dream-riddled sleep tonight.

She found her woolen robe in the closet and went downstairs. In the dark bathroom she turned on a faucet and waited for the icy water to heat. A sense of calm finally settled over her. Somehow she knew that whatever was going to happen would do so before nightfall.

With a warm wet washcloth she wiped the clammy sweat from her body. She wondered if this was the way someone felt after making her tragic choice to take her own life. She was not choosing death, however, but life. She hung the rough towel on the rack and pulled the rose wool robe tightly around her as she walked into the kitchen.

Ryan came in silently a few minutes later. "Do you always eat everything in the refrigerator at—" he squinted blearily at the clock "—three forty-seven in the morning?"

The tiny grin that had been tugging at the corner of her mouth gave up. "Only when I'm scared and can't sleep." The entire contents of her refrigerator was scattered haphazardly over the oak table. She considered the bowl of leftover salad, then shoved it aside. Finally she looked at him.

He'd pulled on the old jeans and his gray sweatshirt. After dragging out the chair opposite her, he straddled it, his arms crossed over the back. He buried a yawn in his arms, then raised his head.

The look of compassionate understanding and love in his sleepy eyes nearly undid her. Ariel got up and began putting the food away.

"What would you like to do?" he asked softly. He knew she wouldn't be able to bear going back to bed.

Pausing before the open door of the refrigerator, she thought for a moment. "You know what I'd really like to do? I'd like to be outside, maybe along the river. I am so *tired* of being cooped up."

Going down to the river might not be a wise move, but Ryan understood what she was feeling. She couldn't stand waiting like a small animal caught in a trap, helplessly anticipating the hunter's return. Besides, four o'clock in the morning should be safe enough.

"Okay." Rising from the chair, he held a hand out to her. "Let's go get dressed."

She had dressed in her warmest clothes, olive wool pants, a heavy tan sweater and hiking boots, and was just shrugging into a fleece-lined brown corduroy coat when Ryan returned from across the hall. He was dressed as warmly as she was. He'd exchanged his jeans for khaki field pants and added a thick gray sweater and a worn cowhide ranch coat. Ariel's eyes widened, but she didn't speak. In his left hand, as if it were a natural extension of his arm, was an automatic rifle she knew you couldn't buy over the counter of the local sporting goods store.

They went into the garage. Ryan turned the dancing Murphy back firmly at the door. "No, girl, no rides today."

Ryan used the keys he had lifted from Ariel's purse and opened the metal cabinet along the side wall. He took out her ancient shotgun and wordlessly handed it over as she was climbing into the truck. Her eyes widened further, and she balked at taking the gun. His quiet tone had a finality that wouldn't brook argument.

"Take it, Ariel."

He would much rather have given her the hunting rifle with the high-powered scope, but she had mentioned once that she had never fired anything but a shotgun. Now was no time to start lessons.

Ryan backed out of the garage and left the truck idling to warm up the engine while he shut the garage door. He stepped out into an eerie scene that was all shades of the same color—gray. The pe-

culiar half light promised that the sun was rising, but it was still too
far below the eastern horizon to add any color to the world.

Ashen pines blurred into the massed pewter clouds crawling over
the charcoal mountains guarding the shadowy valley below. He
could barely distinguish the silvered walls of the schoolhouse
against the slate backdrop of the sky. Even his truck had lost its
bright orange and looked like tarnished silver in the strange light.
His hand on the door handle had a ghoulishly bloodless tint. A
chill ran down his spine that had nothing to do with the wind. It
was, he remembered, the favored hour for executions.

The wind eddied around the schoolhouse. Despite the heavy
frost it was only crispy cool outside. His dark head thrown back,
he sniffed the air like a wild animal. It carried reminders of snow-
covered granite peaks and bottomless, ice-rimmed high-country
lakes. The impossibly clean air began to stir his sluggish blood with
a curious, restless excitement.

Ariel sat on the fraying seat, oblivious to the way the truck was
bouncing over the washboard river road. Numbly she gazed at the
shotgun, as familiar to her as her own body, securely upright between her knees. For the first time since her grandfather had placed
it in her eager hands seventeen years ago and she had brought its
wobbly weight to her shoulder, she was forced to recognize the
gun's true purpose. The dully gleaming steel and aged walnut had
not been fashioned into a game piece for her to use in a harmless
sport. They had been made to be a lethal weapon, an instrument
of death. Never had she aimed it at any living thing. Even in defense of her own life, could she now?

Ryan quietly asked for directions.

"Turn here." Ariel indicated the high, narrow levee road. It
bordered a field of random haystacks that looked like giant loaves
of pale bread iced with frost. They took the road for a few minutes into a wilder stretch along the river. Here the river turned back
toward the steep walls of the valley. There were no farms or any
other sign of man's attempt to domesticate this wilderness, except
the winding road cut into the foot of the mountain. Ryan parked
the truck at a wide spot in the road.

Frozen mud crunched under their boots as they tramped across
a wide flat toward the river. The wooden trestle of the Burlington
Northern railroad bridge loomed out of the river mist like the fos-
silized skeleton of some prehistoric beast. Ariel carried her

shotgun, unloaded, over her shoulder. Ryan's rifle, with a full clip, was resting with deceptive casualness in the crook of his elbow.

He scanned the shadowed valley wall behind them, then the brushlined riverbanks. He saw nothing unusual, yet the short hairs on the back of his neck had risen as soon as they had left the truck. He listened. There were several scattered shots, comfortably distant, probably deer hunters. From nearby came the lazy sounds of the geese resting on the quiet water, and the whisper of the rising wind at their backs.

They stood downwind of the geese, behind a chest-high screen of young willows. The geese had neither seen nor heard their stealthy approach. Because of the hour and the ghostly light they automatically hushed their voices.

They were making it so easy for him. The woods were full of hunters, but they had neglected to put on orange clothing. Who would be surprised if dressed as she was in drab brown, she was mistaken for a deer by an overeager hunter without the courage to step forward and admit what he had done?

He slipped three shiny brass bullets with lethal copper rocket tips into the breech of the rifle. The bolt slid home. He sighted through the scope, centering the cross hairs on the back of her head. Satisfied, he lowered the rifle and melted into the underbrush.

Ariel dug around in her coat pocket for the gloves that should have been under the buckshot shells Ryan had given her. Without taking his eyes from the river, he reached for her cold hand and tucked it with his into the fleece-lined warmth of his jacket pocket.

The scene before them was reminiscent of a busy day at the Los Angeles airport. The big Canadian geese were unusually restless, using the slow water for endless takeoffs and landings. A new squad flew in low, buzzing the trestle and alighting with hardly a splash.

The geese sensed the approach of the winter storm that had built a week ago high above the Arctic Circle. It had moved like a ponderous, invading army down across Canada. Now the first outriders of wind were infiltrating across the U.S. border fanning across the valley, rippling the water and ruffling the geese's feathers. Ariel's hair lifted in the fitful breeze, blond strands tangling with the blue-black of Ryan's.

Engrossed in the geese, Ariel paid no attention to the strong, swift breeze that passed by her cheek, or the two puffs of dirt kicked up a few feet in front of her. Suddenly she was facedown in the mud and cockleburs, a pitiless hand on her head keeping her there. It took all her strength to twist her head out of the dirt so she could breathe. Squirming onto her side, she started to demand furiously what the hell Ryan thought he was doing when she realized he was crouched protectively over her, paying absolutely no attention to her. Blood was welling slowly from a peculiar slash on his neck, just above the collar of his coat.

The deadly looking rifle was ready at his waist as his hooded eyes searched the steep hill behind them, inch by torturous inch. A harsh sound in his throat and a twisted smile said he had found what he was looking for. Halfway up he'd caught a clumsy movement through the trees.

Ryan watched for a few more seconds, then seized Ariel's arm, dragging her up into a half crouch. "Stay down," he commanded, pulling her after him. The limber branches of the tamarisks whipped back as he pushed through them, stinging her cold cheeks and bringing tears to her eyes. Ariel bit her lip, determined not to cry, either from the flogging branches or the paralyzing fear. In the shelter of a massive fir, safe from the eyes of anyone on the mountainside, he halted, his hand still bruising her upper arm.

"Is he here?"

Ryan broke off his continual scanning of the area behind them to spare her a glance. She was tense, yet trembling like a frightened fawn, and her eyes were three times too big for her face, but her whisper had been steady. "Yes, he's here." Ryan looked back to the hillside. His arm rose cautiously, and she followed the direction of his pointing finger. "He was there when he shot, but he's moved off to the right and down now." His arm tracked the killer's progress. "He's probably sure he hit us and is coming to check. As long as he thinks we're dead or wounded, we have the advantage."

Ryan began moving again, and she followed, still tethered to him by that viselike hand. They moved through a thin wall of brush into a tiny glade carpeted with frost-crisped grass. Two more sides were walled by impenetrable brush. The fourth side was the levee, where Ariel could see the top of the orange shell on Ryan's truck. A quick scramble up the sandy slope and they would be safe.

Ryan dropped her arm finally to dig his keys out of his pants pockets. "I want you to take the truck, go back to town and bring back Dye and his men." He said the words casually as if he was sending her out for pizza.

Her chin tilted, and she answered calmly. "No, Ryan."

He began to curse her, driven by the fear and desperation wrenching his gut. His words were all the more terrible because they were delivered in a flat, passionless tone instead of the satisfying shouts of anger he wanted. He didn't dare lose enough control to shout, because if he did, he would touch her. And one touch would be too much. He would shake her until that beautiful stiff neck snapped. Or he would hit her, a solid right on that stubborn chin she was leading with so temptingly. Actually it wouldn't be such a bad idea at that, if he could remember to pull his punch at the last second. He could throw her in the back of the pickup and lock her in, where she would be safe. But he knew he couldn't trust himself. She would probably end up hating him forever.

Her face starkly white, Ariel stood silently letting his words roll over her harmlessly. He truly loved her, she knew. He could never say such awful things if he weren't scared to death of losing her. However, his hot rage was no match for the icy fury consuming her.

Scenes from the past ten months played before her eyes: Dennis in her arms, his bright red blood staining her gray slacks; Murphy's limp brown body on a cold, polished steel table; the charred black bulk of her Blazer; Ryan, the sun finding blue fire in his black hair, as he reached for a piece of poisoned candy. Ryan, standing before her now, the black hair mussed, the beautiful mouth that could smile at her with such love and tenderness hard and cruel as the blood oozed into his sodden, red coat collar. Ryan, who would risk his life once more because he loved her. And the man up on the hill had tried to kill him.

"No, Ryan," she repeated tonelessly. "He's taken a year of my life. He's tried to kill me five times." She looked at him steadily, unaware of the silent tears slipping down her cheeks. "He's even tried to kill you. No one deserves to go after him more than I do." She pumped a shell into the shotgun with cold efficiency. "Coming?"

The iron fingers shackling her upper arm would probably shatter both bones any moment, she thought dispassionately. No matter, she could always shoot with the other. Then the brutal hand slipped up to her cheek in the tenderest of caresses.

Ryan felt the madness drain out of him as he responded to the love her shuttered eyes couldn't quite hide. His hand lightly brushed away the tears she still wasn't aware of, smearing their muddy tracks. "I guess you do deserve it, love. But—" he pulled the collar of her coat up around her ears "—I want you to promise to do exactly as I tell you."

"But—"

"Promise me!"

The searing intensity that blazed in his suddenly gaunt face burned away her protest. "I promise," she whispered.

The flame died as quickly as it flared. The warm, chocolate eyes that melted when they were loving her were now opaque mirrors, showing nothing. They were the eyes of a man who had killed before, and would again—for her. A tiny corner of her brain screamed, frightened at how easily she accepted this side of him. Ruthlessly she strangled the voice into silence.

"You stay here and watch the truck." Ryan delivered his orders in a detached, lifeless voice, so different from the velvet purr that could lick over her skin like a warm, living being. "If he comes, shoot to wound him only. I want him alive."

Holding her eyes, he took her mouth in a harsh, thorough kiss. Without a word he turned and crossed the clearing. Her hesitant voice, calling as loudly as she dared, stopped him.

"You be careful, Ryan Jones! I love you."

There was a quick flash of that rascally, rakish grin. "I know." He turned and faded into the brush.

Ariel discovered that she was a miserable failure as the one who had to stand and wait. Belatedly she realized Ryan's ploy. The killer would never bother with the truck until he determined the success of his ambush. Ryan, of course, planned to intercept him, with her safely out of the way. She paced the clearing, torn by indecision. Should she go after him, risking his wrath and possibly spoiling his plan? Or should she keep her promise and remain here, feeling utterly useless and worried almost out of her mind. She finally decided that she would wait, unless she heard gunfire. Then no promise on earth could be strong enough to keep her from going to him. She was listening so intently for a gunshot that she never heard the small snap of a broken twig behind her.

"Set the shotgun down very carefully, Ariel."

The blood in her veins congealed. She hesitated, gauging her chances, but she knew that even she could never turn and fire fast enough to beat a bullet in the back. Like a sleepwalker, she laid the gun on the frozen grass.

Odd, she could hear the infinitesimal breakage of each blade, but she hadn't heard him approach. Her senses had become acutely sensitive. Was she suddenly so aware because she might have little time left to be aware of anything? She smelled a whiff of a familiar cloying cologne on the ragged breeze and heard the small sigh of relief behind her.

"Good girl. I'd hoped you would be sensible. Now kick it away." Her toe nudged the shotgun away. "You can turn around now," he added, almost as a polite afterthought.

She asked the question as she slowly turned. "Why, Robert?"

Robert DiSanto's red-rimmed green eyes narrowed sharply. "Ah, I see you're not surprised. That may change things a bit. Does anyone else know?"

"The IRS, the D.A. in San Francisco, the L.A. police, to name a few. There are roadblocks up here in the valley," she informed him with quiet satisfaction, then repeated her question. "Why did you kill your own brother, Robert?"

Robert DiSanto pulled away the wig of lank blond hair and gingerly peeled off the scraggly mustache and eyebrows, revealing thick, curly auburn hair. The rifle aimed at her heart wavered only a fraction. "Dennis and I were in business together, cocaine, some other things." His free hand gestured vaguely; then he shrugged. "But you probably already know all that.

"He got cold feet." Robert's low laugh was obscene. "He was afraid you would find out he wasn't as lilly-white as you thought he was. I told him—" his sigh indicated his forbearance "—he shouldn't choose a woman over business, but he wouldn't listen."

"But why kill him, Robert? He never would have told me."

Robert explained with the patience necessary for a backward toddler. "Because he might have decided to bare his soul to you after all, or let something slip. I couldn't take the risk. And then, you'd seen Garza that day in his office with us. Once he was arrested, I knew, if you saw his picture in the paper you'd remember. He saw the flicker of recognition when he mentioned Garza's name. "There, you see?" He'd proved his point. He shrugged eloquently. "You can understand my position. It was nothing personal, Ariel, just business. Just as you must understand—" he sounded confident that she did "—why I can't let you go now, you or your lover."

"They'll catch you, Robert." Ariel edged almost imperceptibly toward the closest thicket. If she could get within five or six feet she could dive for cover. "You'll never even get out of the valley."

"But they're looking for me in this, aren't they?" he said, his hand flicking contemptuously at the wig he had stuffed in the pocket of his scruffy jeans. He saw by the twinge of dismay crossing her face that he was right. "I can leave here easily, as myself, driving the car Jones rented. Nobody's looking—"

"It won't work, Robert," Ariel interrupted, her voice reasonable. "You may get past the roadblocks, but you won't be able to go back to Los Angeles. You'll be on the run, penniless, no one to turn to." She had decided to go not for the brush but for her shotgun when the time came. Just another few inches... "Why don't you just—"

"I think not." The barrel of the rifle gestured warningly, and Ariel froze. He began turning gradually, the rifle leading her in a slow, macabre dance around the clearing, until his unprotected back was to the levee. "I have quite a bit of money in a Bahamian bank," his smile was pleased, "for just such a contingency." His eyes looked past her for a moment, thoughtful. He caught her subtle move toward her gun, and they snapped back to her. "A little plastic surgery, and everything will work out fine." His tone indicated that he forgave her all the trouble she had caused him. "How did they find out?" he asked curiously.

"You weren't quite as clever with your money as you thought, Robert. And then I found a negative Dennis hadn't printed. You were in it, with Reilly, at the park. It was just an accident that you were caught by the camera." She felt a perverse flicker of satisfaction. "I recognized you, even through your disguise." He was holding the gun loosely; maybe if she rushed him, he would be so surprised he would drop it. She tensed, readying her body.

Robert nodded ruefully, his hands tightening their hold on the rifle. "Call your lover, Ariel; tell him you need him. Call him; he'll come."

Ariel's throat was achingly dry. She would get down on her knees and beg, throw herself on his gun, anything, but she wouldn't call

Ryan. She tried to swallow, her voice coming out a harsh rasp. "No, Robert."

Robert raised the rifle, and she couldn't keep from cringing. Then she stiffened her quaking body, using every ounce of willpower that she possessed. "I won't call him. You'll have to shoot me first."

Robert's finger moved to the trigger of the rifle. "Call him, Ariel. Now."

"He's already here, DiSanto." The feral growl came from behind him. "Drop the gun."

Ariel saw the shock blanch Robert's face as she dived for her shotgun. She rolled twice, then scrambled to her feet the gun leveled at his chest.

Robert DiSanto considered his options, then dropped his rifle.

"Back away from it," Ryan ordered. "And turn around."

DiSanto took three steps backward and turned. Slowly he raised his hands. "Pity," he reflected. "I'd thought about hiring you, Jones, if I ever needed a good criminal attorney. I don't suppose you'd be interested now." There was a hint of question in his voice.

Ryan held his gun almost carelessly. Reaching into his jacket pocket, he pulled out the last cigarette in the pack. He lit it, inhaling deeply, and breathed out a long stream of smoke. "No."

DiSanto made a small, indecisive move toward the gun lying on the ground in front of him.

"Go ahead, bastard," Ryan encouraged softly. "I've had you in my sights for the past five minutes. It wouldn't bother me in the least to pull the trigger, and *I*—" Ryan's cruel smile was self-mocking "—would certainly never be found guilty of murder."

"Why didn't you shoot?" The words were torn from DiSanto involuntarily.

Ryan didn't answer immediately. Now there was a question. Why hadn't he? He'd wasted precious minutes before he'd realized that the killer had done the unexpected and was not going to the riverbank. He'd had to waste more time circling back. When he'd topped the levee and seen Robert pointing his gun at Ariel, it was as if he were suddenly back in that Cambodian hut. He'd raised his rifle and sighted through the dull red mist clouding his vision. A small, sane inner voice had struggled to be heard over the bloodthirsty clamor in his brain. Then he'd heard her voice, rigidly controlled, low and rational. He could see she was terrified, her face was bloodless, her eyes enormous, but she'd held her trembling body straight and faced her murderer. And he knew she would never have called him. He'd felt such pride in her...and such love, and he had lowered the rifle.

"Because, as much as you deserve it, the woman you've tried so hard to kill saved you. I don't think she could take another death right now—not even yours. Besides," he added conversationally, "You probably won't be around much longer anyway. Your business associates won't be too happy with you. They're going to be afraid that you might develop a sudden urge to talk to the wrong people. Even in prison you'll have to look over your shoulder all the time."

Ryan watched as fear turned the man's handsome face ugly.

The woman Ryan thought couldn't take another death spoke at last. Ariel had almost fainted at the wild surge of relief and joy she had felt when Robert dropped the gun. She had been ready to fling herself into Ryan's arms. Then an ice-cold aftershock of lingering fury had numbed her emotions and her body. "Turn around, Robert," she said now. "Unlike you, I'm averse to shooting a man in the back."

The hunter turned on his quarry, but now he was the frightened animal at bay. He looked halfway across the little clearing into empty blue eyes. There was no hate in them, no remorse, no mercy for him.

The dark man behind them was forgotten. Only he seemed to hear the approaching sirens. Ryan thought furiously. He saw her eyes, too. She was going to shoot, and there wasn't the slightest hope that she'd miss. If he shot first, just to wound... It was too late. She had raised the gun to her shoulder and taken aim.

Robert DiSanto stood frozen, his green eyes widening in growing horror.

"No, Ariel. Oh, love, no." Ryan's despairing whisper was barely audible, his agile brain already planning her defense.

Her finger stroked the trigger in a lover's caress and tightened.

The shotgun blast shattered the breathless quiet.

Chapter 15

Robert DiSanto screamed and fell. Two more shots echoed across the river. The startled geese milled frantically. They climbed high overhead, honking querulously.

Nothing in the clearing moved. Then, cautiously, Robert Di-Santo uncurled his arms from around his head and rose up on his hands and knees, looking incredulously at the woman with the smoking gun.

"No, Robert," Ariel told him, her voice and smile oddly gentle, almost kind. "I couldn't kill you. Ryan was right. I couldn't bear another death, not even yours."

An avalanche of sand and dirt poured down the face of the levee. The men who had been stricken motionless by the tableau below them were piling out of their vehicles and sliding down the slope. Ariel, feeling strangely detached, saw the chief jerk Robert to his feet, snapping on handcuffs as he read him his rights. Ryan started toward her. He seemed to be moving in peculiarly slow motion. She ejected the last spent shell and handed her shotgun to the sheriff's deputy beside her. Then she quietly fainted.

When Ariel revived she found herself in what seemed to be becoming a common position for her. She was lying cradled in Ryan's arms across his lap. She kept her eyes closed, listening to the words flying over her light head. A game warden had evidently spotted Robert's rental car and called it in. Chief Dye and the sheriff had converged on the area. Coincidentally, Rick Jones and a federal marshall had arrived to take charge of their prisoner.

Ryan felt her relaxed body tighten with the return of consciousness and grinned up at his brother. His brother grinned back happily, then withdrew unobtrusively.

Ryan shifted a little on the cold ground. "Think you can stand up, love?" he murmured near her ear.

Ariel nodded and opened her eyes. The first thing she saw was the bloody collar of Ryan's coat. The bullet graze no longer oozed.

Ryan hauled her to her feet and was immediately called over by the federal marshal. Ted Dye put a stabilizing arm around her shoulders, and Ariel leaned against him gratefully. When he was sure she could stand by herself, he reclaimed his prisoner and marched him up the levee to a police car. Ariel watched as Ryan and his brother moved to the edge of the clearing to speak privately.

"I imagine Davidson will admit he may have been a little narrow-minded when he gets DiSanto's statement," Rick Jones predicted dryly. He watched Ryan's eyes drift back to the woman standing alone in the middle of the glade. His wickedly knowing grin was the identical twin of his older brother's. "I knew you'd like her."

"Yeah." Suddenly Ryan wrapped his brother in a crushing bear hug. Rick hesitated for only a heartbeat, then returned it, clapping Ryan on the back enthusiastically. They broke apart, hands clasping once. "I'll call you as soon as we're home," Ryan promised.

As suddenly as they had appeared, the men and their assorted cars and pickups vanished. Rick, the last man to leave, paused on the top of the levee. He watched as his brother put his arms around the woman he loved and folded her close. Her arms wound around his waist, pulling him closer. Wearily, they leaned on each other. The bloodied but victorious black knight was claiming his lady. With a soft, satisfied smile Rick walked away. The debt was paid at last.

The sun was only minutes below the rim of the valley. The dingy gray clouds were tinted with infinite shades of gold and rose. A few stray feathers of snow drifted down on their heads.

Gently disengaging herself from Ryan's arms, Ariel retrieved her shotgun. Her back to Ryan, she squared her drooping shoulders and drew a deep breath of the chilled air. She feared it was going to take far more courage to face the man she loved than it had taken to face a killer.

Trust, she'd discovered, required a small leap of faith. She'd made the leap and landed safely on her feet. Now she was about to take an even more desperate, sweeter gamble—her happiness on one verbal toss of the dice. "No"—two letters, snake eyes—and her life was going to be as bitter as venom. "Yes" and it was happily-ever-after-time.

"There's something that still has to be settled."

Ryan started toward her. "What's that?"

"Marriage," she said calmly. She leveled the shotgun at his belt buckle, and he halted abruptly.

Ryan eyed the shotgun. It was wobbling just a bit. He knew the gun was empty. He relit the dead cigarette and puffed leisurely. One elegant black brow arched. "Is it going to be a shotgun wedding, then?" He looked totally unconcerned, almost bored, and Ariel felt a shaft of killing pain. "Are we pregnant?"

The shotgun wavered badly. "Not—" her voice cracked "—yet."

He nodded disinterestedly, then moved without warning. The shotgun was jerked from her hands, and she was dragged into his arms. Clamping a ruthless hand on the back of her head, he tilted her face up to his.

"Say it!" he rasped. "It sure as hell took you long enough to admit it the first time, and I want to hear it again."

"I don't know if I will now." She sniffed petulantly. "I think you're trying to evade the issue here, counselor."

"Brat!" he growled in her right ear. "Say it, dammit!"

Two bright tears rolled down her cheeks as she gave him a dazzling smile. "I love you, Ryan Jones. Will you—"

His hand over her mouth silenced her question. "I love you, Ariel Spence." His dark eyes softened with a sweet poignancy. "And I want to be the one to ask. Will you marry me?"

Her yes was lost in an endless kiss. The sun finally broke through the clouds and flooded the little glade with brilliant sunlight.

Swirling snow devils hid the landscape outside the schoolhouse. Ryan stood behind Ariel at the window, his arms loosely around her.

"Isn't there a hot spring on the river, not far from here?"

Ariel watched the silent snow fall for a moment longer. "Mmm. It's supposed to be like a natural jacuzzi."

"The snow's supposed to last all night," he murmured. He tilted his head to look down at her, a sly smile flirting with his mouth. "I've always wondered how accurate certain details of your first book were, Felicia."

Her answering smile was wickedly innocent.

A short while later the steaming water was lapping at their bodies. Huge snowflakes fluttered down like white butterflies, landing on the smooth black rock. They tasted sweet and cool when caught on the tongue, but they tasted even better when they were licked from heated skin, icy hot and tangy.

"Ryan, I'm sinking," Ariel murmured, unconcerned.

"Hold your breath," he counseled. His lips melted a snowflake on her breast.

With a laughing gasp she clutched at his shoulders as she slid precariously lower. His hands were gentle on her hips as he lifted her over him. Delicately her tongue flicked another icy crystal from the black hair on his chest. "I love you." The words were whispered over his wet, warm skin.

"I love you," he echoed, burying his mouth in her throat.

As they sank deeper into the warm water, soft murmurs became even softer sighs of pleasure.

Reality, they discovered, was so much better than fiction.

Silhouette Intimate Moments

COMING
NEXT MONTH

MAN FOR HIRE—Parris Afton Bonds
Alyx needed to hire a man to help her rescue her kidnapped daughter. Khalid Rajhi was a desert sheikh who gave not only his help, but his heart.

THE OLD FLAME—Alexandra Sellers
Sondra had always recognized the power Ben held over her, and never more clearly than now, when there seemed no way to escape him, on the job or off.

SWEET REASON—Sandy Steen
Laine had no intention of falling in love while on vacation in Mexico, much less getting involved with a case of espionage. But Drew Kenyon had a way of blowing intentions and expectations to the wind.

WHEN WE TOUCH—Mary Lynn Baxter
The FBI wanted Blair Browning back, and they knew just how to get her. Caleb Hunt wanted Blair, too, for a very personal reason—and he, too, seemed destined for success.

AVAILABLE NOW:

QUEST OF THE EAGLE
Maura Seger

**TREASURES LOST,
TREASURES FOUND**
Nora Roberts

FLASHPOINT
Patricia Gardner Evans

LADY OF THE NIGHT
Emilie Richards

The Silhouette Cameo Tote Bag Now available for just $6.99

Handsomely designed in blue and bright pink, its stylish good looks make the Cameo Tote Bag an attractive accessory. The Cameo Tote Bag is big and roomy (13″ square), with reinforced handles and a snap-shut top. You can buy the Cameo Tote Bag for $6.99, plus $1.50 for postage and handling.

Send your name and address with check or money order for $6.99 (plus $1.50 postage and handling), a total of $8.49 to:

> **Silhouette Books**
> **120 Brighton Road**
> **P.O. Box 5084**
> **Clifton, NJ 07015-5084**
> **ATTN: Tote Bag**

SIL-T-1R

The Silhouette Cameo Tote Bag can be purchased pre-paid only. No charges will be accepted. Please allow 4 to 6 weeks for delivery.

N.Y. State Residents Please Add Sales Tax

Offer not available in Canada.

FOUR UNIQUE SERIES
FOR EVERY WOMAN YOU ARE . . .

Silhouette Romance

Heartwarming romances that will make you
laugh and cry as they bring you all the wonder
and magic of falling in love.

6 titles
per month

Silhouette Special Edition

Expanded romances written with emotion and
heightened romantic tension to ensure
powerful stories. A rare blend of passion and
dramatic realism.

6 titles
per month

Silhouette Desire

Believable, sensuous, compelling—and
above all, romantic—these stories deliver
the promise of love, the guarantee
of satisfaction.

6 titles
per month

Silhouette Intimate Moments

Love stories that entice; longer, more
sensuous romances filled with adventure,
suspense, glamour and melodrama.

4 titles
per month